Fairy Stories

Chosen by Anna Wilson

Illustrated by Lara Jones

MACMILLAN CHILDREN'S BOOKS

For my dear sister, Carrie, and Dom and Teasel

First published 2006 by Macmillan Children's Books
a division of Macmillan Publishers Limited
20 New Wharf Road, London N1 9RR
Basingstoke and Oxford
www.panmacmillan.com

Associated companies throughout the world

ISBN-13: 978-0-330-43823-0
ISBN-10: 0-330-43823-9

A CIP catalogue record for this book is available from
the British Library.

Typeset by Nigel Hazle
Printed and bound in Great Britain by Mackays of Chatham plc, Kent

Contents

Clem's Dream

Joan Aiken

Clem woke up in his sunny bedroom and cried out, 'Oh, I have lost my dream! And it was such a beautiful dream! It sang, and shouted, and glittered, and sparkled – and I've lost it! Somebody pulled it away, out of reach, just as I woke up!'

1

He looked around – at his bed, his toys, his chair, his open window with the trees outside.

'Somebody must have come in through the window, and they've stolen my dream!'

He asked the Slipper Fairy, 'Did you see who stole my dream?'

But the Slipper Fairy had been fast asleep, curled up in his slipper with her head in the toe. She had seen nobody.

He asked the Toothbrush Fairy, 'Did you see who stole my dream?'

2

But the Toothbrush Fairy had been standing on one leg, looking at herself in the bathroom mirror. She had seen nothing.

Clem asked the Bathmat Fairy. He asked the Soap Fairy. He asked the Curtain Fairy. He asked the Clock Fairy.

None of them had seen the person who had stolen his dream.

He asked the Water Fairy, 'Did you see the person who stole my dream?'

'Look under your pillow, willow,

3

willow, willow!' sang the Water Fairy.

'Open your own mouth and look in, in, in, in! Then, then you'll know, ho, ho, ho, ho!'

Clem looked under his pillow. He found a silver coin.

He climbed on a chair, and looked in the glass, opening his mouth as wide as it would go.

He saw a hole, where a tooth used to be.

'The Tooth Fairy must have come while I was asleep. She took my tooth and paid for it with a silver coin. She must have taken my dream too. But she had no right to do that.'

At breakfast, Clem asked, 'How can I get my dream back from the Tooth Fairy?'

5

The Milk Fairy said, 'She lives far, far away, on Moon Island, which is on the other side of everywhere.'

The Bread Fairy said, 'She lives in a castle made of teeth, at the top of a high cliff.'

The Apple Fairy said, 'You will have to take her a present. Something round and white. Otherwise she will never give back your dream.'

Clem went into the garden. He said, 'How can I find my way to

6

Moon Island, on the other side of everywhere? And what present can I take the Tooth Fairy?'

'Go up to the top of the hill, the hill, the hill, the hill,' sang the Grass Fairy, 'and put your arms round the stone, the stone, the stone that stands there. If your fingers can touch each other, round the other side, then the stone will grant your wish.'

So Clem ran up to the top of the green, grassy hill.

There stood an old grey stone,

tall as a Christmas tree. Clem tried to put his arms round it. But his arms would not quite reach, his fingers would not quite touch.

'You need to grow, to grow, to grow, to grow,' sang the Grass Fairy. 'Ask my sisters to help you, help you, help you, help you.'

So Clem ran back to the house and called for help. The Bread Fairy, the Water Fairy, the Milk Fairy and the Apple Fairy all came to the top of the hill and helped him. They pulled him longways,

8

they pulled him sideways. By and by, when they had pulled and pulled and pulled, he was able to make his fingers meet round the other side of the old grey stone.

'Now you may have your wish,' said the Stone Fairy.

'I wish for a boat,' said Clem, 'to take me to the Tooth Fairy's castle on Moon Island, on the other side of everywhere.'

A laurel leaf fell into the brook, and grew till it was as big as a boat. Clem stepped into it.

'Away you go, you go, you go, you go,' sang the Water Fairy, and the boat floated away with Clem, down the brook, along the river, and into the wide, wide sea.

The sea is all made of dreams. Looking down, into the deep water, Clem could see many, many dreams. They gleamed and shifted under his boat like leaves made of glass – gold, green, black and silver. But nowhere could Clem see his own dream, nowhere in all the wide sea.

10

The boat
travelled on,
day after
day, night
after night.

In the
distance, Clem saw
many monsters. There was the
Spinach Monster, all greeny-black,
the Shoelace Monster, all tangly,
the Stair Monster, all cornery, the
Seaweed Monster, all crackly, and
the Sponge Monster, all soggy.

But the Water Fairy tossed

handfuls of water at them, and they did not dare come too near.

At last the boat came to Moon Island, on the other side of everywhere. Moon Island is round as a wheel. Its rocky beaches are covered with oysters and black stones as big as apples. Up above are high white cliffs. And on top of the highest cliff of all stands the Tooth Fairy's castle, which is all made out of teeth.

'How shall I ever manage to climb up that cliff?' asked Clem.

12

'And what present can I take the Tooth Fairy, so that she will give me back my dream?'

'Sing a song to the oysters on the beach,' the Water Fairy told him. 'They are very fond of songs.'

So Clem sang:

'Night sky
Drifting by
How can I climb the rock so high?
Moon beam
Star gleam
Where shall I find my stolen dream?'

13

All the oysters on the beach sighed with pleasure and opened their shells to listen to Clem's song.

The King of the Oysters said, 'Stoop down, Clem, feel with your finger inside my shell and you will find a pearl. Take it to the Tooth Fairy, and perhaps she will give you back your dream.'

Clem stooped and gently poked his finger inside the big oyster shell. There he found a pearl as big as a plum. It just fitted in the palm of

14

his hand. He also picked up one of the round black stones off the beach.

'Thank you!' he said to the King of the Oysters. 'That was kind of you. I will take this beautiful pearl to the Tooth Fairy, and perhaps she will give me back my dream. But how shall I ever climb up this high cliff?'

'Sing your song again, again, again,' sang the Water Fairy. 'And perhaps somebody else will help you.'

15

So Clem sang:

'Night, sleep,
Ocean deep,
How shall I climb the cliff so steep?
Rain, mist,
Snow, frost,
How shall I find my dream that's
lost?'

The snowflakes came pattering
down out of the sky and built Clem
a staircase of white steps that led,
back and forth, back and forth,

16

criss-cross, all the way up the high cliff.

And so Clem was able to climb up, step by step, step by step, until he came to the very top, where the Tooth Fairy's castle was perched.

The door was made of driftwood, white as paper.

Clem knocked on the door with his black stone. When he shook the stone, it rattled, as if it had loose teeth inside it.

Clem knocked once. He knocked twice. He knocked three times.

'Who is banging on my door?' cried an angry voice.

'It's me, Clem! I have come to ask for my dream!'

Slowly the door opened, and the Tooth Fairy looked out.

The Tooth Fairy is the oldest fairy in the world. Before the last dragon turned to stone, she was building her castle, and she will be building it when the seeds from the last thistle fly off into space. Her eyes are like balls of snow, and her hands are like bunches of thorns.

18

Her feet are like roots. Her teeth
are like icicles.

'Who are you?' said the Tooth
Fairy. 'How dare you come
knocking at my door? I never give
back a tooth. Never!'

'I'm Clem. And I don't want my
tooth back. I want my dream
back!'

The Tooth Fairy gave Clem a
crafty look.

'How can you be certain that I
have your dream?'

'I'm certain,' said Clem.

19

'And if I have it, here in my castle, how can you find it?'

'I'll know it when I see it,' said Clem.

'Oh, very well. You may come in and look for it. But you may stay only seven minutes.'

So Clem went into the Tooth Fairy's castle – along wide halls and into huge rooms.

The fairy shut the door behind him and pulled the bolt, which was made from a serpent's tooth.

Clem wandered all over the castle

20

– up winding stairways, round
corners, through galleries, up on to
the tops of towers, out on balconies,
down into cellars, under arches,
across courtyards.

Everything was white, and there
was not a single sound to be heard.
Not a mouse, not a bird.

He began to fear that he would
never find his dream.

'You have had six minutes!'
called the Tooth Fairy.

Her voice rang like a bell in the
hollow castle.

But then, just after that, Clem heard the tiniest tinkle, like water dripping into a pool.

'Look up,' whispered the Water Fairy. 'Look up, up, up, up!'

Clem looked up, into a round, empty tower. And high, high, high, high, far, far up, he saw something flutter – something that gleamed, and twinkled, and shone, and sparkled.

'It's my dream!' shouted Clem joyfully. 'Oh, oh, oh, it's my beautiful, beautiful dream!'

At the sound of his voice, the

dream came floating and fluttering down from the high cranny where the Tooth Fairy had hidden it; like a falling leaf it came floating and fluttering down, and then wrapped itself lovingly all round Clem.

'This is my own dream,' he told the Tooth Fairy. 'And here is a pearl, which I brought for you. Now I shall take my dream home.'

At the sight of Clem, joyfully hugging his dream, the Tooth Fairy became so sad that she began to

23

melt. She grew smaller, like a lump of ice in the sun.

'Don't, don't, don't take your dream away, Clem! Please, please, leave it with me!' she begged. 'It is the only beautiful thing I have, in all this silent whiteness. It is the most beautiful thing I have ever seen. If you leave it with me I will give you a hundred years!'

'I don't want a hundred years,' said Clem. 'I would rather have my dream.'

'I will give you a carriage, to

24

travel faster than the sun!'

'I would rather have my dream.'

'I will give you a bonfire that you can carry in your pocket.'

'I would rather have my dream.'

'I will give you a ray of light that can cut through stone.'

'I would rather have my dream.'

'I will give you a garden that grows upside down and backwards.'

'I would rather have my dream.'

'I will give you a word that will last for ever.'

'I would rather have my dream.'

When the Tooth Fairy saw that Clem really meant to take his dream away, she grew sadder still.

'Very well,' she said at last. 'Give me the pearl, then.'

She sighed, such a long deep sigh that the whole castle trembled. Then she pulled back the bolt made from a serpent's tooth, and opened the door. Clem walked out of the castle.

When he turned to wave goodbye to the Tooth Fairy, she was sitting huddled up on a tooth. She looked

so old and small and withered and pitiful that he began to feel sorry for her. He stood, thinking.

'Listen!' he called after a minute or two. 'Would you like to *borrow* my dream? Suppose you keep it until the next time you come to take one of my teeth. How about that?'

'Yes! *Yes!* YES!'

Her white eyes suddenly shone like lamps.

So Clem gently let go of his dream and it fluttered away, back into the Tooth Fairy's castle.

27

'Goodbye, Dream – for a little while!' he called. 'I'll see you next Tooth-day.'

'Wait!' called the Tooth Fairy. 'Since you have been so kind, Clem, I'll give you back your pearl.'

'No, no, keep it, keep it! Why would I want a pearl? Put it into the wall of your castle.'

Clem ran down the stair that had built itself of snow. On the stony beach down below, his boat was waiting for him. He jumped into it, and it raced back over the sea, over

28

the floating dreams, red, black, silver and green like leaves.

But Clem looked behind him and saw his own dream waving and fluttering like a flag from the tower of the Tooth Fairy's castle, and the pearl shining like a round eye in the wall.

It won't be many months before she comes with the dream, thought Clem, and he poked with his finger in the gap between his teeth, where already he could feel a new tooth beginning to grow.

When he arrived home the Bread Fairy, the Milk Fairy and the Apple Fairy were there to welcome him.

'I have lent my dream to the Tooth Fairy,' he told them. 'But it won't be many months before she brings it back.'

And he ran upstairs, washed his face, brushed his teeth and jumped into bed.

He took with him the round black stone, which rattled gently when he shook it.

'The Tooth Fairy will look after my dream,' he told the Slipper Fairy and the Clock Fairy. 'She has it safe.' Then he fell asleep.

When Clem was fast asleep, still holding the black stone, which rattled gently to itself, all the fairies came to look at him.

'He doesn't know,' said the Water Fairy, 'he doesn't know that he has brought away the most

precious thing of all, all, all, all, all.'

'If he ever learns how to open up that stone,' said the Bread Fairy, 'he will be more powerful than any of us.'

'He will be able to grow apple trees on the moon,' said the Apple Fairy.

'Or grass on Mars,' said the Grass Fairy.

'Or make the tick-tock Time turn backwards,' ticked the Clock Fairy.

'Well, let us hope that he uses it

32

sensibly, sensibly, sensibly,' said the
Soap Fairy softly.

'Let us hope so,' said the Curtain
Fairy.

'Let us hope so,' said the Bathmat
Fairy.

But Clem slept on, smiling,
holding the black stone tightly in his
hand.

And, by and by, he began to
dream again.

The Hefty Fairy

Nicholas Allan

Deep in an old hidden wood lay
A Fairy Grotto.
In it lived . . .
The Hefty Fairy.

She was the saddest fairy alive. Her legs and arms were as thick as mushroom stalks.

34

Her body was the shape of an egg.

She flew like a balloon and crashed into the other fairies so often they told her she must never fly when they were in the air.

Every evening the fairies set off in a cloud of silvery dust, along a candlelit runway and up into the sky. In their hands they carried twenty-pence pieces from the royal treasury, for they were going to collect the milk teeth that children left under their pillows.

The Hefty Fairy wished she could go too. But the other fairies just laughed at her. 'You're far too fat for such a delicate task,' they said.

So the Hefty Fairy would trot off all by herself to dance round the fairy ring. As she danced she sang the Hefty Fairy song:

'I'm the fairy who's lumpy,
I'm lumpy, frumpy and dumpy.
I dance round the ring
Flapping my wings,
Going bumpety! Bumpety! Bumpety!'

36

One day the Hefty Fairy discovered the Silvery Thing. She was sitting on a puddle bank, wondering if she was really very hefty, when she saw it.

She jumped into the puddle and pulled and pulled and pulled.

Out it came: a brand-new, shiny twenty-pence piece! 'Ooo,' cried Hefty.

She picked it up and hurried back to her grotto. First she found an oak leaf.

37

Next, she gathered some strong blades of grass and some spider's thread and began to sew.

When she'd finished she had a rucksack. She put the twenty-pence piece inside, took a deep breath, spread her wings and fluttered off. She didn't notice the Fairy Queen watching with her royal guard.

Over the wood flew the Hefty Fairy, across a yellow, a gold and a green field, and then beyond. She had never been beyond Further before, let alone further than Beyond.

38

First she came to a river, then a town.

By the time she reached the houses the sun was setting like an apricot on the hill.

As night began to fall, a tired Hefty Fairy flew from window to window.

She saw an old lady gobbling a chocolate cake.

She saw a man making faces in the bathroom mirror.

She saw two girls pulling each other's hair.

Then she saw exactly what she was looking for: a little boy brushing his teeth – and wiggling a tooth with his finger!

The Hefty Fairy watched as he went into the bedroom and wiggled his tooth. As he put on his pyjamas he wiggled his tooth. As he said goodnight to his mother he wiggled his tooth. He wiggled it and wiggled it and wiggled it. Finally the tooth dropped out.

'Ooo,' said the Hefty Fairy.

Hefty knew she had to find the

40

tooth by midnight or the other
fairies would collect it first.

She waited for the lights to go
out, then flew around the house,
found a keyhole and wriggled
into it.

She pushed and she pulled until
she was red in the face. Then she
sucked in her tummy and pressed as
hard as she could.

Pop! She flew in like a
champagne cork and landed on the
kitchen floor.

The journey to the bedroom was full of dangers . . .

Hefty was too tired to fly, but she bravely ran all the way down the long hallway and then struggled to the top of the stairs.

Slowly and quietly, she crept into the little boy's room.

The corner of the white sheet was hanging down like a rope.

She started to climb and climb and climb. And when she reached the top she saw it: something oblong; something white; something

glistening; something that looked like . . .

A TOOTH!

She was far too plump to squeeze through the tunnel made by the pillow, but, with a last effort, she flew up and landed on the little boy's nose.

'Atchoo!' he sneezed, and rolled over.

Now Hefty could crawl into the tunnel.

Further and further she went until her fingers touched the smooth white tooth.

43

She grabbed it, left the twenty-pence piece behind and scurried to the end of the bed. 'Ooo, ooo, ooo,' she cried in a wobbly, worried sort of way.

There was no time to lose. Looking down, she saw the cat snuggled under the bed.

That's the answer, she thought and, with a great jump, landed right on top of its back. 'Giddy up!' she cried.

The cat ran through the kitchen, out of the cat flap and into the

garden where a triumphant Hefty Fairy bounced on to the grass.

And not a moment too soon! Looking back she saw the tooth fairies, like two bright stars, by the door.

Then there was only a faint silver trail of fairy dust lingering in the keyhole.

It was midnight!

The Hefty Fairy had had quite

enough excitement for one night. But there was still the long journey home. She felt lonely as she flew, so she sang to cheer herself up:

'I'm the fairy who's lumpy,
I'm lumpy, frumpy and dumpy.
I dance round the ring
Flapping my wings,
Going bumpety! Bumpety! Bumpety!'

Back in the grotto the fairies were having breakfast and boasting about how many teeth they'd collected,

when they suddenly heard a noise above them.

Something large and round was crashing through the trees. Out of the sky dropped an enormous pink football. Buttercups and saucers went flying; fairies fell off their chairs. Very slowly the football moved. It rolled one way, then another. A plump foot uncurled, then a short leg, another leg, a wing, two wings, two hands, two arms, and, finally, a dazed head popped out. 'It's Hefty!' cried a fairy. Everyone laughed.

'Yes it's me,' Hefty said proudly. 'I've been away to collect a tooth.' She tipped up her rucksack to show her prize . . . but there was nothing there.

It must have fallen out! All the fairies laughed. 'You *silly* great Hefty Fairy,' they cried. 'How could *you* ever collect a tooth!'

'I'm *not* a silly Hefty Fairy,' cried Hefty, waving her arms. Tears welled up in her eyes. She picked herself up and started to run. She ran and she ran, through the

sunbeams, along the fairy paths, across the fairy ring until she came to the fairy palace.

She ran through the pearly hall, through the state rooms and the winter ballroom and into the Fairy Queen's bedroom. There was the Fairy Queen having breakfast in bed.

Hefty put her arms round her and cried and cried and cried. The Fairy Queen loved Hefty very much and felt sad to see her lumpy fairy so upset.

49

'But it really happened, Your Majesty,' said Hefty. 'I did find a tooth, all by myself.'

'I know,' replied the Fairy Queen.

'You do!' cried Hefty in surprise. Then Hefty remembered that the Fairy Queen knew *everything*.

Next the Fairy Queen did an amazing thing. She stood up and went through a little gold door. When she came out, she was pulling behind her:

something oblong;

something white;

something glistening;
something that looked like . . .
Hefty Fairy's tooth!
'Oh, thank you, Your
Majesty,' cried
Hefty, rushing
towards the door.
'Where are you
going?' said the
Queen.
'To show off my
tooth,' replied Hefty
excitedly.
The Fairy Queen

said nothing. But as Hefty reached
the door she stopped and looked
round. All at once she remembered
how nasty the other fairies had been
and wondered if she wanted to
show them her tooth at all!

'Of course,' said the Queen, 'the
tooth could be a Very Special Secret
between ourselves.'

'A completely proper secret?'
whispered Hefty.

'One only you and I will know
about,' replied the Fairy Queen.
And to seal the Very Special Secret

she kissed the Hefty Fairy on the cheek.

To share a secret with the Fairy Queen was the biggest honour in the whole fairy kingdom.

Hefty was the happiest fairy alive.

The Hefty Fairy felt very important. She built a wardrobe and hid her tooth inside.

Whenever she felt unhappy, which wasn't very often, she would lift out her tooth and sit in her chair, looking at it, remembering her amazing adventure.

She knew then that she was just as good as any other fairy and, somehow, the other fairies seemed to know it too!

FLissie and the ELVes ELeVen

Jan Burchett and Sara Vogler

Flissie Flitterdown
stood in her bedroom.
She gazed at
her reflection
in a fresh
dawn dewdrop.
She looked like a

perfect fairy in every way. Her hair sparkled, her dress glittered and her wings twinkled. And the dinky pink foxglove hat that Grandma had given her for her birthday was perched on top of her head at exactly the right angle.

'Yuck!' groaned Flissie, splattering the dewdrop against her bedroom wall.

Ahead of her loomed yet another day of being a good little fairy. How boring! Last week she'd

scattered thistledown all over Buttercup Meadow, sprinkled sixty-six spider webs with fairy dust and collected three thousand, four hundred and seventeen children's teeth. And now it was her task to skip off to Mr Potter's garden and pop up amongst the poppies until she was seen. For some reason humans liked to see fairies at the bottom of their gardens.

Flissie decided she would rather just sit under a cabbage and pick her nose. If only she was old

57

enough to have a wand – a big, long silver one. At least then she could have fun with some spells.

Flissie grabbed her fairy basket and stuffed a few things in it. All at once there was a puff of pink powder and a tinkling of tiny bells, and her mother appeared in front of her, waving her wand.

'Time to go, Flissie!' she chirruped happily. 'Have you got your wing gloss?'

'Yes, Mum,' sighed Flissie.

'And your daisy-leaf sandwiches?'

58

'Yes, Mum.'

'And your Mr Sparkle's Sponge-
It-Off Kit for Getting Rid of
Unsightly Garden Stains?'

'YES, MUM!'

'Have a nice day then!' twinkled
Mrs Flitterdown, fluffing up the
gossamer netting on Flissie's skirt.

'I won't,' muttered Flissie under
her breath.

While her mother stood watching at
the door of the family mushroom,
Flissie skipped merrily down the

winding path. She tripped round the turn that led through the Magic Forest towards Dingly Dell. But as soon as she was out of sight she began to mooch along, swinging her basket crossly and scuffing her pink satin slippers as much as she could.

'Felicity Flitterdown!' came a stern voice. 'What do you think you're doing?'

Flissie looked up. Above her head hovered Miss Prettywick, one of the Fairy Behaviour Inspectors. Oh no, thought Flissie. I'd have kept up the

60

skipping if I'd known that the FBI were on patrol!

'Sorry, Miss Prettywick,' she said in the most sugary voice she could manage. 'I was um . . . just trying to scrape some dirt from my shoes.'

'Are you not carrying your Mr Sparkle's Shine-It-Up Kit for Getting Rid of Unsightly Slipper Stains?'

Flissie shook her head glumly.

'Young fairies today!' sighed Miss Prettywick. 'You'd forget your wings if they weren't sewn on!' She

waved her wand at Flissie's feet and the slippers shimmered anew. 'Now, no shilly-shallying! You'd better fly or you'll be late for Mr Potter.'

'Thank you, Miss Prettywick,' said Flissie, with a sickly smile. She wiggled her wings and took off, feeling crosser than ever.

Soon she came to a sign.

YOU ARE NOW ENTERING
DINGLY DELL
**Dingly Dell welcomes
careful fliers**

62

Just a short flight across Dingly Dell and she'd be in Mr Potter's garden. She knew she'd be there all day. Old Mr Potter never came out of his cottage.

Thump! Something hit Flissie on the head. She fell out of the air and landed with a splat on a damp dock leaf.

'Sorry, mate!' said a cheerful voice. 'You OK?'

Dazed, Flissie looked up. An elf was standing over her. He was wearing the usual green felt jacket

63

and shorts, but he had a big number nine on his chest. He reached down a hand and pulled her to her feet.

'No harm done?' he asked.

'No,' said Flissie, rubbing her head. 'I'm fine. But what happened?'

'Coal there hit you with the conker!' he explained, pointing at a red-faced elf who was twisting his acorn cap about in his hands. 'Shame. It was a fantastic throw-in.'

64

'Conker?' murmured Flissie in confusion. 'Throw-in? I don't understand.'

'We're playing footconker,' said the elf. 'Best game in the Magic Forest. I'm Bex and we're the Elves Eleven. We all live in the Old Oak Tree just over there.'

'I'm Flissie,' said Flissie, 'and I'm a fairy.'

'Well I didn't

think you were a goblin!' laughed Bex. 'Do you want to watch? We're having a practice on our pitch.'

'All right then,' said Flissie. Anything was better than Mr Potter's poppies. She sat down on a tuft of moss. Bex picked up the conker and ran back to join his friends.

Flissie watched. The Elves Eleven kicked the conker about inside a rectangle marked out with snail slime. Some of them were trying to

boot it into a spider's web at one end, and the rest were trying to do the same at the other. They flicked the conker in the air, they trapped it under their little green boots and they kicked it to each other so quickly it made Flissie's head spin. She'd never seen fairies do anything like this! Her feet twitched. She longed to join in.

There was one strange thing about the Elves Eleven. There were only ten of them. Flissie wondered why. Perhaps they'd been hit on the head so many times by the conker they couldn't count any more.

All of a sudden the conker rolled over towards her.

'Knock it back here, will you, Flissie!' yelled Coal, waving.

Flissie stood up, pulled back her leg and kicked the conker just like she'd seen the elves do. It flew through the air and landed right at Coal's feet. It felt great!

All the elves stared at her.

'That was a brilliant punt,' said

Bex in amazement. 'Do you want to play?'

'Yes please!' yelled Flissie. She dashed on to the pitch to join them.

Footconker was wonderful! Flissie was on the team with Bex, and they had to get the conker past a big elf called Banksy, who was guarding his web with his life. Flissie wasted no time. As soon as the conker came her way she made a run up the side of the pitch with it. She had seen Bex do that earlier. She was so fast that none of the

69

elves on the other team could catch her. She kicked the conker across to Bex and ran towards the web. Bex booted it back to her. Remembering what she'd seen the elves do, Flissie trapped it under her slipper and then slammed it hard into the web. To her horror the web broke.

Oh, no! thought Flissie. I've spoilt the game! They'll never let me play again.

Bex and his team rushed over. Everyone was shouting at once.

'That was a great goal!'

'It's got to be the winner.'

'You're a natural on the wing.'

'But I broke your web!' gulped Flissie.

'No problem!' declared Banksy with a huge grin. 'Our team mascot will sort that out.' He gave a

71

whistle. 'Spinner!' he yelled, 'we need you!'

At that a big black spider let itself down on its thread from a tree above. 'OK, Boss!' it grinned, waving its hairy legs in delight. And before you could say Little Miss Muffet it had spun a strong new web.

When the game finished, Flissie's cheeks were glowing. She'd had the time of her life.

The Elves Eleven gathered round her – all ten of them.

'Coal's had a brilliant idea,' Banksy told her. 'We've got a game on Saturday against Gnomes United and since Buster broke his leg we're an elf short. Do you want to play?'

Flissie couldn't believe her dainty little ears!

'That would be magic!' she gasped. Then she frowned. 'How exactly did Buster break his leg? He wasn't playing footconker, was he?'

'Of course not!' laughed Coal. 'He fell out of bed.'

73

'You can't break a leg falling out of bed!' exclaimed Flissie.

'You can if your bed's on the fifteenth branch up!' Bex told her. 'Anyway, we must get home. See you Saturday at three, here at the Dell. Gnomes United won't know what's hit them!'

Flissie flew home in a happy daze. She was going to play in a proper footconker match! But as she got near to her mushroom house she came to a stop and hovered

74

anxiously in the air. What were her parents going to say? Her heart sank to her slippers. She had a feeling that footconker was not for good little fairies.

Her father was in the front garden feeding the ladybirds. He took one look at her and put down his packet of dried aphids.

'Flissie!' he said sternly. 'Where have you been? Miss Prettywick has just sent me a bee-mail. She told me you did not go to Mr Potter's garden as you were supposed to!'

'Sorry, Dad,' said Flissie in a tiny voice. 'I've been playing a nice game called footconker. With some elves.' She took a deep breath. 'And they've asked me to play in a proper match on Saturday at Dingly Dell.'

'Footconker!' Flissie knew she was in trouble when her father started shouting. 'Footconker's not for good little fairies! It's dirty and rough. And with elves! Don't get me started on elves. They're common, they're cheeky and they smell.

Haven't I always told you, Flissie? You can't trust anything with pointed ears.'

There was a puff of pink powder and a tinkling of tiny bells.

'What's going on?' said a chirpy voice.

It was Flissie's mother, come to see what all the noise was about.

'Flissie has not been popping up amongst the poppies in Mr Potter's garden,' exploded her dad. He flapped furiously round in the air,

77

scattering the dandelion clocks in clouds of seeds.

'But that was your fairy task for today, Flissie,' fluttered her mother. 'I am very disappointed that you didn't go!'

'Wait till you hear what she *has* been doing, Tulip,' bellowed her father from above. 'She's been playing footconker! And she wants to do it again! On Saturday! With elves! At the Dell!'

Flissie's mother looked at her. Flissie waited for another explosion.

But Mrs Flitterdown clapped her hands gleefully.

'Then of course she must!' she twinkled.

'What?' spluttered Mr Flitterdown. 'But, Tulip . . . elves . . . footconker!'

Mr Flitterdown was not the only one who was surprised. Flissie gawped at her mother in astonishment. 'Don't stand there with your mouth open, sweetie,' said her mum. 'You'll catch gnats in it. But don't think you're getting out of your duties. Back you go to

79

Mr Potter's garden. When you've finished with the poppies you can do a wee spot of overtime tripping in and out of the trellis.'

'Thanks, Mum!' gasped Flissie. She flew off before her mother could change her mind. She couldn't believe her luck! Now she didn't mind how much popping and tripping she had to do. She was going to play footconker on Saturday!

As soon as she'd gone, Mr Flitterdown zoomed down on to

the pebbly path in front of his wife.

'Have you gone mad, Tulip?' he exclaimed, hopping with rage. 'Letting our Flissie play footconker? The FBI won't like it. And what will the neighbours say if they find out? I'll never be able to hold up my head at the Gardening Club after this!'

'No one's going to find out, Linden,' his wife assured him. 'Fairies keep well away from the Dell when there's a match.'

81

'But . . . but,' spluttered Mr Flitterdown. 'If Flissie plays in a proper match she'll get battered and bashed and . . . and . . . and come home covered in mud!'

'Exactly, dearest,' chirped his wife, patting him on the arm. 'And then she'll never want to play footconker again!'

Saturday dawned bright and sunny. The Elves Eleven – ten elves and Flissie – marched out on to the Dingly Dell footconker pitch.

Flissie's pink dress sparkled in the sunlight. She had a big number eleven on the front. Gnomes United waited for them. They looked big and tough. The referee, a pixie from Babbling Brook, sent them all to their places.

Lots of forest folk had come to watch the match. All the elves' parents were there, shouting and cheering and fighting on the touchline. Spinner the spider did his special Elves Eleven cheer dance.

83

Gnomes United were going to be hard to beat. But the elves had Flissie on their side. And Flissie was fast. She flitted in between them and was off with the conker before they could think about tackling her. The lumbering gnomes just stood there scratching their heads.

Flissie was the star of the game. Everyone was cheering for her – even some of the gnome supporters! (Gnomes aren't very bright.)

Flissie didn't notice the air shimmering slightly at one corner of

the pitch. She didn't see her mum and dad watching as she scored five goals in three minutes. Mr and Mrs Flitterdown had made themselves invisible.

'Look at Flissie!' exclaimed Mr Flitterdown crossly. 'She's playing against gnomes. Don't get me started on gnomes. They're big and lumpy. Never trust anything with gnarly skin! What are we going to do, Tulip? She's not getting battered or bashed, and there's not a spot of mud in sight!'

'Then we need to conjure up some rain,' chirruped his wife. 'Once she gets a speck of dirt on her lovely pink dress she'll be off the pitch before you can say Peter Piper picked a peck of pickled peppers.'

'But we're good fairies, dear. We can't do bad spells.'

'We know someone who can, though!' twinkled Mrs Flitterdown. 'Your Great Aunt Agatha. Do send her a bee-mail.'

The next minute there was a faint

buzzing followed by a *Poommph!* from a nearby primrose.

The Flitterdowns were usually too scared to invite Great Aunt Agatha over. She wasn't quite like other fairies. Most fairies are dainty, even the men. Great Aunt Agatha wasn't. She was  round and dumpy and wore a frightful old moth-eaten black cloak. She claimed to be a direct descendant of Malvolia, the

wicked fairy who'd caused all the
trouble for Sleeping Beauty. And so
she dressed the part with a long
greasy wig and a few warts stuck
on for good measure. But today the
Flitterdowns had an emergency!

Some of the spectators were
beginning to stare. Flissie's mum
waved her wand hurriedly and
Great Aunt Agatha vanished from
everyone's sight. Now the fairies
were the only forest folk who could
still see her.

Great Aunt Agatha rushed over

to Flissie's parents and gave them a big hug.

'Darlings!' she gushed, kissing them on both cheeks. 'Aggie's here. What's the problem?'

Mr and Mrs Flitterdown told her their predicament.

'Flissie is playing footconker and we're very worried about it . . .' began Flissie's dad.

'Say no more, young Linden!' exclaimed Great Aunt Agatha, rubbing her hands with glee. 'You want me to help you out.' She

began warming up her twisted black wand. 'I have to warn you, my bad spells only last a little while. But there's nothing I like better than a bit of harmless mischief, as Malvolia said when she arrived at Sleeping Beauty's christening. Now let me see . . . yes, I have just the spell! Knit Knot Knoots. Tie up the boots!'

On the pitch the gnomes were getting desperate. Flissie had outrun them yet again, passed the ball to Coal, who had slammed it into the

90

web. Six–nil. Then while the gnomes were still gawping at Flissie, Bex had scored after a brilliant long ball from Banksy. Seven–nil.

The gnomes stopped gawping. They had finally worked out how to stop Flissie. Every single gnome on the pitch crowded round her as she sped for the goal. She had no way of getting through.

But all of a sudden it looked as if the gnomes' boots had exploded in a flash of black smoke! They fell to the ground, groaning, and staring

91

at their feet in disbelief. All their bootlaces were tied together! The referee blew his whistle and consulted his rule book. This had never happened before in all his years of footconker.

'Aggie!' hissed Mrs Flitterdown. 'Wrong team! We don't want Flissie to enjoy the footconker.'

'Don't we?' asked Great Aunt Agatha, puzzled.

'No we don't!' insisted Mr Flitterdown. 'We want her to get dirty and have a miserable time!'

92

'Why didn't you say so?' squealed his great aunt. 'This *will* be fun, as Malvolia said when she set up her spinning wheel in the tower!' She waved her wand around her head three times. 'Splish, splash, splosh! Soon we'll be awash!' she shrieked merrily.

The gnomes had only just struggled to their feet when *Poommph!* the sky turned black. Raindrops as big as pebbles fell down. Before you could say Incy Wincy the pitch had turned into a

mudbath. Soon all the players were covered in mud, and Flissie's lovely pink dress and slippers were brown and tattered.

'Well done, Great Aunt Agatha,' said Mrs Flitterdown in relief. 'Now she'll never want to play this silly game again.'

'A pleasure, I'm sure,' beamed Great Aunt Agatha.

Flissie's dad shook her hand. 'Goodbye then, Auntie, and thank you.'

'But I'm not finished yet,' cackled

94

the dumpy fairy. 'I've got a lot more than this up my sleeve, as Malvolia said when she planted that first thorn bush outside the castle.' She warmed up her wand again.

Flissie's parents looked at each other in alarm.

'Are you sure this is wise, Tulip?' whispered Mr Flitterdown. 'Who knows what she'll do next? And you know the old saying: never trust a fairy once she starts cackling!'

On the pitch, the sun was out again
and everything was steaming. It
was lucky that the gnomes were
much bigger and lumpier than
Flissie and the elves, because all the
players were so covered in mud it
was hard to tell who was who.

Flissie had lost her slippers and
her wings were sodden and
weighing her down. But she was
unmarked. Bex lobbed the conker to
her and she began a run – or at
least a squelch – up the field. She
dodged one gnome and then

another. Now the goal was in her sight. The referee was just checking his watch when . . .

. . . *Poommph!* He turned into a small green frog and hopped off in search of a pond.

Poommph! The spectators on the touchline turned into pumpkins.

Poommph! The goal turned into the head of a large fire-breathing dragon!

Flissie turned to Bex. 'You didn't tell me about these rules! What happens if I boot the conker into

97

the dragon's mouth – is it still a goal?'

'Beats me!' said Bex, scratching his head.

Back on the touchline, Mrs Flitterdown clocked Great Aunt Agatha with her basket and Mr Flitterdown sat on her as she fell. The spells stopped. The pumpkins turned back into spectators, the dragon became a web again and the referee hopped back to the pitch. He had pondweed draped over his pixie hat and looked rather puzzled as he blew the final whistle.

'Seven–nil to the Elves Eleven!' he croaked.

Flissie was a dreadful sight. Her dress was tattered and torn and her knee was bleeding. Her

hair looked like rat's-tails and her wings were drooping sadly down her back. All at once there was a puff of pink powder and a tinkling of tiny bells and her mother appeared in front of her.

'I'm sorry about my dress, Mum,' said Flissie, when she had got over her surprise.

'Don't worry, dear,' twinkled Mum.

'And my wings have lost their gloss,' said Flissie.

'Don't worry, dear,' twinkled Mum.

'I must be a terrible sight,' said Flissie.

'Don't worry, dear,' twinkled Mum, raising her wand. 'I'll soon have you back to rights. And you won't ever have to play that nasty game again.'

'Oh, yes I will,' beamed Flissie through the grime. 'I'm in the team for next Saturday. Thanks for letting me play. This is the best day of my life!'

101

Lettuce Fairy

Paeony Lewis

Lollo flew to the top of an iceberg lettuce and called, 'Guess what?'

Three tiny fairies looked up from the vegetable patch.

'Tell us,' called the fairies.

Lollo the Lettuce Fairy twirled, and her skirt of salad leaves

fluttered in the breeze. 'Go on, have a guess.'

'The slugs have tummy ache after munching your lettuces?' asked the Carrot Fairy.

'No!'

'The pigeons have stopped pecking your lettuce seedlings?' asked the Pea Fairy.

'No!'

'You're going to leave us in peace and become a smelly compost fairy?' said Maris, the Potato Fairy. 'You'd be good at that.'

Lollo stuck out her tongue at Maris and grinned. 'No! I'm going to be a wonderful, beautiful, glamorous, sophisticated rose fairy.'

'That's not fair,' moaned Maris. She scowled and kicked at the earth. A shower of soil splattered the side of one of Lollo's lettuces. Maris kicked again.

Lollo flapped her green wings and flew down.

'Don't mess up my lettuces,' said Lollo to Maris. 'I have to keep them

105

perfect for three days. Otherwise I won't get to be a rose fairy.'

Maris's scowl turned into a sneaky smile. 'So you haven't definitely got the rose job?'

'Not quite,' said Lollo. 'The Queen of the Garden Fairies said I'd been working really hard and she felt sure I'd get the job I deserved. Well, I think I deserve to be a beautiful rose fairy. Of course if another fairy also wants to be a rose fairy then . . .' Lollo's voice trailed off. She stared at Maris. 'Do

you know if anybody else has asked to be the Rose Fairy?'

Maris's sneaky smile turned into an innocent smile. 'I'm sure you don't need to worry,' she said. 'However, just in case, I'll help you watch your lettuces.'

'Thank you,' said Lollo. 'But I'll be fine.'

'Oh, I insist,' said Maris.

Lollo couldn't help shuddering at the glint in the eyes of the Potato Fairy.

107

All afternoon Lollo the Lettuce Fairy stood on top of a big cos lettuce. Every time a bird approached she'd wave her wand. If a slug or snail came too near again, she waved her wand and green stars shot out.

'Oi!' grumbled a snail. 'Quit shooting stars. You'll dent my shell.'

'Sorry,' said Lollo. 'I just want to keep my

lettuces safe. I'm going to be a rose fairy.'

'Roses have yucky thorns,' muttered the snail, and he headed towards the plump pea pods.

'Shoo!' shouted the Pea Fairy.

The snail turned around and slithered on to the path. 'Darn fairies. Why can't they let a snail eat in peace?' he muttered. 'Don't know why they bother protecting stuff. Humans can't see fairies. It's all a big waste of time.'

'I so agree with you,' said a voice.

109

The snail swivelled his head. Maris the Potato Fairy stood there. She had her 'I feel so sorry for you' expression on her face.

'I don't like potatoes,' said the snail.

'But you do like lettuces,' said Maris. 'Lovely, juicy, succulent lettuces.'

The snail nodded, drooling with excitement. By the time Maris had finished explaining her plan, he stood in a puddle of drool. 'Yum,' he said for the thirty-third time. 'I'll

wait for you to give me the starry signal.'

Plip plop began the rain. Lollo shook her wand and it turned into a green umbrella. Plip plop. Plip plop. The rain fell harder.

'Come and shelter under one of my potato plants,' called Maris from across the vegetable patch.

Lollo shook her head. 'Thanks, but I've got to keep watch.'

Maris shrugged her shoulders and went back to jumping on a

potato that stuck up out of the soil.

Plip plop, plip plop, plip plop. The rain fell harder. Lollo shivered and thought about curling up in a beautiful, soft rose. In the distance she could just see the glamorous red roses shining through the rain.

'Hey, Lollo,' said a voice in her ear.

Lollo dropped her umbrella. She turned. 'Oh, it's you.'

Maris stood there, wearing an old potato hat. Rain dripped from her

nose. 'I think I saw a slug heading towards your favourite baby lettuces,' she said.

'My lovely Lollo Rossa seedlings?'

'Yeah, those things,' said Maris.

Lollo flew to the top of the highest iceberg lettuce. She squinted through the rain at her little Lollo Rossa seedlings. Was that a brown slimy slug or a mound of wet soil?

'What are you waiting for?' said Maris, who'd crawled up behind her. 'Go protect your precious seedlings. I'll watch your other lettuces.'

113

Lollo looked at Maris. The Potato Fairy smiled her best helpful-looking smile.

'You'll really watch my lettuces?' asked Lollo.

Maris widened her smile. 'I won't take my eyes off them.'

'That's surprisingly kind of you,' said Lollo.

Lollo thanked Maris and flew as fast as she could towards her Lollo Rossa seedlings. Flying was hard work because the rain made her lettuce wings soggy. Lollo landed

with a thump and looked back to see five brown stars shoot out from the Potato Fairy's wand.

'I think Maris just used some of her magic stars to keep my lettuces safe,' said Lollo to her favourite little lettuces (who couldn't talk back, but liked listening). 'How generous of Maris. I hope she has enough magic left for herself.'

The Lollo Rossa seedlings stood in a wet row. All green and red and frilly. Lollo marched up and down the first row, inspecting every baby

lettuce. She lifted dripping leaves and patted the stalks.

'I can't see any slugs or nibbled leaves,' said Lollo to her lettuces. She flicked wet hair from her eyes. 'But I'll check the second row, just to be sure. Maris is watching my other lettuces so I don't need to worry.'

Lollo trudged down the next row, splashing her legs with mud. She thought about being curled up and dry in a gorgeous red rose, sniffing its delicate perfume.

116

THUMP! SPLAT!

Lollo wiped mud off her face and looked around. She remembered stepping on a potato leaf and suddenly she'd fallen down a hole.

The hole was three times the height of Lollo. She tried flapping her wings to fly out. Nothing happened. Her heavy, soggy, muddy wings stayed flopped down her back.

Lollo tried climbing. She grabbed at the side of the hole and pulled herself up. Squelch! Down she

117

slithered. Every time Lollo took a step upwards, the mud oozed away from under her feet and she slid down to the bottom of the hole.

'Help!' called Lollo. 'HELP!'

Nobody came. The rain fell harder. Without the potato leaf to cover the hole, the muddy water began to rise. First it covered Lollo's feet. Then her ankles. Then her knees . . .

'HELP!'

Lollo groaned. Stuff like this didn't happen to glamorous rose fairies. It

was time for magic. Lollo knew that
a spell to get her out of the hole
would use up all the magic in her
wand, but this was an emergency.

Lollo waved her muddy wand.
This time there were no shooting
stars. Just one tired, faint green star
plopped out of the tip of her wand.
It was enough to raise Lollo into
the air. But only for a second.

FLOP! SQUELCH!

All the magic had gone from her
wand. She'd used it up chasing
away birds, snails, slugs and

caterpillars. Now the muddy water reached Lollo's waist. It would be hours before her wand was recharged with enough power to lift her out of the hole.

Lollo sniffed. A stink of mouldy, muddy potatoes filled her nose. Where is Maris? she thought.

'HELP!' yelled Lollo. 'HELP!'

'What are you doing down there?' called a voice.

Lollo looked up to see the Pea Fairy. 'I fell in this hole and I'm stuck.'

120

'Wait there,' called back the Pea Fairy. 'I'll go and find help.'

The Pea Fairy wasn't gone too long, although it felt like ages to Lollo in the hole that had now turned into a muddy swimming pool. Lollo practised her crawl and backstroke to keep her mind off her muddy wet doom.

SPLOSH! The end of something fell in the water. It was a long pea tendril.

'Grab hold,' called the Pea Fairy.

121

'We'll pull you up,' called another voice. It was the Carrot Fairy.

Lollo clung to the pea tendril. Slowly, bit by bit, the fairies pulled her up the side of the muddy hole.

Finally, two wet fairies and one muddy, extra-wet fairy stood at the edge of the hole.

'Poor you,' said the Pea Fairy. 'That's a new hole. I wonder what made it?'

Lollo shook her head, 'I don't know, although it smells of mouldy old potatoes.'

She sighed, opened her muddy wings and stretched out her arms to help the rain wash her clean. Then Lollo looked around. 'Talking of potatoes, where's Maris?'

'I did find her,' said the Pea Fairy. 'She said she was busy watching your lettuces, just like she'd promised.'

'Oh,' said Lollo. Now she felt guilty for doubting the Potato Fairy.

The rain began to ease and

123

together the fairies went to find
Maris.

When they reached the iceberg
lettuces, Lollo wailed.

'My lettuces! They're ruined!'

A snail looked up. So did his
mates.

'Ooops,' said one of the snails.
'Time to go.'

'Thanks for the meal,' called
another snail. 'Delicious.'

'Maris,' said Lollo. 'I can't believe
this. I thought you were watching
my lettuces.'

124

'I did watch them,' said Maris. 'I never stopped watching.' She giggled. 'And I watched the snails eat them. They had such a fun time.'

Lollo sank down on a half-eaten lettuce leaf. She put her soggy head in her hands. 'Now I'll never be a glamorous rose fairy.'

'We'll see,' said a clear, musical voice.

The sun chased away the clouds and a rainbow arched across the freshly washed sky. The rainbow

ended in the vegetable garden. Red, orange, yellow, green, blue, indigo and violet light danced on the munched lettuces.

Lollo jumped up and curtsied. The Pea, Carrot and Potato Fairies curtsied too.

The Queen of the Garden Fairies raised her gold wand. 'There are two vacant jobs. Who wants to be a rose fairy? Who wants to be a daisy fairy?'

'Rose fairy,' said Lollo in a small voice.

'Rose fairy,' said Maris firmly. She glanced at Lollo and smiled a superior smile.

The Queen swirled her wand. Rainbow stars danced above the heads of the Lettuce and Potato Fairies. 'Let's see what you deserve,' said the Queen.

Lollo looked down at her green, muddy lettuce skirt. Slowly it changed into clean, simple white petals. Her tunic was a soft yellow, tinged with pink. She looked across at Maris and saw her dressed in

127

luscious red petals. Maris smiled triumphantly.

'Good,' said the Queen. 'My magic has worked perfectly.'

Lollo groaned. She opened her mouth to disagree.

'Stop!' said the Queen. 'Are you sure you want to argue with the Queen of the Garden Fairies?'

Lollo trembled under the gaze of the Queen. She lowered her head and said nothing. The little fairy just stared at her feet and the new daisy slippers.

★

That evening, Lollo sat on the
lawn, singing to the daisies. She
wasn't alone. Another new daisy
fairy sang with her. Her name was
Flori.

129

'Isn't this lovely!' said Flori to Lollo. 'It's exactly what I wanted. No mean bugs or gross diseases. All we have to do is encourage the daisies to grow quickly.'

'And to have strong stalks,' said Lollo. 'For perfect daisy chains.'

But Lollo couldn't help looking up at the red rose climbing along the fence. Every few moments red sparks shot into the air.

Flori watched too. Her eyes twinkled.

'Looks like the new Rose Fairy is

130

busy,' said Flori. 'I wonder what she did to deserve it? I never enjoyed being a rose fairy.'

Lollo looked at her with amazement. 'Why? Apart from a few thorns, being a rose fairy must be so glamorous and easy.'

Flori snorted. 'No way! It was really hard work chasing away so many pests. Greenfly, whitefly, caterpillars, thrips, froghoppers, sawflies . . . They never stopped coming. There were thousands of them.' Flori made a face. 'And I

had to clean up icky diseases like black spot, mould and rust. You try being glamorous with all that going on. It was such a bore.'

Lollo the Daisy Fairy stroked a white petal and grinned. 'The Queen of the Garden Fairies said we'd get what we deserved. I wonder if Maris the Rose Fairy agrees?'

Fairy Cake

Jonathan Emmett

Jake's granny is an extraordinary cook and the owner of The Conjuror's Cookbook — *a book of mysterious recipes that, when followed, cause magical creatures to appear.*

It is Jake's birthday and Granny is throwing a party for him. Before the

party, Granny gives Jake a special present – a witching-whisk. Made of silver and shaped like a dragon's foot, the wand-like whisk can be used to magically transform cooking ingredients. With the whisk's help, Jake and Granny are able to attempt one of the Cookbook's more troublesome recipes – Fairy Cake.

Jake added the other ingredients and then picked up the witching-whisk. He wasn't sure how to use it. He wondered whether he should just

134

stir it around like a normal whisk. 'What do you think?' he asked, handing it to Granny.

Granny experimented, whipping the whisk in the air. The talons suddenly sprang open, and she let out a shriek and dropped it into the bowl.

135

The whisk made a slurping noise, as if tasting the mixture. Then it pushed itself up on its talons and began scuttling around the bowl.

'Ugh!' said Granny. 'It's like a spider.'

Jake leaned in closer. He could hear the whisk muttering to itself.

'It must be doing an incantation,' he explained.

The whisk scuttled, faster and faster, churning up the coloured mixture until it disappeared in a

kaleidoscopic blur. The incantation grew faster too, speeding up until the words merged into a high-pitched whine.

'Not bad for an antique,' said Jake admiringly, as the bowl began to glow red-hot.

'It beats my old electric mixer any day,' agreed Granny.

After a few minutes the whine stopped abruptly, and the whisk rattled to a halt against the side of the bowl.

The mixture had been

transformed into a luminous paste that glowed like a light bulb.

Jake scraped it carefully out of the bowl and into an old bird's nest that Granny had found in the garden. Granny put the nest on to a baking tray and popped it into the oven. Then she set the timer and began tidying up.

'We better put this somewhere safe!' she said, holding the witching-whisk gingerly as she ran it under the tap. 'We don't want one of your friends picking it up and

accidentally turning themselves into a meringue or something.'

She put the whisk back in its case and tucked it away at the back of the larder.

'That's it!' said Jake, when the timer went off.

Granny opened the oven door and a cloud of smoke billowed out into the kitchen.

'Oh dear,' she coughed. 'The nest's burned. I must have set the temperature too high.'

She fished out the smoking clump of twigs and dropped it on to a cooling rack.

'Heavens!' she gasped, when she saw what was in it.

Curled up inside the charred nest was the tiniest girl they had ever seen.

'A fairy!' whispered Jake.

'Is it alive?' asked Granny. The fairy lay motionless and her eyes were tight shut.

'I shouldn't think so,' said Jake sadly.

140

'I'll see if I can hear it breathing,' said Granny.

She leaned in close until her ear was covering the tiny face.

'BOO!' yelled the fairy, in a surprisingly loud voice.

'Oh, my giddy aunt,' shrieked Granny, falling backwards on to the floor.

Jake helped her back to her feet. He didn't know what to make of the fairy's behaviour.

'What did you do that for?' he

asked. 'You frightened the life out of us.'

'I know,' said the fairy. 'It was good, wasn't it?'

'It was very rude,' said Granny crossly. 'Especially when we hadn't been introduced.'

'My name's Dewlally,' said the fairy. 'I'm your fairy god-daughter. And it was very rude of *you* to keep calling me *it*!'

Jake couldn't help smiling. The fairy was only a few centimetres high, and yet she

didn't seem at all scared of
Granny.

'Sorry,' he said, 'we didn't mean
to offend you. I'm Jake and this is
Granny.'

'Pleased to meet you,' said
Dewlally, holding out her tiny hand.

Jake reached out to shake it, but the fairy pulled it away and thumbed her nose at him instead.

'Gotcha!' she sniggered.

'What charming manners,' said Granny scornfully. 'How *very* grown up.'

'If being grown up means being an old grumpy-knickers like you, then you can stuff it,' retorted Dewlally, sticking out her tongue.

Jake had to stop himself from laughing. The fairy was being very rude to Granny.

144

'You could try to be a little nicer,' he said, 'after all, we did bake you.'

'Hollyhocks!' said Dewlally. 'Are you nice to whoever baked you?'

'I can't answer that,' said Jake. 'I wasn't really baked.'

'No, you're only *half-baked*!' smirked Dewlally. 'Anyway, just because you baked me, doesn't mean you own me. I can do what I like.'

'Not while you're in my cottage, you can't,' said Granny.

145

'Then I'll get out of your stupid cottage. I wouldn't want to hang around with a ho-hum like you anyway. I'm off!'

Dewlally blew a raspberry and then skipped off towards the open window.

'What a pity,' said Granny, 'just when I was beginning to take a real dislike to you.'

But Jake was disappointed. He had never met a fairy before, and he was sad to see Dewlally leaving, even if she was very rude.

'Won't you stay a little longer?'
he asked. 'We've hardly got to
know each other.'

'Let her go,' said Granny. 'We're
better off without her. We've
got a party to get ready for,
remember!'

'A party?' asked Dewlally, who
was about to leap out of the
window. 'Did you say "party"? I
love parties!'

'Yes,' said Jake, 'it's my birthday.
We're having a party this
afternoon.'

147

'And *you're* not invited,' snapped Granny.

'Why not?' asked Dewlally, leaping back into the kitchen. 'After all, I am your fairy god-daughter!'

'You didn't give a fig for us a moment ago,' said Granny accusingly. 'You were just about to leave.'

'But that was before you invited me to your party,' said Dewlally.

'We haven't invited you!' said Granny firmly. 'You're not coming.'

'Why not?' pleaded Dewlally.

'Because you're bound to cause trouble,' said Granny.

'I won't!' said Dewlally. 'Oh please, please, pretty please, I promise I'll be good.'

Jake didn't say anything, but he gave Granny an imploring look. He wanted Dewlally to come to the party too.

'Look, even if she did behave herself,' argued Granny, '– and I don't believe for a moment that she would – she'd cause enough trouble

just by being seen. Most people don't believe in fairies!'

'That's not a problem,' said Dewlally. 'I can make myself invisible, look!'

The fairy vanished and then reappeared a moment later.

'Oh no!' said Granny. 'That settles it. It would be even worse if we couldn't keep an eye on you!'

'That's not fair!' said Dewlally, stamping her foot.

'Well that's how it is!' retorted Granny. 'So off you go!'

'Shan't!' said the fairy. 'I'm going to hold my breath until you let me come!'

'Please yourself,' said Granny.

Dewlally took a deep breath and then clamped her mouth shut. After a few seconds, her face had turned red and her eyes were bulging out of their sockets.

'Can't we do something?' asked Jake. 'She looks like she's going to explode!'

'She's bluffing,' said Granny

coolly. 'I'm not sure that fairies even need to breathe.'

'I hate you!' gasped Dewlally, letting out her breath. 'You're horrid and I don't want to go to your stupid party anyway. I hope you all have a really awful time!'

And she jumped back on to the window sill and disappeared off into the garden.

'Good riddance!' said Granny, shutting the window. But she saw Jake looking a little sad.

'Oh cheer up,' she said, giving

him a hug. 'It's your birthday,
remember. You're supposed to be
enjoying yourself. Let me show you
what I've prepared for your party.'

Granny had been cooking for
days and the kitchen was stuffed
with delicious treats. The fridge was
overflowing with cooked meats,
quiches, jellies and trifles. And the

larder shelves were groaning with sausage rolls, pasties and cakes and puddings of every description.

Jake's mouth was watering so much he had to wipe it on his sleeve.

'Why don't you take it through and lay it out on the table while I make the sandwiches?' Granny suggested. 'And feel free to nibble. There's plenty more.'

By the time they had finished setting out the food the guests were starting

154

to arrive. They were all Jake's school friends. Jake's parents had meant to come, but they had both gone down with the flu.

'Come in! Come in!' said Granny, ushering everyone into the cottage.

Jake's best friend, Nigel, arrived with his mother. Jake often teased Nigel about her because she was always fussing over him.

'Is Niglet sure he'll be all right without Mumsy?' she asked.

'Yes, Mum,' said Nigel, going

155

bright red with embarrassment. 'It's only a birthday party. I'm not climbing Everest!'

'Well, all right then,' said his mum, giving him a big sloppy kiss. 'But promise to phone me, if you feel poorly and want to come home.'

'This is our number,' she said, handing a piece of paper to Granny, 'and Nigel's doctor's and the hospital's and these are his special headache pills. Oh and here's an extra jumper in case he

gets cold. Now have I forgotten anything?'

'There's no need to worry,' said Granny. 'He's only here until seven o'clock.'

'But that's ages,' fussed Nigel's mother. 'Shall I come back a bit earlier, in case you have any trouble?'

'Thank you, but don't bother,' said Granny kindly. 'I'm sure we'll have no trouble at all.'

Jake's friends couldn't believe it when they saw all the food that

157

was waiting for them. They knew that Granny had written cookbooks so they were looking forward to something special, but none of them had expected such a magnificent feast.

An hour later, as the children were polishing off the last few cakes and sandwiches, Granny popped out to the kitchen and came back with her big surprise.

It was a birthday cake, shaped and decorated to look like a castle. There were little flags flying from

every turret and tiny candles burning on top of the walls.

Everyone was silent in admiration, until Granny started singing 'Happy Birthday to You', and then they all joined in.

Jake blew out the candles and Granny handed him a knife. But it seemed a shame to cut up the beautiful cake.

'Let's save it for after the games,' he said. 'Then everyone will have had a chance to look at it.'

The first game that they played was musical statues. Granny put on some music and the children danced around until she turned it off. Then they were all *supposed* to freeze and stay perfectly still. But for one reason or another most of the children were unable to do so.

'Someone was tickling me!' explained Nigel.

'And someone prodded me in the ribs,' complained one of the girls.

'Well whoever it was had better

stop it,' said Granny. 'That's cheating.'

But the tickling and the prodding didn't stop and the children were soon protesting about other things.

'Someone pinched my bottom!' claimed one child.

'Someone stamped on my foot!' complained another.

'And someone pulled my hair!' sobbed a third.

After a couple more turns like this, Granny was getting suspicious. She watched the children carefully

161

when she turned off the music, but saw none of them touch each other. Either they were all lying or something odd was going on. In the end, Jake was the only person who was able to keep still, and so he was the winner.

'What would you like to play next?' Granny asked him.

'Blind man's buff,' said Jake. 'And I think that *you* should go first, since you didn't play the last game.'

Jake tied a blindfold around Granny's head and then spun her around in the middle of the room until she wasn't sure which way she was pointing.

'Ready or not, here I come!' said Granny. And she set off, with her arms outstretched, trying to find someone.

'Whoa!' she cried, as she tripped over on to the carpet.

'Who was that?' she asked, as she groped around her feet.

'Nobody,' laughed Jake, 'you must have caught your shoe.'

Granny picked herself up and set

off once more. But she hadn't gone more than a couple of steps before she was flat on her face again.

'Now stop it,' she said a little crossly, 'someone definitely tripped me up that time.'

'They didn't,' said Jake. 'We were all watching.'

Granny began to feel uneasy, but she got up and set off once more.

'That's enough!' she shouted after she'd been tripped up for a third time. Someone was sniggering loudly in her ear.

She tore off her blindfold, but there was no one there! All the children were on the other side of the room, looking slightly alarmed.

'I think we'd better play something else now!' said Granny as she got to her feet and tried to compose herself.

She took a large package out of a cupboard and handed it to Nigel.

'Pass-the-parcel,' she explained.

The children sat down in a circle and Granny put some more music on so that the game could begin.

To Granny's great relief, the game seemed to be going smoothly. When the music stopped the child that was holding the parcel tore off the paper to discover a small treat hidden between each layer.

By the end of the game, everyone had got a treat except Jake, so Granny was pleased to see that the parcel had stopped with him for the final layer.

Jake tore open the paper and gasped.

Dewlally was lying inside!

Jake had to think fast. There would be all sorts of trouble if the other children found out about the fairy.

'Look!' he said, jumping up and taking the parcel to Granny. 'It's a little *doll*!'

Granny looked into the wrapping paper and gaped.

'Yes,' she croaked, snatching up Dewlally, 'isn't it lovely? I'll put it in the kitchen, where it won't get broken.'

Dewlally looked like she was

about to protest, but Granny
jammed her thumb into the fairy's
mouth.

'I won't be a moment,' she said,
rushing out of the room.

'You little troublemaker!' hissed
Granny when she got the fairy into
the kitchen.

'Let me go!' squealed Dewlally.
'It's not right for you to hold
me.'

'Isn't it?' said Granny. 'Well, it's
not right for *you* to ruin Jake's

party. This is why I said you shouldn't come.'

'But I love parties,' said Dewlally. 'Besides, I was invisible. You would never have guessed that I was there if I hadn't decided to show myself.'

'Are you kidding?' said Granny. 'All that poking and pinching and tickling. That was you, wasn't it? And who was it that kept tripping me up? I guessed as soon as I heard that sniggering.'

'It was just a bit of fun!' smirked Dewlally.

169

'For you, maybe,' said Granny angrily. 'But I'm covered in bruises! Oh no, you've spoiled enough games for one day. The party's over for you, my girl.'

She took Dewlally into the larder, dropped her into a picnic basket and fastened the lid.

Meanwhile, the children had decided to play hide-and-seek.

'I'll go first,' said Jake. He was anxious to see how Granny was getting on with Dewlally. 'I'll wait

in the kitchen while the rest of you find somewhere to hide.'

'Where is she?' he whispered when he joined Granny.

'In there,' said Granny, nodding towards the larder, 'where she can't get up to any more mischief.'

But Granny couldn't have been more wrong!

Dewlally hadn't stayed inside the picnic basket for long. She'd squeezed out through a carrying hole the moment that Granny had left.

She groped across the dark
larder and tried to push open the
door.

It was locked.

'Hollyhocks!' she muttered. The
door was a tight fit and there was
no chance of slipping under it.

She pressed her ear against the
panelling and heard Jake tell
Granny that he was supposed to be
playing hide-and-seek.

'I'll give them a few more
minutes,' he said, 'then I'll go and
look for them.'

It's not fair, thought Dewlally. I want to play too!

She was feeling very sorry for herself.

There were no windows in the larder, so everything was pitch-dark – or almost everything. Dewlally could just see a dim strip of light coming from the back. She groped towards it and was surprised to find that it was coming from inside a small case.

She undid the catch and heaved open the lid.

When she saw what was inside, she squealed with delight.

Just think of the fun I can have with this, she thought.

The light was coming from spots of luminous cake mixture sticking to the scaly surface of the witching-whisk.

Jake left Granny in the kitchen and went to look for his friends. After searching the entire cottage twice, he came back.

'I can't find them,' he said

exasperatedly, 'not one of them.'

'I'll help you,' said Granny, 'they must be somewhere.'

But they couldn't find any of them.

They looked up in the attic and even in the garden, although the children had agreed that they wouldn't hide outside.

'What on earth's happened to them?' wondered Jake.

'I don't know,' said Granny, 'but I've got a good idea who might.'

She unlocked the larder and

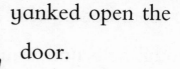

yanked open the door.

They found Dewlally, sitting among a heap of strewn ingredients, clutching the witching-whisk.

Granny nearly exploded.

'Give me that,' she shouted, snatching the whisk from the fairy's hands. 'And tell us what you've done with them.'

'Who?' said Dewlally innocently.

'You know who!' said Granny
hotly.

'My friends,' said Jake.

'Oh, *them*,' said the fairy.
'They're hidden somewhere in the
cottage.'

'Where?' hissed Granny.

'I can't just tell you. You have to
find them yourselves. Isn't that the
point of hide-and-seek?'

Granny lunged at Dewlally,
trying to grab her, but the little fairy
jumped nimbly to one side and
vanished.

177

'Now that wasn't very sporting, was it?' said Dewlally, reappearing in the kitchen behind them. 'If you keep that up, I shan't give you any clues.'

'Clues?' repeated Jake.

'Yes,' said the fairy. 'I thought that would make it more fun.'

'Please can we have one, then?' asked Jake politely. He thought it best to be nice to the fairy. Otherwise, she might disappear for good. Then they'd never find out what she'd done with his friends.

178

'All right, then,' said Dewlally graciously. 'Seeing as you asked so nicely. Here's the first one:

> *What often gets beaten,*
> *But seldom gets thrashed,*
> *Is as smooth as a pebble,*
> *But easily smashed?'*

'What's that supposed to mean?' snapped Granny.

'It's a riddle, isn't it?' asked Jake.

He looked around, but Dewlally

179

had vanished again and wouldn't
answer him.

'I bet she's still here somewhere,'
said Granny suspiciously, 'watching
us!'

'Well, we'd better try and solve
the riddle anyway,' said Jake. 'It's
the only clue we've got. We're
looking for something that's smooth
and fragile.'

They thought about it for a
while.

'A piece of glass,' suggested
Granny.

180

'No,' said Jake. 'That can't be right. You don't *beat* glass, do you?'

'Of course!' said Granny, slapping her forehead. 'It's eggs – they're smooth and fragile, and you beat them. But how does that help us find your friends?'

'I've been thinking about that,' said Jake. 'They can't be their normal size or we'd have found them by now. Dewlally must have used the witching-whisk to *shrink* them—'

'And hide them with the eggs!' exclaimed Granny.

They ran to the fridge and pulled out the egg tray, but there was no sign of the children. They even tried looking *inside* the eggs, breaking them open in their hands, but with no luck.

'Now the *yolk's* on you!' sniggered Dewlally, reappearing on the far side of the kitchen.

'Very funny,' said Jake, keeping his temper, 'but there's nothing here.'

'Of course,' said Dewlally. 'That was only the first clue. There are still three more.'

'Come on then,' said Granny testily, 'give us the next one.'

'What's the "magic word"?' asked Dewlally.

'Please!' said Jake.

'Here you are then,' said Dewlally.

> *'What's always ground,*
> *But not found underfoot,*
> *Is as white as a pearl,*
> *But as powdery as soot?'*

183

And then she vanished again.

'Right,' said Jake. 'We're looking for something white and powdery ...'

'... that's always ground,' added Granny. 'What do you suppose that means? It can't mean soil because you can find that under your feet.'

'Flour!' exclaimed Jake. 'That's *ground* — in a mill!'

They rushed into the larder and searched through all the flour jars, but found nothing.

184

'I didn't think we would,' said Jake. 'Not after what Dewlally said last time.'

'Quite right,' said the fairy, appearing on a shelf high above them. She looked like she was really enjoying herself. 'That would be far too easy. You need to get *all* the answers and put them together if you want to find the hiding place. Here's the next riddle:

What lies before flies
And fingers and cup

And is spread upon bread
Before eating it up?'

'That's easy,' said Granny straight away, 'it's butter.'

'Wow!' said Dewlally, taken aback. 'You're not as stupid as you look.'

'What's the last one?' said Jake, before Granny had a chance to reply.

'What's made out of crystal,
Is sold as a grain,

But grows in the field
As a beet or a cane?'

Both Jake and Granny had got the hang of the riddles now.

'Sugar!' they both said at once.

'Hollyhocks!' cursed Dewlally. 'I didn't think you'd get them that quickly.'

And just then, the doorbell rang.

The bell was so loud and unexpected that it made everyone jump.

187

Dewlally was so startled, she fell off her shelf.

'Got you!' said Granny, lunging across the larder and catching the fairy in her hand. 'Now tell us where you've hidden the children.'

'Never!' said Dewlally, stubbornly. 'Not even if you torture me!'

The doorbell rang loudly again. There was still an hour before the children were supposed to be picked up, so Granny hadn't a clue as to who it could be.

'We'd better go and see,' said
Jake.

'First things first,' said Granny.
She got some clingfilm and wound
it tightly around Dewlally's body,
pinning her arms to her sides. Then
she shut the fairy in the oven and
wedged a chair against the door.

Nigel's mother was on the doorstep.

'I know you said I needn't come
early,' she said, pushing into the
hallway. 'But I was worried about
Niglet and I couldn't bear to wait.

Where is the little darling? It's awfully quiet.'

'Err, he's hidden around here somewhere,' said Granny, trying to sound relaxed, 'along with the other children.'

'We're playing hide-and-seek,' explained Jake. 'Why don't you wait with Granny while I go and find them?'

'What a good idea,' said Granny, steering Nigel's mum into the front room. 'I'm sure they won't be long.'

Jake went back into the kitchen and wondered where to look. There was no point in questioning Dewlally. She was obviously determined not to give in. He would have to work it out from the clues she'd already given them.

Eggs, flour, butter and sugar – Dewlally had said that he needed to put all these answers together to find the hiding place, but what did she mean?

He tried writing all the words on a piece of paper and then mixing

191

up the letters to make new words.
He got 'fur to bug larger guests'
and 'leaf rug bursts ogre gut', but
nothing that made any sense. This
is silly, he thought. There are
hundreds of words I could make.
I could be mixing these letters for
ever.

And then he realized! The
answers did have to be mixed
together, but not as letters. They
were the four basic ingredients for
making a cake!

Jake ran into the hallway and

192

bumped into Nigel's mum. Despite Granny's efforts, she had decided to look for Nigel herself.

'He's probably trapped in a cupboard somewhere, unable to breathe!' she said anxiously.

'Yes, I expect so,' said Granny absently. She was wondering what Jake was up to.

Jake ran into the dining room and made straight for the birthday cake.

It was still sitting in the middle of the table. But it looked slightly different. There were now some small figures standing guard on top of the walls.

Jake peered at the figures closely and recognized the tiny, frozen faces of his friends.

'I've found them!' he whispered.

As soon as he said this, the figures grew larger, swelling outwards like balloons. A couple of seconds later, and the children were tumbling over each other as they reached their proper size.

'Niglet!' said Nigel's mother, who

had just come into the room. 'What on earth are you doing on the table?'

'I don't know,' said Nigel dazedly. 'I think I must have been asleep.'

'On top of a table?' said his mother incredulously. 'And what's that all over your best shoes? It looks like cake.'

Jake and Granny were relieved to find that the children couldn't remember anything that had happened after they'd gone off to

hide. Jake told them that they must have eaten too much and had all dozed off. He said that he and Granny had found them all and carried them into the dining room. Of course, he didn't try to explain why they'd woken up on the table. He pretended to be as puzzled about that as they were.

Fortunately, they all thought that it was hilariously funny and no one could be bothered to find out who was responsible.

When Jake and Granny had seen

196

the last child off, they went back into the cottage to clear up.

'Well I suppose the party was a success, after all,' sighed Granny.

'You bet!' said Jake. 'The food was brilliant and I got lots of smashing presents.'

'Pity about this cake, though,' she said, scraping the trampled remains into a plastic bag. 'You didn't even get to try any. If that fairy hadn't—'

'Dewlally!' exclaimed Jake. 'She's still in the oven!'

197

'Serves her right,' said Granny. But even she felt a little guilty.

Jake eased open the oven door and was surprised when the witching-whisk came tumbling out. There was a scrap of paper wrapped round it, on which had been scrawled a tiny note.

Deer Jake
Thankyoo for a luvly party. I know yoo alwaze ment to invite me even if grumpy-nickers dident. I carnt

198

beeleaf how stoopid she iz. Did
she reely think I wood stay in
this oven?

Eniway, I borrowed the whisk
agane to make you a birfday
present. I hope you like it!
Yor faery godorter
Dewlally

'A present,' said Jake. 'What does
she mean?'

'This!' said Granny, pulling
something out of the oven.

It was another castle-shaped cake.

This one was tiny, little bigger than an egg, but incredibly detailed despite its size. There were dozens of towers and courtyards and silver portcullises across each of the gates. It was the most beautiful cake that Jake had ever seen.

'She's just trying to show mine up!' said Granny. But even she was impressed.

They looked at the cake for nearly an hour before it occurred to them that they might eat it. And then it was another half-hour before

they could bear to take a knife
to it.

Jake cut it in half and discovered
that the icing was filled with a sky-
blue sponge.

'Here goes!' he
said, and they
each popped a
piece into their
mouth.

The cake tasted delicious, but
they hardly noticed the flavour. The
instant they bit into it, a series of
long-forgotten memories started to
flood vividly into their minds.

Jake remembered himself as a baby, crawling across his parents' bed and ripping the paper off what was to become his favourite teddy bear.

Granny was recalling her own childhood. She saw herself coming downstairs one morning to discover her first beautiful cookery set waiting for her in the kitchen.

One after another, they found themselves re-experiencing the happiest memories from every birthday they had ever had.

202

'Now that's what I call a birthday cake,' said Jake, when he eventually came back to his senses.

'I only wish I had the recipe,' sighed Granny wistfully, as she chased the fading memories.

'I think that you probably have!' said Jake, spotting something resting against the oven. 'And lots more that are just as strange and wonderful.'

He bent down and picked up the object.

It was *The Conjuror's Cookbook*.

203

Fairy Soup and Friendship

Anna Wilson

Mr Gripe lived on his own. This suited him down to the ground, as he didn't like other people. He'd never had any friends, and he intended to keep it that way. Friends seemed far too much like hard work to him. He spent his

days growing vegetables in his garden, but he could never be bothered to cook any of them. There was no point when it was just him on his own.

Every evening he would light a fire, turn on the telly and settle into his armchair. Then he would spend a pleasant evening shouting out at the 'fools' who presented the programmes, while he nibbled away at a dry crust or two.

One winter's night, Mr Gripe was enjoying a particularly ridiculous

205

programme called *The Truth About Fairies*.

'Everyone knows fairies are just a figment of the imagination!' Mr Gripe scoffed.

A huge man with an unfeasibly large beard was cheerily explaining that fairies were everywhere, you just had to know where to look.

Mr Gripe was just about to shout, 'Utter nonsense!' at the poor presenter when –

Bang! Bang! Bang!

'Who's knocking on my door at

this unearthly hour?' grumbled Mr Gripe, turning down the volume on the telly. 'No one ever knocks on my door. Ever.'

He huffed and puffed and heaved himself out of his old leather armchair and hobbled to the door. He opened it a crack, looked out into the dark winter's night, and growled: 'Whaddya want?'

But there didn't seem to be anyone there.

'Huh, pesky kids,' Mr Gripe muttered as he slammed the door.

angrily. 'As if I can spend all evening answering the door to Mr Nobody. I ask you.'

He had just turned up the volume on the telly again and was listening to more 'drivel' about how fairies usually appear to people who need them most, when –

Bang! Bang! Bang!

The knocking started up again.

'I'll get you this time, you little varmints!' Mr Gripe shouted, and shuffled to the door with his cold cup of tea, ready to throw it over

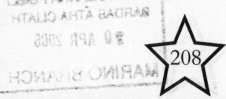

208

the rascals he imagined were picking on him. That would give them a nasty surprise.

But this time, when he opened the door, it was Mr Gripe who got a nasty surprise, for there, hovering in front of his eyes, was . . . A FAIRY!

'You are a very rude little man, aren't you?' the fairy said in a cross, tinkly little voice. 'No wonder you don't have any friends.'

'I – I – how dare you! Are you a fairy? I don't believe in you! Go

away and leave me alone!' Mr
Gripe said rudely.

'There you go, being rude again,'
the fairy answered. 'Well, invite me
in then. I'm freezing
my wings off out
here.'

Mr Gripe
had never met
anyone as rude as
him before. And he had certainly
never met a fairy before. He didn't
know what to do. So he let the
fairy in.

'What do you want?' he asked her.

'How do you do? Nice to meet you. I'm Araminta – honestly, it doesn't cost much to be polite,' the fairy said huffily. She turned to look at the telly. 'Aah, I see you are watching the esteemed Professor Ruxbee-Box. A worthy gentleman who respects us fairy folk. You could learn a thing or two from him. However, we don't have time for that now.' And with that, Araminta switched off the telly and turned back to Mr Gripe.

211

'I must be dreaming,' Mr Gripe muttered to himself. 'I must have fallen asleep in front of the telly, and now I'm dreaming about fairies. It's all the fault of that man with the beard. Such a hypnotic voice, he had . . .'

'Stop muttering to yourself and listen to me, will you?' Araminta demanded. 'I have been travelling all night and I'm absolutely starving.'

'Really? How interesting. I've had my supper already. And if you think

212

you're getting anything out of *me* after talking to me like that—' Mr Gripe said stroppily.

'I don't call a couple of biscuits "supper",' Araminta cut in. 'You need to look after yourself better. Anyway, don't worry, I've brought my own magic ingredients. You won't have to do a thing. All I need is a saucepan and I can make the most delicious soup you've ever tasted in your life.'

'Oh!' said Mr Gripe at a loss for words. No one had ever suggested

213

he look after himself, let alone
offered to cook for him.

'There – I thought that'd shut
you up, dearie,' Araminta said,
cheekily. 'I don't suppose you've
eaten anything but biscuits and
toast for years, have you?'

'Humpf,' replied Mr Gripe. He
didn't like being put in his place by
such a miniature madam, but he *did*
like the sound of the soup . . .

He walked into his tiny kitchen
and scrabbled around in a cupboard.
'Right, here's a saucepan,' he

announced, placing it on the stove.
'Let's see you make this soup then.
It'd better be good after disturbing
me like this.'

Araminta smiled to herself and,
producing a wand from behind one
silvery wing, she muttered a few
words in fairy language and waved
the wand at the saucepan on the
stove.

WHOOSH!

A stream of glittery golden
sparkles flew from the tip of her
wand into the saucepan and

landed in a heap, shimmering and shining.

'Wha– what's that glittery stuff?' Mr Gripe stuttered. All this magic was beginning to make him feel rather weak and weary.

'Magic ingredients for my soup,' Araminta said briskly, flying over to the stove and turning it on. 'Now, I just need a few drops of water to bind it all together.'

'Right, water. Here you go,' said Mr Gripe, and he handed the fairy a cup of water from the tap.

Araminta hovered over the stove and poured the water into the glitter, muttering more magical words under her breath as she stirred. Then, taking a spoon from the pocket in her silvery skirt, she tasted a tiny drop of the soup.

217

'Mmm,' she said thoughtfully. 'That's all right as soup goes, but it could do with a little bit of onion to bring out the flavour. Shame I didn't bring any with me.'

'I've got an onion!' Mr Gripe said excitedly. And he ran out into his garden in the dark and pulled up an onion from his vegetable patch. Then he ran back in and handed it to the fairy.

'Here you are!' he said.

Araminta waved her wand again and the onion sprang apart into

tiny, ready-chopped pieces and flew into the saucepan. She stirred the soup some more and then daintily tasted it.

'Mmm,' she said again. 'It's almost got the flavour I'm looking for, but there's something missing. I know! It could do with a nice juicy carrot . . .'

'I've got a carrot!' Mr Gripe shouted. And he ran out once again into the garden in the dark and pulled up a carrot. Never in all his born days as a gardener had he

thought to use his vegetables in soup before. His mouth was watering away at the thought of tasting this magic meal.

Once again, the fairy waved her wand, and the carrot exploded into small slithers and flew into the pan.

Araminta stirred and tasted as before.

'Mmm,' she said. 'This will be a soup fit for the Fairy Queen herself, if I'm not mistaken. But it could do with a little potato to thicken it a bit.'

Mr Gripe was out of the kitchen door again before you could say 'veg patch', and he soon returned with a lovely white potato, fresh from the soil.

This too got the magic wand treatment and was soon whirring around in the saucepan with the onion and the carrot, the water and, of course, the magic glittery ingredients.

At last Araminta was satisfied. 'It's ready!' she declared. 'Get us two bowls now, will you? Let's eat!'

221

Mr Gripe tucked into his bowl of soup with great gusto. He had never tasted anything so delicious in all his life. He supped and slurped and swallowed, and didn't even look up from his bowl until he'd finished.

'This is wonderful, Araminta!' he exclaimed as he polished off the last spoonful. 'You must give me the recipe – what is in that magic glitter of yours?'

But Araminta had disappeared. Mr Gripe blinked and rubbed his eyes and wondered again if he'd

been dreaming, but there were the two empty soup bowls and the saucepan . . . Then he noticed a tiny envelope propped against his bowl. He tore it open and out floated a letter the size of a postage stamp. Mr Gripe fetched a magnifying glass and sat down to read the note. It said:

Thank you for your hospitality this evening. The magic ingredient you are looking for is — friendship.

223

And to this day, if you ever find yourself passing by Mr Gripe's house and you feel a bit peckish, go and knock on the door. He won't mind a bit. In fact, he'll welcome you with open arms and tell you The Truth About Fairies and Friendship as you enjoy a bowl of his famous fairy vegetable soup.

NeLLie the Fairy

Alan Durant

Nellie was a fairy.

This is how it happened. One day she visited some beautiful fairy-tale gardens and she made a wish at a magical wishing well. She threw in a shiny coin and wished to be a fairy. She knew her wish would

come true, because magic wishes always do.

Next morning, when she woke, Nellie wasn't an ordinary little girl any more, she was a fairy. She had shiny silver wings and a sparkly fairy wand. She had a glittering pink dress and twinkly fairy shoes. She was very happy.

Nellie went to tell her brother Paul. But Paul didn't think that Nellie was a fairy. He thought Nellie was a fool. 'Silly Nellie,' he teased. 'Silly-billy, Nellie-wellie.'

He laughed at Nellie.

Nellie was cross. 'You are the silly one,' she said. She waved her fairy wand and turned her brother into a bee!

'Now, buzz off, you pest,' said Nellie – and he did.

227

Nellie checked her fairy clock.

'It's time for me to fly,' she said – and off she flew, out through the window and up into the sky.

In the street below people looked up in big surprise.

'My, what a huge bird,' said someone.

'It looks like a candyfloss cloud,' said another.

'Is it a plane?' said someone else. (He was a very old man and he wasn't wearing his glasses, because

228

his dog had borrowed them without asking him.)

'No, it's Nellie!' shouted Nellie's best friend, Lisa-Loo. She waved at Nellie and Nellie waved back.

Nellie flew down next to Lisa-Loo.

'Nellie, you're a fairy!' cried Lisa-Loo, and she hopped with delight.

'I am,' said Nellie, 'and I have some jobs to do.'

'I'll help you,' said Lisa-Loo.

'OK,' said Nellie. 'Hold my hand.'

229

So Lisa-Loo held Nellie's hand
and off they flew together.

They flew away to the fairy-tale
garden, where a host of bluebells
was growing all in a ring.

'Those bluebells look dusty,' tutted
Nellie. (Bluebells are the fairies'
favourite flowers and they hate to
see them dusty.)

So Nellie and Lisa-Loo cleaned
the dusty bluebells – and gave them
a drink too.

'Thank you,' chimed the bluebells,
nodding their shiny blue heads.

230

Next Nellie waved her fairy wand and magicked a choir of songbirds to cheer up an arbour of gloomy trees.

'Oh, thank you, Nellie,' creaked the trees.

Then Nellie and Lisa-Loo sprinkled some fairy glitter on a fountain that had lost its sparkle. 'Thank you so much, Nellie,' the fountain gurgled brightly.

Nellie frowned. 'There's something wrong,' she said. 'There's something I haven't done.' She

231

looked around the garden . . . and suddenly she knew!

'I've forgotten to wake up the sun,' she said.

So Nellie and Lisa-Loo shouted to wake up the sleepy sun.

'All right, all right, I'm coming,' yawned the sun, slowly rising.

Nellie looked at her fairy clock.

'Quick Lisa-Loo, we must hurry,' said Nellie, 'or we shall be late for school!'

So Lisa-Loo held Nellie's hand
and off they flew.

Nellie's teacher was a little
surprised to see a fairy in her class.

'Why, Nellie, you're a fairy,' she
said. 'How lovely.'

The children all gathered round
Nellie. They wanted to touch her
wings and look at her fairy
wand.

'Are you really a fairy, Nellie?'
they asked.

'I am,' said Nellie.

'She is,' confirmed Lisa-Loo.

233

'Then do some magic, Nellie,' the children begged. 'Please.'

'Well, all right,' said Nellie.

Nellie waved her sparkly wand and – swish swish! She turned all the chairs into toadstools.

Swish swish! She turned all the tables into tree stumps.

Swish swish! The classroom was lit up by fairy lights.

'Ooh! Ah!' sighed the children. They sat down on the toadstools and gazed at the twinkling fairy lights.

234

'Now, if you're very good, children,' said Nellie's teacher, 'perhaps Nellie will tell us a story.'

'Oh, yes, tell us a story, please, Nellie,' they pleaded.

'Well, all right,' said Nellie.

So Nellie told them a story. It was a fairy story, of course, and it started like this: 'Once upon a time there was a little girl who made a wish to be a fairy.'

The story Nellie told was her own story!

'But, Nellie,' said the children,

when Nellie stopped, 'how does the story end?'

'Happily ever after, of course,' said Nellie, 'like all the best fairy stories.'

'Will you be a fairy for ever?' asked the children.

'Ah, wait and see,' said Nellie, 'wait and see.'

Nellie's dandelion clock went puff. (That was Nellie's alarm going off.)

'I must be off,' sighed Nellie. 'There are lots more jobs to do.'

She waved her wand and off she flew.

Nellie was very, very busy.

First she had to polish the moon

before he came out, because he'd lost his shine.

'Oh, thank you, Nellie,' he beamed.

Next Nellie had to sprinkle some twinkle on the stars.

'Thank you, Nellie,' they twittered.

Then she had to paint a rainbow to make the sky look nice and colourful.

(It took her a long, long time even with her magic and her special fairy paints, because rainbows stretch far across the sky.)

238

There were so many jobs to
do.

'I never knew it was such hard
work being a fairy,' sighed
Nellie.

At last, as the sun lay down to
sleep and the world turned dusky,
Nellie sat on a large sunflower to
rest. A sleepy bee buzzed by and she
thought about her brother Paul. He
was a pest and he made her cross
sometimes, but, well, she missed
him. She thought about Lisa-Loo
and she missed her too. Everyone

needs a best friend, thought Nellie, even a fairy. She yawned. It had been a long day and she was very tired.

Nellie thought and thought and at last she knew what she had to do.

Nellie flew back to the wishing-well in the fairy-tale garden. She waved her fairy wand and magicked a shiny coin. Then she threw the coin into the well.

'Thank you for making my wish come true,' she said. 'I've loved

240

being a fairy, but it's very hard work and now I'm sleepy, and I'd really like to go home and be a little girl again, like my best friend, Lisa-Loo.' And that was Nellie's wish. (She knew it would come true, because magic wishes always do.)

Next day, when Nellie woke up, she wasn't a fairy any more, she was a little girl, and her brother wasn't a bee, he was a little boy (but he was still a pest!). The strange thing was that nobody

remembered that Nellie had ever been a fairy, not even her best friend, Lisa-Loo.

Well, that's magic for you.

The Dull Fairy

Fiona Dunbar

There were once five fairies, and they were all sisters. Four of them were super-sparkly and thrillingly talented, but the middle one, Cimone, was not. She was just . . . nice. And *mellow*. Her sisters considered her dull, because she

243

didn't possess that special Ingredient X, which they had in abundance.

As a result, poor Cimone always felt rather left out of things; her four super sisters would even forget her name, usually calling her 'Ginger' instead. 'I don't even have ginger hair!' Cimone would protest. 'It's auburn; *cinnamon*-coloured!' But no matter how much she complained, they still insisted on calling her 'Ginger' or 'Ginge'.

When they weren't Gingefying Cimone, her sisters mostly ignored

her. Fairies can be like that. If you thought they were all nice, then you are very much mistaken; they can be just as moody, vain, attention-span-challenged and immature as the rest of us. Especially when they are the super-sparkly and thrillingly talented kind.

Fiery-tempered Piper, the eldest, was a passion fairy, which is the kind that inspires people to feel very strongly about Causes, campaigning furiously about such issues as the plight of the Lesser-Spotted

245

Grimble-Plit. Well, somebody has to, as any Lesser-Spotted Grimble-Plit will tell you.

Stella, the second eldest, was a muse fairy. Muse fairies have been responsible for inspiring every great piece of music and important piece of art in the whole history of doing clever stuff. There was a muse fairy sitting on the shoulder of Leonardo da Vinci when he painted the *Mona Lisa*; there was one hovering about the deaf ears of Ludwig van Beethoven as he composed his *Fifth*

Symphony. William Shakespeare would not have written . . . you get the picture. Stella herself had yet to inspire anything world-shattering, but she had got a Mr Dwight Argyll of Bexleyheath to stand in front of his mirror one day in his socks and twang his guitar, which in turn led him to rename himself Digg da Soxx, have a hit single and get himself signed to a major record company. Stella considered herself nothing less than a star too, and never let anyone forget it.

Clovia, the second youngest, was a sports fairy. Her job was to spur people on to be very fast and nimble, enabling them to win races and score goals again and again. She was very impatient and could never sit still for five minutes.

So, you see, there never was a dull moment with Piper, Stella and Clovia around. It was all zip, zip, woweee! All the time! They truly were the spice of life.

The youngest of all, Fenella, was a bit gentler; she was a baby magic

fairy. This kind of fairy is nearly always present when a baby is born, ensuring that its parents fall madly, passionately in love with the squealing purple blob they have just brought into the world. I say *nearly* always, because, like anyone else, the baby magic fairy occasionally fails to show up at the right place and time, with tragic consequences for the infant concerned. I'm sorry I had to mention that, because this isn't that kind of story, but it's true.

But the mildest of all was

249

Cimone. She had tried to be super-sparkly and thrillingly talented, but it didn't work; she just *wasn't*. And so she ended up doing routine odd jobs like filling in for the Tooth Fairy when she got sick and that kind of thing.

When Cimone's four super-sparkly and thrillingly talented sisters went on a trip to the Fairy Fair, but forgot to include her, she decided she had had enough. 'I don't deserve to be treated in this way!' she said crossly when they returned.

'Oh, Ginger's moaning again,' groaned Stella, as she checked herself in the mirror.

'Moan, moan, moan, that's all she ever does!' shrieked Piper. 'I'm not putting up with any more of this; I've got an important job tomorrow. Good night!' And off she flounced.

'Bored now,' yawned Clovia, and she too disappeared off to bed.

This left just Fenella, who did feel rather guilty. 'I'm ever so sorry, Ginger – I mean, Cimone.' At that moment Fenella's fairy mobile rang;

she answered it. 'Bexleyheath?' she
cried. 'Now? But I can't, I was just
going to . . . *yawn* . . . go to
beddy-byes!'

Realizing that a baby was about
to be born, and a baby magic fairy
was needed urgently, Cimone
offered to go in Fenella's place.

'But you can't *do* baby magic,
Ginger – I mean, Cimone,' Fenella
pointed out. 'You haven't got
Ingredient X like me.'

Cimone lowered her eyes. 'No, I
suppose you're right.'

'But you can come with me if you like!' added Fenella.

'OK!' said Cimone, brightening. 'I'm sure I can be of some help.' And off they went.

But time was running out: they had a long way to go, and the baby was due any minute. Poor Fenella fluttered with all her might, but she was tired from her day out and began to fall asleep on the wing. Cimone, however, had plenty of energy since all she'd done that day was to play pretend hide-and-

seek among the toadstools by herself – a pointless activity she had soon given up on. Spotting Fenella flying lower and lower, her eyelids drooping, Cimone swooped to the rescue. She grabbed her wilting little sister around the waist and fluttered extra specially hard to support the two of them. She huffed and puffed; Fenella was a dead weight.

At last, they arrived at the hospital, flying in at the window just seconds after the baby was born.

'*Waaah! Waaah!*' squealed the baby girl, and her mother was staring right at her; there wasn't a moment to lose. Cimone shook her little sister. 'Fenella! Wake up!'

Fenella rubbed her eyes. 'Oh, right!' She stretched out her wings, and immediately set about working her baby magic.

Cimone watched entranced as Fenella flitted around mother and baby, scattering fairy dust.

Gradually, a golden glow appeared around them, radiating

brighter and brighter, forging a bond that would last a lifetime. And now the weary mother's face lit up. 'Oh, my lovely girl! You are so beautiful!' she exclaimed to her squawking purple munchkin.

How wonderful to be able to work such magic! thought Cimone wistfully. She was proud to have helped Fenella, yet seeing the magic at work only made her feel sadder. If only *I* were super-sparkly and thrillingly talented too, she thought. But I'm just dull, dependable

256

Cimone; so forgettable, no one can even remember my name.

But, two weeks later, something happened that was to change Cimone's life for ever . . .

'Cimone, I have to go back to Bexleyheath,' announced Fenella. 'That baby's father is coming home from a long trip, and is about to meet his child for the first time. I need to work some baby magic on him but I'm . . . *yawn!* . . . ever so sleepy. Will you carry me?'

Cimone was glad to be of some use, and off they went.

They arrived at Bexleyheath in the early morning to find the baby's mother, Mrs Argyll, looking absolutely ragged. She had dark circles under her eyes, her hair looked like a bird's nest, and she had baby sick all down her front and didn't seem to care. She was carrying the crying baby on her shoulder as she walked back and forth, going, 'Husshh! Husshh!'

But the baby's father, Mr Dwight

258

Argyll, did not seem to have returned yet. He was in fact the very same Dwight Argyll who had transformed himself into the rock star Digg da Soxx with the help of Stella's muse fairy magic, and he was returning from a concert tour. Fenella and Cimone went from room to room to see if he had arrived yet, but there was no sign of him. Instead they found a thin-looking boy, sitting listlessly in his bedroom, staring at his football boots.

'Big match today,' the boy muttered to himself. 'I can't do it . . . I can't do it. *Mum!*' he cried out. '*I'm hungry!*'

But Mum couldn't hear him over the baby's wailing, and the boy didn't seem to have the energy to go into her room.

'Oh dear,' said Cimone. 'The poor boy's wasting away.'

There was a sound at the front door; Fenella and Cimone went to see if it was Mr Argyll. But instead it was someone posting a leaflet

260

through the door: '*PLEASE HELP SAVE THE LESSER-SPOTTED GRIMBLE-PLIT!*' it said. '*MEETING TONIGHT AT SEVEN P.M. – DON'T MISS YOUR CHANCE TO MAKE A DIFFERENCE!*' It fell on top of a pile of unopened letters and other leaflets about the Grimble-Plit meeting.

A moment later, they heard a key in the front door; this time it *was* Mr Argyll. He was unshaven and had red-rimmed eyes, but he cried out excitedly, 'Honey, I'm

261

home!' dropped his bags and ran upstairs to see his new baby. Fenella and Cimone flitted after him with all their might.

Once again, Fenella worked her baby magic as Mr Argyll laid eyes on his daughter for the first time. 'Oh, my precious girl!' he cried, as he rushed over, arms wide open.

'Oh, Dwight!' cried Mrs Argyll, as she handed over the baby, and collapsed on to the bed, sobbing.

Fenella and Cimone hovered around to see what was the matter.

'I'm at my wit's end!' sobbed Mrs Argyll. 'The baby hardly ever sleeps; I haven't slept for more than half an hour at a stretch in two whole weeks!'

Now the boy appeared at the doorway. 'Oh, Dad!' he cried. 'At last you're home!' Then he too burst into tears, which set the baby off all over again as well.

Fenella covered her ears. 'Ooh, let's go, all this crying's making my ears hurt!'

'No,' said ever-sensible, thoughtful

263

Cimone. 'I think we need to call in some reinforcements.' And she took out her fairy mobile. 'Stella? We've got a bit of an emergency here. Can you come, and bring Piper and Clovia?'

'Right away!' agreed Stella, never one to miss an opportunity to be the star of the show.

While they waited for their sisters to arrive, Fenella and Cimone watched as the Argyll family filled each other in on their woes.

Mrs Argyll was distraught

because, quite apart from being seriously sleep-deprived and failing to feed her son properly, she was supposed to be attending the Very Important Meeting about the Lesser-Spotted Grimble-Plit that night, where she was to give an impassioned speech, which she hadn't even written yet.

Her son was distraught because he was playing in the league final match that afternoon, but he barely had the strength to dress himself for lack of nourishment – and he too

265

had been kept awake night after night by his baby sister.

Finally, Mr Argyll, aka Digg da Soxx, was distraught because he had just agreed to tag one extra concert on to the end of his tour, and it was to be tonight. But Mrs Argyll wanted him to babysit so she could go to her meeting . . . and both of them needed to sleep for most of the day before they could do anything at all.

Meanwhile, the baby cried and cried.

At last the other three fairies arrived, and Cimone told them the situation. 'I thought you could all help by giving these people the extra boost they need,' she explained.

Piper, Stella and Clovia looked in on the Argyll family; everyone was still either arguing or crying, or both. Then the fairies convened outside the bedroom door to decide what to do. 'Well, of course,' declared Piper, 'the most important thing is that Mrs Argyll should attend her meeting. The very future

267

of the Lesser-Spotted Grimble-Plit depends upon it! I am the passion fairy who endowed her with such vision and verve, and I will not have her deprived of her big moment!'

'Excuse me,' said Stella haughtily, 'but I'll have you know that *I* am the very muse fairy who helped Mr Argyll become the Digg da Soxx that he is today, and I say it's far more important for him to appear at that concert tonight. Hundreds of his fans are expecting him! Who

268

cares about your silly Grumble-Squit anyway?'

'What about the boy?' Clovia chipped in. '*I* am the very sports fairy who bestowed upon him his great talent for football, yet the poor child is suffering from neglect. Something must be done, and urgently!'

'Hey! You're all forgetting the most important person here – the baby!' cried Fenella, trembling with rage. 'Everyone knows that baby comes first!'

'You always say that!' snapped Piper. 'Just because *you're* the baby!' And she soon had Fenella in tears, accusing her of being babyish and having no social conscience. Stella and Clovia began arguing with each other about whether music or sport was more important. The fight grew more and more heated, until the four of them were having such a screaming match (none of which the humans could hear, of course) that they'd quite forgotten what they were doing there in the first place.

'QUIET!' yelled Fenella. The three fairies were shocked into silence and stared at her. Then she said, 'Have you noticed something?'

And now that the row had stopped, they did indeed notice something: none of the humans was yelling or crying any more. The fairies flitted into the bedroom and saw that in fact every one of them was fast asleep.

And the air was filled with the gentle sound of a lullaby, sung by none other than Cimone as she sat

271

beside the baby. It wasn't a remarkable singing voice – and nor was it one that the baby, being human, could actually hear. But she sensed the soothing presence of Cimone, felt the vibrations of her song and was lulled into a deep, tranquil sleep.

Mr Argyll had been so exhausted that, as soon as he felt the baby relax in his arms, he had lain down and, without a word, fallen fast asleep.

Mrs Argyll was so relieved at the

prospect of some rest that she, too, just flopped down on top of the duvet and zonked out.

Finally, the boy curled up on the bed beside the rest of his family and drifted off to the land of Nod.

About seven hours later, all the humans woke up feeling much refreshed. Mrs Argyll fed the baby, and Mr Argyll bought some bacon and eggs and cooked a huge breakfast for everyone else. Then he put on his dark glasses (as rock stars tend to do) and took his son to the

football match, where the boy scored two goals, winning the match – and the season's trophy – for his team; Mr Argyll took the baby along too, which meant that Mrs Argyll had time to write her speech on the plight of the Lesser Spotted Grimble-Plit. That evening Mr Argyll took his son along with him to the rock concert, where the boy got to watch his dad, Digg da Soxx, from backstage.

Mrs Argyll attended her meeting with the baby strapped to her in a

274

baby carrier. She was able to do this because Cimone flitted along beside them, and any time the baby stirred, she lulled her back to sleep. Mrs Argyll was on top form, and her speech got a standing ovation. Even this didn't rouse her sleepy little baby. Mrs Argyll won her cause: the local woods would not be cleared for development after all, and the Lesser-Spotted Grimble-Plit was saved.

And it was all thanks to Cimone. Hurray! After three days, the baby

had got into a good sleep pattern and didn't need Cimone any more. But word spread in the fairy community about her extraordinary gift, and soon her fairy mobile was ringing almost constantly. The Lullaby Fairy was in demand! At last Cimone had found her talent, and a very useful one it was too. After all, what use is it being an impassioned speaker, a brilliant musician or a talented footballer, if you never have the energy to do any of those things? Everyone needs sleep, and we are

pretty darned useless without it. Nobody can be super-sparkly and thrillingly talented *all* the time.

Cimone's sisters soon came to appreciate this too, and realized that perhaps being mellow didn't mean you were dull, it just meant you were . . . mellow. It didn't stop them being moody, vain, attention-span-challenged and immature, but they had come to appreciate their quieter sister for her sweet gentle nature. And they never called her 'Ginger' again.

The Tale of the Thirteenth Fairy

Kaye Umansky

Now, let's get one thing straight. I refuse to take the blame. You know what I'm talking about. That business with Sleeping Beauty. I've been held responsible for years, and it's time to set the record straight.

Now, I agree I may have gone a bit far. You shouldn't go playing around with Curses when there are babies around. I admit that. Curses are unpredictable. They can go wrong. I know that now. But I do have a bit of a temper and, remember, I was very, *very* cross at the time. More than cross. Furious.

I mean, how would you feel? Supposing your twelve best friends got invited to a party in a palace and you got left out? You'd be

hopping mad, wouldn't you? And more than a little hurt.

I say best friends, but they're not. Catch me being friends with that lot. The Twelve Good Fairies. That's what they call themselves. It's a sort of club. They all wear ballet dresses and call themselves by flowery names. Every Saturday night, they meet in the woods when the moon's up and skip around in the soppy fairy ring they've built there, pointing their tippy-toes and frightening the owls. When they're

all puffed out, they have tea with dewberry wine and fairy cakes, served on spotty toadstool tables by frog waiters in bow ties. That's when they talk about me behind my back. I know, because I hid behind a bush once and listened.

I never get invited. I wouldn't go anyway. I'm a rotten dancer and pink net doesn't suit me. They can keep their old club, I don't care.

Anyway. I was really fed up when I found out that the King and Queen had a new baby and they

were all invited to the christening!
I wouldn't even have known about
it, except that I bumped into Fairy
Bluebell outside the post office and
she couldn't resist showing off.
Normally, she never speaks to me,
but I could tell she was bursting
with news.

'Good morning, Grizelda,' she

trilled. 'Tra-la-la, what a lovely day.'

'Oh,' I said. 'It's you.'

'Yes,' she simpered. 'What lovely black rags, are they new?'

I could have zapped her there and then, but I didn't want to singe the people in the queue. See how thoughtful I am? So I ignored her. It didn't stop her, though.

'Isn't it too, too exciting?' she twittered.

'No,' I said. 'I find queuing for stamps very dull.'

283

'I'm talking about the Invitation,' she said.

'What invitation?'

'The Invitation to the christening at the palace. There's a new royal baby, didn't you know? Oh, I suppose you don't, living all alone with no friends. *We're* all going. We're getting new dresses and we're going to give lovely magical presents, like Love and Joy and Happiness. It's on Saturday at two o'clock. The Invitation's all in gold. Haven't you got one?'

284

'New postman,' I lied. 'Delayed, I expect.'

It wasn't, of course. It had never been sent in the first place. But I didn't want to give her the satisfaction.

'You'll have to scrub up a bit if you do come,' said Bluebell. 'But they've probably decided not to have you. It is a *palace*, you know. They have to think of the carpets. Perhaps they think your pointy hat won't fit in. Well, it is a bit of a downer at a party.

285

Oh, look here's Primrose! Coo-eee! Primrose!'

Fairy Primrose came fluttering up, clutching a large gold envelope in one hand and a card in the other. The card said, *Yes please, I will come*, in delicate fairy writing. She and Bluebell fell into each other's arms.

'I'm sending off my reply to the Invitation!' cried Primrose, all pink, flustered excitement.

'Me too!' squealed Bluebell. 'Isn't it exciting? Everyone's going. Lilac, Rose, Violet, Snowdrop, Pansy,

Daisy, Poppy, Daffodil, Holly and Marigold. Everyone except Grizelda. She hasn't been invited.'

They both stared at me in a pitying way. Well, they pretended to be pitying. Really, they were delighted.

'That's because there are only twelve gold plates,' said Primrose. 'Remember last year, Bluebell, when we went to the palace as guests of honour? When the King and Queen got married? There were only twelve gold plates, I'm quite sure of it.'

I was thunderstruck. Until now, I hadn't realized I hadn't been invited to the wedding either! Talk about adding insult to injury.

'Twelve gold plates and twelve fairies,' went on Primrose. 'You would make thirteen, you see, Grizelda, and you'd have to eat from the dog's bowl or something.'

They both pealed with charming fairy laughter.

'That's all right, I'll eat off yours,' I said grimly.

288

'I don't *think* so,' said Primrose, smugly tossing her golden hair.

'I don't think it's about plates,' said Bluebell, staring at me. 'I think it's more likely they just don't want you. Thirteen's an unlucky number. And you don't fit in. You don't have nice, pretty clothes, like us. You'll lower the tone.'

'Ah, go stick your head in an acorn,' I said rudely and stomped off in a huff, not bothering about the stamps. I could hear them whispering and giggling behind me.

289

It played on my mind. I shouldn't have let it bother me, but it did. I stewed for a whole week. I lost sleep, thinking about it. That's why I went steaming into the palace like I did on the day of the christening. I was going to have a quiet day at home, reading the paper or boiling up a brew or something, but when it came to it, I couldn't. I had to be there and make my presence felt. I had been insulted and somebody had to pay.

I screeched across the sky on my

290

broomstick and did an emergency stop over the palace gardens. The broom's getting on a bit, not so accurate as it once was, and I landed head first in a rose bush, which put me in an even worse mood. I was scratched and pricked all over by the

thorns, which is probably why I had
getting pricked on my mind when I
delivered the Curse.

They were all in there in the big
hall: King, Queen, baby, celebrities,
courtiers, guests, you name it. The
palace had pulled the stops out.
There were balloons and a great
big christening cake. When I came
charging in, the Twelve Good
Fairies were right in the middle of
giving the baby their soppy gifts.

The baby was a nice little thing,
actually. I could see that. It didn't

292

seem to mind being given Happiness and Wisdom and Health and whatnot, although I suspect it would have been just as happy with a cuddly giraffe or a mashed banana. Anyway, I didn't hang about. I had a Curse to deliver.

Now, the Curse. This needs careful explaining. A lot of people think I said something I didn't. They *think* I said, 'She will prick her finger on a spindle *and die*.' But I didn't. I never said anything about dying. What I was *going* to say was,

293

'She will prick her finger on a spindle *and I* will give her a sticking plaster.' However, I never got it out. I got as far as 'She will prick her finger on a spindle *and I* . . .' And then everyone started screaming and rushing about and the last, all-important words didn't get delivered. It's hard to speak when the Captain of the Guard has you in a headlock.

Surprised, eh? I thought you would be. But you shouldn't believe everything you hear. It's important

to get both sides of a story. I assure you, my honest intention was to wait until she was older and a bit more sensible, then lure her up into a quiet attic, where she would prick her finger, but not *that* badly. Then I would give her a plaster to show her my nice, helpful side, and we'd get chatting and I would tell her all about how mean they were to me sixteen years ago. We would end up with a better understanding of each other and she would be sure not to repeat the mistakes of her

295

thoughtless parents. And she would
begin by inviting me to her
birthday party.

But sadly, everyone misheard.

Anyway, I was bundled out by
the guards and went home to nurse
my wounds. If they were going to
be like that, I would let them think
the worst. Think of all the trouble
the King and Queen would have,
banning spinning wheels and
needles all over the kingdom. It
would hardly make them popular.
Just wait until people's pants started

falling down, then there'd be an outcry. It wouldn't be much of a revenge for not inviting me to the party, but it was better than nothing.

What really put the cat amongst the pigeons was that silly little Fairy Violet got in on the act and made things worse. She still had her gift to give, you see, and decided to be a bit clever and soften the Curse. You are allowed one go at this, according to the magic rules. She changed the '*and I*' bit to '*and fall*

297

asleep for a hundred years'. If she had left well alone, the whole thing would have ended a lot sooner. Princess Beauty would have pricked her finger, we would have had our little chat and the whole thing would have ended there. But, no. Violet interfered.

Anyway, there was nothing I could do about it. The Curse was now well and truly cast, with Violet's bit tagged on. In sixteen years' time, instead of getting a sticking plaster and a new best friend (me), the poor princess was stuck with falling asleep for a hundred years. I had to go along with it. You can't mess about with Fate.

So, on her sixteenth birthday, there I was with my spindle, up in the attic, cackling away and doing it all proper. Beauty wasn't a bit scared – just curious. We had a pleasant little chat, I showed her how the spinning wheel worked, then she pricked her finger and nodded off, right there on the spot.

299

Then there was the whole business of everyone else in the palace falling asleep. That took time. I didn't hang about. I felt a bit guilty, in a way. She seemed a nice little thing. I just packed up the spinning wheel, flew home and had a strong cup of tea with four sugars, which always makes me feel better.

Well, that was a hundred years

ago. A hundred years of Good Fairy dances, and I haven't been invited to any of them. Who cares? Give me the crossword puzzle any time.

Tonight's the night. The Curse will end and of course there will be a happy ending. Violet can never leave things alone. She added a lot of extra details about a prince coming along and waking Beauty with a kiss. I'm not a great one for kissing, I'd sooner be woken with an alarm clock, but I hope Beauty

won't mind. Just imagine sleeping for a hundred years. I bet she's ready for breakfast.

I suppose there will be another royal wedding before long.

They'd better invite me.

the Two Fairy Godmothers

Anna Wilson

Pippa was a very lucky girl, because she had not one but TWO fairy godmothers. The big, bouncy, cuddly one was

called Fairy Milly and the tall,
thin, spiky one was called Fairy
Mona. However,
there was a downside
to having these
particular fairies as
godmothers, because
these two argued
like cat and dog. One
day, their argument
got right out of hand,
and they vowed
never to speak to
each other ever

again. Unfortunately for Pippa, that just happened to be the day she was christened . . .

It had all started when Fairy Milly had decided to tell a few jokes at the party after the baptism. Fairy Mona didn't like Fairy Milly getting all the attention, so she muttered to everyone that Fairy Milly had drunk too much dandelion wine.

Fairy Milly had retaliated by turning Fairy Mona's stupendous chocolate christening cake into a

hippopotamus, which had run riot and flattened the vicar.

Marika, the Head Fairy Godmother, was so angry with both of them that she decided to punish them.

'I am taking away your magic powers, you two!' she thundered at Fairy Milly and Fairy Mona. 'Your behaviour is enough to give all fairy godmothers a bad name.'

The two godmothers were mortified.

'But we haven't even given Pippa

a christening present yet!' cried Fairy Milly.

'Don't answer me back, Fairy Millicent,' warned Marika.

'It's all your fault, Milly,' screeched Fairy Mona. 'You're just too jolly by half. We fairies are meant to be dignified, not delirious.'

'Mona by name, moaner by nature!' laughed Fairy Milly.

'That's it, you two!' Marika declared, stamping her tiny foot in frustration. 'Not only will you lose your magic powers, but your moods

307

will affect the weather wherever
you go! Now, be off with you!'

Fairy Milly sighed as Marika
disappeared in a puff of pink
petals.

'She always was a bit of a drama
fairy, that one,' said Milly and,
looking down into the baby's crib,
she stroked the little one's hair.
'Don't worry, baby Pippa. All your
wishes will come true one day.
After all, every cloud has a silver
lining.'

As the fairies had not been able to grant Pippa any wishes at her christening, they both promised to help look after her one day a week each.

'It's the least we can do,' said Fairy Milly.

'Just as long as I don't ever have to see *her* again,' Fairy Mona said, pointing at Fairy Milly.

'Suits me!' Fairy Milly grinned.

So, Fairy Mona came to look after Pippa every Tuesday. And every

Tuesday it rained — in fact, it didn't just rain, it poured.

One day Pippa asked, 'Can't you wave your wand and make the sun come out, Fairy Mona?'

'No, dear. I've lost all my magic,' Fairy Mona explained impatiently. 'You know what happened at your christening. Oh, how I wish I'd not been rude to Fairy Milly. I hate this rain! Every Tuesday it's the same . . . We can't even go to the park with all the other fairy godmothers. We can't visit anyone. I can't

310

magic us anywhere exciting. We just have to sit here every Tuesday and watch the rain. It's so miserable.'

'Never mind,' Pippa smiled. 'Why don't you teach me how to make your fairy flapjacks? You haven't lost your magic touch when it comes to baking!'

This was certainly true, thought Fairy Mona. She was still renowned throughout the kingdom for her cream puffs and cherry tarts. So every Tuesday while the rain

streamed down the windowpane,
Fairy Mona taught Pippa how to
bake delicious cakes.

When it was Fairy Milly's turn to
look after Pippa, it was quite a
different story. Fairy Milly was
always of a sunny disposition,
which meant the weather was too.
In other words, every Wednesday,
when Fairy Milly came to look
after Pippa, the sun peeped out from
behind the dark and dreary rain-
clouds left behind by Fairy Mona,

then it laughed and chased them all away.

Fairy Milly was always full of the joys of spring and found fun in the simplest activities.

'What a lovely sunny day!' she would cry as she walked up the path to Pippa's house. 'Come on, grab your coat, no time to lose — let's go and feed the ducks. You're such a little sunbeam, Pippa — the sun always shines when I come to see you!'

'You're the sunbeam, Fairy

313

Milly!' Pippa would reply as she ran out to greet her.

One Tuesday, while Pippa was watching the raindrops drip-drip-drop down into the puddles, a bright idea beamed into her head.

'It's always rainy when Fairy Mona comes on Tuesdays and it's always sunny when Fairy Milly comes on Wednesdays. I wonder what would happen if they *both* came together to see me on a Tuesday?'

Pippa thought that maybe, just maybe, she'd come up with a rather perfect plan.

Who needs magic? The combination of Fairy Milly's sunny smiles and Fairy Mona's crumbly cakes might just chase away those Tuesday rain-clouds once and for all, Pippa thought to herself.

Later that afternoon, when Fairy Mona had gone home, Pippa sat down to write two invitations:

315

**PLEASE COME TO A TEA-PARTY
NEXT TUESDAY.
LOVE, PIPPA.**

Then she folded them up and put them into two envelopes and went to post them to her two fairy godmothers.

When Fairy Mona got her invitation in the post she was not best pleased. She didn't like surprises, and she certainly didn't like parties – not after the last party

316

she'd been to, which had been at Pippa's christening.

'What does she mean, "come to a tea-party"? Tuesday's my normal day anyway. And what's the point of a party – it always rains when I go there. Oh, I suppose I may as well bake one of my Strawberry Sugar Sandwich Surprises for the occasion.'

When Fairy Milly got her invitation she was as pleased as a princess. She liked surprises, and she *loved* parties!

317

She hadn't been to one since Pippa's christening either, and she rather missed them.

'Ooh! We can have tea outside in the garden,' she cried, clapping her hands together. She didn't realize it usually rained at Pippa's on a Tuesday.

The day of the tea-party dawned. And the weather was . . . the weather was . . . Well, to tell you the truth, the weather wasn't really one thing or the other. It didn't seem

to know what to do with itself.

Pippa was worried that her plan wouldn't work and that it would rain all day, because rain always seemed to follow Fairy Mona wherever she went. Then she remembered what Fairy Milly always said – 'Every cloud has a silver lining.'

I hope Fairy Milly will remember to bring the lining with her, thought Pippa, because these clouds don't look at all silvery to me.

Just then, Pippa didn't have any

more time to ponder over cloud linings, silver or otherwise, as the doorbell rang and in stormed Fairy Mona, her face like thunder.

'It's started raining AGAIN. AND I've stepped in a puddle right up to my middle! My Strawberry Surprise has turned to Molten Mush! I hate parties anyway. I've made a decision – I'm never coming here again. I've had enough.'

This is going to be a disaster, thought Pippa miserably as she took the soggy sponge-cake from Fairy

320

Mona and went into the kitchen. Whatever did I think I was doing, trying to get my two godmothers together? They are as different as chalk and cheese! They'll never get along.

'So is this it then?' grumbled Fairy Mona. 'Not much of a tea-party, is it? Just you, me and a few saggy teddies.'

'Oh no,' said Pippa brightly, 'I've invited Fairy Milly too.'

'WHAT? That old . . .'

But I can't tell you what Fairy

321

Mona said next because, luckily, it was drowned out by the sound of the doorbell.

It was Fairy Milly, out of breath, soaked to the skin – and laughing her head off as usual.

'Look at this weather! I've never seen anything like it. The funniest thing's just happened to me – I stepped in a puddle right up to my middle!' Then Fairy Milly saw Pippa's face, and she stopped laughing. 'Oh dear. What's the matter, Pippa?

What's happened to my little sunbeam today?'

'I knew this wouldn't work!' Pippa blurted out, and she burst into tears.

'What wouldn't work?' asked Fairy Milly. And then she spotted Fairy Mona, glowering thunderously behind Pippa. 'Oh,' she said hastily. 'Let's put the kettle on, shall we?'

But Pippa had put her boots on instead and was running out into the garden to hide.

'What a washout,' Pippa sobbed as she ran through the puddles, mud

splashing her and tears pouring down her face, making her wetter than ever.

But then she saw something that stopped her in her tracks. She turned and shouted back:

'Look, fairies! Look – behind that cloud!' The sun had come out and was shining through the rain, and the most beautiful rainbow was arching over Pippa's house, framing her two godmothers, who were standing in the doorway, side by side for the first time in years.

Suddenly Fairy Milly looked at Pippa, who was covered in mud from top to toe, and a little smile twitched at the corner of her mouth. Fairy Mona caught a glimpse of it . . . then Fairy Milly looked at

Fairy Mona, and Fairy Mona looked at Fairy Milly – and the pair of them flung their arms around each other and laughed till they cried.

The sound of their laughter lit up the sky and made the rainbow shine more brightly than ever.

'What's that?' Pippa asked with a puzzled expression. She pointed at the rainbow, which seemed to end at the bottom of the garden. A tiny figure was sliding down the rainbow, shouting, 'Wheeeee!' loudly.

'Oh no,' said Fairy Mona. 'We're for it now. It's Marika, the Head Fairy Godmother. Last time we saw her, she took away our magic, turned the weather upside down and made our lives hell, didn't she, Milly?'

Fairy Milly couldn't speak. She was quivering in her boots.

'What are you standing there for, looking like a wet weekday?' Marika called out. 'Here – catch!' And she threw two sparkly silver wands at Pippa's fairy godmothers.

327

'But – what are you giving us these for?' asked Fairy Milly. 'I thought we weren't allowed to do any more magic.'

'I think you've learned your lesson, don't you?' said the Head Fairy Godmother, beaming. 'Thanks to little Pippa here. And she seems to be able to do magic without any help from us! Who'd have thought it? Well done, Pippa!'

'Hurray! Thank you, Marika. Thank you, Pippa! Let's go and slide down the rainbow!' cried Fairy

328

Mona, pulling on her wellies. She waved her wand at Pippa and grabbed her by the hand. 'Come on, dear – follow me! I haven't done this for years!'

A pair of dazzling silver wings sprouted from Pippa's shoulders. Then she found herself whizzing through the air, holding on tightly to Mona as

they both shot up into the sky in the direction of the rainbow.

'What did I tell you, Pippa?' grinned Fairy Milly, catching up with her and taking her by the other hand. 'Every cloud has a silver lining!'

Baldilocks and the Six Bears

Dick King-Smith

There was once a magic forest full of fine tall trees.

In it lived not only animals, but — because it was a magic forest — fairies and pixies and goblins. Some of the goblins were full of mischief and some of the elves were rather

331

spiteful, but on the whole, the fairy people were a happy lot. All except one.

He was a hobgoblin, quite young, not bad-looking; he might even have been thought handsome except for one thing.

He hadn't a hair on his head.

Someone – probably an elf – had named him

332

Baldilocks, and that was what everyone called him.

Baldilocks had never had a great deal of hair, and what he did have had gradually fallen out, till now he had none at all.

How sad he was. How he envied all the other fairy people their fine locks and tresses, each time they met at the full moon.

In a clearing among the trees was a huge fairy ring, and in the middle of this ring sat the wisest fairy of them all. She

was known as the Queen of the Forest.

As usual, everyone laughed when Baldilocks came into the fairy ring.

'Baldilocks!' someone – probably an elf – would shout, and the pixies would titter and the elves would snigger and the goblins would chuckle and the fairies would giggle. All except one.

She was a little red-haired fairy, not specially beautiful, but with such a kindly face. She alone did not laugh at the bald hobgoblin.

334

One night, when everyone was teasing poor Baldilocks as usual, the Queen of the Forest called for silence. Then she said to Baldilocks, 'Would you like to grow a fine head of hair?'

'Oh, I would, Your Majesty!' cried the hobgoblin. 'But how do I go about it?'

'Ask the bear,' said the Queen of the Forest, and not a word more would she say.

The very next morning Baldilocks set out to find a bear. It did not

335

take him long. He came to a muddy pool, and there was a big brown bear, catching frogs.

'Excuse me,' said Baldilocks. 'Could you tell me how to grow a fine head of hair?'

The brown bear looked carefully at the hobgoblin. He knew that the only way a bald person can grow hair is by rubbing bear's grease into his scalp. But he wasn't going to say that, because he knew that the only way to get bear's grease is to kill a bear and melt him down.

336

He picked up a pawful of mud.

'Rub this into your scalp,' said the brown bear.

So Baldilocks took the sticky mud and rubbed it on his head. It was full of wriggling things and it smelt horrid. But it didn't make one single hair grow.

The next bear Baldilocks met was a big black one. It was robbing a wild bees' nest.

337

'Excuse me,' said Baldilocks. 'Could you tell me how to grow a fine head of hair?'

The black bear looked carefully at the hobgoblin. He too knew the only way for a bald person to grow hair. He pulled out a pawful of honeycomb.

'Rub this into your scalp,' said the black bear.

So Baldilocks took the honey and rubbed it on his head. It was horribly sticky and it had several angry bees in it that stung him.

338

But it didn't make one single hair grow.

The third bear that Baldilocks met was a big gingery one that was digging for grubs in a nettle patch.

Baldilocks asked his question again, and the ginger bear, after looking carefully at him, pulled up a pawful of nettles and said, 'Rub these into your scalp.'

So Baldilocks took the nettles and rubbed them on his head. They stung him so much that his eyes

339

began to water, but they didn't make one single hair grow.

The fourth bear that Baldilocks came across, a big chocolate-coloured one, was digging out an ants' nest, and by way of reply to the hobgoblin he handed him a pawful of earth that was full of ants.

When Baldilocks rubbed it on his head, the ants bit him so hard that the tears rolled down his face, but they didn't make one single hair grow.

Baldilocks found the fifth bear by the side of the river that ran through the forest. It was a big, old, grey bear, and it was eating some fish that had been left high and dry on the bank by a flood. They looked to have been dead for a long time, and when Baldilocks's question had been asked and answered, and he rubbed the rotten fish on his head they made it smell perfectly awful. But, once again, they didn't make one single hair grow.

Baldilocks had just about had enough. What with the mud and the honey and all the stings and bites and the stink of the fish, he almost began to hope that he wouldn't meet another bear. But he did.

It was a baby bear, a little golden one, and it was sitting in the sun doing nothing.

'Excuse me,' said Baldilocks. 'Could you tell me how to grow a fine head of hair?'

The baby bear looked fearfully at the hobgoblin. He knew, although

he was so young, that the only way for a bald person to grow hair is by rubbing bear's grease into his scalp. And he knew, although he was so young, that the only way to get bear's grease is to kill a bear and melt him down.

He did not answer, so Baldilocks, to encourage him, said, 'I expect you'll tell me to rub something into my scalp.'

'Yes,' said the baby bear in a small voice.

'What?'

343

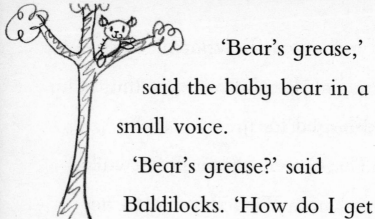

'Bear's grease,' said the baby bear in a small voice.

'Bear's grease?' said Baldilocks. 'How do I get hold of that?'

'You have to kill a bear,' said the baby bear in a whisper, 'and melt him down.'

'Oh!' said Baldilocks. 'Oh no!' he said.

When next the fairy people met, and the hobgoblin came into the fairy ring, someone – probably an

elf – shouted 'Baldilocks!' and everyone laughed, except the little red-haired fairy.

The Queen of the Forest called for silence. Then she said to Baldilocks, 'You haven't grown any hair. Didn't you ask a bear?'

'I asked six, Your Majesty,' said Baldilocks, 'before I found out that what I need is bear's grease and to get that I have to kill a bear and melt him down.'

'That might be difficult,' said the Queen of the Forest, 'but perhaps you could kill a little one?'

She smiled as she spoke, because she knew, being the wisest fairy of them all, that high in a nearby tree a small golden bear sat listening anxiously.

'I couldn't do such a thing,' said Baldilocks. 'I'd sooner stay bald and unhappy.'

Up in the tree, the baby bear hugged himself silently.

After the others had gone away,

346

Baldilocks still sat alone in the fairy ring. At least he thought he was alone, till he looked round and saw that the little red-haired fairy with the kindly face was still sitting there too.

'I think,' she said, 'that bald people are much the nicest.'

'You do?' said Baldilocks.

'Yes. So you mustn't be unhappy any more. If you are, you will make me very sad.'

Baldilocks looked at her, and to his eyes it seemed that she didn't

347

simply have a kind face,
she was beautiful.

He smiled the happiest
of smiles.

'You mustn't be sad,' he said.
'That's something I couldn't bear.'

ACKNOWLEDGEMENTS

The publishers wish to thank the following for permission to use copyright material:

Joan Aiken, 'Clem's Dream', from *The Last Slice of Rainbow and Other Stories* by Joan Aiken, first published by Jonathan Cape 1985. Reprinted by kind permission of A. M. Heath and Co Ltd on behalf of the author, © Joan Aiken Enterprises Ltd 1985; **Nicholas Allan**, 'The Hefty Fairy', first published 1989 by Hutchinson Children's Books. Reprinted by kind permission of The Random House Group Ltd, © Nicholas Allan 1989; **Jan Burchett and Sara Vogler**, 'Flissie and the Elves Eleven', c/o The Agency, 24 Pottery Lane, London W11 4LZ, © Jan Burchett and Sara Vogler 2006; **Fiona Dunbar**, 'The Dull Fairy', c/o The Agency, 24 Pottery Lane, London W11 4LZ, © Fiona Dunbar 2006; **Alan Durant**, 'Nellie the Fairy', c/o The Agency, 24 Pottery Lane, London W11 4LZ, © Alan Durant 2006; **Jonathan Emmett**, 'Fairy Cake', c/o David Higham Associates Limited, 5–8 Lower John Street, Golden Square, London W1F 9HA, © Jonathan Emmett 2006; **Dick King-Smith**, 'Baldilocks and the Six Bears' from *The Ghost at Codlin Castle and Other Stories* by Dick King-Smith, first published by Viking 1992, reprinted by kind permission of A. P. Watt Ltd on behalf of Fox Busters Ltd, © Dick King-Smith 1992; **Paeony Lewis**, 'Lettuce Fairy', c/o The Agency, 24 Pottery Lane, London W11 4LZ, © Paeony Lewis 2006; **Kaye Umansky**, 'The Tale of the Thirteenth Fairy', c/o Caroline Sheldon, Thorley Manor Farm, Thorley, Yarmouth PO41 0SJ © Kaye Umansky 2006; **Anna Wilson**, 'The Two Fairy Godmothers' and 'Fairy Soup and Friendship', c/o The Agency, 24 Pottery Lane, London W11 4LZ, © Anna Wilson 2006.

Princess Stories

Chosen by Anna Wilson

Every princess has a story to tell.

A pretty perfect princess and a badly behaved princess, a princess in love and a princess in BIG trouble . . .

These are just a few of the princesses on parade in this fun, magical story collection.

Nina
Fairy Ballerina

New Girl

Anna Wilson

The first book in a magical new series about a little fairy who brings a lot of sparkle to everything she does – especially ballet.

Nina Dewdrop loves ballet. And when she is accepted into the Royal Academy of Fairy Ballet it looks like Nina's dreams of becoming a prima fairy-ballerina are coming true. First she has to buy everything a budding ballerina needs, from tutus to ballet shoes. Then Nina must say goodbye to her old fairy-friends . . .

When Nina arrives at the Academy, she instantly loves her friendly and funny new room-mate, Peri. In the first ballet class of term, Nina and Peri decide to perform a dance from *Swan Lake*. But magical mayhem descends when snooty, trouble-making Angelica Nightshade waves her wand and tries to turn Nina into a real swan!

Nina
Fairy Ballerina

Daisy Shoes

Anna Wilson

The second book in a magical new series about a little fairy who brings a lot of sparkle to everything she does – especially ballet.

Nina loves the Academy of Fairy Ballet. There are ballet classes every day, and even though the fairies are banned from using magic during their performances, that doesn't stop the girls learning new wand tricks outside lessons!

Now Nina is getting ready for her first end-of-term exam and she is practising her pirouettes to perfection. For if she can pass with flying colours, her mother has promised to buy Nina her dream daisy ballet shoes . . .

Nina
Fairy Ballerina

Best Friends

Anna Wilson

The third book in a magical new series about a little fairy who brings a lot of sparkle to everything she does – especially ballet.

When a new glamorous and graceful fairy ballerina called Bella Glove arrives at the Royal Academy of Fairy Ballet, everybody wants to be her friend. Nina and Peri can't believe their luck when they're asked to share their room with the special visitor! Better still for Nina, Bella wants to be in a pair with her.

But what about poor Peri?

Nina
Fairy Ballerina

Show Time

Anna Wilson

The fourth book in a magical new series about a little fairy who brings a lot of sparkle to everything she does – especially ballet.

Nina Dewdrop and her two best friends have been asked to organize a ballet show – at Queen Camellia's Fairy Palace! They must set the stage, choose the decorations for the after-show party and practise their parts.

But when disaster disrupts rehearsals, Nina's sure someone is sabotaging the show. Will it be all right on the fairies' big night?

Other titles available from
Macmillan Children's Books

The prices shown below are correct at the time of going
to press. However, Macmillan Publishers reserves the right to
show new retail prices on covers, which may differ from those
previously advertised.

Chosen by Anna Wilson

Princess Stories   ISBN-13: 978-0-330-43797-4   £4.99
                      ISBN-10: 0-330-43797-6

By Anna Wilson

NINA FAIRY BALLERINA

New Girl   ISBN-13: 978-0-330-43985-5   £3.99
                      ISBN-10: 0-330-43985-5

Daisy Shoes   ISBN-13: 978-0-330-43986-2   £3.99
                      ISBN-10: 0-330-43986-3

Best Friends   ISBN-13: 978-0-330-43987-9   £3.99
                      ISBN-10: 0-330-43987-1

Show Time   ISBN-13: 978-0-330-43988-6   £3.99
                      ISBN-10: 0-330-43988-X

All Pan Macmillan titles can be ordered from our website,
www.panmacmillan.com, or from your local bookshop and are
also available by post from:

Bookpost, PO Box 29, Douglas, Isle of Man IM99 1BQ
Credit cards accepted. For details:
Telephone: 01624 677237
Fax: 01624 670923
Email: bookshop@enterprise.net
www.bookpost.co.uk

lonely planet

CORK, KERRY & SOUTHWEST IRELAND

ROAD TRIPS

Neil Wilson

HOW TO USE THIS BOOK

Reviews

In the Destinations section:

All reviews are ordered in our authors' preference, starting with their most preferred option. Additionally:

Sights are arranged in the geographic order that we suggest you visit them and, within this order, by author preference.

Eating and Sleeping reviews are ordered by price range (budget, midrange, top end) and, within these ranges, by author preference.

Map Legend

Routes

Trip Route
Trip Detour
Linked Trip
Walk Route
Tollway
Freeway
Primary
Secondary
Tertiary
Lane
Unsealed Road
Plaza/Mall
Steps
)= = Tunnel
Pedestrian Overpass
- - - Walk Track/Path

Boundaries

- - - International
- - - State/Province
——— Cliff

Hydrography

River/Creek
Intermittent River
Swamp/Mangrove
Canal
Water
Dry/Salt/Intermittent Lake
Glacier

Highway Markers

[E44] E-Road Network
[M100] National Network

Note: Not all symbols displayed above appear on the maps in this book

Trips

1 Trip Numbers
9 Trip Stop
Walking tour
Trip Detour

Population

❖ Capital (National)
◉ Capital (State/Province)
● City/Large Town
● Town/Village

Areas

Beach
Cemetery (Christian)
Cemetery (Other)
Park
Forest
Reservation
Urban Area
Sportsground

Transport

✈ Airport
Cable Car/Funicular
Ⓟ Parking
Train/Railway
Tram

Symbols In This Book

 Top Tips   Food & Drink

 Link Your Trips   Outdoors

 Tips from Locals   Essential Photo

 Trip Detour   Walking Tour

History & Culture   Eating

Family   Sleeping

◉ **Sights**   🛏 **Sleeping**

🏖 **Beaches**   ✗ **Eating**

🏃 **Activities**   **Drinking**

📖 **Courses**   ★ **Entertainment**

☞ **Tours**   🛍 **Shopping**

✷ **Festivals & Events**   ❶ **Information & Transport**

These symbols and abbreviations give vital information for each listing:

☎ Telephone number
☻ Opening hours
Ⓟ Parking
⊖ Nonsmoking
❄ Air-conditioning
@ Internet access
🛜 Wi-fi access
🏊 Swimming pool
🍴 Vegetarian selection
📖 English-language menu
👪 Family-friendly

🐾 Pet-friendly
🚌 Bus
⛴ Ferry
🚊 Tram
🚆 Train
apt apartments
d double rooms
dm dorm beds
q quad rooms
r rooms
s single rooms
ste suites
tr triple rooms
tw twin rooms

CONTENTS

Marino Branch
Brainse Marino
Tel: 8336297

Dingle Peninsula Driving the Wild Atlantic Way

WELCOME TO
CORK, KERRY & SOUTHWEST IRELAND

The Southwest contains some of Ireland's most iconic scenery: crenulated coastlines, green fields crisscrossed by tumbledown stone walls, and mist-shrouded mountain peaks and bogs.

This idyllic area claims some of the country's top peninsula drives – the Ring of Kerry and Dingle Peninsula – as well as a shoal of charming fishing towns and villages that have helped establish the southwest as a gourmet heartland, fanning out from the country's spirited second-largest city, Cork.

The region's exquisite beauty makes it one of Ireland's most popular tourist destinations, but there's always an isolated cove or untrodden trail to discover along its roads.

3 **Dingle Peninsula**
Encounter captivating scenery, castles, neolithic monuments and artistic Dingle. **3–4 DAYS**

2 **Ring of Kerry**
Pass jaw-dropping scenery as you circumnavigate the Iveragh Peninsula. **4 DAYS**

Galway Bay
New Qua
Inishmore
Bellharb
Inishmaan
Aran
Islands
Inisheer
Carror

Corof

Liscannor
Liscannor Bay
Inagh

Doo Lough

Doonbeg
Kilkee
Kilrush
Labasheeda
Cross Village   Carrigaholt
Kilbaha
Tarbert
Glin
Mouth of the Shannon   Ballybunion

Listowel

Kerry Head
Ballyheigue Bay   Banna
Abbeyfeale

KERRY

Maharees Islands
Brandon Bay
Tralee

ATLANTIC   Sybil Point   Cloghane

OCEAN   Dingle
                       Peninsula   Castlemaine

Dunquin   Dingle   Inch   Killorglin
Blasket   Point
Islands   Great   Glenbeigh
         Blasket
Dingle Bay   *Lough Caragh*

Castleisland   Newm

Farranfore

Killarney

Mills

Kells

Cahersiveen   Iveragh   Moll's   Killarney
Valentia   Peninsula   Gap   National Park
Island
Saint   Waterville   *Lough Currane*   Sneem   Kenmare
Finan's Bay
Skellig
Islands   Caherdaniel   Lauragh   Glengarriff
Scariff   *Kenmare River*   Dunmanw
Island   Eyeries   Beara   Adrigole
                   Peninsula
         Allihies   Bantry   Drimoleagu
                   Bere   Durrus
         Dursey   Island   Sheep's Head
         Island   Peninsula   Ballydehob   Rossca
                   Bantry Bay
                   *Dunmanus   Goleen   Skibbereen
                   Bay*   Baltimore
                   Mizen Head   *Roaringwater
                   Peninsula   Bay*
                        Cape Clear
                        Island

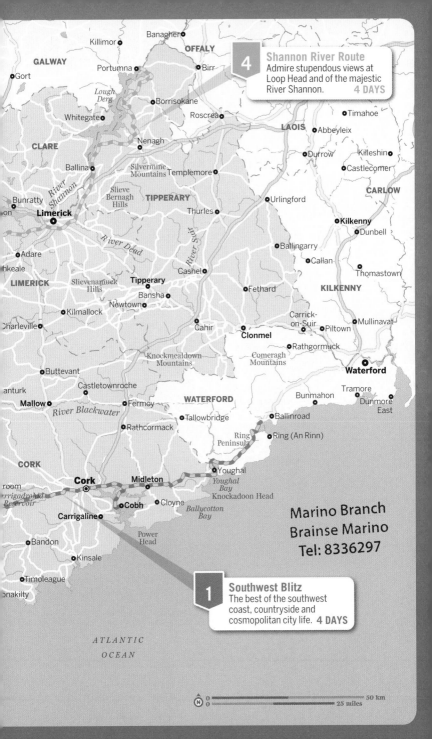

GALWAY

Killimor
Banagher
Portumna
Birr
OFFALY

4 **Shannon River Route**
Admire stupendous views at
Loop Head and of the majestic
River Shannon. **4 DAYS**

Gort
Whitegate
Lough Derg
Borrisokane
Roscrea
Timahoe
LAOIS
Abbeyleix

CLARE
Nenagh
Durrow
Killeshin

Ballina
Silvermine Mountains
Templemore
Castlecomer

Bunratty
River Shannon
Slieve Bernagh Hills
TIPPERARY
Thurles
Urlingford
CARLOW

Limerick
River Dead
River Suir
Ballingarry
Kilkenny
Dunbell

Adare
Callan

hkeale
Slievenamuck Hills
Tipperary
Cashel
Thomastown

LIMERICK
Bansha
Fethard
KILKENNY

Charleville
Kilmallock
Newtown
Carrick-on-Suir
Mullinavat

Cahir
Clonmel
Piltown

Buttevant
Knockmealdown Mountains
Rathgormuck

Castletownroche
Comeragh Mountains
Waterford

anturk
Mallow
Fermoy
WATERFORD
Bunmahon
Tramore

River Blackwater
Tallowbridge
Ballinroad
Dunmore East

Rathcormack
Ring Peninsula
Ring (An Rinn)

CORK

room
Cork
Midleton
Youghal

rrigadrohid Reservoir
Cobh
Cloyne
Youghal Bay
Knockadoon Head

Carrigaline
Power Head
Ballycotton Bay

Bandon
Marino Branch
Brainse Marino
Tel: 8336297

Kinsale

Timoleague

nakilty

1 **Southwest Blitz**
The best of the southwest
coast, countryside and
cosmopolitan city life. **4 DAYS**

ATLANTIC
OCEAN

0 — 50 km
0 — 25 miles

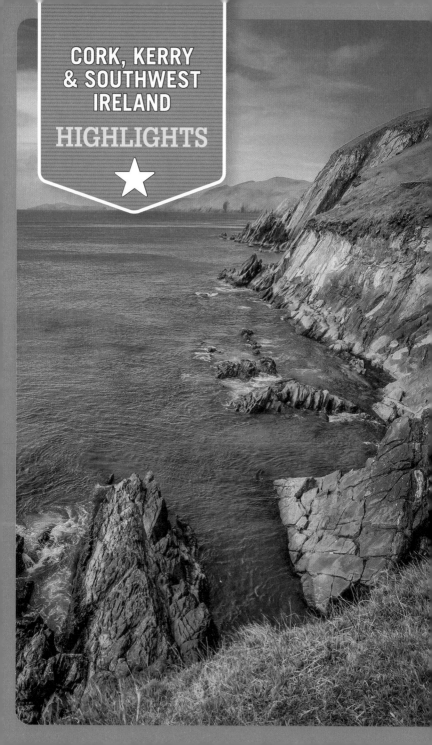

CORK, KERRY
& SOUTHWEST
IRELAND

HIGHLIGHTS

★

Dingle Peninsula (left) This rocky, striated land has a history as compelling as its beauty, prehistoric monuments, scenic spots and fabulous pubs. See it on Trip 3

JORG GREUEL/GETTY IMAGES ©

Cork (above) An appealing waterfront location, some of the best food you'll find, lively craic and a liberal, youthful and cosmopolitan dynamic make Cork hard to resist. See it on Trip 1

Ring of Kerry (right) Yes, it's popular. And yes, it's always choked with bus traffic, especially in summer. But there are 1000 reasons why the Ring of Kerry is the tourist charm bracelet it is. See it on Trip 2

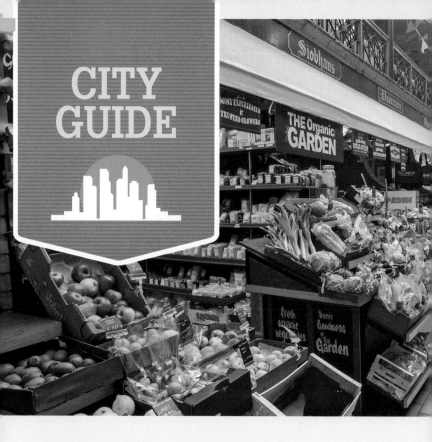

CORK CITY

The Republic of Ireland's second city is second only to Dublin in size; in every other respect it considers itself equal to Dublin (or even better). Great restaurants, top-class galleries and a vibrant pub scene lend credence to its claim, while the people are as friendly and welcoming as you'll find anywhere.

Getting Around

Cork's compact centre and easy-to-follow one-way system makes driving a relatively hassle-free experience.

Parking

Streetside parking requires scratch-card parking discs (€2 per hour), obtained from the tourist office and

some newsagencies. There are several signposted car parks around the central area, with charges of €2 per hour and €12 overnight.

Where to Eat

The narrow pedestrianised streets north of St Patrick's St are packed with cafes and restaurants, and the place hops day and night. The English Market is *the*

GABRIEL12/SHUTTERSTOCK ©

TOP EXPERIENCES

➡ Look Upon Cork
Wander up through Shandon and explore the galleries, antique shops and cafes of the city's prettiest neighbourhood, perched on a hill on the northern side of town.

➡ Eyeball the Best of Irish Art
The Crawford Municipal Art Gallery is small, but it's packed with great art by such top Irish names as Jack B Yeats, Nathaniel Hone, Sir John Lavery and Mainie Jellett.

➡ Indulge Your Taste Buds
Cork's foodie scene is made famous by its collection of terrific restaurants, but don't forget the splendid Victorian English Market.

➡ Have a Night on the Town
Atmospheric old pubs, buzzing music venues and a well-respected theatre scene make for a memorable night.

English Market Cork's produce market

place for great produce and outstanding daytime eats.

Where to Stay

Base yourself in town, as close to St Patrick's St and the South Mall as possible. Once you've exhausted the warren of streets between these two locations, venture west across the Lee and wander up to Shandon, where Corkonians regularly take refuge from the city below.

Useful Websites

Cork City Tourism (www.cometocork.com) Sights, accommodation bookings, discounts.

People's Republic of Cork (www.peoplesrepublicofcork.com) Indie guide to what's on in Cork.

WhazOn? (www.whazon.com) Comprehensive entertainment listings.

Trips Through Cork City

Destination Coverage p60

POCKET
DUBLIN

For more, check out our city and country guides.
www.lonelyplanet.com

11

CURRENCY
Euro (€)

LANGUAGES
English, Irish

VISAS
Not required by most citizens of Europe, Australia, New Zealand, USA and Canada.

FUEL
Petrol (gas) stations are everywhere, but are limited on motorways. Expect to pay €1.35 per litre of unleaded (€1.25 for diesel).

RENTAL CARS
Avis (www.avis.ie)
Europcar (www.europcar.ie)
Hertz (www.hertz.ie)
Thrifty (www.thrifty.ie)

IMPORTANT NUMBERS
Country code (☏353)
Emergencies (☏999)
Roadside Assistance (☏1800 667 788)

Climate

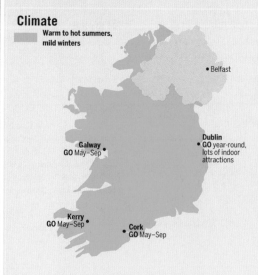

Warm to hot summers, mild winters

Belfast

Dublin
GO year-round, lots of indoor attractions

Galway
GO May–Sep

Kerry
GO May–Sep

Cork
GO May–Sep

When to Go

High Season (Jun–mid-Sep)
» Weather at its best.

» Accommodation rates at their highest (especially in August).

» Tourist peak in Dublin, Kerry and southern and western coasts.

Shoulder (Easter–May, mid-Sep–Oct)
» Weather often good: sun and rain in May, often-warm 'Indian summers' in September.

» Summer crowds and accommodation rates drop off.

Low Season (Nov–Easter)
» Reduced opening hours from October to Easter; some destinations close.

» Cold and wet weather throughout the country; fog can reduce visibility.

» Big city attractions operate as normal.

Your Daily Budget

Budget: Less than €60

» Dorm bed: €12–20

» Cheap meal in cafe or pub: €6–12

» Pint: €4.50–5 (more in cities)

Midrange: €60–150

» Double room in hotel or B&B: €80–180 (more in Dublin)

» Main course in midrange restaurant: €12–25

» Car rental (per day): €25-45

Top End: More than €150

» Four-star hotel stay: from €150

» Three-course meal in good restaurant: around €50

» Top round of golf from €90

Eating

Restaurants From cheap cafes to Michelin-starred feasts, covering every imaginable cuisine.

Cafes Cafes are good for all-day breakfasts, sandwiches and basic dishes.

Pubs Pub grub ranges from toasted sandwiches to carefully crafted dishes.

Hotels All hotel restaurants take nonguests. A popular option in the countryside.

Eating price indicators represent the cost of a main dish:

Eating costs

€ less than €12

€€ €12–25

€€€ more than €25

Sleeping

Hotels From chain hotels with comfortable digs to Norman castles with rainfall shower rooms and wi-fi.

B&Bs From a bedroom in a private home to a luxurious Georgian townhouse.

Hostels Every major town and city has a selection of hostels, with clean dorms and wi-fi. Some have laundry and kitchen.

Sleeping price indicators represent the cost of a double room in high season:

Sleeping costs

€ less than €80

€€ €80–180

€€€ more than €180

Arriving in Ireland

Dublin Airport

Rental cars Rental agencies have offices at the airport.

Taxis Taxis to the city take 30 to 45 minutes and cost €25 to €30.

Buses Private coaches run every 10 to 15 minutes to the city centre (€6).

Cork Airport

Rental cars There are car-hire desks for all the main companies.

Taxis A taxi to/from town costs €22 to €26.

Bus Every half hour between 6am and 10pm to the train station and bus station (€2.80).

Dun Laoghaire Ferry Port

Train DART (suburban rail) takes about 25 minutes to the centre of Dublin.

Bus Public bus takes around 45 minutes to the centre of Dublin.

Mobile Phones

All European and Australasian phones work in Ireland, as do North American phones not locked to a local network. Check with your provider. Prepaid SIM cards cost from €10.

Internet Access

Wi-fi and 3G/4G networks are making internet cafes largely redundant. Most accommodation places have free wi-fi, or a daily charge (up to €10).

Money

ATMs are widely available. Credit and debit cards can be used in most places, but check first.

Tipping

Not obligatory, but 10% to 15% in restaurants; €1 per bag for hotel porters.

Useful Websites

Entertainment Ireland (www.entertainment.ie) Countrywide listings.

Failte Ireland (www. discoverireland.ie) Official tourist-board website for the Republic.

Lonely Planet (www. lonelyplanet.com/ireland, www. lonelyplanet.com/ireland/ northern-ireland) Destination information, hotel bookings, traveller forum and more.

For more, see Road Trip Essentials (p110).

Road Trips

Dingle Peninsula Connor Pass (p47)
ROLF G WACKENBERG/SHUTTERSTOCK ©

Southwest Blitz

Catch the very best of Ireland's southwest along this classic route as it curls from Killarney around the Ring of Kerry coast and across County Cork's lush countryside to charming Dungarvan.

TRIP HIGHLIGHTS

139 km

Kenmare
Board a seal-spotting cruise accompanied by sea shanties

265 km

Cork
Thriving, cultured metropolis made glorious by its location

Killorglin

START
Killarney

5

4

6

7

Cobh

Youghal

FINISH
Dungarvan

183 km

Bantry
Visit Bantry House gardens' enormous 'stairway to the sky'

Caherdaniel
Lush gardens at Derrynane's historic park

92 km

narourke (p20) A high point along the Ring of Kerry

4 DAYS
369KM / 229 MILES

GREAT FOR...

BEST TIME TO GO

Late spring and early autumn for the best weather and manageable crowds.

 ESSENTIAL PHOTO

The view from Beenarourke across rocky coastline and scattered islands.

 BEST FOR FAMILIES

Ride the train or stroll around animal-filled Fota Wildlife Park.

1 Southwest Blitz

This drive around the country's stunning southwest conjures up iconic impressions of Ireland: soaring stone castles, dizzying sea cliffs, wide, sandy beaches, crystal-clear lakes, dense woodlands and boat-filled harbours. Villages you'll encounter en route spill over with brightly painted buildings, vibrant markets and cosy pubs with toe-tapping live music, perfectly poured pints and fantastic craic.

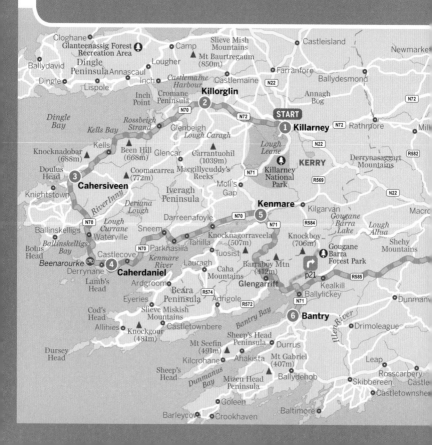

① Killarney (p78)

Killarney's biggest attraction, in every sense, is Killarney National Park (p82), with magnificent Muckross Estate at its heart. If you're not doing the classic Ring of Kerry route that brings you through the park, you should definitely consider a detour here. Right in town, there are pedestrian entrances to the park opposite **St Mary's Cathedral** (www.killarneyparish.com; Cathedral Pl; ⏰8am-6.30pm), a superb example of neo-

Gothic revival architecture, built between 1842 and 1855.

Also worth a visit in the town centre is the 1860s **Franciscan Friary** (www.franciscans.ie; Fair Hill; ⏰8am-8pm), with an ornate Flemish-style altarpiece, some impressive tilework and, most notably, stained-glass windows by Harry Clarke. The Dublin artist's organic style was influenced by art nouveau, art deco and symbolism.

Plunkett and College Sts are lined with pubs;

behind leaded-glass doors, tiny traditional **O'Connor's** (www.oconnorstraditionalpub.ie; 7 High St; ⏰noon-11.30pm Sun-Thu, to 12.30am Fri & Sat; 📞) is one of Killarney's most popular haunts, with live music every night.

The Drive » It's 22km west to Killorglin on the N72. To visit the too-gorgeous-for-words Gap of Dunloe, after 5km turn south onto Gap Rd and follow it for 3km to Kate Kearney's Cottage, where many drivers park in order to walk up to the Gap. You can also hire ponies and jaunting cars here (bring cash).

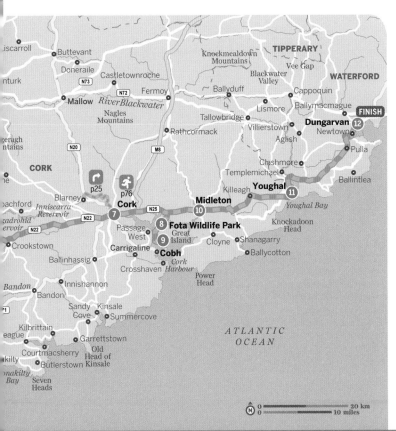

2 Killorglin (p85)

Unless you're here during mid-August's ancient Puck Fair (p85), the main reason to pause at the pretty riverside town of Killorglin (Cill Orglan) is its excellent selection of eateries. These become rather more scarce on the Ring of Kerry coast road until you get to Kenmare, so considering picking up picnic fare here, too.

At smokery **KRD Fisheries** (066-976 1106; www.krdfisheries.com; Tralee Rd; 9am-1pm & 2-5pm Mon-Fri, to 1pm Sat, to 11am Sun) you can buy salmon direct from the premises. Nearby, Jack Healy bakes amazing breads and also makes pâté and beautiful sandwiches at Jack's Bakery (p85).

The Drive » It's 40km from Killorglin to Cahersiveen. En route, you'll pass the turn-off to the little-known Cromane Peninsula, with a truly exceptional restaurant, as well as the quaint and insightful Kerry Bog Village Museum and the turn-off to Rossbeigh Strand, with dazzling views north to the Dingle Peninsula.

3 Cahersiveen

The ruined cottage on the eastern bank of the Carhan River, on the left as you cross the bridge to Cahersiveen, is the humble birthplace of Daniel O'Connell (1775–1847). On the opposite bank there's a stolid bust of the man. Known as 'the Great Liberator', O'Connell was elected to the British Parliament in 1828, but as a Catholic he couldn't take his seat. The government was forced to pass the 1829 Act of Catholic Emancipation, allowing some well-off Catholics voting rights and the right to be elected as MPs. Learn more about it at the **Old Barracks Heritage Centre** (066-401 0430; www.theoldbarracks cahersiveen.com; Bridge St; adult/child €4/2; 10am-5pm Mon-Sat, 11am-4pm Sun Mar-Nov; P), housed in a tower of the former Royal Irish Constabulary (RIC). The barracks were burnt down in 1922 by anti-Treaty forces.

Ballycarbery Castle and ring forts are located here; Cahersiveen is also a jumping-off point for exploring Valentia Island and the Skellig Ring.

The Drive » Continue from Cahersiveen for 17km along the N70 to Waterville. From Waterville the rugged, rocky coastline is at its most dramatic as the road twists, turns and twists again along the 12km stretch to Caherdaniel. At Beenarourke, the highest point of the road, you can stop to enjoy what is plausibly claimed to be 'Ireland's finest view', looking across the rocky coastline and scattered islands to Kenmare River, Bantry Bay and the rugged hills of the Beara Peninsula.

TRIP HIGHLIGHT

4 Caherdaniel (p86)

Hiding between Derrynane Bay and the foothills of Eagles Hill, Caherdaniel barely qualifies as a tiny hamlet. Businesses are scattered about the undergrowth like smugglers, which is fitting since this was once a haven for the same.

There's a Blue Flag **beach**, plenty of activities, good hikes and pubs where you may be tempted to break into pirate talk.

Sublime **Derrynane National Historic Park** (066-947 5113; www.derry nanehouse.ie; Derrynane; adult/child €5/3; 10.30am-6pm mid-Mar–Sep, 10am-5pm Oct, to 4pm Sat & Sun Nov–early Dec; P) incorporates **Derrynane House**, the ancestral home of Daniel O'Connell, whose family made money smuggling from their base by the dunes. Its **gardens** are astonishing, warmed by the Gulf Stream, with palms, 4m-high tree ferns, gunnera ('giant rhubarb') and other South American species. A **walking track** through the gardens leads to wetlands, beaches and cliff tops.

The Drive » The N70 zigzags for 21km northeast to the quaint, colourful little village of Sneem. This area is home to one of the finest castle hotels in the country, the Parknasilla Resort and Spa. It's a further 27km drive along the N70 to Kenmare.

TRIP HIGHLIGHT

5 Kenmare (p87)

Set around its triangular market square, the sophisticated town of Kenmare is stunningly situated by Kenmare Bay.

Reached through the tourist office, the **Kenmare Heritage Centre** (📞064-664 1233; The Square; 🕙10am-5.30pm Mon-Sat Apr-Oct, by appointment Nov-Mar) tells the history of the town from its founding as Neidín by the swashbuckling Sir William Petty in 1670. The centre also relates the story of the Poor Clare Convent, founded in 1861, which is still standing behind Holy Cross Church.

Local women were taught needlepoint lace-making at the convent and their lacework catapulted Kenmare to international fame. Upstairs from the Heritage Centre, the **Kenmare Lace and Design Centre** has displays, including designs for 'the most important piece of lace ever made in Ireland' (in a 19th-century critic's opinion).

Star Outdoors (📞064-664 1222; www.staroutdoors.ie; Dauros) offers activities such as dinghy sailing (from €65 per hour for up to six people; you'll need some prior experience), sea kayaking (single/double per hour €22/38) and hill walking for all levels.

Warm yourself with tea, coffee, rum and the captain's sea shanties on an entertaining two-hour voyage with **Seafari** (📞064-664 2059; www.seafariireland.com; Kenmare Pier; adult/child €25/12.50; 🕙Apr-Oct; 👶) to spot Ireland's biggest seal colony and other marine life. Binoculars (and lollipops!) are provided.

The Drive >> Leave the Ring of Kerry at Kenmare and take the steep and winding N71 south for 44km to Bantry. For an even more scenic alternative, consider driving via the Ring of Beara, encircling the Beara Peninsula. If you don't have time to do the entire Ring, a shorter option is to cut across the Beara's spectacular Healy Pass Rd (R574).

DETOUR:
GOUGANE BARRA FOREST PARK

Start: 6 Bantry

Almost alpine in feel, **Gougane Barra** (www.gouganebarra.com) is a truly magical part of inland County Cork, with spectacular vistas of craggy mountains, silver streams and pine forests sweeping down to a mountain lake that is the source of the River Lee. St Finbarre, the founder of Cork, established a monastery here in the 6th century. He had a hermitage on the island in Gougane Barra Lake (Lough an Ghugain), which is now approached by a short causeway. The small chapel on the island has fine stained-glass representations of obscure Celtic saints. A loop road runs through the park, with plenty of opportunities to walk the well-marked network of paths and nature trails through the forest.

The only place to air your hiking boots is the **Gougane Barra Hotel** (📞026-47069; www.gouganebarrahotel.com; s/d from €79/122; 🕙Apr-Oct; 🅿🛜). There's an on-site restaurant (daytime snacks €6 to €10, two-/three-course dinner menus €26.50/33.50), a cafe and a pub next door.

To reach the forest park, turn off the N71 onto the R584 about 6km north of Bantry and follow it northeast for 23km. Retrace your route to the N71 to continue back to Bantry and on to Cork City.

WHY THIS IS A CLASSIC TRIP
NEIL WILSON, WRITER

Journeying from Killarney to Dungarvan, this trip not only incorporates all of Ireland's definitive elements but also plenty of unexpected ones, from the *Titanic*'s fateful final port to exotic animals roaming free in an island-set zoo to a spine-tingling 9th-century prison – as well as countless opportunities for serendipitous detours (because, of course, serendipity is what makes a road trip a true classic).

Above: Bantry House (p23), County Cork
Right: Cork City Gaol (p24)
Left: Giraffes, Fota Wildlife Park (p24), County Cork

TRIP HIGHLIGHT

⑥ Bantry

Framed by the craggy Caha Mountains, sweeping Bantry Bay is an idyllic inlet famed for its oysters and mussels. One kilometre southwest of the centre of bustling market town Bantry is **Bantry House** (☏027-50047; www.bantryhouse.com; Bantry Bay; house & garden adult/child €11/3, garden only €6/free; ☉10am-5pm daily Jun-Aug, Tue-Sun mid-Apr–May, Sep & Oct; **P**), the former home of Richard White, who earned his place in history when in 1798 he warned authorities of the imminent landing of patriot Wolfe Tone and his French fleet to join the countrywide rebellion of the United Irishmen. Storms prevented the fleet from landing, altering the course of Irish history. The house's **gardens** and the panoramic 'stairway to the sky' are its great glory, and it hosts the week-long **West Cork Chamber Music Festival** (www.west corkmusic.ie) in June/July, when it closes to the public (the garden, craft shop and tearoom remain open).

The Drive » Head north on the N71 to Ballylickey and take the R584 and R585 to Crookstown, then the N22 through rugged terrain softening to patchwork farmland along the 86km journey to Cork city.

❼ Cork City (p60)

Ireland's second city is first in every important respect, at least according to the locals, who cheerfully refer to it as the 'real capital of Ireland'.

A flurry of urban renewal has resulted in new buildings, bars and arts centres and tidied-up thoroughfares. The best of the city is still happily traditional, though – snug pubs with regular live-music sessions, excellent local produce in an ever-expanding list of restaurants and a genuinely proud welcome from the locals.

Cork swings during the **Cork Jazz Festival** (www.facebook.com/corkjazzfestival), with an all-star line-up in venues across town in late October. An eclectic week-long program of international films screens in November during the **Cork Film Festival** (www.corkfilmfest.org).

About 2km west of the city centre, faint-hearted souls may find the imposing former prison, **Cork City Gaol** (☎021-430 5022; www.corkcitygaol.com; Convent Ave; adult/child €10/6; ⌚9.30am-5pm Apr-Sep, 10am-4pm Oct-Mar), grim but it's actually very moving, bringing home the harshness of the 19th-century penal system. An audio tour guides you around the restored cells, with models of suffering prisoners and sadistic-looking guards. The most common crime was simply poverty, with many of the inmates sentenced to hard labour for stealing loaves of bread. The prison closed in 1923, reopening in 1927 as a radio station – the Governor's House has been converted into a Radio Museum (€2).

The Drive ❱❱ Head east of central Cork via the N8 and N25, and take the turn-off to Cobh to cross the bridge to Fota Island and reach Fota Wildlife Park (18km).

---

❽ Fota Wildlife Park (p70)

Kangaroos bound, monkeys and gibbons leap and scream on wooded islands, and cheetahs run without a cage or fence in sight at the huge outdoor **Fota Wildlife Park** (☎021-481 2678; www.fotawildlife.ie; Carrigtwohill, Fota Island; adult/child €16.70/11.20, parking €3; ⌚10am-6pm; P ♿).

A tour train (one way/return €1/2) runs a circuit round the park every 15 minutes in high season, but the 2km circular walk offers a more close-up experience.

From the wildlife park, you can stroll to the Regency-style **Fota House** (☎021-481 5543; www.fotahouse.com; house tours adult/child €9/3.50, house & gardens €13.50/6; ⌚10am-5pm daily Mar-Sep, Sat & Sun Feb & Oct-Dec; P). The mostly barren interior contains a fine kitchen and ornate plasterwork ceilings; interactive displays bring the rooms to life.

Attached to the house is the 150-year-old **arboretum**, which has a Victorian fernery, a magnolia walk and some beautiful trees, including giant redwoods and a Chinese ghost tree.

The Drive ❱❱ From Fota Wildlife Park, head south for 5km to Cobh.

---

❾ Cobh (p71)

For many years Cobh (pronounced 'cove') was the port of Cork. During the Famine, some 2.5 million people left Ireland through the glistening estuary. In 1838 the *Sirius,* the first steamship to cross the Atlantic, sailed from Cobh, and the *Titanic* made its final stop here in 1912.

The original White Star Line offices, where 123 passengers embarked on the *Titanic's* final voyage now houses the unmissable **Titanic Experience Cobh** (☎021-481 4412; www.titanicexperiencecobh.ie; 20 Casement Sq; adult/child €10/7; ⌚9am-6pm Apr-Sep, 10am-5.30pm Oct-Mar; ♿). Admission is by tour, which is partly guided and partly interactive, with holograms, audio-visual presentations and exhibits.

Standing dramatically above Cobh, the massive French Gothic **St Colman's Cathedral** (☎021-481 3222; www.cobhcathedralparish.ie; Cathedral Pl; admission by donation; ⊙8am-6pm May-Oct, to 5pm Nov-Apr) is out of all proportion to the town. Its 47-bell carillon, the largest in Ireland, weighs a stonking 3440kg.

In 1849 Cobh was renamed Queenstown after Queen Victoria paid a visit; the name lasted until Irish independence in 1921. Housed in the old train station, **Cobh, The Queenstown Story** (☎021-481 3591; www.cobhheritage.com; Lower Rd; adult/child €10/6; ⊙9.30am-6pm mid-Apr–mid-Oct, 9.30am-5pm Mon-Sat & 11am-5pm Sun mid-Oct–mid-Apr) has exhibits evoking the Famine tragedy, a genealogy centre and a cafe.

The Drive » Travel north on the R624 then east on the N25 to Midleton (18km in total).

➓ Midleton (p73)

The number-one attraction in Midleton is the former whiskey distillery now housing the **Jameson Experience** (☎021-461 3594; www.jamesonwhiskey.com; Old Distillery Walk; tours adult/child €22/11; ⊙shop 10am-6pm; P), where you can learn how Irish whiskey is made. Attractive cafes, restaurants and a great farmers market (p74) make it worth stopping for a while.

The Drive » Continue east on the N25 for the 28km drive to Youghal.

⓫ Youghal (p74)

The ancient seaport of Youghal (Eochaill; pronounced 'yawl'), at the mouth of the River Blackwater, was a hotbed of rebellion against the English in the 16th century. Oliver Cromwell wintered here in 1649 as he sought to drum up support for his war in England and quell insurgence from the Irish. Youghal was granted to Sir Walter Raleigh during the Elizabethan Plantation of Munster. The curious **Clock Gate** was built in

DETOUR: BLARNEY CASTLE

Start: ➐ Cork City

Blarney Castle (☎021-438 5252; www.blarneycastle.ie; Blarney; adult/child €18/8; ⊙9am-7pm Mon-Sat, to 6pm Sun Jun-Aug, shorter hours Sep-May; P) is one of Ireland's most popular tourist attractions. Queen Elizabeth I is rumoured to have invented the term 'to talk blarney' out of irritation with Lord Blarney's ability to go on and on without ever agreeing to her demands.

The clichéd **Blarney Stone** is located at the top of a slippery spiral staircases. On the battlements, you bend backwards over a long, long drop (with safety grill and attendant to prevent tragedy) to kiss the stone (an act which is said to confer on you the gift of eloquence). Once you're upright, don't forget to admire the stunning views before descending.

If the throngs get too much, vanish into the Rock Close, part of the beautiful and often ignored gardens.

Head out of central Cork via Merchant's Quay and the N20; Blarney is about 10km northwest of the city.

1777 and served as a clock tower and jail concurrently; several prisoners taken in the 1798 Rising were hanged from its windows.

Main St has an interesting curve that follows the original shore; many of the shopfronts are from the 19th century. Further up the street are the almshouses built by Englishman Richard Boyle, who became the first earl of Cork in 1616. Across the road is the 15th-century tower house, **Tynte's Castle**, which originally had a defensive riverfront position before the River Blackwater silted up and changed course.

Built in 1220, **St Mary's Collegiate Church** incorporates elements of an earlier Danish church dating back to the 11th century. The churchyard is bounded by a fine stretch of the 13th-century town wall and one of the remaining turrets.

Beside the church, **Myrtle Grove**, the former home of Sir Walter Raleigh.

The Drive » Rejoin the N25 and cross the River Blackwater. Continue following the N25 northeast for the final run to Dungarvan, a 31km trip in all.

- - - - - - - - - - - - - - - - - - -

⑫ Dungarvan

One of Ireland's most enchanting coastal towns, pastel-shaded Dungarvan is best known by its foodie reputation, but there are some intriguing sights, too. On the waterfront, **Dungarvan Castle** (☎058-48144; www. heritageireland.ie; Castle St; ⊙10am-6pm late May-late Sep) dates back to the 12th century. Admission is by (free) guided tour only.

Housed in a handsome building dating from the 17th century, the **Old Market House Arts Centre** (☎058-48944; www. facebook.com/oldmarkethouse; Lower Main/Parnell St; ⊙11am-1.30pm & 2.30-5pm Tue-Fri, 1-5pm Sat, hours can vary) showcases contemporary art by local artists.

The **Waterford County Museum** (☎058-45960; www.waterfordmuseum.ie; 2 St Augustine St; ⊙10am-5pm Mon-Fri) covers maritime heritage (with relics from shipwrecks), Famine history, local personalities and various other titbits, all displayed in an 18th-century grain store.

Youghal (p25) Clock Gate Tower

Ring of Kerry

Circumnavigating the Iveragh Peninsula, the Ring of Kerry is the most diverse of Ireland's prized peninsula drives, combining jaw-dropping coastal scenery with soaring mountains.

2

TRIP HIGHLIGHTS

.89 km

Muckross Estate
Magnificent garden-set mansion, deer parks, waterfall and abbey

START/FINISH

● Killarney

● Rossbeigh Strand

10

11

● Kenmare

7

Caherdaniel
Aquatic activities galore and horse rides along the beach

90 km

158 km

Gap of Dunloe
Rocky bridges cross crystal-clear streams and lakes

4 DAYS
202KM / 125 MILES

GREAT FOR...

BEST TIME TO GO

Late spring and early autumn for temperate weather free of summer crowds.

 ESSENTIAL PHOTO

Ross Castle as you row a boat to Inisfallen.

✓ **BEST FOR WILDLIFE**

Killarney National Park, home to Ireland's only wild herd of native red deer.

s Castle (p38) Evocative ruins in Killarney National Park

2 Ring of Kerry

You can drive the Ring of Kerry in a day, but the longer you spend, the more you'll enjoy it. The circuit winds past pristine beaches, medieval ruins, mountains, loughs (lakes) and the island-dotted Atlantic, with the coastline at its most rugged between Waterville and Caherdaniel in the peninsula's southwest. You'll also find plenty of opportunities for serene, starkly beautiful detours, such as the Skellig Ring and the Cromane Peninsula.

---

1 Killarney (p78)

A town that's been in the business of welcoming visitors for more than 250 years, Killarney is a well-oiled tourism machine fuelled by the sublime scenery of its namesake national park, with competition helping keep standards high. Killarney nights are lively and most pubs put on live music.

Killarney and its surrounds have likely been inhabited since the Bronze Age, but it wasn't until the mid-18th century that Viscount Kenmare developed the region as an Irish version of England's Lake District; among its notable 19th-century tourists were Queen Victoria and Romantic poet Percy Bysshe Shelley. The town itself lacks major attractions, but the landscaped grounds of nearby Killarney House and Muckross House frame photo-worthy panoramas of lakes and mountains, while former carriage drives around these aristocratic estates now serve as scenic hiking and biking trails open to all.

The town can easily be explored on foot in an hour or two, or you can get around by horse-drawn jaunting car.

The Drive >> From Killarney, head 22km west to Killorglin along the N72,

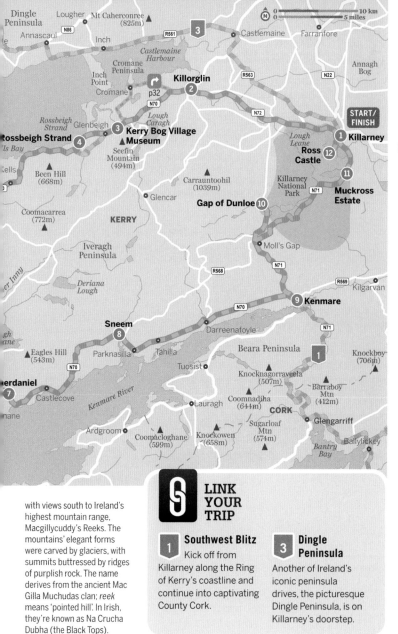

with views south to Ireland's
highest mountain range,
Macgillycuddy's Reeks. The
mountains' elegant forms
were carved by glaciers, with
summits buttressed by ridges
of purplish rock. The name
derives from the ancient Mac
Gilla Muchudas clan; *reek*
means 'pointed hill'. In Irish,
they're known as Na Crucha
Dubha (the Black Tops).

S LINK YOUR TRIP

1 Southwest Blitz

Kick off from
Killarney along the Ring
of Kerry's coastline and
continue into captivating
County Cork.

3 Dingle Peninsula

Another of Ireland's
iconic peninsula
drives, the picturesque
Dingle Peninsula, is on
Killarney's doorstep.

31

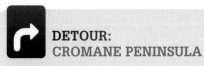

DETOUR:
CROMANE PENINSULA

Start: ② Killorglin

Open fields give way to water vistas and multihued sunsets on the Cromane Peninsula, with its tiny namesake village sitting at the base of a narrow shingle spit.

Cromane's exceptional eating place, **Jack's Coastguard Restaurant** (☎066-976 9102; www.jackscromane.com; Cromane; mains €19-36, 5-course tasting menu €65, 3-course Sun lunch €29; ⊙6-9pm Thu-Sun, 1-3pm Sun, hours can vary; P ♿), is a local secret and justifies the trip. Entering this 1866-built coastguard station feels like arriving at a low-key village pub, but a narrow doorway at the back of the bar leads to a striking, whitewashed contemporary space with lights glittering from midnight-blue ceiling panels, stained glass and metallic fish sculptures, and huge picture windows looking out across the water. Seafood is the standout, but there's also steak, roast lamb and a veggie dish of the day.

Cromane is 9km from Killorglin. Heading southwest from Killorglin along the N70, take the second right and continue straight ahead until you get to the crossroads. Turn right; Jack's Coastguard Restaurant is on your left.

② Killorglin (p85)

Killorglin (Cill Orglan) is quieter than the waters of the River Laune that lap against its 1885-built eight-arched bridge – except in mid-August, when there's an explosion of time-honoured ceremonies at the famous **Puck Fair** (Aonach an Phuic; www.puckfair.ie; ⊙mid-Aug), a pagan festival first recorded in 1603. A statue of King Puck (a goat) peers out from the Killarney end of the bridge.

Killorglin has some of the finest eateries along the Ring – **Bianconi** (☎066-976 1146; www.bianconi.ie; Lower Bridge St; mains €10-28; ⊙kitchen 11.30am-10pm Mon-Sat, 6-9pm Sun; 🛜) and **Jack's Bakery** (Lower Bridge St; dishes €2.50-8; ⊙8am-6.45pm Mon-Fri, to 6pm Sat, 9am-2pm Sun) are both good spots for a late breakfast or early lunch.

The Drive » Killorglin sits at the junction of the N72 and the N70; continue 13km along the N70 to the Kerry Bog Village Museum.

③ Kerry Bog Village Museum

Between Killorglin and Glenbeigh, the **Kerry Bog Village Museum** (www.kerrybogvillage.ie; Ballincleave, Glenbeigh; adult/child €6.50/4.50; ⊙9am-6pm; P) re-creates a 19th-century settlement typical of the small communities that carved out a precarious living in the harsh environment of Ireland's ubiquitous peat bogs. You'll see the thatched homes of the turf cutter, blacksmith, thatcher and labourer, as well as a dairy, and meet rare Kerry Bog ponies.

The Drive » It's less than 1km from the museum to the village of Glenbeigh; turn off here and drive 2km west to unique Rossbeigh Strand.

④ Rossbeigh Strand

This unusual beach is a 3km-long finger of shingle and sand protruding into Dingle Bay, with views of Inch Point and the Dingle Peninsula. On one side, the sea is ruffled by Atlantic winds; on the other, it's sheltered and calm.

The Drive » Rejoin the N70 and continue 25km southwest to Cahersiveen.

⑤ Cahersiveen

Cahersiveen's population – over 30,000 in

1841 – was decimated by the Great Famine and emigration to the New World. A sleepy outpost remains, overshadowed by the 688m peak of **Knocknadobar**. It looks rather dour compared with the peninsula's other settlements, but the atmospheric remains of 16th-century **Ballycarbery Castle**, 2.4km along the road to White Strand Beach from the town centre, are well worth a visit.

Along the same road are two stone ring forts. The larger, **Cahergall**, dates from the 10th century and has stairways on the inside walls, a *clochán* (circular stone building shaped like an old-fashioned beehive) and the remains of a house. The smaller, 9th-century **Leacanabuile** has an entrance to an underground passage. Their inner walls and chambers give a strong sense of what life was like in a ring fort. Leave your car in the parking area next to a stone wall and walk up the footpaths.

The Drive » From Cahersiveen you can continue 17km along the classic Ring of Kerry on the N70 to Waterville, or take the ultrascenic route via Valentia Island and the Skellig Ring, and rejoin the N70 at Waterville.

- - - - - - - - - - - - - - - - - -

⑥ Waterville

A line of colourful houses on the N70 between Lough Currane

DETOUR:
VALENTIA ISLAND & THE SKELLIG RING

Start: ⑤ Cahersiveen

Crowned by Geokaun Mountain, 11km-long Valentia Island (Oileán Dairbhre) makes an ideal driving loop, with some lonely ruins that are worth exploring. Knightstown, the only town, has pubs, food and walks.

The **Skellig Experience heritage centre** (☎066-947 6306; www.skelligexperience. com; adult/child €5/3, incl cruise €35/20; ☉10am-7pm Jul & Aug, to 6pm May, Jun & Sep, to 4.30pm Fri-Wed Mar, Apr, Oct & Nov; 🅿), in a distinctive building with turf-covered barrel roofs, has informative exhibits on the offshore Skellig Islands. From April to September, it also runs two-hour cruises around the Skelligs.

If you're here between April and October, and you're detouring via Valentia Island and the Skellig Ring, a ferry service from Reenard Point, 5km southwest of Cahersiveen, provides a handy shortcut to Valentia Island. The five-minute crossing departs every 10 minutes. Alternatively, there's a bridge between **Portmagee** and the far end of the island.

Immediately across the bridge on the mainland, Portmagee's single street is a rainbow of colourful houses. On summer mornings the small pier comes to life with boats embarking on the choppy crossing to the Skellig Islands.

Portmagee holds **set-dancing workshops** over the May bank holiday weekend, with plenty of stomping practice sessions in the town's **Bridge Bar** (☎066-947 7108; www.moorings.ie; mains €13-18; ☉8am-11.30pm Mon-Sat, to 11pm Sun, kitchen to 9pm; 👣), a friendly local gathering point that's also good for impromptu music year-round and more formal sessions in summer.

The wild and beautiful, 18km-long Skellig Ring road links Portmagee and Waterville via a Gaeltacht (Irish-speaking) area centred on Ballinskelligs (Baile an Sceilg), with the ragged outline of Skellig Michael never far from view.

WHY THIS IS A CLASSIC TRIP
NEIL WILSON, WRITER

In a land criss-crossed with classic drives, the Ring of Kerry is perhaps the most classic of all. Now a key stretch of the Wild Atlantic Way, this trip showcases Ireland's most spectacular coastal scenery, its ancient and recent history, traditional pubs with crackling turf fires and spontaneous, high-spirited trad-music sessions, and the Emerald Isle's most engaging asset: its welcoming, warm-hearted locals.

Above: Derrynane Beach (p86), along the Ring of Kerry
Right: Stone bridge at the Gap of Dunloe (p36), Killarney National Park
Left: Muckross House (p37), Killarney National Park

and Ballinskelligs Bay, Waterville is charm-challenged in the way of many mass-consumption beach resorts. A statue of its most famous guest, Charlie Chaplin, beams from the seafront. The **Charlie Chaplin Comedy Film Festival** (www.chaplinfilmfestival.com) is held in August.

Waterville is home to a world-renowned **links golf course**. At the north end of Lough Currane, **Church Island** has the ruins of a medieval church and beehive cell reputedly founded as a monastic settlement by St Finian in the 6th century.

The Drive » Squiggle your way for 14km along the Ring's most tortuous stretch, past plunging cliffs, craggy hills and stunning views, to Caherdaniel.

- - - - - - - - - - - - - - - -

TRIP HIGHLIGHT

❼ Caherdaniel (p86)

The scattered hamlet of Caherdaniel counts two of the Ring of Kerry's highlights: Derrynane National Historic Park, the childhood home of the 19th-century hero of Catholic emancipation, Daniel O'Connell; and what is plausibly claimed as 'Ireland's finest view' over rugged cliffs and is-lands, as you crest the hill at Beenarourke (there's a large car park here).

Most activity here centres on the Blue Flag beach. **Derrynane Sea**

Sports (📞087 908 1208; www.derrynaneseasports.com; Derryname Beach) organises sailing, canoeing, surfing, windsurfing and waterskiing (from €40 per person), as well as equipment hire (around €15 per hour). **Eagle Rock Equestrian Centre** (📞066-947 5145; www.eaglerockcentre.com; Ballycarnahan; horse riding per hour €40) offers beach, mountain and woodland horse treks for all levels.

The Drive » Wind your way east along the N70 for 21km to Sneem.

----

⑧ Sneem

Sneem's Irish name, An tSnaidhm, translates as 'the knot', which is thought to refer to the River Sneem that twists and turns, knot-like, into nearby Kenmare Bay.

Take a gander at the town's two cute squares, then pop into the **Blue Bull** (📞064-664 5382; South Sq; mains €9-15, dinner €14-24; ⏰kitchen noon-2pm &

6-9.30pm, bar 11.30am-midnight), a perfect little old stone pub, for a pint.

The Drive » Along the 27km drive to Kenmare, the N70 drifts away from the water to take in views towards the Kerry mountains.

----

⑨ Kenmare (p87)

The copper-covered limestone spire of Holy Cross Church, drawing the eye to the wooded hills above town, may make you forget for a split second that Kenmare is a seaside town. With rivers named Finnihy, Roughty and Sheen emptying into Kenmare Bay, you couldn't be anywhere other than southwest Ireland.

In the 18th century Kenmare was laid out on an X-shaped plan, with a triangular market square in the centre. Today the inverted V to the south is the focus. Kenmare River (actually an inlet of the sea) stretches out to the southwest, and there are glorious mountain views.

Signposted southwest of the square is an early Bronze Age **stone circle**, one of the biggest in southwest Ireland. Fifteen stones ring a boulder dolmen, a burial monument rarely found outside this part of the country.

The Drive » The coastal scenery might be finished but, if anything, the next 23km are even more stunning as you head north from Kenmare to the Gap of Dunloe on the narrow, vista-crazy N71, winding between crag and lake, with plenty of lay-bys to stop and admire the views (and recover from the switchback bends).

TRIP HIGHLIGHT

⑩ Gap of Dunloe (p84)

Just west of Killarney National Park, the Gap of Dunloe is ruggedly beautiful. In the winter it's an awe-inspiring mountain pass, squeezed between Purple Mountain and Macgillycuddy's Reeks. In high summer it's a magnet for the tourist trade, with buses ferrying countless visitors here for horse-and-trap rides through the Gap.

On the southern side, surrounded by lush, green pastures, is **Lord Brandon's Cottage** (Gearhameen; dishes €3-8; ⏰8am-3pm Apr-Oct), accessed by turning left at Moll's Gap on the R568, then taking the first right, another right at the bottom of the hill,

TOP TIP:
AROUND (AND ACROSS) THE RING

Tour buses travel anticlockwise around the Ring, and authorities generally encourage visitors to drive in the same direction to avoid traffic congestion and accidents. If you travel clockwise, watch out on blind corners, especially on the section between Moll's Gap and Killarney. There's little traffic on the Ballaghbeama Gap, which cuts across the peninsula's central highlands, with some spectacular views.

KILLARNEY NATIONAL PARK

Designated a Unesco Biosphere Reserve in 1982, **Killarney National Park** (www.killarneynationalpark.ie) is among the finest of Ireland's national parks. And while its proximity to one of the southwest's largest and liveliest urban centres (including pedestrian entrances right in Killarney's town centre) encourages high visitor numbers, it's an important conservation area for many rare species. Within its 102 sq km is Ireland's only wild herd of native red deer, which has lived here continuously for 12,000 years, as well as the country's largest area of ancient oak woods and views of most of its major mountains.

Glacier-gouged Lough Leane (the Lower Lake or 'Lake of Learning'), Muckross Lake and the Upper Lake make up about a quarter of the park. Their crystal waters are as rich in wildlife as the surrounding land: great crested grebes and tufted ducks cruise the lake margins, deer swim out to graze on islands, and salmon, trout and perch prosper in a pike-free environment.

With a bit of luck, you might see white-tailed sea eagles, with their 2.5m wingspan, soaring overhead. The eagles were reintroduced here in 2007 after an absence of more than 100 years. There are now more than 50 in the park and they're starting to settle in Ireland's rivers, lakes and coastal regions. And like Killarney itself, the park is also home to plenty of summer visitors, including migratory cuckoos, swallows and swifts.

Keep your eyes peeled, too, for the park's smallest residents – its insects, including the northern emerald dragonfly, which isn't normally found this far south in Europe and is believed to have been marooned here after the last ice age.

then right again at the crossroads (about 13km from the N71 all up). A simple 19th-century hunting lodge, it has an open-air cafe and a dock for boats from Ross Castle near Killarney. From here a (very) narrow road weaves up the hill to the Gap – theoretically you can drive this 8km route to the 19th-century pub **Kate Kearney's Cottage** (☎064-664 4146; mains €10-24; ⊙ kitchen noon-9pm, bar to 11.30pm Mon-Thu, to 12.30am Fri & Sat, to 11pm Sun; ⓟ 🐾) and back *but* only outside summer. Even then walkers and cyclists have right of way and the precipitous hairpin bends are

nerve-testing. It's worth walking or taking a jaunting car (or, if you're carrying two wheels, cycling) through the Gap: the scenery is a fantasy of rocky bridges over clear mountain streams and lakes. Alternatively, there are various options for exploring the Gap from Killarney.

The Drive ›› Continue on the N71 north through Killarney National Park to Muckross Estate (32km).

– – – – – – – – – – – – – – –

TRIP HIGHLIGHT

⑪ Muckross Estate (p82)

The core of Killarney National Park is Muckross

Estate, donated to the state by Arthur Bourn Vincent in 1932. **Muckross House** (☎064-667 0144; www.muckross-house.ie; adult/child €9.25/6.25, incl Muckross Traditional Farms €15.50/10.50; ⊙9am-7pm Jul & Aug, to 6pm Apr-Jun, Sep & Oct, to 5pm Nov-Mar; ⓟ) is a 19th-century mansion, restored to its former glory and packed with period fittings. Entrance is by guided tour.

The beautiful **gardens** slope down, and a building behind the house contains a restaurant, craft shop and studios where you can see potters, weavers and bookbinders at work. Jaunting cars wait to run you through deer parks and woodland to **Torc Waterfall** and **Muckross Abbey** (about €20 each, return; haggling can reap discounts). The visitor centre has an excellent cafe.

Adjacent to Muckross House are the **Muckross Traditional Farms** (adult/child €9.25/6.25, incl Muckross House €15.50/10.50; ☻10am-6pm Jun-Aug, from 1pm Apr, May & Sep, from 1pm Sat & Sun Mar & Oct). These reproductions of 1930s Kerry farms, complete with chickens, pigs, cattle and horses, re-create farming and living conditions when people had to live off the land.

The Drive » Continuing a further 2km north through the national park brings you to historic Ross Castle.

----

⑫ Ross Castle (p82)

Restored **Ross Castle** (☎064-663 5851; www.heritageireland.ie; Ross Rd; adult/child €5/3; ☻9.30am-5.45pm early Mar–Oct; P) dates back to the 15th century, when it was a residence of the O'Donoghues. It was the last place in Munster to succumb to Cromwell's forces, thanks partly to its cunning spiral staircase, every step of which is a different height in order to break an attacker's stride. Access is by guided tour only.

You can take a motorboat trip (around €10 per person) from Ross Castle to **Inisfallen**, the largest of Killarney National Park's 26 islands. The first monastery on Inisfallen is said to have been founded by St Finian the Leper in the 7th century. The island's fame dates from the early 13th century when the Annals of Inisfallen were written here. Now in the Bodleian Library at Oxford, they remain a vital source of information on early Munster history. Inisfallen shelters the ruins of a 12th-century oratory with a carved Romanesque doorway and a monastery on the site of St Finian's original.

The Drive » It's just 3km north from Ross Castle back to Killarney.

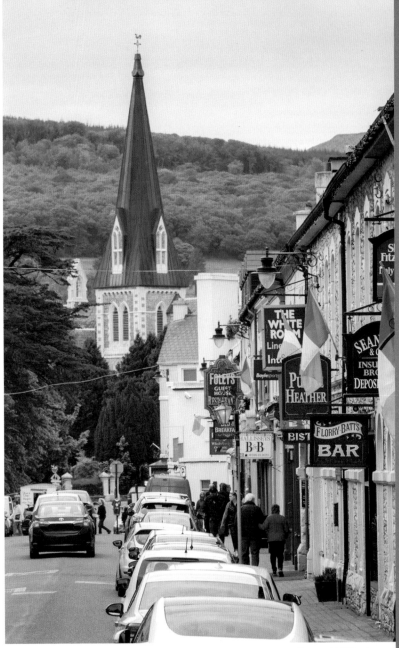

Kenmare (p36) Downtown

Dingle Peninsula

3

Driving around this history-infused headland, you'll encounter churches, castles, neolithic monuments, captivating scenery and artistic little Dingle, the peninsula's delightful 'capital'.

TRIP HIGHLIGHTS

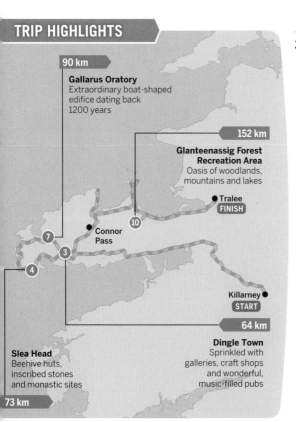

90 km

Gallarus Oratory
Extraordinary boat-shaped edifice dating back 1200 years

152 km

Glanteenassig Forest Recreation Area
Oasis of woodlands, mountains and lakes

● Tralee
FINISH

● Connor Pass

⑩

⑦

③

④

● Killarney
START

64 km

Dingle Town
Sprinkled with galleries, craft shops and wonderful, music-filled pubs

Slea Head
Beehive huts, inscribed stones and monastic sites

73 km

3–4 DAYS
185KM / 115 MILES

GREAT FOR...

BEST TIME TO GO

June to August offer the best beach weather.

 ESSENTIAL PHOTO

Snap a perfect panorama from Clogher Head viewpoint.

BEST FOR HISTORY

Slea Head's astonishing concentration of ancient sites.

e Peninsula View from Clogher Head (p46) to Sybil Head

41

3 Dingle Peninsula

As you twist and turn along this figure-of-eight drive, the coastline is the star of the show. The opal-blue waters surrounding the Dingle Peninsula provide a wealth of aquatic adventures and superbly fresh seafood, and you'll find that where the promontory meets the ocean — at wave-pounded rocks, secluded coves and wide, golden-sand beaches — Dingle's beauty is at its most unforgettable.

❶ Killarney (p78)

The lively tourist town of Killarney is an ideal place to kick off your trip, with a plethora of places to eat, drink and sleep. If you have time, the 102-sq-km **Killarney National Park** (p82), immediately to its south, and the **Gap of Dunloe** (p84), with its rocky terrain, babbling brooks and alpine lakes, are well worth exploring. On a tight schedule, however, you can still get a good overview of the area –

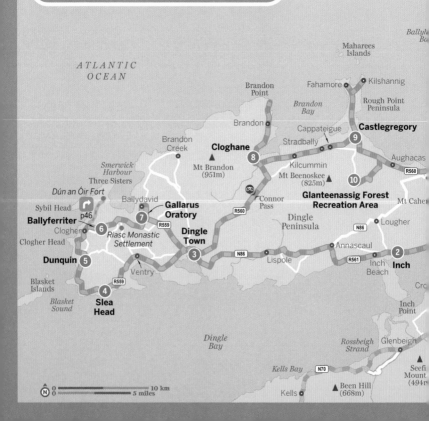

and entertaining commentary, too – aboard a horse-drawn jaunting car, also known as a trap, which comes with a driver called a jarvey. The pick-up point, nicknamed 'the Ha Ha' or 'the Block', is on Kenmare Pl. Trips cost €40 to €80, depending on distance; traps officially carry up to four people.

The Drive >> The quickest route from Killarney to the peninsula is via the R563 to Milltown and Castlemaine. Turn west here onto the R561; you'll soon meet the coast before coming to the vast beach at Inch (41km).

② Inch

Inch's 5km-long sand spit was a location for the movies *Ryan's Daughter* and *Playboy of the Western World*. Sarah Miles, a star of the former film, described her stay here as 'brief but bonny'.

The dunes are certainly bonny, a great spot for windswept walks, birdwatching and bathing. The west-facing Blue Flag beach (lifeguarded in summer) is also a hot surfing spot; waves average 1m to 3m. You can learn to ride them with **Offshore Surf School** (☏087 294 6519; www.offshoresurfschool.ie; lessons adult/child per 2hr from €25/20, board & wetsuit hire per 2hr €15; ⊙9am-6pm Apr–mid-Oct).

Cars are allowed on the beach, but don't end up providing others with laughs by getting stuck.

Sammy's (☏066-915 8118; www.facebook.com/sammysinchbeach; mains €7-15; ⊙10am-6pm Mon-Thu, to 9pm Fri-Sun, shorter hours Oct-Easter; ☎ 🖶), at the entrance to the beach, is the nerve centre of the village. In addition to its beach-facing bar and restaurant, there's a shop, tourist information and trad music sessions during the summer.

The Drive >> Shadowing the coast, about 7km west of Inch, Annascaul (Abhainn an Scáil; also spelled Anascaul) is home to a cracking pub,

LINK YOUR TRIP

1 Southwest Blitz
Killarney is also the jumping-off point for another classic Irish road trip along the Ring of Kerry and a stunning swathe of County Cork.

2 Ring of Kerry
From Tralee it's a quick 22km zip along the N22 to pick up Ireland's most famous driving loop in Killarney.

the South Pole Inn, formerly run by Antarctic explorer Tom Crean in his retirement and now something of a Crean museum. Continuing 18km west of Annascaul brings you into Dingle town.

TRIP HIGHLIGHT

③ Dingle Town (p91)

Fanned around its fishing port, the peninsula's charming little capital is quaint without even trying. Dingle is one of Ireland's largest Gaeltacht (Irish-speaking) towns (although locals have voted to retain the name Dingle rather than go with the officially sanctioned Gaelic version An Daingean) and has long drawn runaways from across the world, making it a surprisingly cosmopolitan, creative place.

This is one of those towns whose very fabric is its attraction. Wander the higgledy-piggledy streets, shop for handcrafted jewellery, arts, crafts and artisan food and pop into old-school pubs. Two untouched examples are **Foxy John's** (Main St; ⊙10am-11pm; 🛜) and **Curran's** (Main St; ⊙10am-11pm), which respectively have old stock of hardware and outdoor clothing on display.

Dingle's most famous 'resident' is Fungie the dolphin. Boats leave Dingle's pier daily for one-hour **dolphin-spotting trips** (📞066-915 2626; www.dingledolphin.com; The Pier; adult/child €16/8). On land, the **Dingle Oceanworld** (📞066-915 2111; www.dingle-oceanworld. ie; The Wood; adult/child/family €15.50/10.75/47; ⊙10am-7pm Jul & Aug, to 6pm Sep-Jun) aquarium has a walk-through tunnel and a touch pool.

Don't leave Dingle without catching traditional live music at pubs such as the **An Droichead Beag** (Small Bridge Bar; www.androicheadbeag.com; Lower Main St; ⊙3pm-2.30am Mon-Thu, from noon Fri & Sat, to 1.30am Sun), where sessions kick off at 9.30pm nightly, and standout seafood at its restaurants.

The Drive ≫ West of Dingle, along the R559, the signposted Slea Head Drive runs around the tip of the Dingle Peninsula. Driving clockwise offers the best views and although it's a mere 47km in length, doing this stretch justice requires a full day, at least.

TRIP HIGHLIGHT

④ Slea Head

Overlooking the mouth of Dingle Bay, Mt Eagle and Ireland's most westerly islands, the Blaskets, Slea Head has fine beaches and superbly preserved structures from Dingle's ancient past, including beehive huts, forts, inscribed stones and monastic sites.

The nearby village of **Ventry** (Ceann Trá), 6km west of Dingle town, is idyllically set next to a wide sandy bay. Full-day boat trips to the Blasket Islands with **Blasket Islands Eco Marine Tours** (📞086 335 3805; www. marinetours.ie; Ventry Pier, Ventry; full-/half-day tour €70/55; ⊙Apr-Oct) depart from Ventry Harbour, with three hours ashore on Great Blasket; shorter trips are available. The **Celtic & Prehistoric Museum** (📞087 770 3280; Kilvicadownig, Ventry; €5; ⊙10am-5.30pm mid-Mar-Oct; 🅿), 4km southwest of the village, squeezes in an incredible collection of Celtic and prehistoric artefacts.

ANGUS MCCOMISKEY/ALAMY STOCK PHOTO ©

Dingle town An Droichead Beag pub

About 4.5km further west, the **Fahan beehive huts** (Fahan; adult/child €3/ free; ☺8am-7pm Easter-Sep, shorter hours Oct-Easter) sit on the inland side of the road. Fahan once had some 48 drystone *clochán* beehive huts dating from AD 500, although the exact dates are unknown. Today five structures remain, including two that are fully intact. The huts are on the slope of Mt Eagle (516m), which still has an estimated 400-plus huts in various states of preservation.

The Drive » Continuing north from Slea Head for just over 2km brings you to Dunmore Head, the westernmost point on the Irish mainland and the site of tiny but pretty Coumeenoole beach. From here it's around 3km to Dunquin.

- - - - - - - - - - - - - - - - - -

⑤ Dunquin

Yet another pause on a road of scenic pauses, Dunquin is a scattered village beneath Mt Eagle and Croaghmarhin.

The Blasket Islands (now uninhabited) are visible offshore. Dunquin's **Blasket Centre** (Ionad an Bhlascaoid Mhóir; ☎066-915 6444; www.

blasket.ie; adult/child €5/3; ☺10am-6pm Easter-Oct; P) is a wonderful interpretive centre with a floor-to-ceiling window overlooking the islands. Great Blasket Island's past community of storytellers and musicians is profiled, along with its literary visitors such as John Millington Synge, writer of *Playboy of the Western World*. The practicalities of island life are covered by exhibits on shipbuilding and fishing. There's a cafe with Blasket views and a bookshop.

The Drive » North from Dunquin is Clogher Head; a short walk takes you out to the head, with stunning views to Sybil Head and the Three Sisters. Follow the road another 500m around to the crossroads, where a narrow paved track leads to Clogher beach. Back on the loop road, head inland towards Ballyferriter (about 9km in all).

6 Ballyferriter

Housed in the 19th-century schoolhouse in the village of Ballyferriter (Baile an Fheirtearaigh), the **Dingle Peninsula Museum** (Músaem Chorca Dhuibhne; ☎066-915 6333; www.westkerrymuseum.com; Ballyferriter; admission by donation; ◷10am-5pm Easter & Jun–mid-Sep, by appointment rest of year; P) has displays on the peninsula's archaeology and ecology. Across the street there's

a lonely, lichen-covered church.

The remains of the 5th- or 6th-century **Riasc Monastic Settlement** are an impressive, haunting sight, particularly the pillar with beautiful Celtic designs. Excavations have also revealed the foundations of an oratory first built with wood and later stone, a kiln for drying corn and a cemetery. The ruins are signposted as 'Mainistir Riaisc' along a narrow lane off the R559, about 2km east of Ballyferriter.

The Drive » The landscape around Ballyferriter is a rocky patchwork of varying shades of green, stitched by miles and miles of ancient stone walls. Wind your way along the R559 some 2km east of the Riasc Monastic Settlement turn-off to reach an amazing dry-stone oratory.

DETOUR: DÚN AN ÓIR FORT

Start: 5 Dunquin

En route between Dunquin and Ballyferriter, turn north 1km east of Clogher, from where narrow roads run to the east of the Dingle Golf Links course to **Dún an Óir Fort** (Fort of Gold), the scene of a hideous massacre during the 1580 Irish rebellion against English rule. All that remains is a network of grassy ridges, but it's a pretty spot overlooking sheltered Smerwick Harbour.

The fort is about 6km from Clogher. Return on the same road to just south of the golf course and turn east to rejoin the R559 and continue to Ballyferriter.

TRIP HIGHLIGHT

7 Gallarus Oratory

The dry-stone **Gallarus Oratory** (www.heritageireland.ie; P) is quite a sight, standing in its lonely spot beneath the brown hills as it has done for some 1200 years. It has withstood the elements perfectly, apart from a slight sagging in the roof. Traces of mortar suggest that the interior and exterior walls may have been plastered. Shaped like an upturned boat, it has a doorway on the western side and a round-headed window on the east. Inside the doorway are two projecting stones with holes that once supported the door.

The Drive » Pass back through Dingle town before cutting across the scenic Connor Pass to reach the northern side of the peninsula. About 6km before you reach Kilcummin, a narrow road leads north to the quiet villages of Cloghane (23km) and Brandon, and finally to Brandon Point overlooking Brandon Bay.

8 Cloghane

Cloghane (An Clochán) is another little piece of peninsula beauty. The village's friendly pubs nestle between Mt Brandon and Brandon Bay, with views across the water to the Stradbally Mountains. For many, the main goal is scaling

951m-high **Mt Brandon** (Cnoc Bhréannain), Ireland's eighth-highest peak. If that sounds too energetic, there are plenty of coastal strolls.

The 5km drive from Cloghane out to **Brandon Point** follows ever-narrower single-track roads wandered by sheep, culminating in cliffs with fantastic views south and east.

On the last weekend in July, Cloghane celebrates the ancient Celtic harvest festival **Lughnasa** with events – especially bonfires – both in the village and atop Mt Brandon. The **Brandon Regatta**, a traditional *currach* (rowing boat race), takes place in late August.

The Drive » Retrace your route to Cloghane and head east to Kilcummin (7km) and continue a further 7km east to Castlegregory, the Dingle Peninsula's water-sports playground.

⑨ Castlegregory

A highlight of the quiet village of Castlegregory (Caislean an Ghriare) is the vista to the rugged hills to the south (a lowlight is the sprawl of philistine holiday homes).

However, things change when you drive up the sand-strewn road along the **Rough Point Peninsula**, the broad spit of land between Tralee Bay and Brandon Bay. Great underwater visibility makes this one of Ireland's best diving areas, where you can glimpse pilot whales, orcas, sunfish and dolphins. Professional dive shop **Waterworld** (📞066-713 9292; www.waterworld.ie; Harbour House, Scraggane Pier; ⊗9am-6pm year-round) is based at Harbour House in Fahamore. **Jamie Knox Watersports** (📞066-713 9411; www.jamieknox.com; Sandy Bay; equipment rental per hour €5-15; ⊗ lessons Apr-Oct, shop year-round) offers surf, windsurf, kitesurf, canoe and pedalo hire and lessons.

The Drive » Continue east on the R560 for 4km then turn right and follow signs to one of the Dingle Peninsula's least-known gems, the Glanteenassig Forest Recreation Area.

TRIP HIGHLIGHT

⑩ Glanteenassig Forest Recreation Area

Encompassing 450 hectares of forest, mountains, lakes and bog, **Glanteenassig Forest Recreation Area** (www.coillte.ie/site/glanteenassig; ⊗8am-10pm May-Aug, to 6pm Sep-Apr) is a magical, little-visited treasure. There are two lakes; you can drive right up to the higher lake, which is encircled by a plank boardwalk, though it's too narrow for wheelchairs or prams.

The Drive » From Glanteenassig Forest Recreation Area, return to the main road and head east through the village of Aughacasla – home to the wonderful Seven Hogs inn – on the coast road (R560),

---

CONNOR PASS

At 456m, Connor (or Conor) Pass is Ireland's highest motor road. On a foggy day you'll see nothing but the road just in front of you, but in fine weather it offers phenomenal views of Dingle Harbour to the south and Mt Brandon to the north. The road is in good shape, despite being very narrow and *very* steep on the north side (large signs portend doom for buses and trucks).

The car park at the pass yields views down to a scatter of lakes in the rock-strewn valley below, plus the remains of walls and huts where people once lived impossibly hard lives. When visibility is good, the 10-minute climb west to the summit of An Bhinn Dubh (478m) is well worthwhile for the kind of vistas that inspire mountain climbers.

which links up with the N86 to Blennerville (27km in total).

⑪ Blennerville

Blennerville, just over 1km southwest of Tralee on the N86, used to be the city's chief port, though the harbour has long since silted up. A 19th-century **windmill** (☎066-712 1064; www.blennerville-windmill.ie; Blennerville; adult/child €7/3; ⊗9am-6pm Jun-Aug, 9.30am-5.30pm Apr, May, Sep & Oct; **P**) here has been restored and is the largest working flour mill in Ireland and Britain. Its modern visitor centre houses an exhibition on grain milling and on the thousands of emigrants who boarded 'coffin ships' from what was then Kerry's largest embarkation point. Admission includes a 30-minute guided windmill tour.

The Drive » Staying on the N86 brings you into the heart of Tralee.

⑫ Tralee (p95)

Although Tralee is Kerry's county town, it's more engaged with the business of everyday life than the tourist trade. Elegant Denny St and Day Pl are the oldest parts of town, with 18th-century buildings, while the Square, just south of the Mall, is a pleasant, open contemporary space hosting **farmers markets** (liveliest on Saturday).

A 15-minute nature-safari boat ride is the highlight of a visit to Tralee's **wetlands centre** (☎066-712 6700; www.traleebaywetlands.org; Ballyard Rd; adult/child €5/2, guided tour €10/5; ⊗10am-7pm Jul & Aug, to 5pm Sep, Oct & Mar-Jun, 11am-4pm Nov-Feb; **P** ⊛). You can also get a good overview of Tralee Bay nature reserve's 30 sq km, encompassing saltwater and freshwater habitats, from the 20m-high viewing tower (accessible by lift/elevator), and spot wildlife from bird hides.

In Ireland and beyond, Tralee is synonymous with the **Rose of Tralee** (www.roseoftralee.ie) beauty pageant, open to Irish women and women of Irish descent from around the world (the 'roses'). It takes place amid five days of celebrations in August.

An absolute treat is the **Kerry County Museum** (☎066-712 7777; www.kerrymuseum.ie; 18 Denny St; adult/child €5/free; ⊗9.30am-5.30pm Jun-Aug, to 5pm Tue-Sat Sep-May), with excellent interpretive displays on Irish historical events and trends. The Medieval Experience recreates life (smells and all) in Tralee in 1450.

Ingeniously converted from a terrace house, **Roundy's** (5 Broguemakers Lane; ⊗6pm-midnight Thu-Sun) is Tralee's hippest little bar, spinning old-school funk, while **Baily's Corner** (30 Lower Castle St; ⊗9am-11.30pm Mon-Thu, to 12.30am Fri & Sat, 4-11pm Sun; 🎵) is deservedly popular for its traditional sessions.

GABRIELA/GETTY IMAGES ©

Blennerville Windmill

49

Shannon River Route

4

Follow the majestic River Shannon as it wends from Lough Derg to the broad estuary at vibrant Limerick city, and take in the stupendous views at Loop Head.

190 km

Loop Head
Awesome Atlantic views extend from this little-visited peninsula

114 km

Foynes
Atmospheric museum devoted to 1940s flying boats

START
Portumna

FINISH
Bunratty
3

Kilkee

Tarbert–Killimer
Ferry Crossing

5

1 km

Limerick City
Has a fabulous castle, gallery, museum and cathedral

4 DAYS
296KM / 184 MILES

GREAT FOR...

BEST TIME TO GO

Even in high summer there are plenty of crowd-free escapes.

 ESSENTIAL PHOTO

The soaring cliffs on the aptly named 'Scenic Loop' road west of Kilkee.

✓ **BEST FOR DOLPHIN SPOTTING**

Estuary-set Kilrush has a nature centre, dolphin trail and cruises.

Head (p56) Spectacular cliffs at County Clare's southernmost point

Shannon River Route

Ireland's longest river provides a stunning backdrop to this route. It begins with gentle lake scenery around the boaters' paradise of Lough Derg, followed by fascinating historical sights in and around Limerick city. A visit to the world's only flying boat museum is followed by a short ferry trip across the Shannon estuary to take in the sweeping white-sand beaches of Kilkee and the dramatic seacliffs of Loop Head.

① Portumna

In the far southeastern corner of County Galway, the lakeside town of Portumna is popular for boating and fishing.

Impressive **Portumna Castle & Gardens** (☎090-974 1658; www.heritageireland.ie; Castle Ave, Portumna; adult/child €5/3; ☺9.30am-6pm Apr-Sep, to 5pm Oct) was built in the early 1600s by Richard de Burgo and boasts an elaborate, geometrical organic garden.

The Drive ≫ From Portumna, cross the River Shannon – also the county border – into County Tipperary. Take the N65 south for 7km then turn right onto the R493, winding through farmland. Briefly rejoin the N52 at the Nenagh bypass, then turn west on the R494, following it to Ballina (52km in all).

② Ballina & Killaloe

Facing each other across a narrow channel, Ballina and Killaloe (Cill Da Lúa) are really one destination, even if they have different personalities (and counties). A fine 1770 13-arch, one-lane **bridge** spans the river, linking the pair. You can walk it in five minutes, or drive it in about 20 (a Byzantine system of lights controls traffic).

Ballina, in County Tipperary, has some of the better pubs and restaurants, while Killaloe typifies picturesque County Clare. It lies on the western banks of lower Loch Deirgeirt (the southern extension of Lough Derg), where it narrows at one of the principal crossings of the Shannon.

The Drive ≫ Continue following the R494 then the M7 southwest to Limerick city (about 24km).

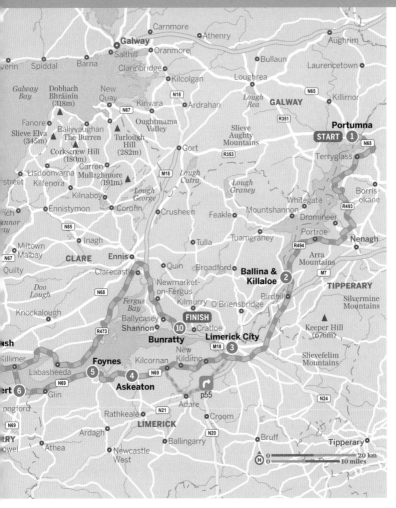

TRIP HIGHLIGHT

3 Limerick City (p98)

Limerick city straddles the Shannon's broadening tidal stream, where the river runs west to meet the Shannon Estuary. Despite some unexpected glitz and gloss, it doesn't shy away from its tough past, as portrayed in Frank McCourt's 1996 memoir *Angela's Ashes*.

Limerick has an intriguing **castle** (☎061-711 222; www.kingjohnscastle. com; Nicholas St; adult/child €13/9.50; ☺9.30am-6pm Apr-Sep, to 5pm Oct-Mar), built by King John of England between 1200 and 1212 on King's Island; the ancient **St Mary's Cathedral** (☎061-310 293; www.saint maryscathedral.ie; Bridge St; adult/child €5/free; ☺9am-5pm Mon-Thu, to 4pm Fri & Sat, from 1.30pm Sun), founded in 1168 by Donal Mór O'Brien, king of Munster; and the fabulous **Hunt Museum** (www.huntmuseum. com; Custom House, Rutland

St; adult/child €7.50/free, free on Sun; ☉10am-5pm Mon-Sat, from 2pm Sun; 🚹), with the finest collection of Bronze Age, Iron Age and medieval treasures outside Dublin.

The dynamic **Limerick City Gallery of Art** (www.gallery.limerick.ie; Carnegie Bldg, Pery Sq; ☉10am-5.30pm Mon-Wed, Fri & Sat, to 8pm Thu, noon-5.30pm Sun) is set in the city's Georgian area. Limerick also has a contemporary cafe culture, and renowned nightlife to go with its uncompromised pubs – as well as locals who go out of their way to welcome you.

The Drive » The narrow, peaceful N69 follows the Shannon Estuary west from Limerick; 27km along you come to Askeaton.

TRIP HIGHLIGHT

④ Askeaton

Hidden just off the N69, evocative ruins in the pint-sized village of Askeaton include the mid-1300s **Desmond Castle** (☉weekends by appointment May-Oct), a 1389-built **Franciscan friary**, and **St Mary's Church of Ireland** and **Knights Templar Tower**, built around 1829, as well as the 1740 **Hellfire** gentlemen's club. The ruins are undergoing a slow process of restoration that started in 2007. The town's **tourist office** (☏086 085 0174; askeaton touristoffice@gmail.com; The Square; ☉ limited hours, call

to check) has details of ruins that you can freely wander (depending on restoration works) and can arrange free **guided tours** lasting about one hour, led by a passionate local historian.

The Drive » Stunning vistas of the wide Shannon estuary come into view as you drive 12km to Foynes.

TRIP HIGHLIGHT

⑤ Foynes

Foynes is an essential stop along the route to visit the fascinating **Foynes Flying Boat Museum** (☏069-65416; www.flyingboatmuseum.com; adult/child €12/6; ☉9.30am-6pm Jun-Aug, to 5pm mid-Mar–Jun & Sep–mid-Nov; 🅿). From 1939 to 1945 this was the landing place for the flying boats that linked North America with the British Isles. Big Pan Am clippers – there's a replica here – would set down in the estuary and refuel.

The Drive » The most scenic stretch of the N69 is the 20km from Foynes to Tarbert in northern County Kerry, which hugs the estuary's edge.

⑥ Tarbert

The little town of Tarbert is where you'll hop on the car ferry to Killimer, in County Clare, saving yourself 137km of driving. Before you do so, though, it's worth visiting the

renovated **Tarbert Bridewell Jail & Courthouse** (www.tarbertbridewell.com; adult/child €5/2.50; ☉10am-6pm Apr-Sep, to 4pm Mon-Fri Oct-Mar), which has exhibits on the rough social and political conditions of the 19th century. From the jail, the 6.1km **John F Leslie Woodland Walk** runs along Tarbert Bay towards the river mouth.

The ferry dock is clearly signposted 2.2km west of Tarbert. Services are operated by **Shannon Ferry Limited** (☏068-905 3124; www.shannonferries.com; cars €20, motorcyclists, cyclists & pedestrians €5;

Foynes Foynes Flying Boat Museum

DETOUR:
ADARE

Start: ❸ Limerick City

Frequently dubbed 'Ireland's prettiest village', Adare centres on its clutch of perfectly preserved thatched cottages built by the 19th-century English landlord, the Earl of Dunraven, for workers constructing Adare Manor (now a palatial hotel). Today the cottages house craft shops and some of the region's finest restaurants (p106).

In the middle of the village, **Adaire Heritage Centre** (📞061-396 666; Main St; ⊘9am-6pm) has entertaining exhibits on the history and the medieval context of the village's buildings and can point you to a number of fascinating religious sites. It also books tours of **Adare Castle** (Desmond Castle; www.heritageireland.ie; tours adult/child €10/8; ⊘tours hourly 11am-5pm Jul-Sep). Dating back to around 1200, this picturesque feudal ruin was wrecked by Cromwell's troops in 1657. Restoration work is ongoing; look for the ruined great hall with its early-13th-century windows. You can view the castle from the main road, the riverside footpath, or the grounds of the Augustinian priory.

From Limerick city, the fastest way to reach Adare is to take the M20 and N21 16km southwest to the village on the banks of the River Maigue. From Adare it's 9km northwest to rejoin the N69 at Kilcornan. Alternatively, you can take the less-travelled N69 from Limerick to Kilcornan and slip down to Adare.

⏱7.30am-8.30pm Mon-Sat, from 9.30am Sun Apr-Sep, longer hours Jun-Aug, shorter hours Oct-Mar; 📞). Ferries depart hourly (every half-hour in high summer).

The Drive ❱❱ The car-ferry crossing from Tarbert in County Kerry to Killimer in County Clare (from where it's an 8km drive west to Kilrush) takes just 20 minutes and, because the estuary is sheltered, you can usually look forward to smooth sailing.

⑦ Kilrush

Some 170-plus bottlenose dolphins swim around in the Shannon; **Dolphin Discovery** (✆065-905 1327; www.discoverdolphins.ie; Kilrush Marina; adult/child €26/14; ⏱late May–mid-Oct) runs trips to see them out of Kilrush Marina. The atmospheric town also harbours the remarkable 'lost' **Vandeleur Walled Garden** (✆065-905 1760; www.vandeleur walledgarden.ie; Killimer Rd; ⏱10am-5pm Tue-Sat), home to a 170-hectare forest with winding trails, a colourful array of plants and a beech maze.

The Drive ❱❱ Continue 14km west along the N67 to the beach haven of Kilkee.

⑧ Kilkee

The centrepiece of Kilkee (Cill Chaoi) is its wide, sheltered, crescent-shaped beach. The bay has high cliffs on the north end; to the south a coastal path leads to natural swimming pools known as the Pollock Holes. The waters are very tidal with sandy expanses replaced by waves in just a few hours.

Kilkee has plenty of guesthouses and B&Bs, though during high season, rates can soar and vacancies are scarce.

The Drive ❱❱ The 26.5km drive from Kilkee south to Loop Head ends in cliffs plunging into the Atlantic.

TRIP HIGHLIGHT

⑨ Loop Head

Capped by a working lighthouse, Loop Head (Ceann Léime) is County Clare's southernmost point, with breathtaking views as well as cycling,

fishing and snorkelling opportunities.

The Drive ❱❱ On the R487, follow the 'Scenic Loop' (an understatement): you'll be struck by one stunning vista of soaring coastal cliffs after another. At Kilkee pick up the N67 east to just after Killimer, before continuing northeast on the looping, coastal R473. Next hop on M18/N18 south to Bunratty (110km all up).

---

⑩ Bunratty

Bunratty (Bun Raite) draws more tourists than any other place in the region. The namesake **castle** (✆061-711 222; www. bunrattycastle.ie; adult/child/ family €16/12/45; ⏱9am-5.30pm) has stood over the area for centuries. In recent decades it's been spiffed up and swamped by attractions and gift shops. A theme park re-creates a clichéd – and sanitised – Irish village of old.

With all the hoopla, it's easy to overlook the actual village, at the back of the theme park, which has numerous leafy spots to eat and sleep.

Bunratty Castle interior

Destinations

County Cork (p60)
From bustling Cork City to the lush landscape dotted with idyllic villages, everything good about Ireland can be found in County Cork.

County Kerry (p78)
County Kerry contains some of Ireland's most iconic scenery: sea cliffs and soft golden strands, emerald-green farmland, mist-shrouded bogs and mountain peaks.

County Limerick (p98)
Limerick's low-lying farmland is framed by swelling uplands and mountains. Limerick City is boisterously urban in contrast, with plenty of historical and cultural attractions.

Limerick city (p98) At dusk
JIM NOLAN/500PX ©

County Cork

Everything good about Ireland can be found in County Cork. Surrounding the country's second city – a thriving metropolis made glorious by location and its almost Rabelaisian devotion to the finer things of life – is a lush landscape dotted with villages that offer days of languor and idyll.

CORK CITY

POP 208,670

Ireland's second city is first in every important respect – at least according to the locals, who cheerfully refer to it as the 'real capital of Ireland'. It's a liberal, youthful and cosmopolitan place that was badly hit by economic recession but is now busily reinventing itself with spruced-up streets, revitalised stretches of waterfront, and – seemingly – an artisan coffee bar on every corner. There's a bit of a hipster scene, but the best of the city is still happily traditional – snug pubs with live-music sessions, restaurants dishing up top-quality local produce, and a genuinely proud welcome from the locals.

The compact city centre is set on an island in the River Lee, surrounded by waterways and packed with grand Georgian avenues, cramped 17th-century alleys, modern masterpieces such as the opera house, and narrow streets crammed with pubs, shops, cafes and restaurants, fed by arguably the best foodie scene in the country.

History

Cork has a long and bruising history, inextricably linked with Ireland's struggle for nationhood.

The story begins in the 7th century, when St Fin Barre (also spelt Finbarr and Finbarre) founded a monastery in the midst of a *corcach* (marshy place). By the 12th century the settlement had become the chief city of the Kingdom of South Munster, having survived raids and sporadic settlement by Norsemen. Irish rule was short-lived and by 1185 Cork was in the possession of the English. Thereafter it changed hands regularly during the relentless struggle between Irish and Crown forces. It survived a Cromwellian assault only to fall to that merciless champion of Protestantism, William of Orange.

During the 18th century Cork prospered, with butter, beef, beer and whiskey exported around the world from its port. A mere century later famine devastated both county and city, and robbed Cork of tens of thousands (and Ireland of millions) of its inhabitants by death or emigration.

The 'Rebel City's' deep-seated Irishness ensured that it played a key role in Ireland's struggle for independence. Mayor Thomas MacCurtain was killed by the Black and

Tans (British auxiliary troops, so-named because their uniforms were a mixture of army khaki and police black) in 1920. His successor, Terence MacSwiney, died in London's Brixton prison after a hunger strike. The British were at their most brutally repressive in Cork – much of the centre, including St Patrick's St, the City Hall and the Public Library, was burned down. Cork was a regional focus of Ireland's Civil War in 1922–23.

Today it's a young city, thanks in part to its university: 40% of the population is under 25, and at just 11%, it has the lowest percentage of over 65s in Europe.

◉ Sights

The best sight in Cork is the city itself – soak it up as you wander the streets. A new conference and events centre, complete with 6000-seat concert venue, tourist centre, restaurants, shops, galleries and apartments, was scheduled to open in 2019, but the project has been delayed by financial problems. It will eventually be the focus of the **Brewery Quarter** (the former Beamish & Crawford brewery site, fronted by the landmark mock-Tudor 'counting house'), a block west of the English Market.

Shandon, perched on a hillside overlooking the city centre to the north, is a great spot for the views alone, but you'll also find galleries, antique shops and cafes along its old lanes and squares. Those tiny old row houses, where generations of workers raised huge families in very basic conditions, are now sought-after urban pieds-à-terre. Pick up a copy of the *Cork Walks – Shandon* leaflet from the tourist office (p69) for a self-guided tour of the district.

★ **Cork City Gaol** MUSEUM
See p24.

Crawford Art Gallery GALLERY
(Map p62; ☑021-480 5042; www.crawfordartgallery.ie; Emmet Pl; ⊙10am-5pm Mon-Wed, Fri & Sat, to 8pm Thu, 11am-4pm Sun) FREE Cork's public gallery houses a small but excellent permanent collection covering the 17th century through to the modern day, though the works on display change from year to year. Highlights include paintings by Sir John Lavery, Jack B Yeats and Nathaniel Hone, and Irish women artists Mainie Jellett and Evie Hone.

Cork Public Museum MUSEUM
(Map p62; ☑021-427 0679; www.corkcity.ie/en/things-to-do/attractions/cork-public-museum;

WORTH A TRIP

BLACKROCK CASTLE

Blackrock Castle (☑021-435 7924; www.bco.ie; Blackrock; adult/child €7/5; ⊙10am-5pm; P) is a restored 16th-century castle that now, rather incongruously, hosts a small hands-on science centre, an inflatable planetarium and a pleasant courtyard cafe. Kids love it and the view from the tower is worth the jaunt. It's on the south bank of the River Lee, 5.5km east of the city centre; take bus 202 from Parnell Pl to Blackrock Pier, from where it's a five-minute walk.

Fitzgerald Park, Mardyke Walk; ⊙10am-4pm Tue-Fri, 11am-4pm Sat, 2-4pm Sun) FREE Located in a Georgian mansion with a modern extension, this museum recounts Cork's history. The diverse collection of local artefacts tells the story from the Stone Age right up to local football legend Roy Keane, with a particularly interesting exhibit on medieval Cork and the growth of the city. There's a good cafe around the back.

University College Cork UNIVERSITY
(UCC; Map p62; ☑021-490 1876; http://visitor scentre.ucc.ie; College Rd; ⊙9am-5pm Mon-Fri, noon-5pm Sat) FREE Established in 1845 as one of three 'queen's colleges' (the others are in Galway and Belfast) set up to provide nondenominational alternatives to the Anglican Protestant Trinity College in Dublin, UCC's campus spreads around an attractive collection of Victorian Gothic buildings, gardens and historical attractions, including a 19th-century astronomical observatory. Self-guided audio tours are available from the visitor centre.

Stone Corridor MUSEUM
(Map p62; ☑021-490 1876; www.ucc.ie; UCC Visitors Centre, Main Quad, College Rd; ⊙9am-5pm Mon-Sat) FREE This covered walkway on the north side of University College Cork's Victorian Gothic main quad houses Ireland's biggest collection of Ogham stones, carved with runic inscriptions dating from the 4th to the 6th century AD.

Lewis Glucksman Gallery GALLERY
(Map p62; ☑021-490 1844; www.glucksman.org; University College Cork, Western Rd; suggested donation €5; ⊙10am-5pm Tue-Sat, 2-5pm Sun;)

Cork City

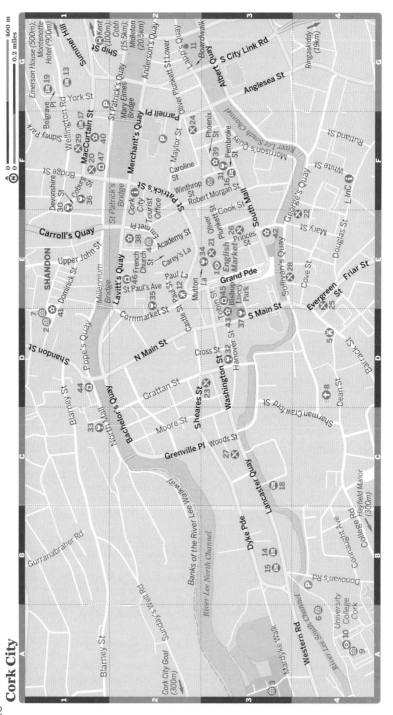

Cork City

This award-winning building is a startling construction of limestone, steel and timber, built in 2004 by Dublin architects O'Donnell and Tuomey. Three floors of galleries display the best in both national and international contemporary art and installation. The on-site **Bobo cafe** (Map p62; ☑ 021-490 1848; www.glucksman.org/visit/cafe; Lewis Glucksman Gallery, Western Rd; mains €6-13; ☉10am-5pm Tue-Sat, noon-5pm Sun;) is excellent.

Elizabeth Fort FORT
(Map p62; ☑ 021-497 5947; www.elizabethfort.ie; Barrack St; ☉10am-5pm Mon-Sat, noon-5pm Sun, closed Mon Oct-May) FREE Originally built in the 1620s, and serving as a *garda* (police) station from 1929 to 2013, this small star-shaped artillery fort once formed an important part of the city's defences. Newly opened to the public, it offers an insight into Cork's military history, and there are good views across the city from the ramparts. Guided tours (per person €3) at 1pm provide additional context.

St Fin Barre's Cathedral CATHEDRAL
(Map p62; ☑021-496 3387; www.corkcathedral.webs.com; Bishop St; adult/child €6/3; ☉9.30am-5.30pm Mon-Sat year-round, 1-2.30pm & 4.30-5pm Sun Apr-Oct) Spiky spires, gurning gargoyles and elaborate sculpture adorn the exterior of Cork's Protestant cathedral, an attention-grabbing mixture of French Gothic and medieval whimsy. The grandeur continues inside, with marble floor mosaics, a colourful chancel ceiling and a huge pulpit and bishop's throne. Quirky items include a cannonball blasted into an earlier medieval spire during the Siege of Cork (1690). The cathedral sits about 500m southwest of the centre, on the spot where Cork's 7th-century patron saint, Fin Barre, founded a monastery.

Cork Butter Museum MUSEUM
(Map p62; ☑021-430 0600; www.corkbutter.museum; O'Connell Sq; adult/child €4/1.50; ☉10am-5pm Mar-Oct) Cork has a long tradition of butter manufacturing – in the 1860s it was the world's largest butter market,

exporting butter throughout the British Empire – and the trade's history is told through the displays and dioramas of the Cork Butter Museum. The square in front of the museum is dominated by the neoclassical front of the **Old Butter Market** (Map p62; O'Connell Sq), and the striking, circular **Firkin Crane** (Map p62; 021-450 7487; www.firkincrane.ie; O'Connell Sq, Shandon; tickets free-€20) building, where butter casks were once weighed (it now houses a dance centre).

🖈 Tours

Cork Walks
WALKING

(Map p62; ✍ 021-492 4792; Daunt Sq) `FREE`
There are four waymarked, self-guided tours covering the City Island, South Parish, University and Shandon districts, all beginning at an information board in Daunt Sq. You can pick up a leaflet and map at the tourist office (p69).

Cork
Culinary Tour
FOOD

(✍ 087 706 8391; www.bonner-travel.com/itinerary/cork-culinary-tour; per person €65) A four-hour tour of Cork's food markets and eating places, including tasting sessions with food and drink sellers and ending with lunch in one of the city's many restaurants.

Atlantic
Sea Kayaking
KAYAKING

(Map p62; ✍ 028-21058; www.atlanticseakayaking.com; Lapp's Quay; per person €50; ⊘ Mar-Sep) Offers guided 'urban kayaking' trips around Cork's waterways from 6.30pm to 9pm (book in advance, minimum two people). It also offers a full-day expedition in two-seater kayaks to Cobh and Spike Island (p71; per person €100).

Cork City Tour
BUS

(✍ 021-430 9090; www.corkcitytour.com; adult/child €15/5; ⊘ Mar-Nov) A hop-on, hop-off open-top bus linking the city's main points of interest. Longer tours (€25 per adult) head to the Jameson Experience (p73) in Midleton.

🎆 Festivals & Events

Cork World
Book Fest
LITERATURE

(www.corkworldbookfest.com; ⊘ late Apr) This huge literary festival combines talks and readings by Irish and international writers with book stalls, music, street entertainment, workshops, film screenings and more.

Cork Midsummer Festival
PERFORMING ARTS

(www.corkmidsummer.com; ⊘ Jun) A week-long arts festival celebrating music, theatre, dance, literature and visual arts.

Cork Oyster
& Seafood Festival
FOOD & DRINK

(www.corkoysterfestival.com; ⊘ Sep) Seafood is king at this three-day event that includes cooking demos, tastings, a Gourmet Trail, an oyster-shucking contest and live music at venues across town.

Cork Folk Festival
MUSIC

(www.corkfolkfestival.com; ⊘ Sep-Oct) A long weekend of foot-stomping fiddle, hushed ballads and big-name headline acts such as Martin Simpson, Dick Gaughan and Kate Rusby.

Cork Jazz Festival
MUSIC

(www.guinnessjazzfestival.com; ⊘ late Oct) Cork's biggest festival has an all-star line-up of jazz, rock and pop in venues across town.

Cork Film Festival
FILM

(www.corkfilmfest.org; ⊘ Nov) Eclectic, week-long program of international films.

🛏 Sleeping

The city has a good range of accommodation, but rooms can be hard to find during major festivals.

🛏 City Centre & Around

Whether you stay on the main island, to the north in Shandon or around MacCurtain St, staying here means you're right in the heart of the action.

Sheila's Hostel
HOSTEL €

(Map p62; ✍ 021-450 5562; www.sheilashostel.ie; 4 Belgrave Pl, off Wellington Rd; dm/tw/f from €16/50/80; @ 🛜) Sheila's heaves with young travellers, and no wonder given its excellent central location, but it's also a great choice for family travel. Facilities include a sauna, lockers, laundry service, a movie room and a barbecue. Cheaper twin rooms share bathrooms. Breakfast is €3 extra.

★ Auburn House
B&B €€

(Map p62; ✍ 021-450 8555; www.auburnguesthouse.com; 3 Garfield Tce, Wellington Rd; s/d €58/90; P 🛜) There's a warm family welcome at this neat B&B, which has smallish but well-kept rooms brightened by window boxes. Try to bag one of the back rooms, which are quieter and have sweeping views over the city. Breakfast includes vegetarian

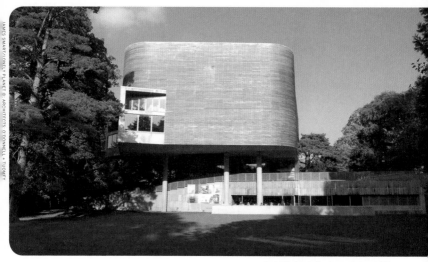

Cork City Lewis Glucksman Gallery (p61)

choices, and the location near the fun of MacCurtain St is a plus.

Isaac's Hotel
HOTEL €€

(Map p62; ☎ 021-450 0011; www.isaacscork.com; 48 MacCurtain St; s/d/apt from €105/153/222; @ 🛜) The central location is the real selling point at this hotel housed in what was once a Victorian furniture warehouse (ask for a room away from the busy street). As well as plain, functional bedrooms, there are self-contained apartments, which come with kitchen and washing machine. There's no air-con, so some rooms can get uncomfortably hot on sunny summer days.

★ Montenotte Hotel
BOUTIQUE HOTEL €€€

(☎ 021-453 0050; www.themontenottehotel.com; Middle Glanmire Rd; d/f from €189/229; P 🛜 🏊) Built as a private residence for a wealthy merchant in the 1820s, the Montenotte has been reimagined as a boutique hotel that skilfully blends its 19th-century legacy with bold designer colour schemes. The hilltop location commands superb views, especially from the roof-terrace bar and restaurant, and guests can enjoy the hotel's sunken Victorian garden, private cinema and luxurious spa.

Imperial Hotel
HOTEL €€€

(Map p62; ☎ 021-427 4040; www.imperialho telcork.com; South Mall; r from €180; P @ 🛜) Having celebrated its bicentenary in 2013 – Thackeray, Dickens and Sir Walter Scott

have all stayed here – the Imperial knows how to age gracefully. Public spaces resonate with period detail – marble floors, elaborate floral bouquets and more – while the 125 bedrooms feature writing desks, understated decor and modern touches including a luxurious spa and a digital music library.

🛏 Western Road & Around

Western Rd runs southwest from the city centre to the large UCC campus; it has the city's biggest choice of B&Bs. You can take a bus from the central bus station or walk (10 to 30 minutes).

★ Garnish House
B&B €€

(Map p62; ☎ 021-427 5111; www.garnish.ie; 18 Western Rd; d/f from €126/165; P 🛜) Attention is lavished on guests at this award-winning B&B where the legendary breakfast menu (30 choices) ranges from grilled kippers to French toast. Typical of the touches here is freshly cooked porridge, served with creamed honey and your choice of whiskey or Baileys; enjoy it out on the garden terrace. The 14 rooms are very comfortable; reception is open 24 hours.

Blarney Stone Guesthouse
B&B €€

(Map p62; ☎ 021-427 0083; www.blarneystone guesthouse.com; Western Rd; s/d from €119/129; P 🛜) The white facade of this tall Victorian townhouse conceals a dazzling interior

THE ENGLISH MARKET

The **English Market** (Map p62; www.englishmarket.ie; main entrance Princes St; ⊙8am-6pm Mon-Sat) – so called because it was set up in 1788 by the Protestant or 'English' corporation that then controlled the city (there was once an Irish Market nearby) – is a true gem, with its ornate vaulted ceilings, columns and polished marble fountain. Scores of vendors set up colourful and photogenic displays of the region's very best local produce, including meat, fish, fruit, cheeses and takeaway food. On a sunny day, take your lunch to nearby Bishop Lucey Park, a popular alfresco eating spot.

The **Farmgate Cafe** (Map p62; ☑021-427 8134; www.farmgatecork.ie; Princes St, English Market; mains €8-14; ⊙8.30am-5pm Mon-Sat) ✐ is an unmissable experience at the heart of the English Market, perched on a balcony overlooking the food stalls below, the source of all that fresh local produce on your plate – everything from crab and oysters to the lamb in your Irish stew. Go up the stairs and turn left for table service, or right for counter service.

crammed with polished period furniture, glittering Waterford crystal chandeliers and curlicued gilt mirrors. The Victorian theme does not extend to the facilities, though – creature comforts include power showers, fast wi-fi, satellite TV and hearty breakfasts.

★ **River Lee Hotel** HOTEL €€€
(Map p62; ☑021-425 2700; www.doylecollection.com; Western Rd; r from €269; P❊⚗☲) This modern riverside hotel brings a touch of luxury to the city centre. It has gorgeous public areas with huge sofas, a designer fireplace, a stunning five-storey, glass-walled atrium and superb service. There are well-equipped bedrooms (nice and quiet at the back, but request a corner room for extra space) and possibly the best breakfast buffet in Ireland.

Hayfield Manor HOTEL €€€
(☑021-484 5900; www.hayfieldmanor.ie; Perrott Ave, College Rd; r from €315; P❊⚗☲) Roll out the red carpet and pour yourself a sherry for *you have arrived*. Just 1.5km southwest of the city centre but with all the ambience of a country house, Hayfield combines the luxury and facilities of a big hotel with the informality and welcome of a small one. The beautiful bedrooms offer a choice of traditional decor or contemporary styling.

✖ Eating

Cork's food scene is reason enough to visit the city. Dozens of restaurants and cafes make the most of County Cork's rightly famous local produce, ranging from beef and pork to seafood and dairy, while the renowned English Market – a cornucopia of fine food – is a national treasure. Well-established places like Nash 19 showcase the best of Irish produce, while newcomer

Ichigo Ichie has added top-end Japanese cuisine to an already heady mix.

Tara's Tea Room TEAHOUSE €
(Map p62; ☑021-455 3742; www.facebook.com/tarastearoom; 45 MacCurtain St; mains €9-15; ⊙9am-6pm Mon-Sat, 10am-5pm Sun; ☎) You'll search long and hard to find a cuter cafe in Ireland than this place. The vintage decor manages to be kitsch yet charming and food is served on vintage china plates. Good for a meal or just a freshly made cake and cup of tea (using real leaves of course). Service is prompt and smiling.

Crawford Gallery Cafe CAFE €
(Map p62; ☑021-427 4415; www.crawfordgallerycafe.com; Crawford Art Gallery, Emmet Pl; lunch mains €10-15; ⊙8.30am-4pm Mon-Sat, 11am-4pm Sun; ☎) An attractive neoclassical room at the back of the city art gallery houses this top-notch cafe. It's managed by the good people from Ballymaloe (p73), so you can expect a deliciously fresh, locally sourced menu that includes the likes of eggs Benedict for breakfast, or crab, chilli and coriander tagliatelle for lunch.

Filter CAFE €
(Map p62; ☑021-455 0050; filtercork@gmail.com; 19 George's Quay; mains €4-7; ⊙8am-6pm Mon-Fri, 9am-5pm Sat, 10am-3pm Sun; ☎) ✐ The quintessential Cork espresso bar, Filter is a carefully curated shrine to coffee nerdery, from the rough-and-ready retro decor to the highly knowledgable baristas serving up expertly brewed shots made with single-origin, locally roasted beans. The sandwich menu is a class act too, offering a choice of fillings that includes pastrami, chorizo and ham hock on artisan breads.

Cork Coffee Roasters
CAFE €

(Map p62; ☑ 021-731 9158; www.facebook.com/
CorkCoffee; 2 Bridge St; mains €3-6; ⊙ 7.30am-
6.30pm Mon-Fri, 8am-6.30pm Sat, 9am-5pm Sun;
🐾) In this foodiest of foodie towns it's not
surprising to find a cafe run by artisan coffee roasters. The brew on offer in this cute
and often crowded corner is some of the
best in Cork, guaranteed to jump start your
morning along with a buttery pastry, scone
or tart.

Quay Co-op
VEGETARIAN €

(Map p62; ☑ 021-431 7026; www.quaycoop.com;
24 Sullivan's Quay; mains €8-11; ⊙ 11am-9pm Mon-
Sat, noon-9pm Sun; ☑ 🖶) 🌿 Flying the flag for
alternative Cork, this cafeteria offers a range
of self-service vegetarian dishes, all organic,
including big breakfasts and rib-sticking
soups and casseroles. It also caters for glu-
ten-, dairy- and wheat-free needs, and is
amazingly child-friendly.

★ Paradiso
VEGETARIAN €€

(Map p62; ☑ 021-427 7939; www.paradiso.res-
taurant; 16 Lancaster Quay; 2-/3-course menus
€39/47; ⊙ 5.30-10pm Mon-Sat; ☑) 🌿 A con-
tender for best restaurant in town of any
genre, Paradiso serves contemporary vegetarian dishes, including vegan fare: how
about corn pancakes filled with leek, parsnip
and Dunmanus cheese with fennel-caper
salsa and smoked tomato? Reservations are
essential. Rates for dinner, bed and breakfast, staying in the funky upstairs rooms,
start from €180/220 per single/double.

★ Nash 19
INTERNATIONAL €€

(Map p62; ☑ 021-427 0880; www.nash19.com;
Princes St; mains €12-22; ⊙ 7.30am-4pm Mon-
Fri, from 8.30am Sat) 🌿 A superb bistro and
deli where locally sourced food is honoured
at breakfast and lunch, either sit-in or take
away. Fresh scones draw crowds early; daily
lunch specials (soups, salads, desserts
etc), free-range chicken pie and platters of
smoked fish from Frank Hederman (p72)
keep them coming for lunch – the Producers Plate (€22), a sampler of local produce,
is sensational.

★ Market Lane
IRISH €€

(Map p62; ☑ 021-427 4710; www.marketlane.ie; 5
Oliver Plunkett St; mains €14-25; ⊙ noon-9.30pm
Mon-Wed, to 10pm Thu, to 10.30pm Fri & Sat,
1-9.30pm Sun; 🐾 🖶) 🌿 It's always hopping at
this bright corner bistro. The menu is broad
and hearty, changing to reflect what's fresh
at the English Market: perhaps roast hake

with wild garlic velouté, or beetroot, walnut
and feta cakes? No reservations for fewer
than six diners; sip a drink at the bar till a
table is free. Lots of wines by the glass.

Miyazaki
JAPANESE €€

(Map p62; ☑ 021-431 2716; www.facebook.com/
miyazakicork; 1A Evergreen St; mains €12-15; ⊙ 1-
3.30pm & 5-9pm Tue-Sun) Here's something
you don't see every day – a takeaway food
joint run by a Michelin-starred chef! You
can sample Takashi Miyazaki's superb dishes – the menu includes sushi rolls, donburi
(rice bowls with your choice of topping),
Japanese curries, udon noodles, dashi etc –
without forking out for the full theatrical
experience at his main restaurant across
the river.

Ichigo Ichie
JAPANESE €€€

(Map p62; ☑ 021-427 9997; www.ichigoichie.ie;
5 Fenns Quay, Sheares St; per person €120-135;
⊙ 6-10.30pm Tue-Sat) More theatre than restaurant, this bold venture by chef Takashi
Miyazaki immerses diners in the art and
craft of Japanese *kappou* cuisine – an
elaborate multicourse meal prepared and
plated by the chef as you watch; expect a
dozen courses spread over three hours or
so. The restaurant was awarded a Michelin
star in 2019.

🍺 Drinking & Nightlife

In Cork pubs, locally brewed Murphy's and
Beamish stouts, not Guinness, are the preferred pints.

Given the city's big student population,
the small selection of nightclubs does a
thriving trade. Entry ranges from free to
€15; most are open until 2am on Fridays
and Saturdays.

Local microbreweries include the long-
established Franciscan Well (p68), whose
refreshing Friar Weisse beer is popular in
summer, and relative newcomer Rising Sons
(p68), whose Mi Daza stout is a new take on
an old recipe.

★ Sin É
PUB

(Map p62; ☑ 021-450 2266; www.facebook.com/
sinecork; 8 Coburg St; ⊙ 12.30-11.30pm Mon-Thu,
to 12.30am Fri & Sat, to 11pm Sun) You could easily spend an entire day at this place, which
is everything a craic-filled pub should be:
long on atmosphere and short on preten-
sion (Sin É means 'that's it!'). There's music
every night from 6.30pm May to September, and regular sessions Tuesday, Friday

and Sunday the rest of the year, most of them traditional but with the odd surprise.

★**Franciscan Well Brewery**   PUB

(Map p62; ☎ 021-439 3434; www.franciscanwellbrewery.com; 14 North Mall; ☉ 1-11.30pm Mon-Thu, to 12.30am Fri & Sat, to 11pm Sun; ☎) The copper vats gleaming behind the bar give the game away: the Franciscan Well brews its own beer (and has done since 1998). The best place to enjoy it is in the enormous beer garden at the back. The pub holds regular beer festivals together with other small independent Irish breweries.

★**Mutton Lane Inn**   PUB

(Map p62; ☎ 021-427 3471; www.facebook.com/mutton.lane; Mutton Lane; ☉ 10.30am-11.30pm Mon-Thu, to 12.30am Fri & Sat, 12.30-11pm Sun) Tucked down the tiniest of alleys off St Patrick's St, this inviting pub, lit by candles and fairy lights, is one of Cork's most intimate drinking holes. It's minuscule, so try to get

in early to bag a table, or perch on the beer kegs outside.

The Oval   PUB

(Map p62; ☎ 021-427 8952; www.corkheritagepubs.com/pubs/the-oval; 25 South Main St; ☉ 3-11.30pm Sun-Thu, to 12.30am Fri & Sat) Come early to grab the seats by the crackling open fire, but even if you're not lucky this time round, it's still a great place to park for a few hours with the perfect pint of stout, enjoying the buzzing atmosphere or an in-depth chat with drinking companions. It's been serving locals for more than 250 years; long may it continue.

Arthur Mayne's Pharmacy   WINE BAR

(Map p62; ☎ 021-427 9449; www.corkheritagepubs.com/pubs/arthur-maynes; 7 Pembroke St; ☉ 10am-2am Sun-Thu, to 3am Fri & Sat) This unusual wine bar's former life as a pharmacy has been lovingly preserved – the window displays are full of vintage cosmetics and memorabilia. The staff are knowledgeable and always happy to recommend a wine pairing from the extensive menu. Combine all that with the delicious sharing plates and soft candlelight and you have an excellent date spot.

Abbot's Ale House   PUB

(Map p62; ☎ 021-450 7116; www.facebook.com/abbotsalehouse; 17 Devonshire St; ☉ 4-11.30pm Mon-Thu, to 12.30am Fri & Sat, to 11pm Sun) A low-key, two-floor drinking den, whose small size contrasts with its huge beer list. There are always several beers on tap and another 300 in bottles. Good for preclubbing.

Rising Sons   MICROBREWERY

(Map p62; ☎ 021-241 4764; www.risingsonsbrewery.com; Cornmarket St; ☉ noon-late; ☎) This huge, warehouse-like, red-brick building houses an award-winning microbrewery. The industrial decor of exposed brick, riveted iron and gleaming copper brewing vessels recalls American West Coast brewpubs. It turns out 50 kegs a week, some of them full of its lip-smacking trademark stout, Mi Daza, and has a food menu that ranges from pizza to weekend brunch.

☆ Entertainment

Cork's cultural life is generally of a high calibre. To see what's happening, check out the *WhazOn?* listings website (www.whazon.com).

Cork's musical credentials are impeccable. Besides theatres and pubs that feature live music, there are also places that are dedicated music venues, and bars known particularly for their live gigs.

For full listings, refer to *WhazOn?*, PLUGD Records, and the event guide at www.peoplesrepublicofcork.com.

★ Cork
Opera House
OPERA

(Map p62; ☑ 021-427 0022; www.corkopera house.ie; Emmet Pl; tickets €30-50; ☺ box office 10am-5.30pm Mon-Sat, preshow to 7pm Mon-Sat & 6-7pm Sun) Given a modern makeover in the 1990s, this leading venue has been entertaining the city for more than 150 years with everything from opera and ballet to stand-up comedy, pop concerts and puppet shows. Around the back, the Half Moon Theatre presents contemporary theatre, dance, art and occasional club nights.

★ Triskel Arts Centre
ARTS CENTRE

(Map p62; ☑ 021-472 2022; www.triskelart.com; Tobin St; tickets €8-30; ☺ box office 10am-5pm Mon-Sat, 1-9pm Sun; ☎) A fantastic cultural centre housed partly in a renovated church building. Expect a varied program of live music, visual art, photography and theatre at this intimate venue. There's also a cinema (from 6.30pm) and a great cafe.

Crane Lane Theatre
LIVE MUSIC

(Map p62; ☑ 021-427 8487; www.cranelaneth eatre.ie; Phoenix St; tickets free-€5; ☺ 2pm-2am Mon-Fri, noon-2am Sat & Sun) Part pub, part vintage ballroom, this atmospheric venue is decked out in 1920s to 1940s decor, with a courtyard beer garden as a central oasis. It stages a wide range of live music gigs and DJ nights, most with free admission.

Everyman Theatre
THEATRE

(Map p62; ☑ 021-450 1673; www.everymancork. com; 15 MacCurtain St; tickets €15-40; ☺ box office noon-5pm Mon-Sat, preshow to 7.30pm Mon-Sat, 4-7.30pm Sun) Acclaimed musical and dramatic productions (it's a great venue for gigs that require a little bit of respectful silence) are the main bill here, but there's also the occasional comedy act or live band.

Fred Zeppelins
LIVE MUSIC

(Map p62; ☑ 086 260 7876; 8 Parliament St; ☺ 4-11.30pm Mon-Thu, to 12.30am Fri & Sat, to 11pm Sun; ☎) There's a hard edge to this dark den of a bar, popular with goths, rockers and anyone who feels uncomfortable leaving the house without a packet of Rizlas. It's been on the go since 1997, and is known for its live gigs

(lots of tribute bands) and DJs at weekends, plus occasional open-mic nights.

🛍 Shopping

St Patrick's St is the retail spine of Cork, housing all the major department stores and malls. But pedestrianised Oliver Plunkett St is the retail heart; it and the surrounding narrow lanes are lined with small, interesting shops.

Vibes & Scribes
BOOKS

(Map p62; ☑ 021-427 9535; www.vibesand scribes.ie/books; 21 Lavitt's Quay; ☺ 10am-6.30pm Mon-Sat, 12.30-6pm Sun) Stocks a vast selection of new, secondhand and remaindered books, including lots of Irish interest titles.

Village Hall
VINTAGE

(Map p62; www.facebook.com/thevillagehallcork; 4 St Patrick's Quay; ☺ 10am-6pm) This Aladdin's cave is stuffed to the brim with unusual vintage clothing, vinyl records, eclectic furniture and assorted oddities. Despite being full of knick-knacks to browse through, it maintains a stylish interior and you could find yourself spending a couple of hours here. There's also delicious coffee and cake to sustain you during your shopping.

PLUGD Records
MUSIC

(Map p62; ☑ 021-472 6300; www.plugdrecords. com; Triskel Arts Centre, Tobin St; ☺ noon-7pm Mon-Sat; ☎) Stocks all kinds of music on vinyl and CD and is the place to keep up with Cork's ever-changing music scene.

20 20 Gallery
ART

(Map p62; ☑ 021-439 1458; www.2020artgal lery.com; Griffith House, North Mall; ☺ noon-5pm Tue-Sat) Commercial fine-art gallery selling paintings, ceramics and photographic prints by a broad range of Irish artists.

❶ Information

Cork City Tourist Office (Map p62; ☑ 1850 230 330; www.purecork.ie; 125 St Patrick's St; ☺ 9am-5pm Mon-Sat; ☎) Information desk, free city maps and self-guided walk leaflets.

People's Republic of Cork (www.peoplesre publicofcork.com) Picking up on the popular nickname for the liberal-leaning city, this indie website provides excellent info.

General Post Office (Map p62; ☑ 021-485 1042; Oliver Plunkett St; ☺ 9am-5.30pm Mon-Sat)

Mercy University Hospital (☑ 021-427 1971; www.muh.ie; Grenville Pl) Has a 24-hour emergency department.

Free wi-fi is available throughout the city centre's main streets and public spaces, including the bus and train stations.

Webworkhouse.com (☐021-427 3090; www. webworkhouse.com; 8A Winthrop St; per hr €1.50-3; ⊘24hr) Internet cafe; also offers low-cost international phone cards.

❶ Getting Around

Street parking requires scratch-card parking discs (€2 per hour, in force 8.30am to 6.30pm Monday to Saturday), available from many city centre shops. Be warned – traffic wardens are ferociously efficient. There are several signposted car parks around the central area, with charges around €2 per hour and €12 overnight.

You can avoid city centre parking problems by using Black Ash Park & Ride on the South City Link Rd, on the way to the airport. Parking costs €5 a day, with buses into the city centre at least every 15 minutes (10-minute journey time).

AROUND CORK CITY

Blarney Castle

If you need proof of the power of a good yarn, then join the queue to get into the 15th-century **Blarney Castle** (☐021-438 5252; www.blarneycastle.ie; Blarney; adult/child €18/8; ⊘9am-7pm Mon-Sat, to 6pm Sun Jun-Aug, shorter hours Sep-May; **P**), one of Ireland's most popular tourist attractions. Everyone's here, of course, to plant their lips on the **Blarney Stone** (also see p25), which supposedly gives one the gift of the gab – a cliché that has entered every lexicon and tour route. Blarney is 8km northwest of Cork and buses run hourly from Cork bus station (€5.60 return, 20 minutes).

The Blarney Stone is perched at the top of a steep climb up claustrophobic spiral staircases. Try not to think of the local lore about all the fluids that drench the stone other than saliva. Better yet, just don't kiss it.

The custom of kissing the stone is a relatively modern one, but Blarney's association with smooth talking goes back a long time. Queen Elizabeth I is said to have invented the term 'to talk blarney' out of exasperation with Lord Blarney's ability to talk endlessly without ever actually agreeing to her demands.

The famous stone aside, **Blarney Castle** itself is an impressive 16th-century tower set

in gorgeous grounds. Escape the crowds on a walk around the **Fern Garden** and **Arboretum**, investigate toxic plants in the Harry Potterish **Poison Garden** or explore the landscaped nooks and crannies of the **Rock Close**.

★**Square Table**   IRISH €€€
(☐021-438 2825; www.thesquaretable.ie; 5 The Square, Blarney; mains €20-30; ⊘6-9pm Wed & Thu, to 10pm Fri & Sat, 12.30-4pm Sun) The sisters who run this cosy little restaurant are passionate about Irish produce, as shown in a menu that puts local seafood, pork and beef, Gubbeen chorizo, Ballyhoura mushrooms and platters of Irish-made salami, black pudding and Irish cheeses front and centre. Best to book in advance.

Fota Island

Fota Island lies in Cork Harbour, connected by short bridges to the mainland and to Great Island, 10km east of Cork on the road to Cobh. Formerly the private estate of the Smith-Barry family, it is now home to gardens, golf courses and Ireland's only wildlife park.

Fota House
Arboretum & Gardens   HOUSE
(☐021-481 5543; www.fotahouse.com; Carrigtwohill, Fota Island; house tours adult/child €9/3.50; house & gardens €13.50/6; ⊘10am-5pm daily Mar-Sep, Sat & Sun Feb & Oct-Dec; **P**) Guided tours of Regency-style Fota House focus on the original kitchen and ornate plasterwork ceilings, but the real highlight here is the arboretum and gardens (a self-guided tour of garden only costs €3). Also see p24.

Fota Wildlife Park   ZOO
See p24.

Fota Island Resort   GOLF
(☐021-488 3700; www.fotaisland.ie; Fota Island; green fees €45-110) Three championship golf courses sprawl within the 315-hectare Fota Island Resort – Deerpark, Belvelly and Barryscourt – anchored by one of Ireland's best known golfing hotels. The resort has hosted the Irish Open three times, most recently in 2014, and welcomes visitors; it's best to book your round in advance. The beautiful old stone clubhouse, set in a converted farmhouse overlooking the lake, is an atmospheric place for a postgolf drink.

SPIKE ISLAND

A low-lying green island in Cork Harbour, **Spike Island** (☑ 021-237 3455; www.spikeisland cork.com; Cork Harbour; adult/child incl ferry €20/10; ⊘ ferry departures 10am-3pm Jun-Aug, noon & 2pm May & Sep, Sat & Sun only Feb-Apr & Oct) was once an important part of the port's defences, topped by an 18th-century artillery fort. In the second half of the 19th century, during the Irish War of Independence, and from 1984 to 2004 it served as a prison, gaining the nickname 'Ireland's Alcatraz'. Today you can enjoy a guided walking tour of the former prison buildings, then go off and explore on your own; the ferry departs from Kennedy Pier, Cobh.

The guided tour takes in the modern prison, the old punishment block, the shell store (once used as a children's prison) and No 2 bastion with its massive 6in gun. Other highlights include the **Gun Park**, with a good display of mostly 20th-century artillery; the **Mitchell Hall**, with an exhibit on the *Aud*, a WWI German gun-running ship that was sunk in the entrance to Cork Harbour; and the **Glacis Walk**, a 1.5km trail that leads around the walls of the fortress, with great views of Cobh town and the harbour entrance. You'll need around four hours to make the most of a visit. There's a cafe and toilets on the island.

Cobh

POP 12,800

Cobh (pronounced 'cove') is a charming waterfront town on a glittering estuary, dotted with brightly coloured houses and overlooked by a splendid cathedral. It's popular with Corkonians looking for a spot of R&R, and with cruise liners – each year around 90 visit the port, the second-largest natural harbour in the world (after Sydney Harbour in Australia).

It's a far cry from the harrowing Famine years when more than 70,000 people left Ireland through the port in order to escape the ravages of starvation (from 1848 to 1950, no fewer than 2.5 million emigrants passed through).

Cobh is on the south side of Great Island. Visible from the waterfront are Haulbowline Island, once a naval base, and the greener Spike Island, formerly a prison and now a tourist attraction.

History

Cobh has always had a strong connection with Atlantic crossings. In 1838 the *Sirius* set out from Cobh, and was the first steamship to cross the Atlantic. The *Titanic* made its last stop here before its disastrous voyage in 1912, and, when the *Lusitania* was torpedoed off the coast of Kinsale in 1915, it was here that many of the survivors were brought and the dead buried. Cobh was also the last glimpse of Ireland for tens of thousands who emigrated during the Famine.

In 1849 Cobh was renamed Queenstown after Queen Victoria paid a visit. The name lasted until Irish independence in 1921 when, unsurprisingly, the local council reverted to the Irish original.

The world's first yacht club, the Royal Cork Yacht Club, was founded here in 1720, but currently operates from Crosshaven on the other side of Cork Harbour. The beautiful Italianate Old Yacht Club now houses an arts centre.

◉ Sights & Activities

Cobh, The Queenstown Story MUSEUM
(☑ 021-481 3591; www.cobhheritage.com; Lower Rd; adult/child €10/6; ⊘ 9.30am-6pm mid-Apr–mid-Oct, 9.30am-5pm Mon-Sat, 11am-5pm Sun mid-Oct–mid-Apr) The howl of the storm almost knocks you off balance, there's a bit of fake vomit on the deck, and the people in the pictures all look pretty miserable – that's just one room at Cobh Heritage Centre. Housed in the old train station, this interactive museum is way above average, chronicling Irish emigrations across the Atlantic in the wake of the Great Famine.

Titanic
Experience Cobh MUSEUM
See p24.

Michael Martin's
Walking Tours WALKING
(☑ 021-481 5211; www.titanic.ie; tours from €13) Michael Martin's 1¼-hour guided Titanic Trail walk leaves from the **Commodore Hotel** (4 Westbourne Pl) at 11am and 2pm, with

BELVELLY SMOKEHOUSE

No trip to Cork is complete without a visit to an artisan food producer, and the effervescent Frank Hederman is more than happy to show you around **Belvelly Smokehouse** (✆ 021-481 1089; www.frankhederman.com; Belvelly; free for individuals, charge for groups; ⊙ by reservation 10am-5pm Mon-Fri) ⚐, the oldest traditional smokehouse in Ireland – indeed, the only surviving one. The smokehouse is 19km east of Cork on the R624 towards Cobh; call ahead to arrange a visit.

Alternatively, stop by Frank's stall at the **Cobh** (✆ 086 199 7643; www.facebook.com/cobhfarmers; The Promenade; ⊙ 10am-2pm Fri) ⚐ or Midleton (p74) farmers markets; you can also buy his produce at Cork's English Market (p66).

Seafood and cheese are smoked here – even butter – but the speciality is fish, particularly salmon. In a traditional process that takes 24 hours from start to finish, the fish is filleted and cured before being hung to smoke over beech woodchips. The result is subtle and delectable.

a free sampling of stout at the end. Martin also runs a ghoulish Ghost Walk (8pm start).

St Colman's Cathedral CATHEDRAL
See p25.

Sleeping & Eating

Gilbert's GUESTHOUSE €€
(✆ 021-481 1300; www.gilbertsincobh.com; 11 Pearse Sq; s/d/penthouse €89/100/180; 🛜) The four rooms at this boutique guesthouse in Cobh's town centre are fresh and contemporary with handmade furniture, pure-wool blankets and rain showers. Rates don't include breakfast, but the penthouse suite has a kitchenette. Gilbert's Bistro, one of Cobh's better restaurants, is just downstairs.

Knockeven House B&B €€
(✆ 021-481 1778; www.knockevenhouse.com; Rushbrooke; d/f from €120/160; 🅿) Knockeven is a splendid Victorian house with huge bedrooms done out with period furniture, overlooking a magnificent garden full of magnolias and camellias. Breakfasts are great too – homemade breads and fresh fruit – and are served in the sumptuous dining room. The decor takes you back to 1st-class passage on a vintage liner. It's 1.5km west of Cobh's centre.

★ Seasalt CAFE €
(✆ 021-481 3383; www.facebook.com/SeasaltCobh; 17 Casement Sq; mains €7-10; ⊙ 9am-5pm Mon-Sat, 10am-5pm Sun) This stylish cafe, run by a skilled chef, brings fresh local produce to brunch dishes such as Gubbeen chorizo hash, or eggs Royale with Belvelly smoked salmon, and lunch specials like croque

madame with West Cork ham and Dubliner cheese. Salads are fresh and inventive, and tart of the day could be spinach and feta, or roast tomato, pesto and mozzarella.

Titanic Bar & Grill IRISH €€
(✆ 021-481 4585; www.titanicbarandgrill.ie; 20 Casement Sq; mains €11-28; ⊙ noon-3pm Mon & Tue, noon-3pm & 6-8.30pm Wed-Sat, noon-5pm Sun; ♿) Around the back of the Titanic Experience (p24), with a huge deck overlooking the harbour, this is a stunning spot for something to eat. The menu lives up to the stylish glossy timber surrounds with posh versions of pub-grub classics such as fish and chips, bangers and mash, and steak with pepper sauce.

Drinking & Nightlife

Roaring Donkey PUB
(✆ 021-481 1739; www.facebook.com/RoaringDonkeyCobh; Orilia Tce; ⊙ 5-11.30pm Mon-Thu, to 12.30am Fri, 3pm-12.30am Sat, 3-11pm Sun) It's a steep walk from the seafront but the pay-off is plenty of craic – and often live music – at the wonderfully named Roaring Donkey (allegedly so called because former patrons' donkeys made their presence known outside). It's 500m north of Cobh Pier.

❶ Information

The **tourist office** (✆ 021-481 3301; www.visitcobh.com; Market House, Casement Sq; ⊙ 9am-5pm Mon-Fri) is housed in the building with an archway through it, opposite the Titanic Experience.

Midleton & Around

POP 12,495

Aficionados of a particularly fine Irish whiskey will recognise the name Midleton, and
the main reason to linger in this bustling
market town is to visit the old Jameson
whiskey distillery, along with a meal at one
of the town's famously good restaurants.
The surrounding region is full of pretty villages, craggy coastlines and heavenly rural
hotels.

Sights

Jameson Experience
MUSEUM

(☑ 021-461 3594; www.jamesonwhiskey.com; Old
Distillery Walk; tours adult/child €22/11; ☺ shop
10am-6pm; P) Coachloads pour in to tour
this restored 200-year-old distillery building. Exhibits and 75-minute tours (run
between 10am and 4pm) explain the process of taking barley and creating whiskey
(Jameson is today made in a modern factory
in Cork). There's a well-stocked gift shop,
and the **Malt House Restaurant** (☺ noon-
3pm) has live music on Sundays.

🛏 Sleeping

There are some good places to stay in town,
but most visitors overnight in Cork city or
head for one of the lovely country-house
hotels in the nearby countryside.

An Stór Midleton Townhouse
B&B €

(☑ 021-463 3106; www.anstortownhouse.com; Dru-
ry's Lane; s/d/f from €50/70/116; P 🛜) Housed
in a former wool store, this place straddles
the boundary between upmarket hostel and
budget guesthouse, offering competitively
priced accommodation in bright, recently redecorated rooms. Family rooms have
a double bed and either two or four bunk
beds. Breakfast is provided, and there's a
self-catering kitchen too. The location is
bang in the town centre.

Oatencake Lodge B&B
B&B €€

(☑ 021-463 1232; www.oatencakelodge.com; Cork
Rd; s/d €50/90; P 🛜) This suburban villa offers superb-value accommodation in crisp,
clean, Ikea-furnished bedrooms. The owners
are warm and welcoming, and ready with
advice on the local area. It's a 10-minute walk
into Midleton town centre, and there's a bus
stop at the door for travel into Cork city.

🍴 Eating

Midleton was one of the hotbeds of Cork's
'eat local' food scene that emerged in the last
decades of the 20th century, pioneered by
the late Myrtle Allen of Ballymaloe House

WORTH A TRIP

THE GOURMET HEARTLAND OF BALLYMALOE

Drawing up at wisteria-clad **Ballymaloe House** (☑ 021-465 2531; www.ballymaloe.ie;
Shanagarry; r from €280; P 🛜 ♨ 🐾) you know you've arrived somewhere special. The
Allen family has been running this superb hotel and restaurant in the old family home for
decades. Rooms are individually decorated with period furnishings and breakfast good-
ies include bread from their own bakery, eggs from the farm and honey from their own
hives. The house is 12km southeast of Midleton, off the R629.

Myrtle Allen (1924–2018) was a legend in her own lifetime, acclaimed internationally for her near single-handed creation of fine Irish cooking. The menu at Ballymaloe
House's celebrated restaurant (three-course lunch €45, five-course dinner €80, open
1pm to 2pm and 7pm to 9.30pm) changes daily to reflect the availability of produce from
its own farms and other local sources. The hotel also runs wine and gardening weekends.

Nonresidents can get a taste of local produce at the Ballymaloe Cafe, next door to
the hotel.

Part of the famous Ballymaloe House empire, the always busy **Ballymaloe Cafe**
(☑ 021-465 2032; www.ballymaloeshop.ie/ballymaloe-cafe; mains €8-14; ☺ 10am-5pm) 🍴
serves freshly prepared seasonal and organic produce from its own farms and gardens
(and from elsewhere in County Cork), including tasty quiche, salads, open sandwiches
and daily blackboard specials. The neighbouring shop (open 9am to 6pm) sells foodstuffs, kitchenware, crafts and gifts.

and championed by the original Farmgate Restaurant – parent of the more famous Farmgate Cafe in Cork city's English Market – and by one of Ireland's oldest farmers markets.

BiteSize BAKERY €
(☎021-463 6456; www.bitesize.ie; 35 Main St; snacks €2-5; ☺8am-6pm Mon-Sat, 9am-6pm Sun; 🛜🚻) This artisan bakery in the middle of the high street is the ideal place to start the day with a Danish pastry served Scandi-style (ie with a luxurious dollop of whipped cream) and a perfectly poured cappuccino. For lunch you'll find soups, sandwiches and savoury tarts, plus cakes galore to take away.

★Farmgate Restaurant IRISH €€
(☎021-463 2771; www.farmgate.ie; Broderick St; mains lunch €13-20, dinner €20-30; ☺9am-5pm Tue-Sat, 5.30-9.30pm Thu-Sat) 🌿 The original, sister establishment to Cork city's Farmgate Cafe (p66), the Midleton restaurant offers the same superb blend of traditional and modern Irish cuisine. Squeeze through the deli (open 9am to 6pm Tuesday to Saturday) selling amazing baked goods and local produce to the subtly lit, art-clad, 'farmhouse shed' cafe-restaurant, where you'll eat as well as you would anywhere in Ireland.

Greenroom CAFE €€
(☎021-463 9682; www.sagerestaurant.ie/greenroom; 8 Main St; mains €9-16; ☺9am-9pm Tue-Thu, to 10pm Fri & Sat, 11am-7pm Sun; 🛜🚲🚻) 🌿 Tucked behind the Sage restaurant, this cafe is one of the town's social hubs, with a popular breakfast menu (excellent poached eggs on sourdough toast) and a convivial outdoor courtyard bar where you can enjoy a drink or two before tucking into gourmet burgers, chicken wings or fish and chips.

Sage IRISH €€€
(☎021-463 9682; www.sagerestaurant.ie; 8 Main St; mains €21-29; ☺5.30-9pm Tue-Thu, to 9.30pm Fri, noon-3pm & 5.30-9.30pm Sat, noon-3.30pm & 4.30-8.30pm Sun) 🌿 Stylish modern decor set off with polished wood and copper makes an elegant setting for relaxed fine dining at this deservedly popular restaurant. Simple-sounding dishes such as homemade black pudding with egg yolk and mushroom, or beer-brined chicken breast with barley and smoked cheese, turn out to be colourful miniature works of art. Reservations strongly recommended.

Shopping

Midleton

Farmers Market MARKET
(Main St; ☺9am-1pm Sat) 🌿 Midleton's farmers market is one of Cork's oldest and best, with bushels of local produce on offer and producers who are happy to chat. It's behind the big roundabout at the north end of Main St.

❶ Information

The **tourist office** (☎021-461 3702; www.ringofcork.ie; Distillery Walk; ☺10am-5pm Mon-Fri Apr-Oct, to 4pm Nov-Mar) is by the entrance gate to the Jameson Experience.

Youghal

POP 7965

Youghal (Eochaill; pronounced 'yawl'), at the mouth of the Blackwater River, has a rich history that may not be instantly apparent, especially if you coast past on the N25. In fact, even if you stop, it may just seem like a humdrum Irish market town. But take a little time and you'll sniff out some of its once-walled past and enjoy views of the wide Blackwater estuary.

◉ Sights & Activities

Youghal Heritage Centre, in the same building as the tourist office, has an interesting exhibition on the town's history. Pick up a **Youghal Walking Trail** leaflet, which will guide you around the various historical sites. Youghal has two Blue Flag **beaches**, ideal for building sandcastles modelled after the Clock Gate. Claycastle (2km) and Front Strand (1km) are both within walking distance of town, off the N25.

Clock Gate Tower HISTORIC BUILDING
(☎024-20769; www.youghalclockgate.ie; 89 North Main St; tours adult/child €9.50/5; ☺11am-4pm daily Jun-Sep, Thu-Sat Mar-May & Oct) The Clock Gate straddles the middle of Youghal's main street. Built in 1777, it served as a town gate, clock tower and jail. One-hour guided tours (tickets from the nearby tourist office) lead you through four floors of exhibits to a rooftop viewpoint while telling the tale of Youghal's colourful past. Also see p26.

Blackwater Cruises BOATING
(☎087 988 9076; www.blackwatercruises.com; The Quays; adult/child €20/10; ☺Apr-Nov) Runs 90-minute cruises upstream from Youghal

YOUGHAL TOWN WALK

Youghal's history is best understood through its landmarks. Heading along Main St from the south, the curious **Clock Gate Tower**.

The beautifully proportioned **Red House**, on North Main St, was designed in 1706 by the Dutch architect Leuventhen, and features some Dutch Renaissance details. Across the road is the 15th-century tower house **Tynte's Castle** (North Main St; ⊘ closed to the public).

A few doors further along, at the side street leading to the church, are six **almshouses** built by Englishman Richard Boyle, who bought Walter Raleigh's Irish estates and became the first Earl of Cork in 1616 in recognition of his work in creating 'a very excellent colony'.

St Mary's Collegiate Church (also see p26) was built in 1220. The Earl of Desmond and his troops, rebelling against English rule, demolished the chancel roof in the 16th century.

Hidden behind high walls to the north of the church, 15th- to 18th-century **Myrtle Grove** (not open to the public) is the former home of Raleigh, and a rare Irish example of a late medieval Tudor-style house.

The churchyard is bounded to the west by a fine stretch of the old **town wall** – follow the parapet until you can descend stairs to the outer side, then enter the next gate along to descend back to Main St through the 17th-century **College Gardens**, now restored and in use as a public park.

---

along the lovely Blackwater River, past ruined castles and abbeys as far as grand Ballynatray House.

🛏 Sleeping & Eating

⭐ **Roseville**   B&B €€
(☑ 087 294 7178; www.rosevilleyoughal.com; New Catherine St; d from €118; 🛜) Despite being right in the middle of town, this B&B feels like a secret hideaway with its two luxurious guest suites beautifully furnished in modern style with country farmhouse touches, and opening onto a private walled garden. Sumptuous breakfasts include eggs all ways, and fruit and vegetable smoothies.

**Aherne's
Townhouse**   INN €€
(☑ 024-92424; www.ahernes.net; 163 North Main St; d/f from €145/200; ❷🛜) The 12 rooms here are extremely well appointed; larger ones have small balconies, where you can breathe in the sea air. Rates include a fabulous breakfast (fresh-squeezed OJ, free-range eggs, locally caught fish) that will keep you going all day. The establishment includes an upmarket seafood restaurant and a stylish, cosy bar.

Sage Cafe   CAFE €
(☑ 024-85844;   www.facebook.com/sagecafe youghal; 86 North Main St; mains €7-14; ⊘ 9.30am-5.30pm Mon-Sat; 🖉) 🌿 Everything at this luscious little cafe is homemade: cod and chips, lentil-and-nut loaf, quiche, cakes and more. Vegetarians in particular will be in heaven.

**Aherne's Seafood Bar
& Restaurant**   SEAFOOD €€
(☑ 024-92424; www.ahernes.net; 163 North Main St; bar meals €14-25, restaurant mains €29-34; ⊘ bar meals noon-9.30pm, restaurant 6.30-9.30pm; 🛜🚸) Three generations of the same family have run the award-winning Aherne's. Seafood is the star, but there are also plenty of meat and poultry dishes. Besides the upmarket restaurant there's a cosy bar, all mahogany and polished brass, where you can enjoy fresh local seafood with wine by the glass. Kids' menu available.

ℹ Information

The **tourist office** (☑ 024-20170; www.youghal.ie; Market Sq; ⊘ 9am-5pm daily May-Sep, to 4pm Mon-Fri Oct-Apr) – housed in an attractive old market house on the waterfront, down from the clock tower – has tourist info, a small heritage centre and free town maps.

STRETCH YOUR LEGS CORK CITY

Start/Finish: Lewis Glucksman Gallery

Distance: 4.7km

Duration: 3 hours

The River Lee flows around Cork's central island of grand Georgian parades, 17th-century alleys and modern masterpieces. As you criss-cross between galleries and architecture, you'll discover that the single-best sight is the city itself.

Take this walk on Trips

1

Lewis Glucksman Gallery

Situated on the leafy campus of prestigious University College Cork (UCC), the award-winning limestone, steel and timber **Lewis Glucksman Gallery** (021-490 1844; www.glucksman.org; University College Cork, Western Rd; suggested donation €5; 10am-5pm Tue-Sat, 2-5pm Sun;) displays the best in national and international contemporary art.

The Walk » From UCC, head south on Donovan's Rd and then east on Connaught Ave and Gill Abbey St, to reach St Fin Barre's Cathedral.

St Fin Barre's Cathedral

Spires, gargoyles and sculpture adorn Cork's Protestant **St Fin Barre's Cathedral** (021-496 3387; www.corkcathedral.webs.com; Bishop St; adult/child €6/3; 9.30am-5.30pm Mon-Sat year-round, 1-2.30pm & 4.30-5pm Sun Apr-Oct). Local legend says the golden angel on the eastern side will blow its horn when the Apocalypse is due to start.

The Walk » Go east along Dean St and turn left on Barrack St to find the entrance to Elizabeth Fort.

Elizabeth Fort

Originally built in the 1620s, this small star-shaped artillery **fort** (021-497 5947; www.elizabethfort.ie; Barrack St; 10am-5pm Mon-Sat, noon-5pm Sun, closed Mon Oct-May) once formed an important part of the city's defences. Exhibits offer an insight into Cork's military history, and there are good views across the city from the ramparts. Free guided tours at 1pm provide additional context.

The Walk » Head downhill to the riverside quays and turn right. Cross the bridge north at Mary St to reach the English Market.

English Market

Cork's ornate Victorian English Market (p66), crammed with colourful stalls selling fine foodstuffs from around the county, is a must-see. You're also spoiled for dining options, which range from gourmet sandwiches to the famous Farmgate Cafe (p66).

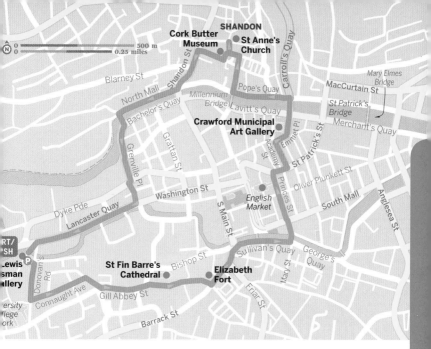

The Walk ›› Princes St meets St Patrick's St, the main shopping and commercial area. Turn left onto Academy St and right on Emmet Pl to the city's premier gallery.

Crawford Municipal Art Gallery

Highlights of the excellent permanent collection at Cork's public gallery, **Crawford Municipal Art Gallery** (☏021-480 5042; www.crawfordartgallery.ie; Emmet Pl; ⊗10am-5pm Mon-Wed, Fri & Sat, to 8pm Thu, 11am-4pm Sun), covering the 17th century to today, include works by Sir John Lavery, Jack B Yeats, Nathaniel Hone and a room devoted to Irish women artists, including Mainie Jellet and Evie Hone. The Sculpture Galleries contain plaster casts of Roman and Greek statues, given to King George IV by the pope in 1822.

The Walk ›› Continue on Emmet Pl, passing Cork Opera House, cross the river and turn west to the hillside neighbourhood of Shandon, with galleries, antique shops and cafes along its side lanes and squares lined with tiny old row houses.

St Anne's Church

Shandon is dominated by the 1722 **St Anne's Church** (☏021-450 5906; www.shandonbells.ie; John Redmond St; tower incl bells adult/child €5/2.50; ⊗10am-5pm Mon-Sat, 11.30am-4.30pm Sun Jun-Sep, shorter hours Oct-May), aka the 'Four-Faced Liar', so called as each of the tower's four clocks used to tell a different time. Ring the bells on the 1st floor and continue up the 132 steps to the top for 360-degree views of the city.

The Walk ›› It's a short walk south on Exchange St and right on John Redmond St to the Cork Butter Museum.

Cork Butter Museum

Cork's long tradition of butter manufacturing is related through displays and dioramas in the **Cork Butter Museum** (☏021-430 0600; www.corkbutter.museum; O'Connell Sq; adult/child €4/1.50; ⊗10am-5pm Mar-Oct). The square in front is dominated by the round **Firkin Crane** building, central to the old butter market and now housing a dance centre.

Marino Branch
Brainse Marino
Tel: 8336297

County Kerry contains some of Ireland's most iconic scenery: surf-pounded sea cliffs and soft golden strands, emerald-green farmland criss-crossed by tumbledown stone walls, mist-shrouded bogs and cloud-torn mountain peaks.

County Kerry

KILLARNEY

POP 14,504

Mobbed in summer, Killarney is perhaps at its best in late spring and early autumn when the crowds are manageable, but the weather is still good enough to enjoy its outdoor activities.

History

The Killarney area has been inhabited since at least the early Bronze Age, when copper ore was mined on Ross Island. In the 7th century St Finian founded a monastery on Inisfallen in Lough Leane, and the region became a focus for Christianity. The lands around the lough were occupied by the Gaelic clans of McCarthy Mór and the O'Donoghues of Ross, who built Ross Castle, before coming into the possession of the Herberts of Muckross and the Earls of Kenmare.

It wasn't until the mid-18th century that Sir Thomas Browne (1726–95) began to develop the region as an Irish version of England's Lake District. It was later bolstered by the arrival of famous visitors including Sir Walter Scott (1825) and Queen Victoria and Prince Albert (1861), as well as the railway (1853). By 1895 Killarney was on the Thomas Cook package-tour itinerary.

⊙ Sights & Activities

★ **Killarney House & Gardens**   HISTORIC BUILDING

(Map p80; www.facebook.com/killarneynational park; Muckross Rd; ⊙8.30am-7.30pm May-Sep, 9am-5.30pm Oct-Apr) **FREE** Dating from the early 18th century, Killarney House was once part of a much larger residence that was later demolished; it was restored in 2016 and now houses the Killarney National Park visitor centre. There are free guided tours of the house every half-hour, and seasonal guided walks in the vast gardens, which sweep majestically towards a gorgeous view of the Kerry mountains.

Knockreer House & Gardens   GARDENS

The original Knockreer House, built for the Earl of Kenmare in the 1870s, burned down in 1913; the present house was built on the same site in 1958 and is now home to a national-park education centre. It isn't open to the public, but its terraced gardens have magnificent views across the lakes to the mountains.

From the park entrance opposite St Mary's Cathedral, follow the path forking right, past the cute thatched cottage of **Deenagh Lodge**, built in 1834.

Killarney Golf & Fishing Club
GOLF

(☑ 064-663 1034; www.killarneygolfclub.com; Mahony's Point; green fees €60-125) This historic club, which has hosted the Irish Open on several occasions, has three championship golf courses with lakeside settings and mountain views. It's 3.4km west of Killarney on the N72.

O'Neill's
FISHING

(Map p80; ☑ 064-663 1970; www.facebook.com/oneillsofkillarney; 6 Plunkett St; ⊙ 9.30am-10pm Mon-Fri, to 9pm Sat, 10.30am-8pm Sun) Information, tackle, permits, licences and rental equipment (rod hire per day €10) can be obtained at O'Neill's, which looks like a gift shop but is a long-established fishing centre.

Tours

Jaunting Car Tours
TOURS

(Map p80; ☑ 064-663 3358; www.killarneyjauntingcars.ie; Kenmare Pl; per jaunting car €40-80) Killarney's traditional horse-drawn jaunting cars provide tours from the town to Ross Castle and Muckross Estate, complete with amusing commentary from the driver (known as a 'jarvey'). The cost varies depending on distance; cars can fit up to four people. The pickup point is on Kenmare Pl.

Killarney Guided Walks
WALKING

(Map p80; ☑ 087 639 4362; www.killarneyguidedwalks.com; adult/child €12/6) Guided two-hour walks through the national-park woodlands leave at 11am daily from opposite **St Mary's Cathedral** (Cathedral Pl) at the western end of New St; advance bookings are required from November to April. Tours meander through Knockreer gardens, then to spots where Charles de Gaulle holidayed, David Lean filmed *Ryan's Daughter* and Brother Cudda slept for 200 years.

Festivals & Events

Killarney Mountain Festival
OUTDOORS

(www.killarneymountainfestival.com; ⊙ Mar) Three days of cultural and historical walks and talks, film screenings, guest speakers, photography and art exhibits, and family fun, focused on the theme of outdoor activities and adventure sports.

The Gathering
MUSIC

(www.inec.ie/festival/the-gathering; ⊙ late Feb/early Mar) On the go for more than 20 years, this is a rousing five days of traditional Irish music, ranging from intimate fireside sessions to large-scale foot-stomping concerts.

Sleeping

★ Black Sheep Hostel
HOSTEL €

(Map p80; ☑ 064-663 8746; www.blacksheephostel.ie; 68 New St; dm/apt from €23/110; 🛜) 🧴 This hostel was designed by travellers, and it shows – custom-made bunks with built-in lockers, reading lights, charging points and privacy curtains; a fully equipped kitchen with free breakfast; an organic garden with free-range chickens (eggs for breakfast!); and a comfortable lounge with sofas, fireplace, communal guitar and library. Three-night minimum from May to October.

★ Fleming's White Bridge Caravan & Camping Park
CAMPGROUND €

(☑ 064-663 1590; www.killarneycamping.com; White Bridge, Ballycasheen Rd; unit plus 2 adults €28, hiker or cyclist €12; ⊙ mid-Mar–Oct; 🛜🐾) A lovely, sheltered family-run campsite 2.5km southeast of the town centre off the N22, Fleming's has a games room, bike hire, campers' kitchen, laundry and free trout fishing on the river that runs alongside it. Reception can arrange bus, bike and boat tours.

★ Crystal Springs
B&B €€

(☑ 064-663 3272; www.crystalspringsbandb.com; Ballycasheen Cross, Woodlawn Rd; s/d from €98/120; 🅿🛜) The timber deck of this wonderfully relaxing B&B overhangs the River Flesk, where trout anglers can fish for free. Rooms are richly furnished with patterned wallpapers and walnut timber; private bathrooms (most with spa bath) are huge. The glass-enclosed breakfast room also overlooks the rushing river. It's about a 15-minute stroll into town.

Killarney

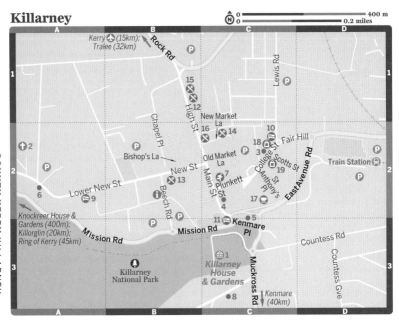

Killarney

⊙ Top Sights
1 Killarney House & Gardens C3

⊙ Sights
2 St Mary's Cathedral............................... A2

⊙ Activities, Courses & Tours
3 Corcoran's C2
4 Deros Tours C2
  Gap of Dunloe Tours..................... (see 16)
5 Jaunting Car Tours C2
6 Killarney Guided Walks A2
7 O'Neill's C2
8 Wild Kerry Day Tours C3

⊟ Sleeping
9 Black Sheep Hostel A2
10 Fairview C2

11 Killarney Plaza Hotel C3

⊗ Eating
12 Brícín.. B1
13 Celtic Whiskey Bar & Larder B2
14 Curious Cat Café C2
15 Gaby's Seafood Restaurant.................. B1
16 Murphy Brownes C2

⊙ Drinking & Nightlife
  Celtic Whiskey Bar & Larder .... (see 13)
17 Lir Café.. C2
  O'Connor's .... (see 16)

⊙ Shopping
  Brícín .... (see 12)
18 Dungeon Bookshop.............................. C2
19 Variety Sounds C2

Killarney Plaza Hotel   HOTEL €€
(Map p80; ☑064-662 1111; www.killarneyplaza.
com; Kenmare Pl; s/d/ste from €140/175/275;
P@⌂⌀) Although it dates only from 2002,
this large 198-room hotel channels the style
of the art deco era. Classically furnished
guest rooms and public areas are in keeping with its luxury reputation; besides the
marble lobby and lavishly tiled indoor pool,
there's a sauna, steam room and spa.

★**Cahernane
House Hotel**   HERITAGE HOTEL €€€
(☑064-663 1895; www.cahernane.com; Muckross
Rd, Muckross; d/ste from €230/310, 4-course dinner menu €60; P⌂) A tree-lined driveway
leads to this magnificent manor 2km south
of town, dating from 1877. A dozen of its 38
antique-furnished rooms (some with claw-
foot bath or Jacuzzi) are in the original
house; garden-wing rooms have balcony or
patio. Fishing is possible in the River Flesk,

which flows through the grounds. Its restaurant (nonguests by reservation) is sublime.

Fairview GUESTHOUSE €€€
(Map p80; 📞 064-663 4164; www.fairview killarney.com; College St; s/d/f from €199/229/239; 🅿 @ 🛜) Reflected in polished wooden floors, the individually decorated rooms (some with classical printed wallpaper, some with contemporary sofas and glass) at this boutique guesthouse offer more bang for your buck than bigger, less personal places. A veritable feast is laid on at breakfast.

Eating

Curious Cat Café CAFE €
(Map p80; 📞 087 663 5540; www.facebook.com/ curiouscatcafe; 4 New Market Lane; mains €9-15; ⊙ 9am-9pm Fri & Sat, to 4pm Sun & Mon) Tucked away on New Market Lane, this quirky little cafe serves a varied menu that ranges from breakfast smoothies with banana-chocolate bread, to sweet and savoury pancakes, to homemade soups and lunch dishes such as chicken wings with blue-cheese dip and steak sandwiches. Good coffee too.

★ **Murphy Brownes** INTERNATIONAL €€
(Map p80; 📞 064-667 1446; www.facebook.com/ murphybrownesrestaurant; 8 High St; mains €14-25; ⊙ 5-9.30pm Mar-early Jan) Elegant and candlelit, but pleasantly informal, this place is ideal for a relaxing dinner. Service is smiling and attentive without being overbearing, and the crowd-pleasing menu is a mix of Irish and international favourites, with local mussels, Kerry lamb shank and fish and chips sitting alongside beef lasagne, chicken curry and Caesar salad.

Gaby's Seafood Restaurant SEAFOOD €€€
(Map p80; 📞 064-663 2519; www.gabys.ie; 27 High St; mains €30-50; ⊙ 6-10pm Mon-Sat) Gaby's is a refined dining experience serving superb seafood in a traditional manner. Peruse the menu by the fire before drifting past the wine racks to the low-lit dining room to savour exquisite dishes such as lobster in cognac and cream. The wine list is long and the advice unerring.

Drinking & Nightlife

★ **Celtic Whiskey Bar & Larder** BAR
(Map p80; 📞 064-663 5700; www.celticwhis keybar.com; 93 New St; ⊙ 10.30am-11.30pm Mon-Thu, to 12.30am Fri & Sat, to 11pm Sun; 🛜) Of the thousand-plus whiskeys stocked at this stunning contemporary bar, over 500 are Irish, including 1945 Willie Napier from County Offaly and 12-year-old Writers' Tears from County Carlow. One-hour tasting sessions and masterclasses (from €15) provide an introduction to the world of Irish whiskey. A dozen Irish craft beers are on tap; sensational **food** (Map p80; 📞 064-663 5700; www.celtic whiskeybar.com; 93 New St; mains €9-27; ⊙ noon-9.45pm; 🛜) is available too.

★ **O'Connor's** PUB
(Map p80; www.oconnorstraditionalpub.ie; 7 High St; ⊙ noon-11.30pm Sun-Thu, to 12.30am Fri & Sat; 🛜) Live music plays every night at this tiny traditional pub with leaded-glass doors, one of Killarney's most popular haunts. There are more tables upstairs, and in warmer weather the crowds spill out onto the adjacent lane.

Lir Café CAFE
(Map p80; 📞 064-663 3859; www.lircafe.com; Kenmare Pl; ⊙ 8am-9pm Mon-Sat, to 7pm Sun; 🛜) Contemporary Lir Café brews some of Killarney's best coffee. Food is limited to toasties, cakes, biscuits and the real treat, handmade chocolates, including Baileys truffles.

Shopping

Variety Sounds MUSICAL INSTRUMENTS
(Map p80; 📞 064-663 5755; 7 College St; ⊙ 9am-6pm Mon-Sat, from noon Sun) A good range of traditional instruments are stocked at this eclectic music shop along with sheet music and hard-to-find recordings.

Dungeon Bookshop BOOKS
(Map p80; 99 College St; ⊙ 8am-8pm Mon-Sat, from 9am Sun) This secondhand bookshop is hidden above a newsagent (take the stairs at the back of the shop).

Brícín ARTS & CRAFTS
(Map p80; www.bricin.ie; 26 High St; ⊙ 10am-9pm Mon-Sat) Interesting local craftwork, including jewellery and pottery, are stocked alongside touristy wares (shamrock aprons and mugs) at Brícín, which also houses a traditional Irish **restaurant** (Map p80; 📞 064-663 4902; mains €19-28; ⊙ 6-9pm Tue-Sat early Mar-Dec).

Information

The closest accident and emergency unit is at **University Hospital Kerry** (📞 066-718 4000;

www.hse.ie; Cloon More) in Tralee, 32km north-west of Killarney.

SouthDoc (☑ 1850 335 999; www.southdoc.ie; Upper Park Rd; ⊘ 6pm-8am Mon-Fri, 1pm Sat-8am Mon) provides a family doctor service outside normal hours, for urgent medical needs. The clinic is 500m east of Killarney's centre, just east of the roundabout on the N22.

Killarney's **tourist office** (Map p80; ☑ 064-663 1633; www.killarney.ie; Beech Rd; ⊘ 9am-5pm Mon-Sat; ☎) can handle most queries and is especially good with transport intricacies.

ⓘ Getting Around

Bicycles are ideal for exploring the scattered sights of the Killarney region, many of which are accessible only by bike or on foot. And the town centre can be thick with traffic at times.

Many of Killarney's hostels and hotels offer bike rental. Alternatively, try **O'Sullivan's Bike Hire** (☑ 064-663 1282; www.killarneyrentabike.com; Beech Rd; per day/week from €15/85).

AROUND KILLARNEY

Killarney National Park

Sprawling over 102 sq km, the sublime **Killarney National Park** (www.killarneynationalpark.ie) FREE is an idyllic place to explore. Ross Castle and Muckross House draw big crowds, but it's possible to escape amid Ireland's largest area of ancient oak woods, with panoramic views of its highest mountains and the country's only wild herd of native red deer.

Muckross Estate is the main part of the park, and was donated to the state by Arthur Bourn Vincent in 1932; the park was designated a Unesco Biosphere Reserve in 1982. The **Killarney Lakes** – Lough Leane (the Lower Lake, or 'Lake of Learning'), Muckross (or Middle Lake) and the Upper Lake – make up about a quarter of the park, and are surrounded by natural oak and yew woodland, and overlooked by the high crags and moors of **Purple Mountain** (832m) to the west and **Knockrower** (552m) to the south.

⊙ Sights

★**Ross Castle**   CASTLE
(☑ 064-663 5851; www.heritageireland.ie; Ross Rd; adult/child €5/3; ⊘ 9.30am-5.45pm early Mar-Oct; ℗) Lakeside Ross Castle was the residence of the O'Donoghue family back in the 15th century. The entertaining, 45-minute guided tour combines an easily digested history lesson with real insight into life in medieval Ireland. The castle is a lovely 2.6km walk or bike ride southwest of the St Mary's Cathedral pedestrian park entrance; you may well spot deer along the way.

★**Muckross House**   HISTORIC BUILDING
(☑ 064-667 0144; www.muckross-house.ie; Muckross Estate; adult/child €9.25/6.25, incl Muckross Traditional Farms €15.50/10.50; ⊘ 9am-7pm Jul & Aug, to 6pm Apr-Jun, Sep & Oct, to 5pm Nov-Mar; ℗) This impressive Victorian mansion is crammed with fascinating objects (70% of the contents are original). Portraits by John Singer Sargent adorn the walls alongside trophy stag heads and giant stuffed trout, while antique Killarney furniture, with its distinctive inlaid scenes of local beauty spots, graces the grand apartments along with tapestries, Persian rugs, silverware and china specially commissioned for Queen Victoria's visit in 1861. It's 5km south of Killarney, signposted from the N71.

★**Muckross Abbey**   RUINS
(Muckross Estate; ⊘ 24hr) FREE Signposted 1.5km northeast of Muckross House, this well-preserved ruin (actually a friary, though everyone calls it an abbey) was founded in 1448 and burned by Cromwell's troops in 1652. There's a square-towered church and a small, atmospheric cloister with a giant yew tree in the centre (legend has it that the tree is as old as the abbey). In the chancel is the tomb of the McCarthy Mòr chieftains, and an elaborate 19th-century memorial to local philanthropist Lucy Gallwey.

Muckross Traditional Farms   MUSEUM
(☑ 064-663 0804; www.muckross-house.ie; Muckross Estate; adult/child €9.25/6.25, incl Muckross House €15.50/10.50; ⊘ 10am-6pm Jun-Aug, from 1pm Apr, May & Sep, from 1pm Sat & Sun Mar & Oct) These re-creations of 1930s farms evoke authentic sights, sounds and smells – cow dung, hay, wet earth and peat smoke, and a cacophony of chickens, ducks, pigs and donkeys. Costumed guides bring the traditional

MUCKROSS LAKE LOOP TRAIL

You could easily spend most of a day ambling around this waymarked 9.5km loop trail (anticlockwise only for cyclists), which takes in some of the most photogenic parts of Killarney National Park. Starting from Muckross House, you head west through lovely lakeshore woods (with lots of side trails to explore) to reach postcard-pretty Brickeen Bridge, which spans the channel linking Lough Leane and the Middle Lake.

Continue to the sylvan glades that surround the Meeting of the Waters, where channels from all three of Killarney's lakes merge. Don't miss the 10-minute side trail (no bikes) to Old Weir Bridge, where you can watch tour boats powering through the narrow, rocky channel beneath its twin arches (here, a swiftly flowing current links the Upper and Middle Lakes).

On the return leg along the south shore of Middle Lake, the trail passes through woods before reaching the N71 Killarney–Kenmare road. Here, walkers have the option of climbing uphill on the other side of the road to visit **Torc Waterfall** before returning to Muckross House. Cyclists have to follow the main road east for 1km before regaining the off-road trail. Between the road and Muckross House you can detour along the **Old Boathouse Nature Trail**, which leads around a scenic peninsula.

Maps and details are available from Killarney tourist office and Muckross House ticket office.

---

farm buildings to life, and the petting area allows kids to get close to piglets, lambs, ducklings and chicks. Allow at least two hours to do justice to the self-guided tour. A free shuttle loops around the farms, which are just east of Muckross House.

🎣 Activities

Killarney's tourist office stocks walking guides and maps. Killarney Guided Walks (p79) leads guided explorations.

Killarney Lake Tours   CRUISE
(MV Pride of the Lakes; ☑ 064-663 2638; www.killarneylaketours.ie; Ross Castle Pier; adult/child €10/5; ⊙ Apr-Oct) One-hour tours of Lough Leane in a comfortable, enclosed cruise boat depart four times daily (11am, 12.30pm, 2.30pm and 4pm) from the pier beside Ross Castle, taking in the island of Inisfallen (no landing) and O'Sullivan's Cascade (a waterfall on the west shore).

Ross Castle
Traditional Boats   BOATING
(☑ 085 174 2997; Ross Castle Pier; ⊙ 9.30am-5pm Apr-Oct, by reservation Nov-Mar) The open boats at Ross Castle offer engaging trips with boaters who define the word 'character'. Rates are around €10 per person for a trip to Inisfallen or the Middle Lake and back; it's €20 for a tour of all three lakes.

Outdoors Ireland   ADVENTURE
(☑ 086 860 4563; www.outdoorsireland.com) Guided kayak tours of the Killarney lakes

lasting three/seven hours (€60/100 per person; no previous experience needed) generally depart from Ross Castle Pier. The company also runs three-hour sunset kayak trips (€60) and two-day beginner rock-climbing courses (€200).

❶ Getting There & Away

There are two pedestrian/bike entrances in Killarney town: opposite St Mary's Cathedral (p79), with 24-hour access; and the so-called Golden Gates at the roundabout on Muckross Rd (open 8am to 7pm June to August, to 6pm April, May and October, to 5pm November to March).

Vehicle access is via Ross Rd on the southern edge of Killarney town centre, leading to Ross Castle car park; and the Muckross Estate entrance on the N71 5km south of Killarney, leading to the Muckross House car park; parking is free.

❶ Getting Around

Walking, cycling and boat trips are the best ways to explore the park.

From the cathedral entrance it's 2.5km (a 30-minute walk) to Ross Castle; to reach Muckross Estate on foot or by bike you have to follow the cycle path beside the N71 south for 3km where it veers off towards the lake (it's 5km all up to Muckross House).

Jaunting cars depart from Kenmare Pl in Killarney town centre, and from the Jaunting Car Entrance to Muckross Estate, at a car park 3km south of town on the N71. Expect to pay around €15 to €20 per person for a tour from Killarney to Ross Castle and back. There are no set prices; haggle for longer tours.

Gap of Dunloe

The Gap of Dunloe is a wild and scenic mountain pass – studded with crags and bejewelled with lakes and waterfalls – that lies to the west of Killarney National Park, squeezed between Purple Mountain and the high summits of Macgillycuddy's Reeks.

Although it's outside the national park boundary, it's been a vital part of the Killarney tourist trail since the late 18th century when, inspired by the Romantic poets, wealthy tourists came in search of 'sublime' and 'savage' landscapes.

During this period, the legend of Kate Kearney first arose: Kate, a fabled local beauty based on a popular song, supposedly lived in a cottage in the pass and dispensed *poteen* (illegally distilled whiskey) to weary travellers. The 19th-century pub at the northern end of the Gap is still known as Kate Kearney's Cottage; there's a busy car park here, where you can rent jaunting cars (cash only).

Lord Brandon's Cottage
CAFE €

(Gearhameen; dishes €3-8; ⊙ 8am-3pm Apr-Oct) At the Gap's southern end, the road twists steeply down to the remote Black Valley and Lord Brandon's Cottage, a 19th-century hunting lodge surrounded by lush, green water meadows with a simple open-air cafe and a dock for boats to Ross Castle, near Killarney. By car, it's reached via a steep minor road from the R568 near Moll's Gap.

★ Heather
CAFE €€

(☑ 064-664 4144; www.moriartys.ie/heather; mains €9-18; ⊙ 10.30am-5pm; P 🛜 🅿) 🍴 In a glorious setting, this light-filled cafe adjoins a farm that provides produce from its fields and polytunnels, while seafood and meat are locally and sustainably sourced. Fantastic food includes sweet treats such as Skelligs white chocolate and roasted-hazelnut cake to gourmet sandwiches and filling dishes like Kerry lamb burger or chickpea, spinach and potato curry.

Kate Kearney's Cottage
PUB FOOD €€

(☑ 064-664 4146; mains €10-24; ⊙ kitchen noon-9pm, bar to 11.30pm Mon-Thu, to 12.30am Fri & Sat, to 11pm Sun; P 🍴) This 19th-century pub at the northern end of the Gap of Dunloe serves decent pub classics including sausage and mash, Irish stew, steaks and burgers, and has a kids' menu. Kitchen hours can be reduced at short notice, so call ahead if you're counting on dining here. The bar hosts live Irish music every night in summer.

❶ Getting There & Away

The traditional way to explore the Gap is via a tour from Killarney – by bus to Kate Kearney's Cottage, then either on foot or by jaunting car through the Gap to Lord Brandon's Cottage on the Upper Lake, and finally by boat to Ross

Killorglin King Puck by Alan Ryan Hall

PATRICK MANGAN/SHUTTERSTOCK ©

Castle and then bus back to town (€30 per person, plus €20 for jaunting car). Most hostels, hotels and pubs in Killarney can set up these tours, or try **Gap of Dunloe Tours** (Map p80; 064-663 0200; www.gapofdunloetours.com; 7 High St; ☺Mar-Oct).

Despite a road sign at Kate Kearney's Cottage implying that cars are forbidden, it is perfectly legal to drive through the Gap of Dunloe – it's a public road. However, driving the Gap is not recommended, at least from Easter to September. The road is very narrow, steep and twisting, and is usually crowded with walkers, cyclists, ponies and jaunting cars; the drivers of the latter will give you short shrift. Early morning or after 5pm is best.

RING OF KERRY

This 179km circuit of the Iveragh (pronounced *eev*-raa) Peninsula winds past pristine beaches, medieval ruins, mountains and loughs, with ever-changing views of the island-dotted Atlantic, particularly between Waterville and Caherdaniel in the peninsula's spectacular southwest.

The smaller but equally scenic Skellig Ring, which spins off the loop, is less travelled as the roads are too narrow for tour buses.

Centred on the Ring, the 700-sq-km Kerry International Dark-Sky Reserve (www.kerry darksky.com) was designated in 2014. Low, light pollution offers fantastic stargazing when skies are clear.

If you want to get further off the beaten track, explore the interior of the peninsula – on foot along the eastern section of the Kerry Way from Killarney to Glenbeigh, or by car or bike on the minor roads that cut through the hills, notably the Ballaghisheen Pass between Killorglin and Waterville, or the Ballaghbeama Gap from Glenbeigh to Gearha Bridge on the R568.

ⓘ Getting Around

Although you can cover the Ring in one day by car or three days by bicycle, the more time you take, the more you'll enjoy it.

The road is narrow and twisty in places, notably between Killarney and Moll's Gap. Tour buses travel the Ring in an anticlockwise direction. Getting stuck behind one is tedious, so you could consider driving clockwise; just note it goes against the advice of authorities – and watch out on blind corners (especially between Moll's Gap and Killarney).

Killorglin

POP 2199

Travelling anticlockwise from Killarney, the first town on the Ring is Killorglin (Cill Orglain, meaning 'Orgla's Church'). For most of the year, it's pretty quiet. In August, however, there's an explosion of ceremonies at the famous pagan festival, the Puck Fair (a statue of King Puck – a goat – stands on the north side of the river). Author Blake Morrison documents his mother's childhood here in *Things My Mother Never Told Me*.

Kerry Bog
Village Museum   MUSEUM
See p32.

Puck Fair   CULTURAL
(Aonach an Phuic; www.puckfair.ie; ☺mid-Aug)
First recorded in 1603, with hazy origins, this lively three-day festival centres on the custom of installing a billy goat (a poc, or puck), the symbol of mountainous Kerry, on a pedestal in the town, its horns festooned with ribbons. Other entertainment ranges from a horse fair to street theatre, concerts and fireworks; the pubs stay open until 3am.

🛏 Sleeping & Eating

Coffey's
River's Edge   B&B €€
(066-976 1750; www.coffeysriversedge.com; Lower Bridge St; s/d from €70/100; P🐾) You can sit out on the balcony overlooking the River Laune at this contemporary B&B with 10 spotless spring-toned rooms and hardwood floors. Cots are available. It's in a central location next to the bridge.

Jack's Bakery   BAKERY €
(Lower Bridge St; dishes €2.50-8; ☺8am-6.45pm Mon-Fri, to 6pm Sat, 9am-2pm Sun) 🌿 Jack Healy bakes amazing artisan breads, and also serves killer coffee and beautiful sandwiches (using homemade pâtés) at this popular spot. There's no indoor seating, but a couple of tables are set up on the pavement in good weather.

Bianconi   GASTROPUB €€
(066-976 1146; www.bianconi.ie; Lower Bridge St; mains €10-28; ☺kitchen 11.30am-10pm Mon-Sat, 6-9pm Sun; 🐾) This Victorian-style pub has a classy ambience and an equally refined menu. Its spectacular salads, such as Cashel Blue cheese, apple, toasted almonds and

pancetta, are a meal in themselves. Upstairs, stylishly refurbished guest rooms (singles/doubles from €95/125) have olive and truffle tones and luxurious bathrooms (try for a roll-top tub).

Giovannelli   ITALIAN €€€

(☑ 087 123 1353; www.giovannellirestaurant. com; Lower Bridge St; mains €19-34; ⊗ 6.30-9pm Mon-Sat) Northern Italian native Daniele Giovannelli makes all his pasta by hand at this simple but intimate little restaurant. Highlights of the blackboard menu might include seafood linguine with mussels in the shell and beef ravioli in sage butter. Wonderful wines are available by the bottle and glass.

ⓘ Information

The **tourist office** (☑ 066-976 1451; www. reeksdistrict.com; Library Pl; ⊗ 9am-1pm & 1.30-5pm Mon-Fri) sells maps, walking guides, fishing permits and souvenirs.

Caherdaniel

POP 76

The road between Waterville and Caherdaniel climbs high over the ridge of Beenarourke, providing grandstand views of some of the finest scenery on the Ring of Kerry. The panorama extends from the scattered islands of Scarriff and Deenish to Dursey and the hills of the Beara Peninsula.

Caherdaniel, a tiny hamlet hidden among the trees at the head of Derrynane Bay, is the ancestral home of Daniel O'Connell, 'the Liberator', whose family made money smuggling from their base by the dunes. The area has a Blue Flag beach, good hikes and activities including horse riding and water sports. Lines of wind-gnarled trees add to the wild air.

⦿ Sights & Activities

★ **Derrynane National Historic Park**   HISTORIC SITE

(☑ 066-947 5113; www.derrynanehouse.ie; Derrynane; adult/child €5/3; ⊗ 10.30am-6pm mid-Mar–Sep, 10am-5pm Oct, to 4pm Sat & Sun Nov–early-Dec; ℗) Derrynane House was the home of Maurice 'Hunting Cap' O'Connell, a notorious local smuggler who grew rich on trade with France and Spain. He was the uncle of Daniel O'Connell, the 19th-century campaigner for Catholic emancipation, who

grew up here in his uncle's care and inherited the property in 1825, when it became his private retreat. The house is furnished with O'Connell memorabilia, including the impressive triumphal chariot in which he lapped Dublin after his release from prison.

Derrynane Beach   BEACH

Derrynane's Blue Flag beach is one of the most beautiful in Kerry, with scalloped coves of golden sand set between grassy dunes and whaleback outcrops of wave-smoothed rock. From the car park at Derrynane House, you can walk 1km along the beach to explore **Abbey Island** and its picturesque cemetery – look inside the ruined chapel to find the tomb of Daniel O'Connell's wife, Mary.

Atlantic Irish Seaweed   FOOD & DRINK

(☑ 086 106 2110; www.atlanticirishseaweed.com; per person €60) A three-hour 'seaweed discovery workshop' involves a guided walk along the Derrynane foreshore at low tide, foraging for edible seaweed (instruction on identification and sustainable harvesting is provided), followed by a lunch (tasting session) of seaweed-based dishes and drinks. Workshops are tide and weather dependent, and booking is essential.

Derrynane Sea Sports   WATER SPORTS

(☑ 087 908 1208; www.derrynaneseasports.com; Derrynane Beach) Derrynane Sea Sports offers sailing, windsurfing and water-skiing lessons for all levels (from €40 per person). Equipment hire spans stand-up paddleboards, surfboards, windsurfers (€10 to €20 per hour), canoes, small sailboats (€25 to €40) and snorkelling gear. Snorkelling tours (€40 per person) last two hours. In July and August ask about fun half-day pirate camps for children (€95).

🛏 Sleeping & Eating

Wave Crest   CAMPGROUND €

(☑ 066-947 5188; www.wavecrestcamping.com; hiker €10, vehicle & 2 adults €29; ℗ @ 🛜) Just 1.6km southeast of Caherdaniel, this year-round campground has a superb setting right on the rocky waterfront with front-row sunset views. From June to August, there's an on-site cafe and an attached shop selling fishing supplies, beach equipment, basic food supplies and wine. Book ahead during high season.

Travellers' Rest Hostel   HOSTEL €
(☑ 066-947 5175; www.hostelcaherdaniel.com; dm/d from €18.50/43; ☺ Mar–early-Nov) All low ceilings, gingham curtains and dried flowers in the grate, Travellers' Rest has the quaint feel of a country cottage, with an open fire and a self-catering kitchen (breakfast isn't included; bring supplies as there are no supermarkets nearby). Shower early: there are just two shared bathrooms. Call at the petrol station opposite if there's nobody about.

Olde Forge   B&B €€
(☑ 066-947 5140; www.theoldeforge.com; s/d/f from €60/80/120; P ﹫) Fantastic views of Kenmare Bay and the Beara Peninsula unfold from this ivy-covered B&B, both from the garden terrace out front and from most of the spacious and comfortable bedrooms. Family rooms sleep two adults and one or two children. It's 1.2km southeast of Caherdaniel on the N70.

Blind Piper   PUB FOOD €€
(☑ 066-947 5126; www.blindpiperpub.ie; mains €13-24; ☺ kitchen noon-7pm Mon-Thu, to 8pm Fri-Sun, bar to midnight daily; ﹅) This local institution is a great family pub with a lovely beer garden set beside the tiny Coomnahorna River, serving quality pub fare like deep-fried monkfish and rib-eye steak. On Thursday evenings from 9.30pm and most weekends from June to August, locals and visitors crowd inside, and music sessions strike up.

Kenmare

POP 2376

Kenmare (pronounced 'ken-*mair*') is the thinking person's Killarney. Ideally positioned for exploring the Ring of Kerry (and the Beara Peninsula), but without the coach-tour crowds of its more famous neighbour,

Kenmare (or Neidín, meaning 'little nest' in Irish) is a pretty spot with a neat triangle of streets lined with craft shops, galleries, cafes and good-quality restaurants.

One of the few planned towns in Ireland, Kenmare was laid out on an X-shaped street plan in the late 18th century by the Marquis of Lansdowne as the showpiece of his Kerry estates. It earned its living as a market town and fishing port, and from ironworks, lead mining and quarrying. The Market House and the Lansdowne Arms Hotel still survive from this period – pick up a copy of the *Kenmare Heritage Trail* from the tourist office (p90) to discover more.

◉ Sights & Activities

Kenmare Heritage Centre   MUSEUM
See p21.

Holy Cross Church   CHURCH
(Old Killarney Rd; ☺ 8am-8pm Easter–mid-Oct, shorter hours mid-Oct–Easter) Begun in 1862 and consecrated in 1864, this church has a splendid wooden roof with 14 angel carvings. Intricate **mosaics** adorn the aisle arches and the edges of the stained-glass window over the altar. The architect was Charles Hansom, collaborator and brother-in-law of Augustus Pugin (the architect behind London's Houses of Parliament).

Dromquinna Stables   HORSE RIDING
(☑ 064-664 1043; www.dromquinna-stables.com; Sneem Rd; treks per hr €30; ☺ mid-Mar–mid-Oct) One-hour, 90-minute and two-hour treks follow trails up into the hills and along Kenmare Bay's beaches with views over the Beara and Iveragh Peninsulas from this stable, which has been in the same family for generations. The stables are 4.5km west of Kenmare on the N70.

SKELLIG ISLANDS

The twin wave-battered pinnacles of the Skellig Islands (Oileáin na Scealaga) are the site of Ireland's most remote and spectacular ancient monastery. The 12km sea crossing can be rough, and the climb up to the monastery is steep and tiring. Due to the sheer (and often slippery) terrain and sudden wind gusts, it's not suitable for young children or people with limited mobility. Bring something to eat and drink, and wear sturdy shoes with good grip and weatherproof clothing.

The jagged, 217m-high rock of **Skellig Michael** (www.heritageireland.ie; ⊙ mid-May–Sep) FREE (Michael's Rock; like St Michael's Mount in Cornwall and Mont St Michel in Normandy) is the larger of the two Skellig Islands and a Unesco World Heritage site. Early Christian monks established a community and survived here from the 6th until the 12th or 13th century. The monastic buildings perch on a saddle in the rock, some 150m above sea level, reached by 618 steep steps cut into the rock face.

The astounding 6th-century oratories and beehive cells vary in size; the largest cell has a floor space of 4.5m by 3.6m. You can see the monks' south-facing vegetable garden and their cistern for collecting rainwater. The most impressive structural achievements are the settlement's foundations – platforms built on the steep slope using nothing more than earth and drystone walls.

Influenced by the Coptic Church (founded by St Anthony in the deserts of Egypt and Libya), the monks' determined quest for ultimate solitude led them to this remote, wind-blown edge of Europe. Not much is known about the life of the monastery, but there are records of Viking raids in AD 812 and 823. Monks were kidnapped or killed, but the community recovered and carried on. In the 11th century a rectangular oratory was added to the site, but although it was expanded in the 12th century, the monks abandoned the rock around this time.

After the introduction of the Gregorian calendar in 1582, Skellig Michael became a popular spot for weddings. Marriages were forbidden during Lent, but since Skellig used the old Julian calendar, a trip to the islands allowed those unable to wait for Easter to tie the knot. In the 1820s two lighthouses were built on the island, together with the road that runs around the base.

Skellig Michael famously featured as Luke Skywalker's Jedi temple in *Star Wars: The Force Awakens* (2015) and *Star Wars: The Last Jedi* (2017), attracting a whole new audience to the island's dramatic beauty.

Star Outdoors WATER SPORTS
See p21.

🛏 Sleeping

Kenmare Fáilte Hostel HOSTEL €
(☑ 087 711 6092; www.kenmarehostel.com; Shelbourne St; dm/s/d from €21/48/56; ⊙ May-Oct; 🛜) Perfectly located in a Georgian townhouse, this hostel is fitted out with quality furnishings and equipment – there's even an Aga cooker in the kitchen – a pleasant change from the utilitarianism of most budget accommodation. Wi-fi is available in common areas only, however, and there's a 1.30am curfew.

★ **Dromquinna Manor** TENTED CAMP €€
(☑ 064-664 2888; www.dromquinnamanor.com; Sneem Rd; d/f €160/190; ⊙ May-Aug; 🅿) This country estate on the shores of Kenmare River, 4.5km west of Kenmare, has 14 sturdy safari-style tents, luxuriously outfitted with plush double beds and antique furniture (but shared showers and toilets), on a gorgeous landscaped site sloping down to the sea. A picnic-hamper breakfast is delivered each morning. There are also converted Victorian potting sheds (from €190) to rent.

★ **Brook Lane Hotel** BOUTIQUE HOTEL €€
(☑ 064-664 2077; www.brooklanehotel.com; Sneem Rd; s/d/f from €125/165/200; 🅿🛜) Chic rooms

There are no toilets on the island.

Small Skellig is long, low and craggy: from a distance it looks as if it's shrouded in a swirling snowstorm. Close up you realise you're looking at a colony of over 23,000 pairs of breeding gannets, the second-largest breeding colony in the world. Most boats circle the island so you can see the gannets and you may see basking seals as well. Small Skellig is a bird sanctuary; no landing is permitted.

Getting to Skellig Michael

Boat trips to the Skelligs usually run from mid-May to September (dates are announced each year by Heritage Ireland), weather permitting (there are no sailings on two days out of seven, on average). You can depart from Portmagee, Ballinskelligs or Caherdaniel. There is a limit on the number of daily visitors, with boats licensed to carry no more than 12 passengers each, so it's wise to book ahead; it costs around €100 per person. Check to make sure operators have a current licence; the OPW (Office of Public Works; www.opw.ie) can provide advice.

Morning departure times depend on tide and weather, and last around five hours in total with two hours on the rock, which is the bare minimum to visit the monastery, look at the birds and have a picnic. The crossing takes about 1½ hours from Portmagee, 35 minutes to one hour from Ballinskelligs and 1¾ hours from Caherdaniel.

If you just want to see the islands up close and avoid actually having to clamber out of the boat, consider a 'no landing' cruise with operators such as **Skellig Experience** (☑066-947 6306; www.skelligexperience.com; adult/child €5/3, incl cruise €35/20; ☺10am-7pm Jul & Aug, to 6pm May, Jun & Sep, to 4.30pm Fri-Wed Mar, Apr, Oct & Nov; ℗) on Valentia Island.

The Skellig Experience heritage centre, local pubs and B&Bs will point you in the direction of boat operators, including the following:

Force Awakens (p87) Star Wars–themed tours; based in Ballinskelligs.

Sea Quest (☑087 236 2344; www.skelligsrock.com; per person €100; ☺mid-May–Sep) Based in Portmagee; also runs a nonlanding wildlife-watching eco-cruise.

Skellig Tours (☑087 689 8431; www.skelligtours.com; Bunavalla Pier, Bealtra; Skellig tour €100; ☺10am mid-May–Sep) Based at Bunavalla Pier, near Caherdaniel.

warmed by underfloor heating are individually decorated with bespoke furniture and luxurious fabrics at this contemporary olive-green property on the northwestern edge of town. Public areas mix vintage and designer pieces. Run by the same owners as Kenmare's superb restaurant No 35, its adjoining stone-and-brick gastropub, Casey's, is first-rate. It's a 750m stroll from the centre.

Hawthorn House B&B **€€**
(☑064-664 1035; www.hawthornhousekenmare. com; Shelbourne St; s/d/f from €60/120/150; ℗ ⊛) This stylish house has eight spacious pine-furnished rooms, all named after local towns and decked out with fresh flowers. It's set back from busy Shelbourne St behind a low wall.

Park Hotel HERITAGE HOTEL **€€€**
(☑064-664 1200; www.parkkenmare.com; Shelbourne St; d/ste from €440/740; ℗ ⊛ ⊞) Overlooking Kenmare Bay, this 1897 Victorian mansion has every conceivable luxury: an indoor swimming pool, heavenly spa, tennis and croquet courts and even its own cinema. Antiques and original art fill its 46 rooms and suites, which have goose-down duvets and pillows. Those in the deluxe category face the water, while superior rooms and suites have balconies and patios.

✕ Eating & Drinking

Jam CAFE **€**
(☑064-664 1591; www.jam.ie; 6 Henry St; mains €7-12; ☺8am-5pm Mon-Sat) Cheerful and bustling Jam makes a great breakfast venue, with a menu that includes granola with

fruit, pancakes with bacon and maple syrup, and scrambled eggs on toast, along with an excellent flat white. There are good cakes and pastries, and a range of hot lunch dishes such as Irish stew, shepherd's pie and lasagne.

★ Boathouse
Bistro   BISTRO €€

(☑ 064-664 2889; www.dromquinnamanor.com; Dromquinna Manor, Sneem Rd; mains €15-28; ⊙ 12.30-9pm daily mid-Mar–Sep, Fri-Sun only Oct–mid-Mar; 🅿) 🥾 At the water's edge, this blue-and-white 1870s boathouse 4.5km west of Kenmare has been stunningly converted to a beach-house-style bistro specialising in local seafood delivered daily to its own wharf. Expertly cooked dishes (Kenmare Bay crab claws in chilli and garlic butter, beer-battered fish and chips) are accompanied by a great selection of by-the-glass wines and craft gins.

★ Tom Crean
Fish & Wine   IRISH €€

(☑ 064-664 1589; www.tomcrean.ie; Main St; mains €17-31; ⊙ 5-9.30pm Thu-Mon Sep-Jun, daily Jul & Aug; 🗟) 🥾 Named for Kerry's pioneering Antarctic explorer, and run by his granddaughter, this venerable restaurant uses only the best of local organic produce, cheeses and fresh seafood. Sneem lobster is available in season, the oysters *au naturel* capture the scent of the sea, and the seafood gratin served in a scallop shell is divine.

Mews
                                         IRISH €€€

(☑ 064-664 2829; www.themewskenmare.com; 3-4 Henry Ct; mains €20-33; ⊙ 6-9pm Tue-Sun) Two of Kerry's top restaurateurs helm this stylish, palm-filled spot hidden in a laneway off Henry St. Vermouth-cream chowder with citrus oil, Kerry beef fillet with a parsnip rösti and clove-poached pear with homemade peanut-brittle ice cream are among the menu highlights. There's a three-course early-bird menu (€34, before 7pm).

Puccini's
Coffee & Books   CAFE

(29 Henry St; ⊙ 8.30am-4pm Mon-Fri, from 9.15am Sat, closed 12.30-1pm daily; 🗟) Puccini's is a tiny coffee bar and bookshop with just a handful of stools at the window counters, but it's the social hub of Kenmare on weekday mornings as folk drop in for an expertly prepared espresso before work.

🛍 Shopping

Soundz of Muzic   MUSICAL INSTRUMENTS
(www.soundzofmuzic.ie; 9 Henry St; ⊙ 11am-5.30pm Mon-Sat, to 4pm Sun) Traditional instruments (accordions, harmonicas, banjos, tin whistles and more) are stocked alongside modern ones (including electric fiddles) at this decades-old shop. It also sells sheet music, CDs and vinyl, and DVDs of live performances.

Kenmare Bookshop   BOOKS
(www.facebook.com/kenmarebookshop; Shelbourne St; ⊙ 10am-5.30pm) Irish history and literature, bestsellers and kids' books are stocked at this independent shop, as well as a good selection of maps and local walking guides.

ℹ Information

Kenmare's seasonal **tourist office** (☑ 1850 230 330; The Square; ⊙ 9.30am-12.30pm & 1.30-5.30pm Mon-Wed, Fri & Sat Mar-Oct) has stacks of information about the town, its surrounds and the Ring of Kerry. Pick up free maps detailing a heritage trail around town and longer walks.

DINGLE PENINSULA

One of the highlights of the Wild Atlantic Way, the Dingle Peninsula (Corca Dhuibhne) culminates in the Irish mainland's westernmost point. In the shadow of sacred Mt Brandon, a maze of fuchsia-fringed *boreens* (country lanes) weaves together an ancient landscape of prehistoric ring forts and beehive huts, early Christian chapels, crosses and holy wells, picturesque hamlets and abandoned villages.

But it's where the land meets the ocean – whether in a welter of surf-pounded rocks, or where the waves lap secluded, sandy coves – that Dingle's beauty truly reveals itself.

Centred on charming Dingle town, the peninsula has long been a beacon for those of an alternative bent, attracting artists, craftspeople, musicians and idiosyncratic characters who can be found in workshops, museums, festivals and unforgettable trad sessions throughout Dingle's tiny settlements.

👉 Tours

Killarney-based tour operators including **Corcoran's** (Map p80; ☑ 064-663 6666; www.corcorantours.com; 8 College St; ⊙ Mar-Oct),

Dingle town Murphy's (p93)

Deros Tours (Map p80; ☑ 064-663 1251; www.derostours.com; 22 Main St; ☉ Mar-Oct) and **Wild Kerry Day Tours** (Map p80; ☑ 064-663 1052; www.wildkerry-daytours.ie; Ross Rd) offer day trips to the Dingle Peninsula. Walking and cycling tours are possible with **Go Visit Ireland** (☑ 066-976 2094; www.govisit ireland.com).

Dingle Town

POP 1440

In summer, Quaint Dingle town's hilly streets can be clogged with visitors; in other seasons its authentic charms are yours for the savouring.

Although Dingle is one of Ireland's largest Gaeltacht towns, the locals have voted to retain the name Dingle rather than go by the officially sanctioned – and signposted – Gaelige name of An Daingean.

 ## Sights

**Dingle
Distillery**   DISTILLERY

(☑ 066-402 9011; www.dingledistillery.ie; Ventry Rd; tour €15; ☉ tours noon-4pm Mar-Sep, from 2pm Oct-Feb) An offshoot of Dublin's Porterhouse microbrewery, this small-scale craft distillery went into operation in 2012, and began bottling its distinctive single malt whiskey in 2016. It also produces award-winning artisan gin and vodka.

An Díseart   CULTURAL CENTRE

(Map p92; ☑ 066-915 2476; www.diseart.ie; Green St; ☉ 9am-5pm Mon-Sat) **FREE** Set in a neo-Gothic former convent, this Celtic cultural centre has impressive stained-glass windows by Dublin artist Harry Clarke (1889–1931) depicting 12 scenes from the life of Christ (audioguide available).

 ## Activities

Dingle Traditional Rowing   BOATING

(Naomhòg Experience; Map p92; ☑ 087 699 2925; www.dinglerowing.com; Dingle Marina; lessons €25) *Naomhòg* is the Kerry name for a *currach*, a traditional Irish boat made from a wooden frame covered with tarred canvas (originally animal hides). They were used by the Blasket islanders for fishing, and are now maintained and raced by local enthusiasts. You can book a one-hour session in Dingle Harbour (minimum two people) to learn how to row one.

Dingle Boat Tours   CRUISE

(Map p92; ☑ 066-915 1344, 087 672 6100; www.dingleboattours.com; Dingle Marina; ferry adult/child return €50/25, ecotour €60/30; ☉ Apr-Sep) Dingle Marine & Leisure operates a 50-minute passenger ferry from Dingle Marina to **Great Blasket Island**, and a 4½-hour ecotour with a one-hour stop on the island. En route look out for seals, dolphins, gannets, puffins, whales and, if you're lucky, basking sharks.

Dingle Town

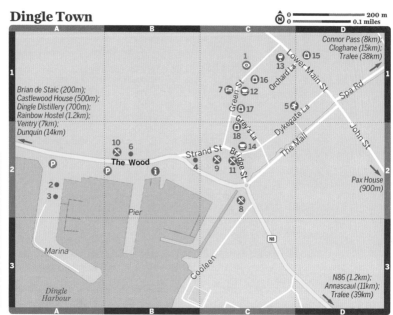

Dingle Town

◉ Sights
1 An Díseart	C1

✪ Activities, Courses & Tours
2 Dingle Boat Tours	A2
3 Dingle Traditional Rowing	A2
4 Mountain Man Outdoor Shop	B2
5 Paddy's Bike Shop	C1
6 Wild SUP Tours	B2

⊜ Sleeping
7 An Capall Dubh	C1

✪ Eating
8 Chart House	C2
9 Murphy's	C2
10 Out of the Blue	B2
11 Reel Dingle Fish Co.	C2

⊙ Drinking & Nightlife
12 Bean in Dingle	C1
Dick Mack's	(see 12)
13 Foxy John's	C1
14 My Boy Blue	C2

✪ Entertainment
Blue Zone	(see 16)

⊜ Shopping
15 Dingle Candle	D1
16 Dingle Record Shop	C1
17 Lisbeth Mulcahy	C1
18 Little Cheese Shop	C2

Wild SUP Tours WATER SPORTS
(Map p92; ☑ 083 476 6428; www.wildsuptours.com; Strand St; half-/full-day tour €49/115; ⊙ Apr-Oct) This outfit offers stand-up paddleboard adventures around the Dingle coastline. All equipment is provided and the full-day tours include a picnic lunch.

Mountain Man Outdoor Shop CYCLING
(Map p92; ☑ 087 297 6569; www.themountainmanshop.com; Strand St; bike rental per hour/day €4/15) Mountain Man rents bikes and runs guided cycling tours (from €30) around the Dingle Peninsula, with themes ranging from archaeology to food.

⭐ Festivals & Events

Dingle Regatta SPORTS
(www.facebook.com/dingleregatta2016; ⊙ mid-Aug) Crews of four race traditional Irish *naomhóg* around the harbour. It's Kerry's

largest event of its kind and inspired the trad song of the same name.

Dingle Races
SPORTS

(www.dingleraces.ie; N86, Ballintaggart; ⊙ mid-Aug) Held over the second weekend in August, Dingle's horse-racing meet brings crowds from far and wide. The racetrack is at Ballintaggart, 2km southeast of the centre.

Dingle Food
& Wine Festival
FOOD & DRINK

(www.dinglefood.com; ⊙ early Oct) Held over four days, this fabulous foodie fest features a 'taste trail' with sampling at over 70 locations around town, plus a market, cooking demonstrations, workshops and a foraging walk. There are also beer, cider, whiskey and wine tastings, a bake-off competition and street entertainment, as well as children's events.

🛏 Sleeping

This tourist town has hostels, hotels and loads of midrange B&Bs. A number of pubs also offer accommodation.

Rainbow Hostel
HOSTEL €

(☑ 066-915 1044; www.rainbowhosteldingle.com; Milltown; dm/d/tr from €17/44/66, camping per person €10; 🅿@🛜♨) This brightly refurbished bungalow, set in large gardens 1.5km northwest of town on the road towards Brandon Creek, offers basic but comfortable accommodation in doubles, twins, triples and dorms (12-bed mixed and six-bed female-only), and is the nearest place to town where you can pitch a tent (a 20- to 30-minute walk).

★ Castlewood
House
BOUTIQUE HOTEL €€

(☑ 066-915 2788; www.castlewooddingle.com; The Wood; s/d/f €130/150/198; 🅿🛜) Book well ahead to secure a berth at Dingle's top hotel, a haven of country-house quiet and sophistication, yet less than 10 minutes' stroll from the town centre. Decor is stylish but understated; the luxury bedrooms have sea views and marble bathrooms with spa baths, while art and antiques adorn the public areas. Breakfast is a thing of beauty.

An Capall Dubh
B&B €€

(Map p92; ☑ 066-915 1105; www.ancapalldubh. com; Green St; d/tw/f €130/130/180; 🅿🛜) Entered via a 19th-century coaching gateway leading into a cobbled courtyard where

breakfast is served in fine weather, this airy B&B has five simple rooms furnished with light timbers and checked fabrics.

★ Pax House
B&B €€€

(☑ 066-915 1518; www.pax-house.com; Upper John St; d €130-230; ⊙ Mar-Dec; 🅿🛜) From its highly individual decor (including contemporary paintings) to the outstanding views over the estuary from the glass-framed terrace and balconies opening from some rooms, Pax House is a treat. Breakfast incorporates produce grown in its own garden; families can be accommodated with fold-out beds. It's 1km southeast of the town centre.

🍴 Eating

★ Reel Dingle Fish Co
FISH & CHIPS €

(Map p92; ☑ 066-915 1713; Bridge St; mains €5-15; ⊙ 1-10pm) 🍴 Locals queue along the street to get hold of the freshly cooked local haddock (or cod, or monkfish, or hake, or mackerel...) and chips at this tiny outlet. Reckoned to be one of the best chippies in Kerry, if not in Ireland.

Murphy's
ICE CREAM €

(Map p92; www.murphysicecream.ie; Strand St; 1/2/3 scoops €4.50/6.50/8.50; ⊙ 11.30am-10pm May-Oct, to 8pm Nov-Apr; 🛜) Made here in Dingle, Murphy's sublime ice cream comes in a daily changing range of flavours that include brown bread, sea salt, Dingle gin and whiskey-laced Irish coffee, along with sorbets made with rainwater. In addition to a second Dingle branch at the pier opposite the tourist office (p94), its runaway success has seen it expand Ireland-wide.

★ Out of the Blue
SEAFOOD €€€

(Map p92; ☑ 066-915 0811; www.outoftheblue.ie; The Wood; mains €19-39; ⊙ 5-9.30pm Mon-Sat, 12.30-3pm & 5-9.30pm Sun) 🍴 Occupying a bright blue-and-yellow waterfront fishing shack, this rustic spot is one of Dingle's top restaurants, with an intense devotion to fresh local seafood (and only seafood). If staff don't like the catch, they don't open, and they resolutely don't serve chips. Highlights might include Dingle Bay prawn bisque with lobster or chargrilled whole sea bass flambéed in cognac.

Chart House
IRISH €€€

(Map p92; ☑ 066-915 2255; www.thechart housedingle.com; The Mall; mains €22-32; ⊙ 6-10pm Jun-Sep, hours vary Oct-Dec & mid-Feb–May)

Window boxes frame this free-standing stone cottage, while inside dark-red walls, polished floorboards and flickering candles create an intimate atmosphere. Creative cooking uses Irish produce: Cromane mussels and Dingle Bay prawns, Annascaul black pudding and Brandon Bay crab, fillet of Kerry beef and Cashel Blue cheese. Book up to several weeks ahead at busy times.

Drinking & Entertainment

★ Dick Mack's · PUB
(Map p92; www.dickmackspub.com; Green St; ⊙11am-11.30pm Mon-Thu, to 12.30am Fri & Sat, noon-11pm Sun) Stars in the pavement bear the names of Dick Mack's celebrity customers. Ancient wood and snugs dominate the interior, while the courtyard out back hosts a warren of tables, chairs and characters, plus artisan food trucks in summer. In 2017 the adjacent 19th-century brewhouse was restored and now creates the pub's very own craft beers.

Bean in Dingle · COFFEE
(Map p92; www.beanindingle.com; Green St; ⊙8am-5pm Mon-Sat, 10am-3pm Sun; 🛜) Coffee specialist Bean in Dingle roasts its own Brazilian, Ethiopian and Guatemalan blend of beans. There's a communal table and a handful of seats; arrive early before it sells out of its sweet and savoury pastries – flaky sausage rolls, sugar-dusted cinnamon scrolls and a daily vegan special such as raw chocolate and caramel slice.

My Boy Blue · COFFEE
(Map p92; www.facebook.com/myboybluedingle; Holyground; ⊙8.30am-5pm Mon, Tue & Thu-Sat, 10am-4pm Sun; 🛜) This bright and artsy corner spot is the place to head for some of Dingle's best coffee, supplied by the 3FE roastery in Dublin. Good choice of cakes and snacks too.

Blue Zone · JAZZ
(Map p92; www.facebook.com/bluezonedingle; Green St; ⊙5.30-10.30pm Thu-Tue) Upstairs from Dingle Record Shop, this great late-night hangout is part jazz venue, part pizza restaurant and part wine bar, with moody blue and red surrounds.

Shopping

Little Cheese Shop · FOOD
(Map p92; www.facebook.com/thelittlecheeseshop; Grey's Lane; ⊙11am-6pm Mon-Fri, to 5pm Sat) Swiss-trained cheesemaker Maja Binder's tiny shop overflows with aromatic cheeses from all over Ireland, including her own range of Dingle Peninsula Cheeses.

Brian de Staic · JEWELLERY
(www.briandestaic.com; The Wood; ⊙9.30am-5.30pm Mon-Sat) This renowned local designer's exquisite modern Celtic work includes symbols such as the Hill of Tara, crosses and standing stones, as well as jewellery inscribed with Ogham script. All of de Staic's jewellery is individually handcrafted.

Dingle Candle · ARTS & CRAFTS
(Map p92; www.dinglecandle.com; Main St; ⊙10am-5.30pm Mon-Sat May-Sep, shorter hours Oct-Apr) Hand-poured, long-burning candles made in Dingle come in 12 different scents inspired by the peninsula, including fuchsia, honeysuckle, smoky turf fire, Atlantic salt and sage, and peated whiskey. Browse for body scrubs, shower mousses, bath salts and perfumes, which are also handmade here.

Dingle Record Shop · MUSIC
(Map p92; www.dinglerecordshop.com; Green St; ⊙11am-5pm Mon-Sat) Tucked off Green St, this jammed music hub has all the good stuff you can't download yet. Live bands play every couple of weeks; podcasts recorded in-store are available online. Hours can be erratic.

Lisbeth Mulcahy · HOMEWARES
(Map p92; www.lisbethmulcahy.com; Green St; ⊙9.30am-7pm Mon-Sat, noon-4pm Sun Jun-Sep, 10am-5pm Mon-Sat Oct-May) Beautiful wall hangings, rugs and scarves are created on a 150-year-old loom by this long-established designer. Also sold here are ceramics by her husband, who has a workshop at **Louis Mulcahy Pottery** (☎066-915 6229; www.louismulcahy.com; Clogher, Ballyferriter; ⊙9am-5.30pm Mon-Fri, from 10am Sat & Sun year-round, longer hours Easter-Oct), 17km west of Dingle on Slea Head.

❶ Information

Busy but helpful, Dingle's **tourist office** (Map p92; ☑1850 230 330; www.dingle-peninsula.ie; The Pier; ⊙9am-5pm Mon-Sat) has maps, guides and plenty of information on the entire peninsula.

❶ Getting Around

Dingle is easily covered on foot. Bike-hire places include **Foxy John's** (Map p92; Main St;

CONNOR PASS

Topping out at 456m, the R560 across the Connor (or Conor) Pass from Dingle town to Cloghane and Stradbally is Ireland's highest public road. On a foggy day you'll see nothing but the tarmac just in front of you, but in fine weather it offers phenomenal views of Dingle Harbour to the south and Mt Brandon to the north. The road is in good shape, despite being narrow in places and steep and twisting on the north side (large signs portend doom for buses and trucks; caravans are forbidden).

The summit car park yields views down to glacial lakes in the rock-strewn valley below, where you can see the remains of walls and huts where people once lived impossibly hard lives. From the smaller, lower car park on the north side, beside a waterfall, you can make a 10-minute climb to hidden Pedlar's Lake and the kind of vistas that inspire mountain climbers.

The pass is a classic challenge for cyclists; it's best to start in Dingle town, from where the road climbs 400m over a distance of 7km. The climb from the north is more brutal, and has the added problem of being single track at the final, steepest section, so you'll be holding up the traffic.

⊙10am-11pm; 🛜), **Paddy's Bike Shop** (Map p92; ☑066-915 2311; www.paddysbikeshop. com; Dykegate Lane; bike rental per day/week from €15/75; ⊙9am-7pm May-Sep, to 6pm Mar, Apr & Oct) and the Mountain Man Outdoor Shop (p92).

Parking is free throughout town, with metered parking at the harbour.

NORTHERN KERRY

Consisting mainly of farmland, Northern Kerry's landscapes can't compare to the spectacular Killarney region, the Ring of Kerry or the Dingle Peninsula. But there are some interesting places that merit a stop: Kerry's county town, Tralee, has a great museum.

Tralee

POP 23,691

Founded by the Normans in 1216, Tralee has a long history of rebellion. In the 16th century the last ruling earl of the Desmonds was captured and executed here. His head was sent to Elizabeth I, who spiked it on London Bridge. The Desmond castle once stood at the junction of Denny St and the Mall, but any trace of medieval Tralee that survived the Desmond Wars was razed during the Cromwellian period. Elegant Denny St and Day Pl are the oldest parts of town, with 18th-century Georgian buildings, while the Square is contemporary.

⊙ Sights

★**Banna Strand** BEACH
(Banna) A favourite weekend getaway for Tralee residents, Banna is one of the biggest and best Blue Flag beaches in Ireland, a 6km stretch of fine golden sand backed by 10m-high dunes, with fantastic views southwest to Mt Brandon and the Dingle hills. The beach is 13km northwest of Tralee, signposted off the R551 Ballyheigue road.

★**Tralee Bay
Wetlands Centre** NATURE RESERVE
See p48.

★**Kerry County
Museum** MUSEUM
See p48.

**Blennerville Windmill
& Visitor Centre** WINDMILL
See p48.

**Ardfert
Cathedral** CATHEDRAL
(☑066-713 4711; www.heritageireland.ie; adult/child €5/3; ⊙10am-6pm late Mar-Sep) The impressive remains of 13th-century Ardfert Cathedral are notable for the beautiful and delicate stone carvings on its Romanesque door and window arches. Set into one of the interior walls is an effigy, said to be of St Brendan the Navigator, who was educated in Ardfert and founded a monastery here. Other elaborate medieval grave slabs can be seen in the visitor centre. Ardfert

Tralee

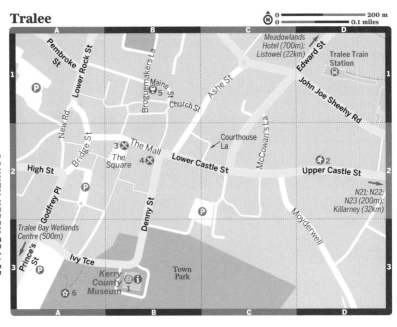

is 9km northwest of Tralee on the Bally-heigue road.

Festivals & Events

Rose of Tralee   CULTURAL
(www.roseoftralee.ie; ⊙ Aug) The hugely popular beauty pageant is open to Irish women
(and women of Irish descent) from around
the world (the eponymous 'roses'). More
than just a beauty contest, it's a five-day-
long festival bookended by a gala ball and a
'midnight madness' parade led by the newly
crowned Rose of Tralee, followed by a fireworks display.

Kerry Film Festival   FILM
(www.kerryfilmfestival.com; ⊙ Oct) The five-
day Kerry Film Festival includes a short
film competition and screenings at venues
around town.

Sleeping

★ **Meadowlands**
Hotel   HOTEL €€
(☑ 066-718 0444; www.meadowlandshotel.com;
Oakpark Rd; s/d/f from €95/125/178; P 🕈)
Strolling distance from town but far
enough away to be quiet, Meadowlands
is an unexpectedly romantic four-star hotel with stunning vintage-meets-design-
er public areas. Rooms have autumnal
hues and service is spot-on. Its beamed-
ceilinged bar (mains €13 to €29), serving
top-notch seafood (the owners have their
own fishing fleet), is at least as popular
with locals as it is with visitors.

Eating

Roast House   CAFE €
(Map p96; ☑ 066-718 1011; www.theroasthouse.
ie; 3 Denny St; mains €8-13; ⊙ 9am-5pm Mon-

Sat; 🛜 🍴) The name comes from its own custom-built coffee roaster, but Roast House is even better known for its food, which spans breakfasts of homemade buttermilk pancakes with bacon and maple syrup to lunch dishes like barbecue pulled-pork sandwiches, sloppy joes, and a curry-spiced mushroom and quinoa burger.

★ Quinlan's Fish   SEAFOOD €€
(Map p96; ☑ 066-712 3998; www.kerryfish.com; The Mall; mains €10-19; ⊙ noon-9pm Sun-Thu, to 10pm Fri & Sat) Quinlan's is Kerry's leading chain of fish shops. It has its own fleet so you know everything here is fresh. The fish and chips are great; alternatives include Dingle Bay squid and chips with sweet-chilli sauce. Lighter pan-fried options are available. The Delft-blue, scrubbed-timber and exposed-brick premises has a handful of wine-barrel tables, or head to Tralee's Town Park.

🍷 Drinking & Entertainment

★ Roundy's   BAR
(Map p96; 5 Broguemakers Lane; ⊙ 6pm-midnight Thu-Sun) Ingeniously converted from a terrace house (with a tree still growing right through the courtyard-garden-turned-interior), this hip little bar has cool tunes, regular DJs spinning old school funk and live bands.

Siamsa Tíre   THEATRE
(Map p96; ☑ 066-712 3055; www.siamsatire. com; Town Park; tickets €15-35; ⊙ booking office 10am-6pm Mon-Sat & preperformance) Siamsa Tíre, the National Folk Theatre of Ireland, re-creates dynamic aspects of Gaelic culture through song, dance, drama and mime. There are several shows a week year-round.

ℹ️ Information

University Hospital Kerry (p81) has an accident and emergency department.

The **tourist office** (Map p96; ☑ 066-712 1288; traleetio@failteireland.ie; Denny St; ⊙ 9am-5pm Mon-Sat) is in the same building as the Kerry County Museum (p95).

ℹ️ Getting Around

O'Halloran Cycles (Map p96; ☑ 066-712 2820; 83 Boherbee; bike rental per day from €15; ⊙ 9am-6pm Mon-Sat) hires out bikes.

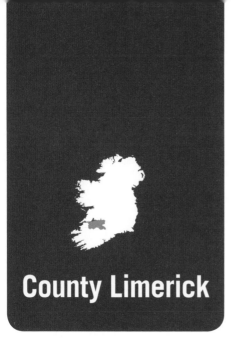

Limerick's low-lying farmland is framed on its southern and eastern boundaries by swelling uplands and mountains. Limerick city is boisterously urban in contrast and has enough historic and cultural attractions for a day's diversion.

County Limerick

Limerick straddles the tidal reaches of Ireland's longest river, the Shannon, where it swings west to join the Shannon Estuary. Following the city's tough past, as narrated in Frank McCourt's Angela's Ashes, its medieval and Georgian architecture received a glitzy makeover during the Celtic Tiger era, but the economic downturn hit hard.

Limerick City

POP 58,319

'There once was a city called Limerick...' Umm, no, can't think of anything that rhymes with Limerick. And no one is quite sure why those humorous five-line verses are named after this Irish city, though the term dates from the late 19th century.

Limerick straddles the tidal reaches of Ireland's longest river, the Shannon, where it swings west to join the Shannon Estuary. Following the city's tough past, as narrated in Frank McCourt's *Angela's Ashes,* its medieval and Georgian architecture received a glitzy makeover during the Celtic Tiger era, but the economic downturn hit hard.

The city is recovering rapidly, however. Limerick was chosen as the first-ever Irish City of Culture in 2014, and the subsequent

investment saw a rejuvenated waterfront complete with stylish boardwalk. There's a renovated castle, an art gallery and a developing foodie scene to complement its traditional pubs, plus locals who can't wait to welcome you.

History

Viking adventurers established a settlement on an island in the River Shannon in the 9th century. They fought with the native Irish for control of the site until Brian Ború's forces drove them out in 968 and established Limerick as the royal seat of the O'Brien kings. Brian Ború finally destroyed Viking power and presence in Ireland at the Battle of Clontarf in 1014. By the late 12th century, invading Normans had supplanted the Irish as the town's rulers. Throughout the Middle Ages the two groups remained divided.

From 1690 to 1691 Limerick acquired heroic status in the saga of Ireland's struggle against occupation by the English. After their defeat in the Battle of the Boyne in 1690, Jacobite forces withdrew west behind the famously strong walls of Limerick town until the Treaty of Limerick guaranteed religious freedom for Catholics. The English later reneged and enforced fierce anti-Catho-

Limerick city King John's Castle

lic legislation, an act of betrayal that came to symbolise the injustice of British rule, while Limerick gained the nickname 'Treaty City'.

During the 18th century the old walls of Limerick were demolished and a well-planned and prosperous Georgian town developed. Such prosperity had waned by the early 20th century, however, as traditional industries fell on hard times. Several high-profile nationalists hailed from here, including Eamon de Valera.

◉ Sights

Limerick's main places of interest cluster to the north on King's Island (the oldest part of Limerick and once part of Englishtown), to the south around the Crescent and Pery Sq (the city's noteworthy Georgian area), and all along the riverbanks.

If you have time, the best approach (on foot) from the city centre to King John's Castle is to cross Sarsfield Bridge and follow the riverside walk north to Thomond Bridge – there are great views across the river to the city and castle.

★ **King John's Castle**   CASTLE
(Map p102; ☑ 061-711 222; www.kingjohnscastle.com; Nicholas St; adult/child €13/9.50; ⊘ 9.30am-6pm Apr-Sep, to 5pm Oct-Mar) An obdurate and brooding Norman mass looming over the River Shannon, Limerick's showpiece castle, with its vast curtain walls and towers, was built on the orders of King John of England

between 1200 and 1212. The massive twin gate towers still stand to their full height. A multimedia experience that provides an excellent potted history of Ireland in general, and Limerick in particular, is followed by exposed archaeology in the undercroft and a tour of the courtyard and fortifications.

★ **Hunt Museum**   MUSEUM
(Map p102; www.huntmuseum.com; Custom House, Rutland St; adult/child €7.50/free, Sun free; ⊘ 10am-5pm Mon-Sat, from 2pm Sun; ⍾) Although named for its benefactors, this museum, opened in 1997, is also a treasure hunt. Visitors are encouraged to open drawers and poke around a fine collection of ancient and modern art treasures. Highlights include a Syracusan coin claimed to have been one of the 30 pieces of silver paid to Judas for his betrayal of Christ, a Renoir study, a Gauguin painting, a Giacometti drawing and works by Picasso and Jack B Yeats.

Limerick City
Gallery of Art   GALLERY
(Map p102; www.gallery.limerick.ie; Carnegie Bldg, Pery Sq; ⊘ 10am-5.30pm Mon-Wed, Fri & Sat, to 8pm Thu, noon-5.30pm Sun) **FREE** Limerick's art gallery adjoins the peaceful People's Park (p100) in the heart of Georgian Limerick. Among its permanent collection of paintings from the last 300 years are works by Sean Keating and Jack B Yeats.

Temporary exhibitions of conceptual and thought-provoking contemporary art fill the other well-lit galleries. The gallery is the home of **EVA International** (www.eva.ie; ☉ Sep-Nov), Ireland's contemporary art biennial held across the city in even-numbered years. Check the website for dates.

Frank McCourt Museum · MUSEUM
(Map p102; www.frankmccourtmuseum.com; Leamy House, Hartstonge St; adult/child €5/2.50; ☉ 11am-4.30pm Mon-Fri year-round, 2-4pm Sat & Sun Apr-Aug) This museum dedicated to Frank McCourt, author of *Angela's Ashes*, can be found in his former school building in Limerick's Georgian quarter. The museum contains a re-creation of a 1930s classroom and of the McCourt household, plus an assortment of memorabilia.

People's Park · PARK
(Map p102; www.limerick.ie; Pery Sq; ☉ 8am-dusk Sep-Apr, to 9pm May-Aug) This lovely wooded park in Pery Sq at the heart of Georgian Limerick is an excellent place for collapsing onto the grass with a chunky novel when the sun pops out. Check out the restored 19th-century red-and-white drinking fountain. The statue on the column in the middle of the park is of Thomas Spring Rice, a former MP for Limerick.

St Mary's Cathedral · CATHEDRAL
(Map p102; ☎ 061-310 293; www.saintmarys cathedral.ie; Bridge St; adult/child €5/free; ☉ 9am-5pm Mon-Thu, to 4pm Fri & Sat, from 1.30pm Sun)

Limerick's ancient cathedral was founded in 1168 by the king of Munster, Donal Mór O'Brien. Parts of the 12th-century Romanesque western doorway, nave and aisles survive, and there are splendid 15th-century black-oak misericords (for supporting 'clerical posteriors') in the Jebb Chapel, unique examples of their kind in Ireland and each fabulously carved with creatures and mythical animals. Check the website for upcoming musical events.

Thomond Park Stadium · STADIUM
(☎ 061-421 109; www.thomondpark.ie; Cratloe Rd; adult/child combined tour & museum €10/8; ☉ 9am-5pm Mon-Fri, also Sat & Sun for prebooked groups of 6 or more) From 1995 until 2007, the Munster province rugby team was undefeated in this legendary stadium; it was also the venue for their famous victories over New Zealand's All Blacks in 1978 and 2016. Tours of the hallowed ground include the dressing rooms, dugouts and pitch, and its memorabilia-filled museum. It's an easy 1km walk northwest of the centre along High St.

🏃 Activities

★ Limerick City

Kayaking Tours · KAYAKING
(Map p102; ☎ 086 330 8236; www.limerickad ventures.com; Rutland St; short/long tour €25/35; ☉ Sat & Sun) Departing from behind the Hunt Museum (p99), these 1½- or 2½-hour kayak tours take you along the River Shannon and beneath the walls of King John's Castle

---

FRANK MCCOURT
....

Since the 1990s, no name has been so closely intertwined with Limerick as Frank McCourt (1930–2009). His poignant autobiographical novel *Angela's Ashes* was a surprise publishing sensation in 1996, bringing him fame and honours (including the Pulitzer Prize).

Although he was born in New York City, McCourt's immigrant family returned to Limerick four years later, unable to survive in America. His childhood was filled with the kinds of deprivations that were all too common at the time: his father was a drunk who later vanished, three of his six siblings died in childhood, and at age 13 he dropped out of school to earn money to help his family survive.

At age 19, McCourt returned to New York and later worked for three decades as a high-school teacher. Among the subjects he taught was writing. From the 1970s he dabbled in writing and theatre with his brother Malachy. He started *Angela's Ashes* only after retiring from teaching in 1987. Its early success was thanks to a bevy of enthusiastic critics, but in Limerick the reaction was mixed, with many decrying the negative portrait it painted of the city.

Today McCourt's legacy in Limerick is celebrated. Limerick city's tourist office (p104) has information about city sights related to the book, you can join Angela's Ashes walking tours, visit the Frank McCourt Museum and drink in South's (p104), one of the watering holes mentioned in the book.

(p99), offering an entirely new perspective on the city. Book in advance; no previous experience needed. Tour times depend on the tide and weather.

Limerick Walking Tours
WALKING

(Map p102; ☎ 061-312 833; www.huntmuseum.com/limerick-walking-tours; per person €10) Highly popular and entertaining guided walks around town with knowledgeable Declan, who moonlights at the Hunt Museum (p99). Tours start and finish outside Brown Thomas on Patrick St, near the intersection with Sarsfield St. Book by phone or email.

Angela's Ashes
Walking Tour
WALKING

(Map p102; ☎ 083 300 0111; www.limerick.ie; per person €10) Noel Curtin runs entertaining and informative walking tours of the city covering locations featured in *Angela's Ashes,* departing from the Frank McCourt Museum at 2.30pm. Book a tour at the tourist office (p104).

Riverbank Walkway
WALKING

Opened in 2016, this 3km all-abilities walkway links the city centre to the University of Limerick campus, following a picturesque route along a former canal and later the south bank of the River Shannon. It begins from Lock Quay, just east of Abbey Bridge.

🛏 Sleeping

The city has a decent range of quality, midrange accommodation – aim to stay near the city centre, for the convenience and the nightlife.

Alexandra Tce on O'Connell Ave (which runs south from O'Connell St) has several midrange B&Bs. Ennis Rd, leading northwest towards Shannon, also has a selection, although most are at least 1km from the centre.

★ No 1 Pery Square
HOTEL €€

(Map p102; ☎ 061-402 402; www.onepery square.com; 1 Pery Sq; club/period r from €145/195; P 🐾) Treat yourself to a night in Georgian Limerick at this elegant hotel right on the corner of Pery Sq. Choose between very well-presented club rooms (each named after an Irish poet) in the modern extension and one of the four period rooms in the classic Georgian townhouse, each a feast of huge sash windows, high ceilings and capacious bathrooms.

TRACING YOUR ANCESTORS

Genealogical centres in County Limerick (and in neighbouring Tipperary) can help trace your ancestors; contact the centres in advance to arrange a consultation.

Limerick Genealogy (☎ 061-496 542; www.limerickgenealogy.com; Dooradoyle Rd, Lissanalta House, Dooradoyle) Professional genealogical research service.

Tipperary Family History Research (☎ 062-80555; www.tfhr.org; Mitchell St, Excel Heritage Centre, Tipperary town) Family research in Tipperary.

Tipperary South Genealogy Centre (☎ 062-61122; www.tipperarysouth. rootsireland.ie; Brú Ború Heritage Centre, Cashel) Comprehensive family-history research service.

George Boutique Hotel
HOTEL €€

(Map p102; ☎ 061-460 400; www.georgelim erick.com; Shannon St; s/d/tr/f from €129/139/164/179; P 🐾) 'Boutique' might be overstating things a bit, but the rooms at this brisk, buzzing and centrally located hotel – with a decor of blond wood, caramels and browns, and the occasional splash of designer colour – are stylish and comfortable. It's frequently booked solid, so reserve well in advance.

Savoy
HOTEL €€

(Map p102; ☎ 061-448 700; www.savoylimer ick.com; Henry St; r from €175; P @ 🐾 ☸) This five-star hotel is beginning to show its age and feels more like four-star, but it's smart enough, with comfy king-size beds and a turn-down service, a spa that specialises in Thai massages, a small swimming pool and a couple of top-notch in-house restaurants.

Absolute Hotel
HOTEL €€

(☎ 061-463 600; www.absolutehotel.com; Sir Harry's Mall; d from €120; P @ 🐾) Exposed brick walls, polished limestone bathrooms and contemporary art give this gleaming hotel overlooking the River Abbey a smart, modern edge. There's a light-filled atrium in the lobby and a cocooning in-house spa, plus a bar and grill. Check in early: secure parking is free but limited.

Boutique
HOTEL €€

(Map p102; ☎ 061-315 320; www.theboutique.ie; Denmark St; s/d from €75/85; @ 🐾) Rotating works of art by Limerick-based Claire De

Limerick

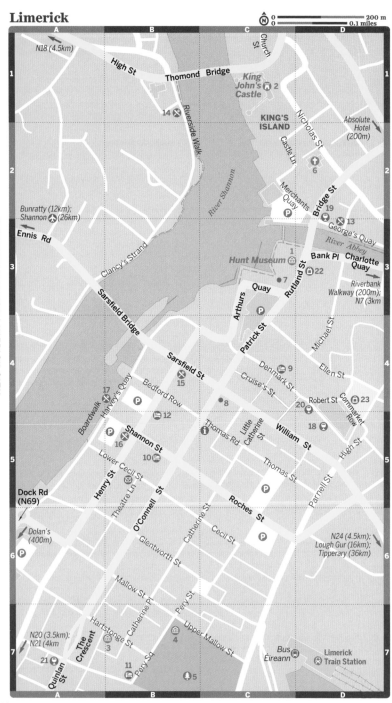

N 0 ____ 200 m
0 ____ 0.1 miles

N18 (4.5km)

High St

Thomond Bridge

Church St

King John's Castle

2

KING'S ISLAND

Nicholas St

Absolute Hotel (200m)

14

Riverside Walk

Castle Ln

6

Bunratty (12km); Shannon ✈ (26km)

Ennis Rd

River Shannon

Merchants Quay

Bridge St

19

13

George's Quay

River Abbey

Clancy's Strand

Hunt Museum

1

Ruttland St

Bank Pl

Charlotte Quay

22

Riverbank Walkway (200m); N7 (3km

Sarsfield Bridge

Arthurs Quay

7

Patrick St

Michael St

Ellen St

Sarsfield St

Denmark St

9

15

Cruise's St

Robert St

20

Commarket Row

23

Boardwalk

17

Bedford Row

8

18

Harvey's Quay

12

William St

Shannon St

Thomas Rd

Little Catherine St

High St

16

Lower Cecil St

10

Parnell St

Dock Rd (N69)

Henry St

Theatre Ln

O'Connell St

Thomas St

Roches St

Dolan's (400m)

Catherine St

Cecil St

N24 (4.5km); Lough Gur (16km); Tipperary (36km)

Glentworth St

Mallow St

Pery St

N20 (3.5km); N21 (4km

Hartstonge St

The Crescent

Catherine Pl

Upper Mallow St

4

3

21

Quinlan St

11

Pery Sq

5

Bus Éireann

Limerick Train Station

102

Limerick

Lacy, a fish tank in the lobby and a glassed-in breakfast room on the 1st-floor balcony set this groovy hotel apart from the pack. Its central location in the heart of the city's nightlife district means it can get noisy on weekends – be aware that it caters to stag and hen parties!

Eating

Limerick has many excellent eateries focusing on fresh Irish produce, an excellent weekly food market (p104), and a small street-food scene with a Wednesday **street-food market** (Map p102; Harvey's Quay Boardwalk; mains €4-7; ⊙11am-4pm Wed May-Sep) on the boardwalk in summer.

★ **Hook & Ladder**   CAFE €€
(Map p102; 061-413 778; www.hookandladder.ie; 7 Sarsfield St; mains €11-15; ⊙8am-5pm Mon-Wed, to 6pm Thu-Sat, 9am-5pm Sun) A haven of understated style and a champion of local produce, this cafe set in a converted bank building epitomises Limerick's foodie scene. Exquisite sandwiches include Doonbeg crab with lemon mayo on honey and pumpkin-seed bread, while hot lunch dishes range from sausage and mash to falafel and hummus wrap. There are associated cookery schools in Limerick and Waterford.

★ **Azur**   IRISH, EUROPEAN €€
(Map p102; 061-314 994; www.azurrestaurant.ie; 8 George's Quay; mains €13-27; ⊙5-9pm Tue-Thu, to 9.30pm Fri & Sat, 11am-8pm Sun;) Georgian architecture meets modern design at this elegant venue – one of Limerick's best

dining experiences. Service is professional but relaxed, the wine list is exemplary, and the menu lends a continental twist to the finest Irish produce, such as roast cod with wild garlic gnocchi and pea velouté, or chicken fillet with chorizo and chickpea cassoulet. Also does Sunday brunch.

La Cucina Centro   ITALIAN €€
(Map p102; 061-517 400; www.lacucina.ie; Henry St; mains €10-15; ⊙10am-9pm Mon-Wed, to 10pm Thu & Fri, from noon Sat, to 8pm Sun;) If you have a hankering for Italian comfort food, this modern diner is the place to head – hearty helpings of authentic pizza and pasta dishes sit alongside quality burgers, chicken salads and fish and chips.

Curragower Bar   GASTROPUB €€
(Map p102; 061-321 788; www.curragower.com; Clancy's Strand; mains €10-25; ⊙food served noon-8pm Mon-Tue, to 9pm Wed-Sun;) Ask a local for a lunch recommendation and they'll likely send you over the river to this appealing pub, which sports a superb outdoor terrace with views across the river to King John's Castle, and a menu that leans heavily towards Irish seafood, from rich and creamy chowder to baked sole with potted prawn, parsley root and pomegranate.

Drinking & Nightlife

Pubs such as Flannery's (p104) are famous for their range of Irish whiskeys, but craft beers are making an impact. Ales from Limerick's own Treaty City Brewery (www.treatycitybrewing.com) can be found at several bars, including Flannery's and Nancy Blake's (p104).

★ Nancy Blake's
PUB

(Map p102; ☑061-416 443; www.facebook.com/nancyblakesbar; 19 Upper Denmark St; ☉11am-midnight Mon & Tue, to 2am Wed-Sun) There's sawdust on the floor and peat on the fire in the cosy front bar of this wonderful old pub, but be sure to head out the back to enjoy a vast covered drinking zone that often features live music or televised sports.

Flannery's Bar
PUB

(Map p102; ☑061-436 677; www.flannerysbar.ie; 17 Upper Denmark St; ☉10am-11pm Sun-Wed, to 2am Thu-Sat) Housed in a former soap factory, this large and lively pub is a magnet for connoisseurs of Irish whiskey – there are more than 100 varieties on offer, and you can book a tasting session for €20 per person. Don't miss the roof terrace, a real suntrap on a summer afternoon.

Locke Bar
PUB

(Map p102; ☑061-413 733; www.lockebar.com; 3 George's Quay; ☉9am-11.30pm Mon-Thu, to 12.30am Fri & Sat, 10am-11pm Sun; 🛜🍴) With its attractive riverside setting, a maze of stone-walled and wood-panelled rooms, outdoor tables overlooking the water, and a menu that runs from breakfast to dinner, the Locke is rightly one of Limerick's most popular pubs. Hosts the Big Limerick Seisiún (session) nightly, with traditional Irish music and dancing from 5pm to 7pm and 9pm to 11pm.

South's
PUB

(WJ South; Map p102; ☑061-314 669; www.facebook.com/southspublimerick; 4 Quinlan St; ☉8.30am-11.30pm Mon-Thu, to 12.30am Fri, from 9.30am Sat, 12.30-11pm Sun) Frank McCourt's father knocked 'em back in South's (Frank himself had his first pint here) and the *Angela's Ashes* connection is worked for all it's worth – even the toilets are named Frank and Angela. Check out the fabulous (though reproduction) neoclassical interior.

☆ Entertainment

Lime Tree Theatre
THEATRE

(☑061-953 400; www.limetreetheatre.ie; Mary Immaculate College, Courtbrack Ave; ☉box office 2-5.30pm Mon-Fri) This 510-seat state-of-the-art theatre is set on a college campus on the southern edge of the city. It stages drama, music and comedy performances by local and international artists, and in 2017 premiered a musical version of *Angela's Ashes* (now touring Ireland and the UK).

University Concert Hall
CONCERT VENUE

(UCH; ☑061-331 549; www.uch.ie; University of Limerick; ☉box office 10am-5pm Mon-Fri, longer hours on performance dates) Permanent home of the Irish Chamber Orchestra, with regular concerts from visiting acts, plus opera, drama, comedy and dance. The campus is 4.5km east of the city.

Dolan's
LIVE MUSIC

(☑061-314 483; www.dolanspub.com; 3 Dock Rd; tickets €10-55; ☉noon-2am Mon-Fri, from 10am Sat & Sun) Limerick's best spot for live music promises authentic trad sessions and an unbeatable gig list – including occasional big-name artists such as Paul Young and Lloyd Cole – as well as cutting-edge stand-up comedians in two adjoining venues.

Shopping

Milk Market
MARKET

(Map p102; www.milkmarketlimerick.ie; Cornmarket Row; ☉10am-3pm Fri, from 8am Sat, from 11am Sun) 🍴 Pick from organic produce and artisan foods including local fruits and vegetables, preserves, baked goods and farmhouse cheeses, browse the flower and craft stalls, or grab a bite at one of the hot-food tables at this busy market held in Limerick's old market buildings. There's usually traditional live music as well.

Celtic Bookshop
BOOKS

(Map p102; ☑061-401 155; http://celticbookshop-limerick.ie; 2 Rutland St; ☉noon-5pm Mon-Sat) Crammed with specialist titles on local and Irish topics.

❶ Information

Limerick Tourist Office (Map p102; ☑061-317 522; www.limerick.ie; 20 O'Connell St; ☉9am-5pm Mon-Sat, hours vary) Helpful staff provide advice and information on Limerick and the rest of Ireland.

Main Post Office (Map p102; Lower Cecil St; ☉9am-5.30pm Mon & Wed-Sat, from 9.30am Tue)

University Hospital Limerick (☑061-301 111; www.hse.ie; Dooradoyle) Has a 24-hour accident and emergency department; south of the city centre.

❶ Getting Around

Limerick city is compact enough to get around on foot or by bike. To walk across town from St Mary's Cathedral to the train station takes about 15 minutes.

LIMERICK CITY TO TARBERT VIA THE SCENIC N69

The narrow, peaceful N69 road follows the Shannon Estuary along the Wild Atlantic Way west from Limerick for 58km to Tarbert (p54) in northern County Kerry. There are some fantastic views of the broadening estuary and seemingly endless rolling green hills laced with stone walls.

At the small village of **Clarina**, west of Mungret on the N69, hang a right to head north for around 1.5km to a crossroads, then turn left and you'll see the haunting ruin of **Carrigogunnell Castle** (⊘dawn-dusk) FREE high up on a ridge. You'll soon see a road to your right that heads past the castle, beyond the hedgerow and the fields. The 15th-century castle was blown up with gunpowder in 1691 and the fabulous wreck famously adorns the back cover of the U2 album *The Unforgettable Fire*.

Further along off the N69 is the village of Askeaton (p54), with evocative ruins including the mid-1300s **Desmond Castle** (⊘weekends by appointment May-Oct), perched dramatically on an island in the River Deel next to the **Hellfire Gentlemen's club**, once home to an 18th-century brothel and drinking club. Restoration of the ruins started in 2007 and is ongoing, with no public access to the site. On the edge of town is the atmospheric 1389-built **Franciscan friary** (⊘dawn-dusk) FREE, with a beautifully preserved cloister. The **Askeaton Tourist Office** (☑086 085 0174; askeatontouristoffice@gmail.com; The Square; ⊘limited hours, call to check) can arrange eye-opening free **guided tours** of the town's historic sites lasting about one hour, led by the very knowledgeable Anthony Sheehy.

At Foynes (p54) is the fascinating **Foynes Flying Boat Museum** (☑069-65416; www.flyingboatmuseum.com; adult/child €12/6; ⊘9.30am-6pm Jun-Aug, to 5pm mid-Mar-Jun & Sep-mid-Nov; ℗).

Taxis can be found at Arthurs Quay, at the bus and train stations, and in Thomas St, or try **Castletroy Cabs** (☑061-332 266; www.castletroycabs.com).

Limerick's Coca-Cola Zero **bike-share scheme** (www.bikeshare.ie/limerick.html), with 23 stations around town is, for visitors, €3 (€150 deposit) for three days. The first 30 minutes of each hire is free.

Adare & Around

POP 1129

Adare's fame centres on its string of thatched cottages built by 19th-century English landlord, the Earl of Dunraven, for workers constructing Adare Manor. Today the pretty cottages are shops and restaurants, while prestigious golf courses nearby cater to golf enthusiasts. The Irish name for Adare is Áth Dara – the Ford of the Oak.

The village is 16km southwest of Limerick. Tourists arrive here by the busload, clogging the roads (the busy N21 is the village's main street). As it's thronged with visitors at weekends, book accommodation and restaurants in advance.

◉ Sights & Activities

Before the Tudor dissolution of the monasteries (1536–39), Adare had three flourishing religious houses, the ruins of which can still be seen, but the main attraction here is the row of thatched cottages lining the main street.

Adare Castle CASTLE
(Desmond Castle; ☑tour bookings 061-396 666; www.heritageireland.ie; tours adult/child €10/8; ⊘tours hourly 11am-5pm Jul-Sep) Highlights include the **great hall** with its early 13th-century windows, and the huge kitchen and bakery. Also see p55.

Franciscan Friary RUINS
(Adare Golf Club; ⊘9am-5pm) The ruins of this friary, founded by the Earl of Kildare in 1464, stand serenely in the middle of Adare Golf Club beside the River Maigue. Public access is assured, but let them know at the clubhouse that you intend to visit. A track leads away from the clubhouse car park for about 400m – watch out for flying golf balls. There's a handsome tower and a fine sedilia (row of seats for priests) in the southern wall of the chancel.

Adare Heritage Centre
MUSEUM

See p55.

Augustinian Priory
ABBEY

(☉ 9am-5pm Mon-Sat) North of Adare village, on the N21 and close to the bridge over the River Maigue, is the Church of Ireland parish church, once the Augustinian priory, founded in 1316 and also known as the Black Abbey. The interior of the church is agreeable enough, but the real joy is the atmospheric little cloister.

A pleasant, signposted riverside path, with wayside seats, starts from just north of the priory gates. Look for a narrow access gap and head off alongside the river. After about 250m, turn left along the road to return to the centre of Adare.

Adare Golf Club
GOLF

(☑ 061-605 200; www.adaremanor.com/golf; green fees €300-375) This prestigious golf club enjoys a spectacular setting within the vast and serene grounds of Adare Manor.

🛏 Sleeping

Adare Village Inn
INN €

(☑ 087 251 7102; www.adarevillageinn.com; Upper Main St; s/d weekday €45/60, weekend €50/70; ᴘ🛜) This cordial place has five excellent-value rooms that are cosy and comfortable and come with power showers. Run by Seán Collins, the inn is a few doors down from his namesake bar (p108), where you check in, round the corner from Main St towards Rathkeale Rd.

★ Dunraven Arms
INN €€

(☑ 061-605 900; www.dunravenhotel.com; Main St; r from €165; 🛜⛱) This jewel of an inn, built in 1792, exudes old-fashioned charm, with cottage-style gardens, hanging baskets, open fires and a comfortable lobby. Smart bedrooms are decorated with antiques, high-thread-count linens and – for the choosy – four-poster beds. Service is warm and helpful, and there's a great restaurant and bar.

Berkeley Lodge
B&B €€

(☑ 061-396 857; www.adare.org; Station Rd; s/d/f €70/90/135; ᴘ🛜) This detached house around 400m north of the village centre has six homely and antique-styled rooms – each in a different colour – with great breakfasts. It's just a three-minute walk to the heritage centre, pubs and restaurants.

Adare Manor
HOTEL €€€

(☑ 061-605 200; www.adaremanor.com; Main St; r from €700; ᴘ@🛜⛱) Built in the mid-19th century for the Earl of Dunraven, this magnificent manor house now houses a luxury hotel. After extensive renovations in 2017 it sports a new bedroom wing and a huge ballroom to complement an already elegant property dripping in antique furniture and class. The manor's superb Oakroom Restaurant (p108) and lavish high tea are also open to nonguests.

🍴 Eating

Good Room Cafe
CAFE €

(☑ 061-396 218; www.thegoodroomadare.ie; Main St; mains €9-11; ☉ 8.30am-5.30pm Mon-Sat, from 10am Sun; 🖨) This homely but busy place prepares inventive breakfasts, soups, salads, hot sandwiches, bruschetta, baked goods, homemade jams, kids' menus and huge cups of coffee in a thatched-cottage location. It's always busy, so arrive early before its famous scones sell out.

★ Restaurant
1826 Adare
MODERN IRISH €€

(☑ 061-396 004; www.1826adare.ie; Main St; mains €20-27; ☉ 6-9.30pm Wed-Sat, 3-8pm Sun; 🖊) One of Ireland's most highly regarded chefs, Wade Murphy continues to wow diners at this art-lined, 1826-built thatched cottage. His passion for local seasonal produce is an essential ingredient in dishes such as pan-seared halibut with Connemara clams and pickled samphire. A three-course early-bird menu (€36) is served daily until 7pm.

Wild Geese
IRISH €€

(☑ 061-396 451; www.thewild-geese.com; Main St; mains lunch €7-16, dinner €22-32; ☉ 11am-3pm & 6-9.30pm Tue-Sat, 12.30-3pm Sun; 🖊) The ever-changing menu at this inviting cottage restaurant celebrates the best of southwest Ireland's bounty, from a lunch of crab cakes followed by cod fillet with creamed leeks, to dinner dishes of succulent scallops and sumptuous racks of lamb. The service is genial, preparations are imaginative and the bread basket is divine.

Maigue Restaurant
IRISH €€

(☑ 061-605 900; www.dunravenhotel.com; Main St; mains restaurant €16-28, bar €14-17; ☉ 7-9.30pm daily, 12.30-2.30pm Sun) The restaurant in the charming Dunraven Arms hotel has an ambitious menu (roast chicken with caramelised fennel and celeriac puree, hake with

Adare Blue Door (p108)

BALLINGARRY

Attractive village Ballingarry is home to one of County Limerick's hidden dining gems, **Mustard Seed at Echo Lodge** (☑069-68508; www.mustard seed.ie; Ballingarry; 4-course dinner €64; ☺7-9.15pm mid-Feb–mid-Jan; P ☎). Produce is picked fresh from this 19th-century former convent's orchards and kitchen gardens, and incorporated into seasonal dishes like wood pigeon with apple and parsnip puree and smoked pearl barley, or venison cooked with coffee and Szechuan pepper. Ballingarry is on the R519, 13km southwest of Adare.

To avoid having to move too far afterwards, book one of the lodge's elegant, country-style rooms, some with four-poster bed (double from €180).

lemon and chervil velouté), but the food in its sedate, wood-panelled Hunter's Bar (beef burger, fish and chips) offers a worthy and more affordable alternative. Hours can vary; reservations are advised.

Blue Door IRISH €€
(☑061-396 481; www.bluedooradare.com; Main St; mains lunch €10-22, dinner €21-27; ☺noon-5pm & 5.30-10pm; ♣) Hearty salads, open sandwiches and lasagne appear on the lunch menu at this upmarket thatched cottage restaurant, while dinner ups the ante with dishes such as confit of duck with black pudding and Guinness sauce, and pan-seared scallops with saffron cream.

Oakroom Restaurant IRISH €€€
(☑061-605 200; www.adaremanor.com/dining; Adare Manor; afternoon tea €55, 3-course dinner €90; ☺afternoon tea 1.30-3.30pm, dinner 6-9.30pm) Dine like a lord at the atmospheric restaurant of Adare Manor (p106), where dinner service is lit only by candles. The superb Irish menu is backed by a fabulous setting with views overlooking the grounds and the River Maigue. Alternatively, try the afternoon tea served on tiered plates in the stately drawing room. Dress code: smart casual.

Drinking & Nightlife

Seán Collins PUB
(www.seancollinsbaradare.com; Upper Main St; ☺10am-11.30pm Mon-Thu & Sun, 10.30am-1.30am

Fri & Sat) A friendly, family-run pub with good craic, good food (served 12.30pm to 9.30pm), and live music on Monday and Friday at 8.30pm.

Bill Chawke's Lounge Bar PUB
(☑061-396 160; www.billchawke.com; Main St; ☺9am-11.30pm Mon-Thu, to 12.30am Fri & Sat, to 11pm Sun) Decked out in GAA (hurling and Gaelic football) memorabilia, this place has a good beer garden and hosts regular trad-music sessions and singalongs.

① Information

The Adare Village website (www.adarevillage. com) is a handy source of information.

Otherwise there's the **tourist office** (☑061-396 255; www.adareheritagecentre.ie/tourist-point; Adare Heritage Centre, Main St; ☺9am-6pm).

① Getting There & Away

Hourly **Bus Éireann** (Map p102; ☑061-313 333; www.buseireann.ie) services link Limerick with Adare (€5, 25 minutes). Many continue on to Tralee (€9, two hours, every two hours). Others serve Killarney (€9, two hours, every two hours).

Lough Gur

The area surrounding this picturesque, horseshoe-shaped lake is rich in Neolithic, Bronze Age and medieval archaeological sites. Short walks along the lake's edge lead to burial mounds, standing stones, ancient enclosures and other points of interest (admission free) and the whole area is ideal for walking and picnics.

Lough Gur Heritage Centre MUSEUM
(☑087 285 2022; www.loughgur.com; adult/child €5/3; ☺10am-8pm Mon-Fri, from noon Sat & Sun Feb-Oct, to 4pm Nov-Jan; P) This thatched replica of a Neolithic hut contains a helpful information desk and good exhibits on prehistoric monuments and settlements in the surrounding area, plus a small museum displaying Neolithic artefacts and a replica of the bronze Lough Gur shield dating from around 1000 BC (the original is in the National Museum in Dublin). It's a good idea to come here first to get some context before exploring the surrounding sites.

Grange Stone Circle ARCHAEOLOGICAL SITE
(☺dawn-dusk) FREE This stone circle, known as the Lios, is a superb 4000-year-old circular enclosure made up of 113 embanked

upright stones, the largest prehistoric circle of its kind in Ireland. It's a 3km walk or drive southwest of the heritage centre; there's roadside parking and access to the site is free (there's a donation box).

ℹ Getting There & Away

There is no public transport to Lough Gur, which is 21km south of Limerick. Driving from Limerick, take the R512 road south towards Kilmallock 16km to find the Grange stone circle.

Around 1km further south along the R512, at Holycross garage and post office, a left turn takes you another 2km to the main car park beside Lough Gur itself, from where it's a short walk to the Lough Gur Heritage Centre.

Kilmallock & Around

POP 1668

Kilmallock was Ireland's third-largest town during the Middle Ages (after Dublin and Kilkenny), and is today the country's best-preserved medieval town. It developed around a 13th-century abbey and from the 14th to the 17th centuries was the seat of the Earls of Desmond. The village lies beside the River Lubach, 26km south of Limerick and a world away from the city's urban racket.

Coming into Kilmallock from Limerick, the first thing you'll see (to your left) is a **medieval stone mansion** – one of 30 or so that housed the town's prosperous merchants and landowners. Further on, the main street bends around the four-storey **King's Castle**, a 15th-century tower house with a ground-floor archway through which the pavement now runs.

Kilmallock Museum   MUSEUM

(📞 063-91300; Sheares St; ⊙ 10am-1pm & 2-4pm Mon-Thu, to 5pm Fri & Sat, noon-5pm Sun) FREE A lane leads down from the main street (opposite the King's Castle) to this tiny museum, which houses a random collection of historical artefacts and a model of the town in 1597. The museum is the base for the history trail around town, and provides tourist information.

Kilmallock Abbey   HISTORIC SITE

FREE A footbridge leads across the river from Kilmallock Museum to the atmospheric ruins of this 13th-century Dominican friary. Much of the arcaded cloister remains standing, as does the church tower, and in the choir stands the arched wall-tomb of the White Knight, Edmund John Fitzgibbon (1552–1608).

⭐ **Kilmallock**
Medieval Tours   HISTORY

(📞 087 395 2895; www.facebook.com/kilmallock medievaltours; adult/child €10/free; ⊙ 9am-5pm Sat & Sun) Historian Trevor McCarthy, dressed in full medieval garb, provides entertaining guided walking tours of Kilmallock's medieval buildings. Tours must be booked in advance.

Ballyhoura
Trail Centre   MOUNTAIN BIKING

(www.coillte.ie/site/ballyhoura; parking €5, coins only) FREE The most extensive, purpose-built mountain-bike centre in the Republic, Ballyhoura has cross-country trails ranging from 6km to a thigh-burning 51km in length. There are showers, toilets, bike hire and a cafe at the car park.

ROAD TRIP ESSENTIALS

Ireland Driving Guide

The motorway system makes for easy travelling between major towns, but the spidery network of secondary and tertiary roads makes for the most scenic driving.

DRIVING LICENCE & DOCUMENTS

EU licences are treated like Irish ones. Holders of non-EU licences from countries other than the US or Canada should obtain an International Driving Permit (IDP) from their home automobile association.

You must carry your driving licence at all times.

INSURANCE

All cars on public roads must be insured. Most hire companies quote basic insurance in their initial quote. If you are bringing your own vehicle, check that your insurance will cover you in Ireland. When driving your own car, you'll need a minimum insurance known as third-party insurance.

HIRING A CAR

Compared with many countries hire rates are expensive in Ireland; you should expect to pay around €250 a week for a small car (unlimited mileage), but rates go up at busy times and drop off in quieter seasons. The main players:

Avis (www.avis.ie)

Budget (www.budget.ie)

Europcar (www.europcar.ie)

Hertz (www.hertz.ie)

Sixt (www.sixt.ie)

Thrifty (www.thrifty.ie)

The major car-hire companies have different web pages on their websites for different countries, so the price of a car in Ireland can differ from the same car's price in the USA or Australia. You have to surf a lot of sites to get the best deals. **Nova Car Hire** (www.novacarhire.com) acts as an agent for Alamo, Budget, European and National, and offers greatly discounted rates.

➡ Most cars are manual; automatic cars are available, but they're more expensive to hire.

➡ If you're travelling from the Republic into Northern Ireland, it's important to be sure that your insurance covers journeys to the North.

➡ The majority of hire companies won't rent you a car if you're under 23 and haven't had a valid driving licence for at least a year.

➡ Some companies in the Republic won't rent to you if you're aged 74 or over; there's no upper age limit in the North.

➡ Motorbikes and mopeds are not available for hire in Ireland.

Driving Fast Facts

➡ **Right or left?** Drive on the left

➡ **Legal driving age** 18

➡ **Top speed limit** 120km/h (motorways; 70mph in Northern Ireland)

Ireland Playlist

Virtually every parish and hamlet has a song about it. Here are our favourites:

Carrickfergus Traditional Irish folk song

Galway Girl Steve Earle

Raglan Road Luke Kelly

Running to Stand Still U2

The Fields of Athenry Paddy Reilly

The Town I Loved So Well The Dubliners (about Derry)

BRINGING YOUR OWN VEHICLE

It's easy to take your own vehicle to Ireland and there are no specific procedures involved, but you should carry a vehicle registration document as proof that it's yours.

MAPS

You'll need a good road map; we recommend getting one even if you have a sat-nav system.

Michelin's 1:400,000-scale Ireland map (No 923) is a decent single-sheet map, with clear cartography and most of the island's scenic roads marked. The four maps (North, South, East and West) that make up the Ordnance Survey Holiday map series at 1:250,000 scale are useful if you want more detail. Collins also publishes a range of maps covering Ireland.

The Ordnance Survey Discovery series covers the whole island in 89 maps at a scale of 1:50,000.

These are all available at most big bookshops and tourist centres throughout Ireland as well as at www.osi.ie.

ROADS CONDITIONS

Irish road types and conditions vary wildly. The road network is divided into the following categories:

Road Distances (Km)

	Athlone	Belfast	Cork	Derry	Donegal	Dublin	Galway	Kilkenny	Killarney	Limerick	Rosslare Harbour	Shannon Airport	Sligo	Waterford
Belfast	227													
Cork	219	424												
Derry	209	117	428											
Donegal	183	180	402	69										
Dublin	127	167	256	237	233									
Galway	93	306	209	272	204	212								
Kilkenny	116	284	148	335	309	114	172							
Killarney	232	436	87	441	407	304	193	198						
Limerick	121	323	105	328	296	193	104	113	111					
Rosslare Harbour	201	330	208	397	391	153	274	98	275	211				
Shannon Airport	133	346	128	351	282	218	93	135	135	25	234			
Sligo	117	206	336	135	66	214	138	245	343	232	325	218		
Waterford	164	333	126	383	357	163	220	48	193	129	82	152	293	
Wexford	184	309	187	378	372	135	253	80	254	190	19	213	307	61

Regional Roads Indicated by an R and (usually) three numbers on a white background, these are the secondary and tertiary roads that make up the bulk of the road network, generally splintering off larger roads to access even the smallest hamlet. Blind corners, potholes and a width barely enough for two cars are the price for some of the most scenic routes in all of Ireland; whatever you do, go slow. In Northern Ireland, these are classified as B-roads.

National Roads Indicated by an N and two numbers against a green background, these were, until the construction of the motorway network, the primary roads in Ireland. They link most towns and are usually single lane in either direction, widening occasionally to double lane (usually on uphill stretches to allow for the overtaking of slower vehicles). In Northern Ireland, these are classified as A-roads.

Motorways Indicated by an M and a single digit against a blue background, the network is limited to the major routes and towns. Most motorways are partially tolled. Motorways in Northern Ireland are not tolled.

ROAD RULES

A copy of Ireland's road rules is available from tourist offices. Following are the most basic rules:

➡ Drive on the left, overtake to the right.

➡ Safety belts must be worn by the driver and all passengers.

➡ Children aged under 12 aren't allowed to sit on the front seats.

➡ Motorcyclists and their passengers must wear helmets.

➡ When entering a roundabout, give way to the right.

➡ On motorways, use the right lane for overtaking only.

➡ Speed limits are 120km/h on motorways (70mph in Northern Ireland), 100km/h on national roads (60mph in Northern Ireland), 80km/h on regional and local roads (60mph in Northern Ireland) and 50km/h (30mph in the North) or as signposted in towns.

➡ The legal alcohol limit is 50mg of alcohol per 100ml of blood or 22mg on the breath (roughly two units of alcohol for a man and one for a woman); in Northern Ireland the limit is 80mg of alcohol per 100ml of blood.

PARKING

All big towns and cities have covered and open short-stay car parks that are conveniently signposted.

➡ On-street parking is usually by 'pay and display' tickets available from on-street machines or disc parking (discs, which rotate to display the time you park your car, are usually provided by rental agencies). Costs range from €1.50 to €6 per hour; all-day parking in a car park will cost around €25.

➡ Yellow lines (single or double) along the edge of the road indicate restrictions. Double yellow lines mean no parking at any time. Always look for the nearby sign that spells out when you can and cannot park.

➡ In Dublin, Cork and Galway, clamping is rigorously enforced; it'll cost you €85 to have

Road Trip Websites

AUTOMOBILE ASSOCIATIONS

Automobile Association (AA; www. theaa.ie) Roadside assistance and driving tips.

Royal Automobile Club (RAC; www.rac.co.uk) Roadside assistance, route planner and accommodation.

ROAD RULES

Road Safety Authority (www.rsa. ie) Rules, tips and information in case of accident.

CONDITIONS & TRAFFIC

AA Roadwatch (www.theaa.ie) Up-to-date traffic info.

Traffic Watch Northern Ireland (www.trafficwatchni.com) Traffic news, maps and live cameras.

MAPS

AA Route Planner (www.theaa.ie) Map your route for the whole island.

APPS

Both the AA and the RAC have mobile apps for Android and IOS that track traffic and allow you to report breakdowns.

the yellow beast removed. In Northern Ireland, the fee is £100 for removal.

FUEL

The majority of vehicles operate on un-leaded petrol; the rest (including many hire cars) run on diesel.

Cost In the Republic, petrol costs range from €1.30 to €1.50 per litre, with diesel usually €0.10 cheaper. Fuel is marginally more expensive in Dublin. In Northern Ireland, petrol costs between £1.20 and £1.30 per litre, but diesel is slightly more expensive (between £1.25 and £1.35 per litre).

Service Stations These are ubiquitous on all national roads, usually on the outskirts of towns. They're increasingly harder to find in cities, and the motorway network has only three or four spread across the entire system. In the North, the big supermarket chains have gotten into the fuel business, so you can fill your car before or after you shop. There are service stations along the North's motorway network.

SAFETY

Although driving in Ireland is a relatively pain-free experience, hire cars and cars with foreign registrations can be targeted by thieves looking to clean them of their contents. Don't leave any valuables, including bags and suitcases, on display. Overnight parking is safest in covered car parks.

BORDER CROSSINGS

Border crossings between Northern Ireland and the Republic are unnoticeable; there are no formalities of any kind. This may change, however, once Brexit occur.

RADIO

The Irish love radio – up to 85% of the population listens in on any given day. Following are the national radio stations:

Newstalk 106-108 (106–108FM) News, current affairs and lifestyle.

RTE Radio 1 (88.2–90FM) Mostly news and discussion.

RTE Radio 2 (90.4–92.2FM) Lifestyle and music.

Local Expert: Driving Tips

Conor Faughnan, Director of Consumer Affairs with the Automobile Association, shares his tips for hassle-free driving in Ireland:

➡ The motorway network is excellent, but there aren't nearly enough rest areas, so check that you have a full tank of fuel before setting off. Off the motorway network there is a good supply of service stations, often open 24 hours, but less so in more remote areas.

➡ The real driving fun is on Ireland's network of secondary roads, where road conditions vary – make sure you're equipped with a good map along with your sat-nav, and beware of potholes, poor road surfaces and corners obscured by protruding hedges! You may also encounter farm machinery and even livestock on rural roads.

➡ Although it rarely snows, winter conditions can be testing (particularly when roads are icy).

➡ A driver may flash their hazard lights once or twice as an informal way to say 'thank you' for any kind of road courtesy extended to them.

Driving Problem-Buster

What should I do if my car breaks down? Call the service number of your car-hire company and a local garage will be contacted. If you're bringing your own car, it's a good idea to join the Automobile Association Ireland, which covers the whole country, or, in Northern Ireland, the Royal Automobile Club (RAC), which can be called to attend breakdowns at any time.

What if I have an accident? Hire cars usually have a leaflet in the glovebox about what to do in case of an accident. Exchange basic information with the other party (name, insurance details, driver's licence number, company details if the car's a rental). No discussion of liability needs to take place at the scene. It's a good idea to photograph the scene of the accident, noting key details (damage sustained, car positions on the road, any skid markings). Call the police (☎999) if required.

What should I do if I get stopped by police? Always remain calm and polite: police are generally courteous and helpful. They will want to see your passport (or valid form of ID), licence and proof of insurance. In the Republic, breath testing is mandatory if asked.

What if I can't find anywhere to stay? If you're travelling during the summer months, always book your accommodation in advance. If you're stuck, call the local tourist office's accommodation hotline.

How do I pay for tollways? Tolls are paid by putting cash in the bucket as you pass. If you don't have exact change, at least one booth is staffed.

IRELAND DRIVING GUIDE **RADIO**

RTE Lyric FM (96–99FM) Classical music.
Today FM (100–102FM) News, chat and music.

Regional or local radio is also very popular, with 25 independent local radio stations available, depending on your location.

In Northern Ireland, the BBC rules supreme, with BBC Radio Ulster (92.7–95.4FM) flying the local flag in addition to the four main BBC stations.

Ireland
Travel Guide

GETTING THERE & AWAY

AIR

Ireland's main airports:

Cork Airport (☏021-431 3131; www.cork airport.com) Airlines servicing the airport include Aer Lingus and Ryanair.

Dublin Airport (☏01-814 1111; www. dublinairport.com) Ireland's major inter-national gateway airport, with direct flights from the UK, Europe, North America and the Middle East.

Shannon Airport (SNN; ☏061-712 000; www.shannonairport.ie; ☏) Has a few direct flights from the UK, Europe and North America.

Northern Ireland's airports:

Belfast International Airport (Alder-grove; ☏028-9448 4848; www.belfastairport. com; Airport Rd) Has direct flights from the UK, Europe and North America.

Car hire firms are well represented at all major airports. Regional airports will have at least one internationally recognised firm as well as local operators.

SEA

The main ferry routes between Ireland and the UK and mainland Europe:

➡ Belfast to Liverpool (England; eight hours)
➡ Belfast to Cairnryan (Scotland; 1¾ hours)
➡ Cork to Roscoff (France; 14 hours; April to October only)
➡ Dublin to Liverpool (England; fast/slow four/8½ hours)
➡ Dublin & Dun Laoghaire to Holyhead (Wales; fast/slow two hours/3½ hours)
➡ Larne to Cairnryan (Scotland; two hours)
➡ Larne to Troon (Scotland; two hours; March to October only)
➡ Larne to Fleetwood (England; six hours)
➡ Rosslare to Cherbourg/Roscoff (France; 18/20½ hours)
➡ Rosslare to Fishguard & Pembroke (Wales; 3½ hours)

Competition from budget airlines has forced ferry operators to discount heavily and offer flexible fares. A useful website is www.ferrybooker.com, which covers all sea-ferry routes and operators to Ireland.
    Main operators include the following:

Brittany Ferries (www.brittanyferries.com) Cork to Roscoff; April to October.

Irish Ferries (www.irishferries.com) It has Dublin to Holyhead ferries (up to four per day year-round) and France to Rosslare (three times per week).

P&O Ferries (www.poferries.com) Daily sail-ings year-round from Dublin to Liverpool, and Larne to Cairnryan. Larne to Troon runs March to October only.

Stena Line (www.stenaline.com) Daily sailings from Holyhead to Dublin Port, from Belfast to Liverpool and Cairnryan, and from Rosslare to Fishguard.

Arriving in Ireland

Dublin Airport Private coaches run every 10 to 15 minutes to the city centre (€6). Taxis take 30 to 45 minutes and cost €20 to €30.

Dun Laoghaire Ferry Port Public bus takes around 45 minutes to the centre of Dublin; DART (suburban rail) takes about 25 minutes. Both cost €3.

Dublin Port Terminal Buses are timed to coincide with arrivals and departures; they cost €3.50 to the city centre.

Belfast International Airport Airport Express 300 bus runs hourly (one way/ return £8/11.50, 30 to 55 minutes). A taxi costs around £30.

George Best Belfast City Airport Airport Express 600 bus runs every 20 minutes (one way/return £2.60/4, 15 minutes). A taxi costs around £10.

DIRECTORY A–Z

ACCOMMODATION

Accommodation options range from bare and basic to pricey and palatial. The spine of the Irish hospitality business is the ubiquitous B&B, in recent years challenged by a plethora of midrange hotels and guesthouses. Beyond Expedia, Booking.com, Trivago and other hotel price comparison sites, Ireland-specific online resources for accommodation include the following:

Daft.ie (www.daft.ie) Online property portal includes holiday homes and short-term rentals.

Elegant Ireland (www.elegant.ie) Specialises in self-catering castles, period houses and unique properties.

Imagine Ireland (www.imagineireland.com) Holiday cottage rentals throughout the whole island, including Northern Ireland.

Irish Landmark Trust (www.irishlandmark.com) Not-for-profit conservation group that rents self-catering properties of historical and cultural significance, such as castles, tower houses, gate lodges, schoolhouses and lighthouses.

Lonely Planet (www.lonelyplanet.com/Ireland/hotels) Recommendations and bookings.

Dream Ireland (www.dreamireland.com) Lists self-catering holiday cottages and apartments.

B&Bs & Guesthouses

Bed and breakfasts are small, family-run houses, farmhouses and period country houses, generally with fewer than five bedrooms. Standards vary enormously, but most have some bedrooms with private bathroom at a cost of roughly €40 to €60 (£35 to £50) per person per night (at least €100 in Dublin). In luxurious B&Bs, expect to pay €70 (£60) or more per person. Off-season rates – October through to March – are usually lower, as are midweek prices.

Guesthouses are like upmarket B&Bs, but a bit bigger. Facilities are usually better and sometimes include a restaurant.

Other tips:

➡ Facilities in B&Bs range from basic (bed, bathroom, kettle, TV) to beatific (whirlpool baths, rainforest showers) as you go up in price. Wi-fi is standard and most have parking (but check).

➡ Most B&Bs take credit cards, but the occasional rural one might not; check when you book.

➡ Advance reservations are strongly recommended, especially in peak season (June to September).

➡ Some B&Bs and guesthouses in more remote regions may only be open from Easter to September or other months.

➡ If full, B&B owners may recommend another house in the area (possibly a private house taking occasional guests, not in tourist listings).

➡ To make prices more competitive at some B&Bs, breakfast may be optional.

Camping & Caravan Parks

Camping and caravan parks aren't as common in Ireland as they are elsewhere in Europe. Some hostels have camping space for tents and also offer house facilities, which makes them better value than the main camping grounds.

At commercial parks the cost is typically somewhere between €15 and €25 (£12 to £20) for a tent and two people. Prices given for campsites are for two people unless stated otherwise. Caravan sites cost around €20 to €30 (£17 to £25). Most parks are open only from Easter to the end of September or October.

Hostels

Prices quoted for hostel accommodation apply to those aged over 18. A high-season dorm bed generally costs €12 to €25, or €18 to €30 in Dublin (£15 to £20 in Northern Ireland). Many hostels now have family and double rooms.

Relevant hostel associations:

An Óige (www.anoige.ie) HI-associated national organisation with 26 hostels scattered around the Republic.

HINI (www.hini.org.uk) HI-associated organisation with five hostels in Northern Ireland.

Independent Holiday Hostels of Ireland (www.hostels-ireland.com) Fifty-five tourist-board-approved hostels throughout all of Ireland.

Independent Hostel Owners of Ireland (www.independenthostelsireland.com) Independent hostelling association.

ELECTRICITY

220V/50Hz

FOOD

The 'local food' movement was pioneered in Ireland in the 1970s, notably at the world-famous Ballymaloe House (p73). Since then the movement has gone from strength to strength, with dozens of farmers markets showcasing the best of local produce, and restaurants all over the country highlighting locally sourced ingredients.

A 'Standard' Hotel Rate?

There is no such thing. Prices vary according to demand – or have different rates for online, phone or walk-in bookings. B&B rates are more consistent, but virtually every other accommodation will charge wildly different rates depending on the time of year, day, festival schedule and even your ability to do a little negotiating. The following price ranges have been used in our reviews of places to stay. Prices are all based on a double room with private bathroom in high season.

Budget	Rest of Ireland	Dublin
Budget (€)	<€80	<€150
Midrange (€€)	€80–180	<€150-250
Top end (€€€)	<€180	<€250

When to Eat

Irish eating habits have changed over the last couple of decades, and there are differences between urban and rural practices.

Breakfast Usually eaten before 9am, as most people rush off to work (though hotels and B&Bs will serve until 10am or 11am Monday to Friday, and till noon at weekends in urban areas). Weekend brunch is popular in bigger towns and cities.

Lunch Urban workers eat on the run between 12.30pm and 2pm (most restaurants don't begin to serve lunch until at least midday). At weekends, especially Sunday, the midday lunch is skipped in favour of a substantial mid-afternoon meal (called dinner), usually between 2pm and 4pm.

Tea Not the drink, but the evening meal – also confusingly called dinner. This is the main meal of the day for urbanites, usually eaten around 6.30pm. Rural communities eat at the same time but with a more traditional tea of bread, cold cuts and, yes, tea. Restaurants follow international habits, with most diners not eating until at least 7.30pm.

Supper A before-bed snack of tea and toast or sandwiches, still enjoyed by many Irish folk, though urbanites increasingly eschew it for health reasons. Not a practice in restaurants.

Vegetarians & Vegans

Ireland has come a long, long way since the days when vegetarians were looked upon as odd creatures; nowadays, even the most militant vegan will barely cause a ruffle in all but the most basic of kitchens. Which isn't to say that travellers with plant-based diets are going to find the most imaginative range of options on menus outside the bigger towns and cities – or in the plethora of modern restaurants that have opened in the last few years – but you can rest assured that the overall quality of the homegrown vegetable is top-notch and most places will have at least one dish that you can tuck into comfortably.

LGBTQI+ TRAVELLERS

Ireland is a generally tolerant place for the LGBTQI+ community. Bigger cities such as Dublin, Galway and Cork have well-established gay scenes, as do Belfast and-

Eating Price Ranges

The following price indicators, used throughout this guide, represent the cost of a main dish:

Budget	Price
Budget (€)	<€12
Midrange (€€)	€12–25
Top end (€€€)	>€25

Derry in Northern Ireland. Same-sex marriage has been legal in the Republic since 2015; Northern Ireland is the only region of the United Kingdom where it is not.

While the cities and main towns tend to be progressive and tolerant, you'll still find pockets of homophobia throughout the island, particularly in smaller towns and rural areas.

Resources include the following:

Gaire (www.gaire.com) Message board and info for a host of gay-related issues.

Gay & Lesbian Youth Northern Ireland (www.cara-friend.org.uk) Voluntary counselling, information, health and social-space organisation for the gay community.

Gay Men's Health Service (☑01 921 2730; www.hse.ie/go/GMHS) Practical advice on men's health issues.

National LGBT Federation (NLGF; ☑01-671 9076; http://nxf.ie) Publishes the monthly *Gay Community News* (www.gcn.ie).

Northern Ireland Gay Rights Association (☑028-9066 5257; www.nidirect.gov.uk; 9-13 Waring St) Represents the rights and interests of the LGBTQI+ community in Northern Ireland. It offers phone and online support, but is not a call-in centre.

Outhouse (☑01-873 4999; www.outhouse.ie; 105 Capel St; ⊙10am-6pm Mon-Fri, noon-5pm Sat; 🚇all city centre) Top LGBTQI+ resource centre in Dublin. Great stop-off point to see what's on, check noticeboards, visit the cafe and library, and meet people. The website has listings and support links.

Dining Etiquette

The Irish aren't big on restrictive etiquette, preferring friendly informality to any kind of stuffy to-dos. Still, the following are a few tips to dining with the Irish:

Children All restaurants welcome kids up to 7pm, but pubs and some smarter restaurants don't allow them in the evening. Family restaurants have children's menus; others have reduced portions of regular menu items.

Returning a dish If the food is not to your satisfaction, it's best to politely explain what's wrong with it as soon as you can. Any respectable restaurant will offer to replace the dish immediately.

Paying the bill If you insist on paying the bill for everyone, be prepared for a first, second and even third refusal to countenance such an exorbitant act of generosity. But don't be fooled: the Irish will refuse something several times even if they're delighted with it. Insist gently but firmly and you'll get your way!

HEALTH

No jabs are required to travel to Ireland. Excellent health care is readily available. For minor, self-limiting illnesses, pharmacists can give valuable advice and sell over-the-counter medication. They can also advise when more specialised help is required and point you in the right direction.

EU citizens equipped with a European Health Insurance Card (EHIC), available from health centres or UK post offices, will be covered for most medical care – but not non-emergencies or emergency repatriation. While other countries, such as Australia, also have reciprocal agreements with Ireland and Britain, many do not.

In Northern Ireland, everyone receives free emergency treatment at accident and emergency (A&E) departments of state-run NHS hospitals, irrespective of nationality.

INTERNET ACCESS

Wi-fi and 3G/4G networks are making internet cafes largely redundant (except to gamers). The few that are left will charge around €6 per hour. Most accommodation places have wi-fi, either free or for a daily charge (up to €10 per day).

MONEY

The Republic of Ireland uses the euro (€). Northern Ireland uses the pound sterling (£), though the euro is also accepted in many places. Although notes issued by Northern Irish banks are legal tender throughout the UK, many businesses outside of Northern Ireland refuse to accept them and you'll have to swap them in British banks.

ATMs

All banks have ATMs that are linked to international money systems such as Cirrus, Maestro or Plus. Each transaction incurs a currency-conversion fee, and credit cards can incur immediate and exorbitant cash-advance interest-rate charges. Watch out for ATMs that have been tampered with, as card-reader scams ('skimming') have become a real problem.

Credit & Debit Cards

Visa and MasterCard credit and debit cards are widely accepted in Ireland. American Express is only accepted by the major chains, and very few places accept Diners or JCB. Smaller businesses, such as pubs and some B&Bs, prefer debit cards (and will charge a fee for credit cards), and a small number of rural B&Bs only take cash.

Exchange Rates

The Republic of Ireland uses the euro.

Australia	A$1	€0.62
Canada	C$1	€0.68
Japan	Y100	€0.83
New Zealand	NZ$1	€0.60
UK	£1	€1.12
USA	US$1	€0.89

OPENING HOURS

Banks 10am–4pm Monday to Friday (to 5pm Thursday)

Pubs 10.30am–11.30pm Monday to Thursday, 10.30am–12.30am Friday and Saturday, noon–11pm Sunday (30 minutes 'drinking up' time allowed); closed Christmas Day and Good Friday

Restaurants noon–10.30pm; many close one day of the week

Shops 9.30am–6pm Monday to Saturday (to 8pm Thursday in cities), noon–6pm Sunday

PHOTOGRAPHY

➡ Natural light can be very dull, so use higher ISO speeds than usual, such as 400 for daylight shots.

➡ In Northern Ireland get permission before taking photos of fortified police stations, army posts or other military or quasi-military paraphernalia.

➡ Don't take photos of people in Protestant or Catholic strongholds of West Belfast without permission; always ask and be prepared to accept a refusal.

➡ Lonely Planet's *Guide to Travel Photography* is full of helpful tips for photography while on the road.

PUBLIC HOLIDAYS

Public holidays can cause road chaos as everyone tries to get somewhere else for the break. It's wise to book accommodation in advance for these times.

The following are public holidays in both the Republic and Northern Ireland:

New Year's Day 1 January

St Patrick's Day 17 March

Easter March/April

May Holiday 1st Monday in May

Christmas Day 25 December

St Stephen's Day (Boxing Day) 26 December

St Patrick's Day and St Stephen's Day holidays are taken on the following Monday when they fall on a weekend. Nearly everywhere in the Republic closes on Good Friday even though it isn't an official public holiday. In the North most shops open on Good Friday, but close the following Tuesday.

June Holiday 1st Monday in June

August Holiday 1st Monday in August

October Holiday Last Monday in October

SAFE TRAVEL

Ireland is safer than most countries in Europe, but normal precautions should be observed.

➡ Don't leave anything visible in your car when you park.

➡ Skimming at ATMs is an ongoing problem; be sure to cover the keypad with your hand when you input your PIN.

➡ In Northern Ireland exercise extra care in 'interface' areas where sectarian neighbourhoods adjoin.

Practicalities

Smoking Smoking is illegal in all indoor public spaces, including restaurants and pubs.

Time Ireland uses the 12-hour clock and is on Western European Time (UTC/GMT November to March; plus one hour April to October).

TV & DVD All TV in Ireland is digital terrestrial; Ireland is DVD Region 2.

Weights & Measures In the Republic, both imperial and metric units are used for most measures except height, which is in feet and inches only. Distance is measured in kilometres, but people can refer to it colloquially in miles. In the north, it's imperial all the way.

→ Avoid Northern Ireland during the climax of the Orange marching season on 12 July. Sectarian passions are usually inflamed and even many Northerners leave the province at this time.

TAXES & REFUNDS

Non-EU residents can claim Value Added Tax (VAT, a sales tax of 21% added to the purchase price of luxury goods – excluding books, children's clothing and educational items) back on their purchases, so long as the store operates either the Cashback or Taxback refund program (they should display a sticker). You'll get a voucher with your purchase that must be stamped at the *last point of exit* from the EU. If you're travelling on to Britain or mainland Europe from Ireland, hold on to your voucher until you pass through your final customs stop in the EU; it can then be stamped and you can post it back for a refund of duty paid.

VAT in Northern Ireland is 20%; shops participating in the Tax-Free Shopping refund scheme will give you a form or invoice on request to be presented to customs when you leave. After customs have certified the form, it will be returned to the shop for a refund and the cheque sent to you at home.

TELEPHONE

When calling Ireland from abroad, dial your international access code, followed by ✆353 and the area code (dropping the 0). Area codes in the Republic have three digits, eg ✆021 for Cork, ✆091 for Galway and ✆061 for Limerick. The only exception is Dublin, which has a two-digit code (✆01).

To make international calls from Ireland, first dial 00 then the country code, followed by the local area code and number. Always use the area code if calling from a mobile phone, but you don't need it if calling from a fixed-line number within the area code.

In Northern Ireland the area code for all fixed-line numbers is ✆028, but you only need to use it if calling from a mobile phone or from outside Northern Ireland. To call Northern Ireland from the Republic, use ✆048 instead of ✆028, without the international dialling code.

Country Code	✆353
International ccess Code	✆00
Directory Enquiries	✆11811/✆11850
International Directory Enquiries	✆11818

Mobile Phones

→ Ensure your mobile phone is unlocked for use in Ireland.

→ Pay-as-you-go mobile phone packages with any of the main providers start around €40 and usually include a basic handset and credit of around €10.

→ SIM-only packages are also available, but make sure your phone is compatible with the local provider.

TOURIST INFORMATION

In both the Republic and the North there's a tourist office or information point in almost every big town. Most can offer a variety of services, including accommodation and attraction reservations, currency-changing services, map and guidebook sales and free publications.

In the Republic the tourism purview falls to **Fáilte Ireland** (✆Republic 1850 230 330, UK 0800 039 7000; www.discoverireland.ie); in Northern Ireland, it's **Discover Northern Ireland** (✆head office 028-9023 1221; www.discovernorthernireland.com). Outside Ireland both organisations unite under the banner Tourism Ireland (www.tourism ireland.com).

TRAVELLERS WITH DISABILITIES

All new buildings have wheelchair access, and many hotels (especially urban ones that are part of chains) have installed lifts, ramps and other facilities such as hearing loops. Others, particularly B&Bs, may not be equipped with accessible facilities.

In big cities, most buses have low-floor access and priority space on board, but the number of kneeling buses on regional routes is still relatively small.

Trains are accessible with help. In theory, if you call ahead, an employee of Irish Rail (Iarnród Éireann) will arrange to accompany you to the train. Newer trains have audio and visual information systems for visually impaired and hearing-impaired passengers.

The **Citizens' Information Board** (✆0761 079 000; www.citizensinformation board.ie) in the Republic and **Disability Action** (✆028-9029 7880; www.disability action.org; 189 Airport Rd W, Portside Business Pk; ☐28) in Northern Ireland can give some advice to travellers with disabilities. Lonely Planet's free Accessible Travel guide can be downloaded at: http://lptravel.to/ AccessibleTravel.

VISAS

If you're a European Economic Area (EEA) national, you don't need a visa to visit (or work in) either the Republic or Northern Ireland. Citizens of Australia, Canada, New Zealand, South Africa and the US can visit the Republic for up to three months, and Northern Ireland for up to six months. They are not allowed to work, unless sponsored by an employer.

Full visa requirements for visiting the Republic are available online at www.dfa. ie; for Northern Ireland's visa requirements see www.gov.uk/government/organisa tions/uk-visas-and-immigration.

To stay longer in the Republic, contact the local *garda* (police) station or the **Garda National Immigration Bureau** (✆01-666 9100; www.garda.ie; 13-14 Burgh Quay, Dublin; ☺8am-9pm Mon-Fri; ☐all city centre). To stay longer in Northern Ireland, contact the Home Office (www.gov.uk/ government/organisations/uk-visas-and -immigration).

BEHIND THE SCENES

SEND US YOUR FEEDBACK

We love to hear from travellers – your comments help make our books better. We read every word, and we guarantee that your feedback goes straight to the authors. Visit **lonelyplanet. com/contact** to submit your updates and suggestions.

Note: We may edit, reproduce and incorporate your comments in Lonely Planet products such as guidebooks, websites and digital products, so let us know if you don't want your comments reproduced or your name acknowledged. For a copy of our privacy policy visit lonelyplanet.com/privacy.

ACKNOWLEDGMENTS

Climate map data adapted from Peel MC, Finlayson BL & McMahon TA (2007) 'Updated World Map of the Köppen-Geiger Climate Classification', *Hydrology and Earth System Sciences*, 11, 163344.

Cover photographs: Front: Jaguar driving between Kenmare and Killarney, Pete Seaward/Lonely Planet ©; Back: St Colman's Cathedral and coloured houses, Cobh, Maurizio Rellini/AWL Images ©

THIS BOOK

This 1st edition of *Cork, Kerry & Southwest Ireland Road Trips* was researched and written by Neil Wilson. This guidebook was produced by the following:

Destination Editor Clifton Wilkinson

Senior Product Editors Sandie Kestell, Jessica Ryan

Product Editor Rachel Rawling

Senior Regional Cartographer Mark Griffiths

Cartographer Alison Lyall

Book Designer Gwen Cotter

Assisting Editors Andrew Bain, Imogen Bannister, Nigel Chin, Melanie Dankel, Carly Hall, Victoria Harrison, Kellie Langdon, Rosie Nicholson, Kristin Odijk, Simon Williamson

Cover Researcher Naomi Parker

Thanks to Will Allen, Sasha Drew, Susan Paterson, Wibowo Rusli, Angela Tinson, Amanda Williamson

OUR STORY

A beat-up old car, a few dollars in the pocket and a sense of adventure. In 1972 that's all Tony and Maureen Wheeler needed for the trip of a lifetime – across Europe and Asia overland to Australia. It took several months, and at the end – broke but inspired – they sat at their kitchen table writing and stapling together their first travel guide, *Across Asia on the Cheap*. Within a week they'd sold 1500 copies. Lonely Planet was born.

Today, Lonely Planet has offices in Franklin, London, Melbourne, Oakland, Dublin, Beijing and Delhi, with more than 600 staff and writers. We share Tony's belief that 'a great guidebook should do three things: inform, educate and amuse'.

INDEX

OUR WRITER

NEIL WILSON
Neil was born in Scotland and has lived there most of his life. Based in Perthshire, he has been a full-time writer since 1988, working on more than 80 guidebooks for various publishers, including the Lonely Planet guides to Scotland, England, Ireland and Prague. He has climbed and tramped in four continents, including ascents of Jebel Toubkal in Morocco, Mount Kinabalu in Borneo, the Old Man of Hoy in Scotland's Orkney Islands and the North-west Face of Half Dome in California's Yosemite Valley.

Published by Lonely Planet Global Limited
CRN 554153
1st edition – Mar 2020
ISBN 978 1 78868 648 8
© Lonely Planet 2020   Photographs © as indicated 2020
10 9 8 7 6 5 4 3 2 1
Printed in China